Florence Fox

"You ... s on a gr... . I am lo... Her name is Rella Sandringham, and she stole money from me down in Texas."

"You have come a long way looking for her," Rella whispered.

"She's become an obsession with me. She won't get away."

Even in the muted light, Rella could see the firm set of his jaw as he spoke of his quarry. She shuddered and prayed he would not see beyond her gypsy disguise.

"As a matter of fact," Cort said, his voice softening, "she was all I could think of until the other night when I came upon an exotic, wild-eyed beauty. Now it is another woman who fills my mind."

Rella swallowed. So he carried the images of two women in his head, did he? Once he discovered the truth, Cort Ramsey would be a terrifying enemy.

"Are she and I so different?" she couldn't help but ask.

He reached out for her. "Very different." He sank to his knees in front of her and held her lightly. "She would never have allowed me to do this," he whispered, kissing the pulse point at her throat. "Or this." His lips trailed feather kisses across her cheeks and at the corners of her mouth.

"No," she moaned, even as her hands clutched at his shirt. She felt lost in a mad world that had no future or past. Reason fled. She could not understand the powerful need that sent her into her enemy's embrace, yet she could not deny it. She could not deny him. . . .

Lawman's Lady

KELLER GRAVES

ZEBRA BOOKS
KENSINGTON PUBLISHING CORP.

ZEBRA BOOKS

are published by

Kensington Publishing Corp.
475 Park Avenue South
New York, NY 10016

First printing: November, 1988

Printed in the United States of America

To Wendy McCurdy

Chapter One

Rella Sandringham suspected she was in trouble the moment she looked up from the dead body of her employer, Perry Tuttle, and saw, watching her from the slowly opening door, a man wearing a badge.

Mesmerized by the brown hand on the white china doorknob, she opened her mouth but couldn't speak. Tall and lean, the man flicked inquiring eyes about the sunlit law office, then took a step forward.

"I'm U.S. Marshal Cort Ramsey." He waved to a short, pot-bellied man standing behind him. "This is the deputy sheriff of Galveston County, Ernest Bowles. Mind telling me what you're doing here?"

Rella continued to kneel beside the body, the full skirt of her gown covering Tuttle's outstretched arm. On the bare wooden floor in front of the desk lay a gun. Rather unfortunate circumstances in which to be found, she admitted. She'd been in a play once where the villain had been discovered by a lawman in much the same way. Not only was she faced with a United States marshal, but a sarcastic one as well.

"I was trying to determine if Mr. Tuttle might still be alive," she managed, proud that her voice was strong. She'd been dependent on her own resources too long to give in to girlish vapors now.

Cort studied the woman carefully. With the window

at her back, her face was in shadows, but he could make out a pair of wide-set eyes, high cheekbones, and a gracefully formed chin. All in all, an angelic face from what he could see; it certainly didn't go with the full, rich voice.

He turned to the deputy. "Bowles, see if you can find Tuttle's son. And bring a doctor from the medical school while you're at it."

Bowles retreated, muttering as best Rella could make out something about Yankee interference. Paying him no mind, the marshal strode toward her, his long legs bringing him quickly across the room, his boots hitting sharply against the floor. Behind him another figure materialized out of the shadows of the second-floor hallway, and Rella recognized him as Tuttle's law clerk, Marcus Clapper. Marcus always seemed to be hovering, Rella thought vaguely as she looked back at the lawman kneeling across the body from her. He felt for a pulse, just as she had done moments before.

"Still warm," he said.

"It wasn't ten minutes ago I heard the shot from downstairs," Marcus said. "When I found Mr. Tuttle stretched out that way, I went running right away for the jail."

Ten minutes ago, Rella thought, Perry Tuttle had been alive and probably scheming at some new deal for making money. Little good his schemes would do him now.

"Mr. Tuttle is dead. Shot," she said, looking at the gun.

Cort nodded. He'd known the lawyer was dead the moment he stepped into the room, even before he'd gotten a close look at the bloodied hole in Perry Tuttle's chest. Checking the pulse had been a formality. Cort felt an anger at the waste of life. This was one part of his job he never got used to, this investigation of death.

He turned his attention to the woman. Up close, she was even prettier than she'd looked from across the room but not quite as angelic as he'd thought. There was decided spirit in her eyes, backed by an incongruous sense of isolation. She seemed to be daring anyone to mention she might be lonely.

The Galveston summer sun streamed in through the window at Rella's back and illuminated the marshal's face like a stage light. With the instinct of an actress, she picked out the details: strong jaw, piercing blue eyes a shade darker than her own, red-brown hair brushing against the collar of his shirt. Rella was good at reading faces. Cort Ramsey was a smart man who would put up with no dissembling, which was fine with her. She had nothing to hide.

"You're mighty calm," he said.

Calm, was she? Rella had enough presence of mind to realize that she was in truth close to shock. Death on the stage was always separated from reality, no matter the skill of the actor. In life it was cold and final.

"I'm—"

"Damn!"

Cort's attention had been drawn behind her to the open safe against the wall by Tuttle's feet. Rella followed his gaze, but all she could see were some papers she'd put there shortly before leaving for a solitary lunch in the park. The packet of money that had been beside the papers was gone.

Cort stood, his long legs planted apart, his eyes pinning her to the floor. She realized with a start that he was angry. Apparently the marshal had a temper and was taking the open safe as a personal affront.

"Looks like there's been a robbery, too," he said

sharply. "Maybe you better tell me just who you are."

Rella's eyes made a quick trip up the marshal's well-formed legs, paused at the gun strapped to his thigh, then moved even more quickly, past the badge pinned to his chest to settle on his grim face. What was Ramsey trying to do, she thought, intimidate her with his manhood? From her angle on the floor, his smooth-fitting trousers offered obvious proof of his sex, but Rella was not impressed, no more than she had been by his gun. Refusing to be intimidated, she stood up to meet his stare straight on. Whatever shock she'd suffered dissipated with the growing certainty she needed to defend herself.

"Rella Sandringham. I work for Mr. Tuttle as bookkeeper."

Forgetting for a moment the body on the floor, she held out her hand. Let Ramsey shake it or ignore it, whatever he chose. She hardly expected him to kiss it in the European style. Americans didn't really know what to do with a woman's hand.

Ramsey didn't seem at all unsure of what to do. All signs of his anger gone, he took her hand in his and studied it, concentrating for a long moment on the small scar at the base of her thumb. His skin felt warmer and smoother than most men who worked and traveled in the harsh western climes.

"The bookkeeper?" he asked, looking up. "That means you take care of the money."

"She sure does," Marcus Clapper said, stepping closer to them. "I never was allowed close to it, at least not after she was hired."

Rella ignored the clerk. Pulling her hand free, she said, "I keep the books, that's all. I'm well aware, Marshal, that there's some cash missing from the safe. It was there when I left for lunch." She saw the look of skepticism on the marshal's face. "Surely you don't think I had anything to do with this?"

"It's a little early to rule out any possibilities."

"I was going to call for help when I found him," Rella said. "I arrived just before you. The first thing I thought of was seeing if I could help Mr. Tuttle. Would a guilty person have felt for a pulse?" She gave him no chance to answer. "Marcus said the gunshot was ten minutes ago. Would a guilty person have chanced being caught with the body?"

"You sound like someone who has been accused of something, Miss Sandringham. Or who maybe expects to be."

Stung by the marshal's implications, Rella snapped, "I just want to help you rule out at least one possibility: the possibility that I am responsible for what happened here."

"Watch her," Marcus warned. "She's a real actress. Been on the stage and everything."

"I've nothing to hide," Rella interjected. "When I was injured a couple of months ago, Mr. Tuttle's son Aaron treated me at the medical school." She rubbed at her scarred hand. "As I was forced to take temporary leave from the traveling troupe that brought me here, Aaron kindly convinced his father to employ me."

"How were you hurt?" Cort asked.

Rella couldn't suppress a shudder. "A . . . fire. At the boardinghouse."

"Still trouble you, does it?"

She'd been right. The marshal didn't miss much. A remembrance of smoke and flames flashed through her mind, and she settled for a nod.

"Don't be fooled by all that innocence," Clapper said from the post he'd taken close to the late lawyer's desk. "She may look like an angel, but I know for a fact she's not."

Rella brushed a blond lock from her face. Innocence was her stock in trade, that was for sure. After she lightened her naturally dark hair and perfected a simpering look, she'd received most of the ingenue roles offered by Templeton's Traveling Thespians. But there was absolutely no reason to discuss that now.

"Marcus," she said, leveling a scornful stare at the officious clerk, "if you've got something to say, say it."

It was Marcus's curse to have spindly arms and legs and a rounded body which made his legs appear all the thinner and gave him the appearance of a bird. When he pursed his lips as he was doing now, his mouth looked very much like a beak.

"You may have started here to earn a little money, but you got higher ideas than that soon enough," he declared. "Angling to reel in Mr. Tuttle, you were. Get him to propose marriage. But he was too smart an old fish to get caught by the likes of you. Not," he added, his narrow eyes glancing at her body, "that he didn't like the bait."

Holding back her own temper, Rella raised her skirts and walked well around the prone form of the man who had been her boss. She was tempted to flee down the stairs to the Strand and keep on running to the docks where she had friends who would get her on the first boat leaving the island. Not quite believing she could really be in trouble, she settled for venting her frustration on Clapper. Surely he wouldn't stand by the lies he was telling.

As she advanced, he was forced to edge away from her. The movement brought a look of satisfaction to her face—until she turned and saw Cort Ramsey watching with those all-seeing eyes of his. He was a hard man to ignore; the thought that he could suspect her of anything so horrible as murder unleashed the anger she'd held in check.

Standing in the door to the little office she shared with Clapper, she freed her wrath on the hapless clerk. "Marcus, you're a liar. Mr. Tuttle may have tried to pat my backside a few times, but most assuredly not because I encouraged him to do so. He was a lecherous man." She paused and muttered, "May he rest in peace," before continuing her assault. "And you're no better. Don't think I haven't seen you eyeing me when you thought I wasn't looking. The only difference between you and him is that he had the nerve to find out how much I would allow."

"There is one other difference," Cort said from his vantage point a few feet away. "Clapper is still alive."

Rella caught her breath. How callous she must appear to act so shrewishly in the very room where tragedy had struck. "If we must discuss this, let's do it away from here." As if seeking a bulwark against her foes, she moved quickly across the adjoining office to stand near her own desk and wait for the men to follow. The marshal shut the door behind him.

The second room was narrow with only enough space for desks at either end facing each other. Rella pointed to an outside door behind Clapper's desk. "That was open when I returned," she said. "The stairs go down into the alley. I usually come and go that way to avoid Mr. Tuttle's attentions. I'm sure I locked it when I went to lunch."

"Proving nothing," said the marshal. "You could have as well unlocked it."

Clapper settled uneasily behind his desk, and Cort began to prowl the room, which was just as drab as the first, with a single curtained window, brown walls and bare floor. It was 1871; after the harsh war years, many people were indulging in the extravagances of Victorian decor. Obviously, Cort thought as he stared at the room's lone attempt at aesthetics, an amateurish painting of the beach at sunset, Perry Tuttle hadn't believed in wasting money on such frills.

Rella gave up trying to read the lawman's thoughts. Away from the sight of Tuttle's corpse, she felt the sadness of the day's tragedy. He had been an old reprobate who alienated his son and took advantage of more than one client—and who recently showed signs of political ambitions—but he had also helped her when she needed it. He'd threatened to terminate her employment if she didn't "cooperate" as he phrased it, but he'd been mostly bluffing. He certainly didn't deserve what had happened to him, and she said a silent prayer that his spirit really was at peace.

From somewhere deep in the recesses of her mind came the remembrance of her grandmother, the Gypsy queen Esmeralda who'd spent her days traveling the English countryside. Her hand went automatically to the moonstone brooch she wore at her neck. A simple piece and probably worthless, it had belonged to Esmeralda and somehow offered comfort. Rella had never known the woman, but her mother had filled her with stories of the Gypsy ways. Gypsies wailed and cried for the dead, then put the sad memories away and got on with living. She saw the wisdom of their ways.

A feeling of exhaustion washed over her, and she moved to her desk. How strange to start trembling now, she thought as she sank into the chair. Marcus perched in his chair across the narrow room; to his left, Ramsey, having abandoned his search, leaned against the frame of the open door.

She studied the marshal once again. He seemed to fill the doorway. He must be six feet tall, half a foot taller than she. His skin was the tan of timeless pearls and went well with his thick, copper hair—if she were inclined to think flattering thoughts of him, which of course she wasn't. Thin lines marked the edges of his blue eyes, making him appear to squint. Rella figured he must ride often into the sun, but his face was not weathered. Its only other marks were around his mouth, faint creases like parentheses that might be caused by frequent laughter. Right now he was looking grim.

She could imagine what he would think if she told him of Esmeralda Scamp. He'd looked sharply at her when Marcus had mentioned she performed on the stage. If he knew she was not only an actress but part Gypsy as well, he would toss her in jail and throw away the key.

"All right, Clapper," Cort said. "Let's start with when you heard the shot. One, you said?"

Marcus nodded. He was up to something. Rella knew it from the way his thin lips twitched into a smirk.

"I was on the street floor having lunch with Ralph," he said. "He works for another lawyer in the building. There wasn't any mistaking that sound. Echoed down the stairs, it did. We both ran up the inside stairway as fast as we could, but whoever did it"—he glanced at Rella, then back to the lawman—"must have gone out the back door. Ralph headed down the alley stairs, in case he could see anyone, and I tried to take care of Mr. Tuttle."

"Was he dead?"

"Not right away. Had just enough strength to whisper one name. Didn't think much about it at the time. Thought he was calling for help."

"You took a damned long time to mention this," Cort said brusquely. "Just whose name did you hear?"

"Rella, is what he said. Kind of unusual name." Clapper's smirk widened. "Guess we both know who he meant."

Rella rose from her chair. If only she possessed Esmeralda's ability to cast the evil eye, she would strike Marcus Clapper dumb on the spot.

"Marshal," she said in the haughtiest stage voice she could manage, "that sniveling law clerk is a liar. He's been envious of the work and money I've received ever since Aaron Tuttle brought me to meet his father."

Marcus's eyes widened. "My family has been on Galveston Island for more than forty years. I don't think Marshal Ramsey is going to believe an actress over me. Even if he was appointed by that Reconstruction governor in Austin." He glanced at Ramsey. "No offense intended."

"None taken. Now, Miss Sandringham—" Cort was interrupted by a knock on the hall door in Tuttle's office. Excusing himself, he returned in a minute followed by a young woman, short and plump where Rella was tall and slender, her soft face furrowed and her brown eyes round with worry.

"Greta!" Rella exclaimed. "What are you doing here?"

"I was with Aaron when Deputy Bowles came for him at the hospital."

"And Aaron?"

"He's in tending to his father." Her large eyes watered. "Oh, Rella, it looks like it's too late to do him any good."

The two women embraced for a moment, then Greta asked in a tremulous voice, "What happened? Was it an . . . an accident?"

"We don't know exactly," Cort said. "Apparently Tuttle was shot and a packet of money taken from the safe."

"Gott in Himmel!" Greta exclaimed. Her wide eyes settled on the open door between the two offices, through which came the muted sound of voices. "The

poor man didn't approve of me. He thought since Papa and I came in a boat and the only work Papa could get was on the docks. . . . Well, he just didn't approve of Aaron being my special friend. But for his life to end this way—"

Rella interrupted before Greta talked her way into being the marshal's primary suspect.

"This is Greta Maas," she said, "a good friend who wouldn't harm another human being no matter how provoked."

"Thanks for the character description, Miss Sandringham," Cort said solemnly. "I'll be sure to keep it in mind." He turned to Greta. "Are you all right? All this must have come as a great shock."

How solicitous he sounded, Rella decided, far more than he had toward her, and she thought about giving him a more personal description, one of himself. She would start with sarcastic, vain, and short-sighted. Discretion prevailed, and she turned toward the wide-eyed young woman. Greta looked saddened but nowhere near collapse, and Rella said, "The marshal was just about to ask me where I was at the time of the shooting." Her blue eyes flashed at him. "Is that not true?"

"It's true, all right. So tell me."

"From what Marcus said about the time of the . . . accident, I was on my way back from having lunch in the park."

"Marshal Ramsey, Rella couldn't hurt anyone," Greta wailed.

Cort ignored her. "Anyone with you?" he asked Rella.

Rella shook her head. "I was by myself."

"Not much of a alibi."

"I didn't know I would need one. Please tell me why I would do such a thing and then return to the scene."

Cort shrugged. "You might have left to hide the money and returned to pose as the innocent discoverer of the murder. Clapper here beat you to it and summoned the law. Of course you had no idea that he had heard the victim whisper your name. Or that I was on the way."

Deputy Bowles, his flat, lined faced broken by a grin, appeared in the doorway. "Sounds like you got the murderer already, Ramsey. For a Yankee, you work fast."

Rella stared in disbelief first at the deputy, then Ramsey. "You both have twisted minds. I would never think of anything so devious as that."

"The money must be somewhere," Cort said.

"Then search my desk. And Marcus's, too, of course."

"Of course," Cort said. "Although Clapper has an alibi. He was with a friend when the shot was fired." Bowles started into the room, but Cort waved him away. "Stand guard at the door to the hall and make sure no gawkers come into the office," he ordered in dismissal. A quick but thorough examination turned up nothing that would solve the mystery.

"Satisfied?" Rella asked.

Ramsey's eyes drifted down her body. "Not really."

Rella knew right away what he was thinking. "Meaning I could have the packet on my person."

"Not likely. But I really can't rule out the possibility, can I? Not without investigating."

Without batting an eyelash, Rella turned to the open-mouthed Greta. "If you don't mind, I'd like you to help Aaron for a few minutes," she said. "He may need you in there. And Marcus, I would appreciate your taking a short trip down to the alley."

She gave the clerk no chance to answer, but hustled him out the door, shutting it firmly at his back. When his face appeared at the window, a dangerous feat since he must be leaning far over the rail, she quickly lowered the shades.

Next she gently shuffled her bewildered friend through the inner door. She caught a glimpse of Aaron bent over his father's body and fought the urge to offer him sympathy. The young man was a brilliant student of medicine. She'd heard that often enough when she was a patient at the school. But, in her limited observations, she'd seen he also didn't have the vaguest idea how to get on in life. Skipped meals, forgotten appointments, conversations drifting into silence as his mind turned to his studies, he would need help from both her and Greta to get through the next few days.

First Rella needed to finish with the galoot who had become her adversary. Closing the door firmly on the sad scene, she turned to the marshal.

"Search me."

Cort started. If Rella Sandringham had committed the murder and robbery, she was doing a damned fine job of feigning innocence.

He moved close. "Now that's an offer I don't think I can refuse. If you don't prefer a woman for the job."

"I'm not embarrassed, if that's what you're thinking. After all, I'm an actress. Surely you've heard we have no shame. Besides, I don't intend to get down to the altogether. The packet of money was rather bulky. It would be difficult to hide."

Cort's eyes drifted slowly from her slender shoulders to the high and nicely rounded breasts, then stopped at the narrow waist. He had a definite preference for such a figure. Under different circumstances, he would have been enjoying the scene.

But there was the money. And Perry Tuttle's body in the other room.

"It's definitely not where I can detect it," he said. "Unless, of course, you've hidden it under your skirt."

"I thought you would eventually mention that part of my anatomy," Rella said, noticing the way he was studying her. He wasn't thinking solely of law enforcement. Somehow she wasn't as insulted as she should have been. Without giving her actions a second thought, she reached down and grasped the lower hem of her skirt, pulling it up to her waist. If he'd expected a flash of skin, he must surely be disappointed. The jaconet petticoat covered her person quite as thoroughly as had her dress, although not with as much fullness. The sharp-eyed marshal could see she was concealing no bulky wad of bills.

She turned and lifted the back of her dress in the same manner, crushing it to her waist. "Satisfied?" she said over her shoulder.

Cort felt a decidedly unprofessional warmth at the sight of the lovely lady's underwear. It didn't take too much imagination to picture the soft skin that it covered.

"Hardly," he said and decided to see just how far the actress would go. "But of course you could be carrying the money between your legs."

Rella dropped her gown and whirled on him. "In which case I would be walking decidedly bowlegged. Which I am not."

"That's one of the advantages to a dress. A man doesn't know what's underneath until he actually inspects a woman with his hands."

"Which you will not do." Rella again lifted her skirt, this time including the petticoat, and gave the marshal a brief look at her stockinged legs.

"Definitely not bowlegged," Cort said, for the moment enjoying his investigation of the outspoken actress. He had to remind himself Rella Sandringham was still a suspect in a murder, and a strong one, considering the law clerk's testimony about Tuttle's last words. Not that he instantly believed the clerk, whose bobbing head reminded him of a gull. Clapper needed closer questioning before his testimony could be taken as the truth.

A timid knock was heard on the door leading to the larger office. "Rella," came the soft voice of Greta, "are you all right in there? Is that marshal hurting you?"

Cort opened the door. "Not at all, Miss Maas. We try to save our beatings for the jail."

He looked beyond the young woman and saw that Aaron Tuttle had taken himself away from the body of his father and was now standing by the window. A tall, spare man with thinning pale hair, he nevertheless didn't appear to be over twenty-five. Tuttle had told him about his displeasure with Aaron concerning his determination to be a doctor. "Quacks, that's what they all are," he'd said. "No better than an Indian medicine man."

Cort went in to console the young man on his loss, then, with Greta taking over, spent a few minutes with the doctor who'd come with Aaron from the medical school. He introduced himself as Phillip Bruster and reported that Tuttle had been killed by a bullet through his heart. The gun found by the desk had apparently been the weapon used. Aaron had identified it as one his father kept in a top drawer.

"Could the death have been suicide?" Cort asked.

Bruster shook his head. "I don't think so. Did anyone move the weapon?"

Cort eyed Rella speculatively. "No one admits to it."

"If Tuttle had shot himself, it would have fallen closer when he fell to the floor."

"I figured the same thing. You sound like a lawman."

"Just been called to a few scenes like this. Too damned many. Be glad when this state gets civilized. You from around here?"

Cort shook his head. "I grew up in Missouri. Yankee territory to most of the people around here. I work out of Houston, although I occasionally come down to the island."

"Lots of folks around here are still fighting the war," Bruster said in disgust. "Don't imagine you've been made to feel welcome."

"Perry Tuttle was one of the few who didn't seem to mind my background. We had a few dealings that had nothing to do with the law."

"Perry was a sharp businessman, all right, which is another reason for ruling out suicide. He was proud of what he did. I wasn't what you would call a close friend, but we met at some of the social events around town. Got into many an argument about our respective professions." Bruster shook his head sadly. "It was murder all right, and not long ago."

"How about that clerk of Tuttle's? Is he known to lie?"

"Never heard he does. Family's straight as a die."

Cort nodded, his eyes mere slits as he studied the room. "Usually I find it's someone close to the victim who's guilty."

"Like maybe someone who worked close beside him," Bowles said from his position by the hallway door.

"The townsfolk will be hoping you find it was a Yankee," said the doctor, picking up his bag. "Nothing I can do for the poor fellow now. He's in God's hands."

And, Cort thought, *his murderer is in mine. Or soon will be.*

His thoughts turned to Rella Sandringham. Tuttle had possibly spent his last breath calling her name. In

Cort's experience, there was only one reason a man did that: to identify his killer. And she'd looked damned guilty when he walked into the room. And then mighty innocent. An actress, was she? She'd better be good if she hoped to fool him.

Cort paused beside Bowles. He didn't have much professional respect for the man, but with the sheriff out of town, he was the highest ranking local lawman and for that fact alone deserved consideration. "What makes you so sure we've solved the case?"

"I've been listening to the evidence. If you don't arrest her, I will."

But Cort wasn't quite ready to go that far, not just yet, even with the irritating Bowles pushing him. He walked back to the smaller office to find the object of his suspicions sitting at her desk and staring into space.

"Do you live near here?"

Rella nodded. "A boardinghouse not far off the Strand."

"I'd like to search your room."

"Marshal Ramsey."

Cort turned to face Aaron Tuttle, whose arm was tight in the grip of his worried lady friend. The younger Tuttle wore a vague look that Cort figured was probably natural to him, the look of a dreamer, not a doer, but he would reserve judgment on that. He looked at the mound on the floor. Aaron had covered his father with a blanket.

Aaron ran his fingers through sparse, sandy hair. He swallowed. "I understand you're questioning Rella . . . Miss Sandringham. I'm just as likely to be responsible for this."

"That's gallant of you," Cort said, "but the doctor gave you an alibi. You couldn't have killed him."

"And neither could Rella," Greta said with a stamp

of her foot. "Anyone would be a . . . a *dummkopf* to suspect her."

Rella cringed. The normally placid Greta was doing neither of them any good. Reaching for the purse she'd left on her desk, she pulled out a key. "Here," she said. "The landlady might object if you kicked down the door. And I certainly don't object if you look through my belongings."

If she thought that her cooperation would buy her sympathy, she thought wrong. Ramsey took the key, asked Bowles to take them all downstairs to wait for his return, and made a quick exit.

In herding them toward a corner of the busy restaurant, Deputy Bowles proved to be just as officious as Marcus Clapper, who traipsed into the downstairs restaurant and announced he'd visited the funeral parlor down the street. "I made arrangements for the remains of that poor man upstairs to be cared for. I hope you don't mind, Aaron."

Aaron nodded absentmindedly, and Rella wondered where his thoughts were traveling. Certainly not to one of the weighty medical books he usually had with him. More likely he was remembering some time in the past with his father, a time when they hadn't been at odds. In unspoken agreement, she and Greta gave him that time of remembrance, and they sat in silence as the minutes dragged past. Even Marcus had the good sense to be quiet.

"Kinda looks like you're in trouble," Bowles said at last to Rella. His drawled words sliced into the quiet. "I'm surprised the Yankee marshal was smart enough to find you out so quickly, but folks around here will be glad enough he did."

"You seem ready to take me to the gallows."

"We do things legal around here," Bowles replied, then stood to greet a gray-haired, portly gentleman who had made his way to the corner table of the restaurant. "Alderman Hayes, good afternoon."

"Heard about the trouble here," the alderman said. "Aaron, let me extend my sympathies. Terrible, terrible thing. I understand Marshal Ramsey is in town."

"Interfering, as usual," Bowles said, "but it looks like this time his ways are paying off." He nodded at Rella. "Got a suspect already."

Rella looked at the middle-aged deputy without answer. His mid-section had turned to paunch, and his hairline receded, a fact he tried to hide by combing a few soft strands across the top of his head; but there was nothing gentle about his eyes. Steely, they were, and they studied her with scorn. What was there about lawmen's eyes, she wondered, that made a suspect feel guilty even when she had nothing to hide? Did such a look come with the job, or was it a requisite to being hired?

When Ramsey returned, he didn't waste words.

"I'm taking you to the jail," he said to Rella. "For further questioning."

Rella waved aside the protests of her friends as she stood to face the all-powerful marshal. She mustn't panic. Somehow she would get out of this predicament. She was *innocent!* That ought to count for something.

"On what basis are you arresting me?" she asked with a tremor. The effort drained her of strength.

"Just questioning, for now." He extended an envelope. "Found it hidden in your room."

Rella knew what it was—the steamship ticket she'd bought for St. Louis, where she hoped to join up with the troupe. She'd forgotten it was tucked in the bottom of her lingerie drawer waiting to be used in a week's time.

"Are you afraid I'll skip town?" she asked.

"Are you saying you wouldn't? You obviously had already made plans to leave."

"I was planning to resume my acting career."

"And needed funds, perhaps, to speed you on your way. It could be Tuttle caught you at the safe."

The anger of injustice refueled her waning strength. "You've got it all figured out, haven't you? Did you find the missing money?"

"Not yet. But I timed myself coming back. Nine and a half minutes it took, without hurrying. You had time to hide that packet somewhere."

"You seem convinced I'm guilty. Will you even bother with a trial?"

"Even in Texas, we try to do things right. And you're not charged with anything yet. I'm just investigating all likely suspects. Right now that just means you. Unless you can tell me why Tuttle would have called your name with his last breath."

Rella gritted her teeth. He had her there. Surely there were a hundred reasons, but she couldn't think of even one. Tuttle had held no affection for her; she was merely a game.

"Do you have any relatives, Miss Sandringham?"

"None living. Both my parents are dead." Rella felt almost relief that her starry-eyed parents were not here to see her in such straits. Both actors, they brought her as a child to America from England. They'd been killed in a boating accident in the East years before.

"And your full name?"

"Cinderella Sandringham," she said sharply. If he so much as smirked, she would slap him in the face and laugh at a charge of assault. "My mother," she added, "was partial to French fairy tales."

Cort had the good sense to nod. As he guided her to the door, Rella came to a halt.

"Marshal," she said, turning on him, "I must be picking up your suspicious nature. Upstairs in the office when you got a look at the safe, you knew right away some money was missing. You even knew it was a bulky packet. Mr. Tuttle didn't normally keep large sums in his safe. What made you so sure it wasn't papers that had been taken?"

"Because I'd visited Tuttle early this morning on a private matter. I know exactly how much money was stolen from that safe," Cort said, his eyes darkening. "Six thousand dollars. And every penny of it belonged to me."

Chapter Two

"What's a lawman doing with so much money?"

Cort glanced sideways at the slender prisoner handcuffed to his left wrist and looked directly into a pair of scornful blue eyes. Cinderella Sandringham might be shackled and on her way to the county jail, but she showed no sign of being cowed.

Rella persisted in her verbal attack. It was virtually all she could do, pulled along as she was down the rough boardwalk past hordes of wide-eyed strangers and across the carriage-crowded streets. On this balmy Saturday afternoon, half of Galveston must have congregated in the business section of town. She'd performed on many a stage with fewer onlookers than watched her progress today.

"Six thousand dollars is a lot of cash for an honest man to accumulate. Especially," she added, raising her voice in case any eavesdropper was hard of hearing, "one like yourself who is supposedly devoted to the public good."

Cort had sighted many an angry Rebel visage in his service with the Army of the West, and more than a few hateful stares from the men he'd arrested in his term as marshal. None matched the fiery stare directed at him now. As a Yankee lawman appointed by a Reconstruction governor, he was already none too popular in the Southern coastal town. At best he was considered an outsider, and Rella was doing nothing to make him more welcome.

Overlooking the obvious physical differences from his previous prisoners—and he'd managed to do that, if only because she was such a sharp-tongued shrew—this one was proving a handful. She was even trying to switch their roles and interrogate him. His only answer was a twitch of his lips. He didn't care to hear what she would say if she knew how rich he really was.

Cort had come a long way since his youthful days on a Missouri farm. He'd left his widowed father to serve his country when war broke out between the states. Josiah Ramsey had been a pacifist, had argued Missouri wasn't even in the war. But Cort had been sure of his mission, thinking in a few months he would be back, filled with glorious memories of how he'd served in a time of need. Lord, but he'd been young and innocent. He'd returned four years later, his fighting skills honed and his need for peace equal to his father's.

But Josiah wasn't there to greet him. He had found only a bitterly divided people unable to forget the hard times of the war. Cort never found out whether Southern sympathizers or abolitionists had raided the farm; the only thing for sure was that Josiah was dead, shot down in the night by the unidentified marauders. Grief and anger drove him to find the killers; he'd failed. The year-old trail had grown cold. He'd sold the farm and become a lawman. Through the years he'd tracked down criminals, although they were never the ones he longed to bring to justice, the slayers of Josiah.

Ruthless in his pursuit of criminals, he found another talent he'd never suspected in himself: the ability to make money. Income from the Missouri farm sale had gone for quarter horses in Texas and cattle he occasionally sold to the Army. All his investments had paid off. He'd even found some land he wanted, a run-down plantation deep in the pine woods of East Texas. It could be had for back taxes.

Not that he was ready to settle down—he was far too restless for that—but the land was rich for farming, and he saw the profit to be made from the acres of timberland that went with the house. Cort had traveled Texas enough to know that even under the yoke of a Reconstruction government, the state was ready for boom times.

He needed cash for the sale and had gone to auction with some of his prized stock to raise it fast. The final transaction had been scheduled for that afternoon between the tax man and Tuttle, who'd made the arrangements for him. The deal would have to be postponed.

But not canceled. He would find that bundle of money if he had to turn over every shovelful of shell and sand and dirt that covered Galveston Island. Unconsciously he gave a tug on the handcuffs and widened his step.

A yelp from his prisoner slowed him down.

"I'm sure you want to toss me into your dungeon as soon as possible," Rella said, blowing an errant blond curl from her brow, "but you would attract less attention if you didn't drag me behind you."

Cort broke his silence. "Dungeon, eh? Do actresses always lean toward the dramatic?"

"I hardly need to embellish on this situation, Marshal. It's quite dramatic enough as it is."

"Lady, you haven't seen anything yet. Wait until you get to the jail."

If Cort hadn't been so angry, he would have felt

sorry for what awaited the fair-haired young beauty. The jail was long overdue for maintenance work, what with the number of drunks and vagrants regularly incarcerated inside. Broken glass had been strewn atop the surrounding brick wall to discourage unscheduled departures of the county's criminal guests.

Gamblers and prostitutes, whose numbers were many on the free-wheeling island, were more likely to pay a fine, thus enriching the city coffers, and be on their way through the front door. Cort didn't avail himself of the women's services—he found willing enough partners back in Houston—but he considered some of them his friends, occasionally helping them out when the customers got too rough. The gamblers he avoided, except when complaints about crooked games came his way. He preferred his poker playing confined to a game with a few of his friends.

But the jail's crowded conditions didn't result just from arrests. The beauty shackled to him would find that out soon enough. Cinderella Sandringham would most likely find her cellmates not the thieves or whores she no doubt envisioned, but rather some deluded soul with far different problems.

Right now Rella wasn't thinking much about a cellmate. She didn't care where the marshal pitched her as long as this journey ended soon. Unfriendly faces along the way were evidence that neither she nor Marshal Ramsey were any too popular with the crowd, with the possible exception of a few young women who eyed the broad-shouldered marshal with something warmer than scorn.

Try as she might to maintain her balance, she kept bumping into him. The brute. As tall as she was, her head barely came to his chin. Each brush against his muscled arm reminded her anew he could snap her in half if he chose—and he'd been angry enough to do just that when he said the stolen money was his.

Men! They either showered a girl with shallow attention or treated her with disdain. As a touring actress, Rella had been treated both ways—more approaches than rejections, for certain—but she was smart enough to know that most of her admirers, assuming low morals in such a one as she, only wanted her for a night of pleasure.

At least the marshal hadn't made any indecent suggestions to her, maybe a little swap, the "cooperation" Perry Tuttle had been after, for quick release from jail. That is, he hadn't made such a proposal yet, but she didn't count out the possibility. From the looks he received along the way, he obviously appealed to the women. Probably thought of himself as some sort of extraordinary lover.

And so he very well might be. He had the outward physical attributes, but he wasn't very smart, not if for one minute he thought her capable of murder and theft. And, while she was on the subject of his shortcomings, what had he been doing with so much cash? Her tauntings along the way hadn't been idle. She'd heard Greta complaining of some kind of graft her father had encountered on the dock, underhanded dealings that maybe involved public officials. Maybe Cort Ramsey wasn't as much for law and order as he seemed, not if by straying he could line his own pockets with money.

Her maunderings were interrupted when they came to another cross street, this one different in that it was covered with crushed oyster shells. Rella was used to such streets by now—if she could cross them gingerly, placing her slippers carefully on the sharp surface. Cort Ramsey's boots hit the lethal shells solid and fast.

Rella let out a howl of protest. Cort came to a halt in the middle of the street, sending a horse-drawn carriage into a wide arc around them, the air filled with the driver's imprecations about "gol-durned pedestrians" who ought to stay out of the way.

"What's wrong now, Miss Sandringham?"

Rella would have walked over hot coals rather than tell him the truth, not with that supercilious look on his face.

"Absolutely nothing, Marshal Ramsey. Shall we proceed?"

He fought back a grin. The job of lawman sure took unusual twists and turns. "Forgot about those thin shoes of yours."

"How did you—" Rella stopped. Of course he knew about her shoes; she had exposed them and a great deal more when she had lifted her skirts.

He swung her to face him and before she could protest slung her over his shoulder.

Rella beat on his back and tried to kick him. Cort was unimpressed. He clamped her knees firmly to his chest and paused to await the passing of a one-horse carriage. Politely tipping his wide-brimmed hat to the occupants, he ignored his prisoner's protests.

"Won't be a second," he said, eyeing her backside.

Rella spluttered against his idea of kindness but was unable to express her opinion in any terms she considered adequate. Her stomach muscles had the strength of youth, but they contracted painfully as they met the harder curve of his shoulder and rendered her speechless. Helplessly she bounced there as he strode across the treacherous shells to place her on the wooden walk.

She opened her mouth to rail at him, but he gave her no chance to voice her rabid thoughts. Before she could catch her breath, he was off down the sidewalk, forcing her to keep up or be dragged willy-nilly behind him by the handcuffs.

In the one glimpse of her face that he allowed himself when he put her down, Cort saw nothing but the outrage of injured dignity, nothing to confirm that she was capable of planning a cold-blooded murder and robbery, and then carrying it out. Damned if he could tell. The evidence was strong against her, but that didn't mean he was through with the investigation. There was something righteous in her denial that spoke of innocence. Before the case was settled, he would have to find out how good an actress she was.

When Bowles met them at the jailhouse door, Cort suppressed his irritation. The deputy carried a lot of bitterness around with him. He'd lost the family money and business in the war and taken the long comedown to his current job when his plans had been to take over the once prosperous Bowles Mercantile Store. The company was no more.

Bowles wasn't the kind to give thanks, but he'd been lucky to get the job, considering the way most Southerners were faring under Governor Davis's Reconstruction government. What galled him almost as much as his own poor condition was his knowledge that a Yankee lawman had come down here to outrank him and make money off of Texas land.

" 'Bout time you got here," Bowles said by way of greeting. "Ben and I got a special place picked out for the prisoner."

Cort nodded. Ben Woods was jailer, a middle-aged deputy who'd been, according to local legend, quite a lawman before the war. But, like so many others, he'd lost most of his family and all of his ambition. Now he was content to mutter imprecations against the criminals and express his puzzlement about the non-prisoners he was forced to house. He seemed close to his fellow Southerner Bowles, echoing his complaints all too often, but Cort had no real quarrel with the man, except for the fact his false teeth were a bad fit and clicked when he talked. As far as Cort could tell, Ben did his job.

Gray-headed and with muscles grown lax, Ben greeted them at the opening to the long, dimly lit corridor which ran between the two row of cells. A ring of keys was clasped in his hand.

"Hear we got a female killer," he said with a shake of his head, as if he were asking what the world was coming to.

"A suspect, at least," Cort said, ignoring the familiar click of wooden teeth and unlocking the handcuffs that bound him to his prisoner.

The jailer's eyes turned to Rella, then widened in surprise. "Don't look like no killer I ever saw."

"I've harmed no one," Rella said through taut lips. She rubbed at her arm and stared down the dingy corridor. Somewhere along its depths awaited her resting place, at least for the night. Surely this boor of a marshal would come to his senses by dawn and let her free.

Ben stepped aside. "Puttin' you in the back with another female," he said, the keys jangling in his hand.

"The little lady'll do jes' fine in here" came a slurred male voice from one of the cells as they passed.

"Settle down, Tom," Ben said with a click. "Alcohol has pickled your parts so much, I doubt you could do much if she was in there for a week."

The jailer continued to shuffle down the corridor, ignoring similar suggestions that came from out of the dimness, not stopping until they arrived at the last cell on the right. A solid wall separated it from the adjoining cell and gave whoever might occupy it a modicum of privacy.

Light from a kerosene lamp, attached high on the corridor wall, flickered into the enclosure. On one of the two cots in the narrow quarters, Rella could make out the huddled figure of a woman, a black shawl covering a black dress. Even the clank of the opening door failed to draw the woman's attention.

"Widow Welch," Ben said cheerfully, "brought you company." The woman didn't move. Ben turned to Rella. "The widow don't talk much to folks that's living. Been waiting here almost two months, matter of fact, and not heard so much as a half dozen words from her."

"What has the woman done?" Rella asked in puzzlement.

"Been widowed, best I can tell. Don't like it one bit. Talks to her late husband. That's more than she was able to do when he was with her, I reckon. Welch was drunk most of the time, paid more than a few visits here. Broke his neck when he tried to race his nag down the beach. Folks say the widow ain't been the same since."

Rella turned angrily on Cort. "Since when is widowhood a crime?"

Cort shook his head. "The widow isn't charged with anything."

"Then why is she incarcerated?"

"She's waiting for a room to open up at the mental ward in Austin. This is the only place for such folks to stay."

"How barbaric!"

"Don't be so quick to judge. Mrs. Welch is suffering from a sickness of the mind. The state has determined she needs care and watching, but there are too many others like her for the facilities. Hence her stay here. We've got a few more patients likewise awaiting removal to Austin, but she's the only female. If," Cort added, the harshness returning to his eyes, "I had any choice, I'd not put a criminal in with the poor woman.

Even a suspected one. I better not hear you've disturbed her in any way."

With those warning words, Rella was escorted into the dim cell and the door slammed shut at her back. The harsh, metallic sound echoed down the corridor. She stared at Cort through the bars.

"I might give you the same advice you gave me, Marshal," she said. "Don't be so quick to judge. The problem is that with your own money involved, you're just too close to this case to pick out the facts."

With that, she turned to meet the Widow Welch. Even this poor, deluded woman would be better company than the arrogant lawman who had so callously thrown her in jail and then had the nerve to issue a warning about behaving herself.

The Widow Welch proved a poor companion, spending the evening hours wringing a handkerchief in her hands and talking with her late husband about the chores that needed doing around the house. Rella decided he must never have listened to his wife when he was alive. The widow figured she had his attention now.

A thin mattress covering Rella's cot offered unsatisfactory comfort for a body needing rest, and when she awoke the next morning, she was more exhausted than she'd been during the sleepless nights following her injury in the boardinghouse fire. She huddled beneath a thin blanket. Somehow the stone walls held in a damp cold that belied the summer outside.

For a moment she gave in to reflection, her hand moving automatically to the moonstone brooch at her throat. Here she was, the granddaughter of a Gypsy queen and an English earl, thrown into the depths of a Texas jail. Her grandparents never had their brief joining recognized by the clergy, but according to the daughter that had been born to them, theirs had been a union of love. Only the strictures of society—and a tyrant of a father—had forced the earl to abandon Esmeralda and their child.

At least that was Mama's tale. Nara Scamp bore her mother Esmeralda's last name—to save the earl embarrassment had been the story. She had traveled the route of fairs and carnivals, telling fortunes alongside her Gypsy mother. One look at Jonathan Sandringham, a touring actor at one of the fairs, and she was in love for life.

Papa had taught her to read and write and to "tread the boards," as he put it, "giving life to the Bard's great words." Nara had taken to Shakespeare the way she had to fortune telling. When Rella came along to bless their union, the Sandringhams, in their flamboyant way, decided to transport culture to the new world. Unfortunately, they hadn't listened to the rumbles of an American civil war, which had echoed even in England. Their activities had been confined to the northeast part of the country.

Once the war was done, it had been up to Rella to take care of the day-to-day problems of their lives, while Nara and Jonathan planned on a loftier plane. They would carry Shakespeare into the wild interior of America. The boating accident had ended their dreams.

What a curious assortment of ancestors she had, Rella thought. Somehow she'd gained strength from the mixture. She wouldn't meet her end on a stretch of sand and shell in the underbelly of Texas.

Shaking off the effects of a restless night, Rella stood and stretched. A trickle of light came into the cell from a high, dirty window at the end of the corridor. Rella stared down at the Widow Welch, who hadn't, as far as she could tell, even attempted to sleep, instead sitting at the edge of her cot and rocking her body back and forth.

"Good morning," Rella said, although what was good about it she hadn't yet decided. Perhaps it was that she couldn't hear a lynch mob forming outside.

The widow stared silently up at her, an act that Rella considered progress. At least her existence was recognized.

"Looks like we're going to be companions for a while."

Still silence.

"I'm Rella Sandringham." Nothing. She went for shock effect. "Marshal Ramsey is apparently charging me with murder and robbery. Charges of which I am innocent."

"Of course you are, my dear."

Rella stared. "What did you say?"

"Simply that you're innocent. Anyone can see that by looking at you. I've seen enough bad ones go through here in the past two months to know."

Rella smiled, the first time she'd done anything so cheerful in twenty-four hours. The act made her feel giddy.

"No one here thinks you notice much."

The woman's lined face broke into an answering smile. "But I do. Mr. Welch and I discuss everything that goes on here. He advises me sometimes. When I ask. I didn't need any advice about you."

Rella studied her unlikely cellmate. The widow must be close to sixty, judging from her wrinkled face and hands and the gray hairs on her head. When she stood and walked to the bolted door, Rella saw they were almost the same height, although the widow's shoulders were bent and she carried a little more weight on her frame.

"Morning, ladies." Ben Woods's voice, as well as the click of his teeth, startled them from the corridor. "One of you's got visitors. Reckon it won't do no harm to let them come on back."

Rella smoothed her wrinkled frock and, giving up on her tangled mass of hair, looked past the jailer. "Greta! And Aaron. What are you two doing here?"

Greta edged her short, plump body past Ben. "I brought you something," she said, winking broadly and extending a square package neatly wrapped in brown paper and twine. "And you know Aaron. He wouldn't let me come to such a place alone. Not," she hastened to add, "that it's so bad. I'm sure they're treating you well enough."

Rella shook her head. "You don't have to make me feel better about being here. No one has abused me. Yet. But of course I haven't seen my almighty accuser yet today."

"The marshal will be along soon, I reckon," Ben said, then bent an approving eye on Greta. "Things certainly are improving around here."

Greta's soft femininity and air of helplessness had won another admirer, Rella noted. Maybe if she shared a little of that gentle goodness, she might not be where she was.

But then again, maybe she would. Cort Ramsey didn't seem the type to be taken in by feminine charm—or by much of anything else.

She turned to Aaron. "How are you doing today?"

Aaron shook his head slowly. "Just trying to believe what's happened. Marcus is taking care of . . ." As was his wont, he let his voice trail into silence, leaving others to finish his thought.

"Good for Marcus," Rella said wryly. She could picture the law clerk making the arrangements for Perry Tuttle's funeral. When he was alive, the attorney hadn't let Marcus do much that was important. But circumstances had changed. Marcus would be quick to take advantage.

Silently Rella chastised herself. Here she was judging another's actions without a great deal of evidence, something she'd thrown up to Cort Ramsey. Maybe Marcus was acting from the goodness of his heart.

"Ben," Rella said, "could you let my visitors in for a while? I'm sure they couldn't help me escape."

Ben shook his head. "Against the rules."

"What about my package?" Greta asked, looking up at the jailer with eyes wide.

Before she had finished, Ben was reaching for his keys.

"Just the lady," he said, as though the frail Aaron presented some kind of threat.

Greta smiled at him and bustled inside. Rella introduced her to the Widow Welch, who moved to the back of the cell, seemingly withdrawn once more into her own thoughts.

"Here," Greta said, again winking. "I baked you a cake. Maybe you and your friend could have a piece of it when we're all gone." Another wink.

Rella almost dropped the unexpectedly heavy package. When she had a good grip on it, she looked at it with more interest. "What have you got in here, a bomb?"

Greta laughed self-consciously. "You always tease." She glanced over her shoulder at Ben. "Can't listen to a thing she says."

Rella placed the curiously heavy cake on the bed. Greta was a good cook. What on earth had she brought? And why was she acting so nervous?

The visitors quickly excused themselves.

The widow spoke when they were gone. "You've got a strange friend."

Rella unwrapped the cake. "I've got a good friend. Care for breakfast?"

"Thank you. More than likely it'll be better than the gruel Ben will be passing out in a while."

Rella attempted to break off a piece. Her fingers struck something hard. She split the cake in half and saw the reason for Greta's wink. Inside the cake had been baked a steel file.

How like Greta to come up with such a scheme. The girl possessed a dangerous pair of characteristics: a lively imagination and more nerve than most men.

Quickly Rella wrapped up the butchered cake and hid the file beneath her mattress. What she planned to do with it, she hadn't the faintest idea. Somehow she couldn't see employing it as an effective means of escape.

Chapter Three

Cort reined his bay gelding to a stop on the narrow residential street near the docks and glanced at the dark clouds forming over the Gulf. Galveston had already been hit by one storm in June, and from the looks of the thunderheads on the horizon, another was on the way. Folks were fond of saying that one day the whole island would be washed to kingdom come by one of those hurricanes. Folks just passing through, that is. The residents swore the city, largest in Texas, would someday be another New York.

Lifting his hat, he wiped sweat from his brow with a forearm. The breeze on this Sunday morning had stilled; the air, heavy with the smell of salt and fish, pressed in on him until he couldn't breathe. Oppressive as the weather was, it seemed appropriate for investigating a man's death.

And for finding a man's stolen goods. He tried not to let the fact that the money belonged to him influence his search, as his unrepentant suspect had claimed. But hell's fire, he hated to let a thief take advantage of him, especially one who refused to admit she'd been caught.

What he'd like to do is turn that termagant suspect over his knee and apply a little persuasion to her enticing behind until he found out what he needed to know. Cort wasn't a violent man, but there was something about the woman that brought out the beast in him. Cinderella, was she? In his present state, he hardly filled the bill of Prince Charming. Nor was he her fairy godmother, willing to finance her own particular dreams.

Still, as he thought back over the evidence, he didn't share Ernest Bowles' opinion that the murder had been solved. Things didn't work out so easily. A little more investigating, he figured, was in order before he went by the jail to question her this morning.

Dismounting, he let his attention wander down the row of small-frame homes. Each one was raised on stilts, Galvestonians having learned such architecture was good protection against the oftentimes rising Gulf waters. His destination, the neatest structure on the street, was the home of Gerhardt and Greta Maas.

The Maas home wore a fresh coat of white paint, and a border of blooming oleanders clustered against the stilts. Cort had already done a little probing before heading out for the house. Maas and his daughter had come to Texas from Germany a year ago. An educated man, he'd landed a good job on the docks as timekeeper for the gangs of screwmen who were charged with getting bales of cotton crammed into the holds.

There were growing rumors of trouble on the waterfront where Maas worked, of thefts and doctored records, but never had Cort heard Perry Tuttle linked to them. Sometime later he would have to question Maas about those rumors, but not today, not with another, weightier matter on his mind.

Cort gave a thought to Greta and her protective attitude toward Rella Sandringham. If he listened to that wide-eyed young woman, he would be giving his only suspect an award for tolerating the late lawyer.

He'd learned at Rella's boardinghouse that she spent some nights at the Maas abode. He was looking for anything and everything that might tell him more about her. All he knew right now was that in contrast to her wide blue eyes and fine-chiseled face, she had a sharp tongue and more nerve than good sense. And she could assume different roles.

Gerhardt Maas met him at the door. A massive man, shorter and wider than Cort and a decade older than Cort's thirty-five years, Maas sported a full head of gray hair and a beard to be proud of. On this Sunday morning, he wore a vested black suit and a bowed cravat.

"Sorry to disturb you," Cort said after introducing himself.

"I was expecting you, Marshal Ramsey," Maas said in a clipped German accent. He held open the screened door. "Please do me the honor of entering my home."

Cort nodded and removed his hat as he stepped inside. Maas had a well-bred air about him that said welcome and made the occasion seem less than the somber official business it was.

Seated in the parlor were his daughter Greta and Aaron Tuttle. The latter rose and extended his hand.

"Marshal—" Aaron began.

"Ramsey," Cort finished as the young man's voice trailed into silence. A day after his father's death, the angular medical student still wore the same bewildered pain that Cort had noticed at the scene of the crime.

From her place on the sofa, Greta had a worried look about her. "Have you been to the jail yet this morning?"

Cort shook his head. "I wanted to talk to you and your father first." He studied the girl. "Something wrong?"

Greta's eyes widened. "Not anything I know of." Her round face settled into a frown. "Except that Rella is being held in that awful place. All the way in the back with those men saying such awful things."

"You've been to see her?"

Greta swallowed. "Just for a few minutes. Aaron took me by."

"My daughter," Maas interrupted, "feels as I do. To arrest Fraulein Sandringham is a terrible injustice. For such acts as this I left Germany."

"I assure you, Mr. Maas, that injustice is just as hateful to me," Cort said, holding back his temper. Somehow every time Rella Sandringham's name came up, he was the one who ended up needing a defense.

Maas gestured toward a chair. "Won't you take a seat? It's early yet, but perhaps a glass of schnapps? It seems to take the edge off such a day as today."

Cort shook his head. He had no time for socializing. "I understand Rella Sandringham spent some time in your home," he said.

"That is correct. She is a quiet young lady—"

Cort swallowed a cynical retort.

"—who has always exhibited the highest character. I am proud that Greta could call her friend."

"The fact that she's touring with a troupe of actors doesn't bother you?"

"My former homeland is not without its strengths. In the old country, Marshal Ramsey, those who give life to the words of poets are honored."

Cort remembered the last play he'd seen, a farce about husbands and other men's wives. Obviously Maas was remembering far more serious performances than usually were seen at the Tremont Opera House. Still, the man had a point. Actresses might lead a more unorthodox life than other women, but that didn't make them necessarily corrupt. It wasn't Rella's calling that Cort held against her; he had far more serious evidence that threatened to keep her in jail.

"Did you happen to see her yesterday around noon?"

"My work on the docks does not permit me even a brief visit home during the day. I have not seen Rella for close to a week."

"Does she have a key?"

"Of course. I told you. Fraulein Sandringham has the complete trust of both myself and Greta."

"*Ja,* Papa," Greta said from her perch at the edge of the sofa.

Aaron supported her view with a nod.

Cort looked from Greta to her father. "Then both of you are certain she could not have made a quick visit here yesterday to leave a packet."

Greta rose, her bosom heaving with indignation. "To leave the money, you mean. *Mein Gott!*"

"Greta! Herr Ramsey is a guest in our home."

"My father is correct, of course. I am sure he would have no objection if you were to examine Rella's belongings. There is a small room at the top of the stairs where she sometimes stays."

"Thank you, Miss Maas, Cort said, "for your cooperation. We both want to uncover the truth."

He made short work of the search. Furnishings included a small bed and bureau, the top drawer of which yielded the only thing of any interest to him: a bank slip indicating that three days earlier the angelic-looking Rella had withdrawn from a Galveston bank the sum of three hundred dollars. It was enough to leave Galveston and travel to rejoin her friends, but it wouldn't go much farther. Maybe it wasn't her entire savings. Had she, without realizing he could check, made another deposit yesterday before the bank closed? He knew it wasn't likely.

Greta said she knew nothing of the three hundred dollars and refused to discuss the slip of paper, but he could tell from the look in her eyes that she was holding something back. The bank was closed today; like most island folks on a Sunday afternoon, even one that held the threat of an approaching storm, the manager would probably be somewhere on the beach. He would have to postpone learning the status of Rella's account.

His search of the law office and the close appraisal he'd given to her person had offered up no sign of money, either hers or his. Likely Greta had the smaller amount, but he could hardly demand to search her rooms. Even if he did turn up the cash, there was nothing it would prove.

In the meantime, a visit to the Galveston jail was definitely in order. He felt a curious pleasure at the thought of facing the suspect again. The noose seemed to be tightening around her lovely neck. Maybe if she realized the seriousness of the evidence against her, she would confess, turn over her ill-gotten gains, and throw herself on the mercy of the court. Perry Tuttle could have made advances that frightened her. Cort remembered the way she'd lifted her skirts in brazen innocence—or so it seemed as he looked back on it. Without meaning to, she might easily have provoked her employer into doing something stupid.

Marcus Clapper seemed to think Rella had thrown herself at Tuttle. From so enticing a woman as Rella Sandringham, however, the poor man couldn't have expected a bullet in the chest.

Cort offered Maas thanks for the cooperation he'd received, requested that Greta visit him should she remember some potentially valuable details concerning her friend, and headed his gelding for the jail. Deputy Bowles and the jailer Ben Woods met him in the outer office.

"Had a quiet night around here," Ben said with a click.

"Yep," Bowles agreed. "That actress didn't cause any kind of a ruckus."

"I figured the pair of you could handle her," Cort said. "Especially since you had her behind bars."

Bowles frowned. "No need to ridicule, Marshal. Women in a jail can cause havoc. Stir the men up just by being close by."

A woman who looked like Rella Sandringham certainly could, Cort thought.

"Looks like we got the case about wrapped up," the deputy continued, shifting his belt to a more comfortable position beneath his paunch. "We can file charges in the morning, or maybe even round up a judge this afternoon."

Cort felt the irritation which always nettled him whenever Bowles tried to talk business. He'd tried to analyze it once. Bowles rarely did anything on his own initiative, kept a coterie of young toughs around him—"getting 'em to go into law enforcement," he explained to Cort—and never seemed to be around when there was trouble. All in all, there wasn't much to recommend him as a lawman.

"I've got a little investigating to do before we hang her," Cort said.

Bowles's eyes narrowed. "What kind of investigating?"

"Just a few loose ends."

"We got that clerk's testimony. A man's dying words ought to count for something. At least that's the way we've always looked at it down here on the island. Maybe you Yankees got other ideas."

"Maybe," Cort said, "we like to check out all the evidence. Alibis, for instance. What if she can come up with one?" He remembered the long ago injustice that had driven him to be a marshal, the unsolved murder of Josiah Ramsey. "I'd hate for the real murderer to go free."

Bowles muttered an imprecation under his breath. Cort had seldom seen him so agitated.

"We got the real murderer back in that cell," Bowles said through gritted teeth.

"Probably," Cort said, trying to be fair. "Ben, you mind getting Miss Sandringham? I'm taking her out for a while."

Ben looked from one man to the other and disappeared through the door leading to the cells.

"And why would you take her out of jail?" Bowles growled. "It's not the usual way we treat prisoners around here."

Cort's temper flared. "I don't have to answer to you, Bowles."

The deputy drew himself taller. "With the sheriff out of town, I am in charge. If you don't file charges, I will."

Which of course he could do. A beautiful actress from England charged with the murder of a prominent Galvestonian—Cort could see the headlines in the *Daily News* now. He even felt sorry for Rella Sandringham with a lawman like Bowles convinced of her guilt. Still, antagonizing the man would make his job of determining her guilt or innocence beyond any doubt all the harder, and he forced himself to be conciliatory.

"Let's hold off until tomorrow, until I can check out her story. Then we'll go together before a judge. You'll get more credit if I make it known you helped me prove a case of murder that'll stand up in court."

"I just think it's a damned fool idea," Bowles said with a scowl.

Cort looked steadily at the deputy. "Ernest, the last case I was on, chasing a gang of robbers that held up a Houston bank, took me halfway across West Texas. Had to take on a small band of Apaches and a half-starved wildcat defending her cubs before I was through. I'm a peaceable man. Interrogating a beautiful woman, even a murderess, will be a relief."

"As long as you don't forget what she's done."

Cort thought of the missing money. "I'm not likely to forget."

When Ben brought the suspect into the office, her blue eyes flaring defiance and a mane of blond hair tumbling in disarray abut her shoulders, Cort took one look and forgot all about the money, remembering for the moment only his troubles with the wildcat.

"Thought we'd go for a walk this morning," he said. "The air's a little close, but I imagine it's better than back in the cell."

Rella extended a slender wrist, exposing the burn scar on her hand. "I don't suppose I have any choice. You'll want to shackle me, of course."

"Good idea," barked Bowles.

Cort patted the revolver strapped to his thigh. "Not today. I'll just gun you down if you try to escape."

"I would expect nothing less."

Rella took a quick survey of her oppressor. Copper hair rested against the column of his neck; a paler shade of red curled at the open throat of his shirt. Solemn-faced and watchful, he looked even taller today than he had the last time she'd seen him. Taller and stronger and certainly no less sarcastic.

Still, there was something gentle in the depths of those probing eyes, something he couldn't hide even with his taunts. And there were those laugh lines around his mouth that she'd noticed yesterday. She couldn't bring herself to believe he would be unfair.

Aware of his manliness, she gave in to a moment of womanly vanity. "You'll have to excuse my appearance," she said, tossing back her hair. "The facilities here aren't designed for a woman's ablutions."

Cort studied the full picture she presented. Even wrinkled, the gown followed the curves of her body as it was obviously designed to do. His body warmed the way it had yesterday—until he remembered what she had most likely done.

"Let's go," he said curtly, clamping a flat-crowned hat low on his forehead and directing her toward the door.

As they walked down the sidewalk, she realized he'd been right about the weather outside. The smell of oleanders, normally refreshing on the breeze off the ocean, hung cloyingly sweet on the morning's still air. She noticed the storm clouds on the horizon and shuddered. She'd been through one of those hurricanes already this month. All she needed was another one rattling the bars of her cell to make her misery complete.

To her dismay, Cort directed her toward Perry Tuttle's law office.

"I want you to walk through everything you did yesterday," he said as they mounted the inside stairs.

What did he expect her to do, she wondered, reenact the crime?

She paused in the doorway leading from the hallway into Tuttle's office. The body had been removed, but there were still blood stains on the wooden floor. She averted her eyes.

"What's the purpose of all this?" she asked.

"Maybe," he said, studying her from beneath the rolled rim of his hat, "you'll remember something you forgot. Think of someone who saw you in the park. That is where you claimed to be when the shots were fired, isn't it?"

Rella was torn between gratitude that he was giving her a chance to prove her innocence and anger that he so obviously doubted she could manage the feat. She hurried through the office and into the small room she shared with Marcus Clapper. She heard the marshal lock the outer door before joining her.

"On Saturdays I come in late. Obviously I arrived after your appointment. I spent most of the morning in here going over the books."

"Is this a normal practice for the weekend?"

"I've already told you I planned to leave soon. I wanted everything to be in order."

"You told me you were leaving," Cort reminded her, "only after I found the ticket for your passage."

Rella lifted her chin. "An understandable oversight on my part, given the circumstances of yesterday."

"Perhaps there are others. That's why we're here. When did you see Tuttle?"

"We kept to our separate offices. Except for the time I went in to ask him about a particular entry he'd made."

"And what was he doing?"

"He was kneeling before the safe. That's when I saw the packet of money."

"You don't deny it."

"There wouldn't be any point. If you recall, I mentioned its disappearance yesterday."

"I recall. After talking with Tuttle, what did you do?"

"Marcus and I both left for lunch. We went our separate ways, of course. Mr. Tuttle said he had some business to take care of and probably wouldn't be back for the rest of the day."

"You have no idea what that business was? Perhaps an appointment with someone?"

Rella wondered if the marshal might be offering her a chance to come up with another suspect, a mysterious visitor who had done the dreadful deed, but try as she might she couldn't. And convinced as she was that her innocence would be proven, she couldn't lie. "He always had business to take care of," she said. "He could have had an appointment, but that's no more than speculation."

"When you left here, where exactly did you go?"

"I had packed a small lunch in my reticule. I headed for the park. The weather was nice, and from there you can hear the ocean. It makes a welcome contrast to these four walls."

Her eyes took on a faraway look, and Cort felt a brief sympathy for her. She was used to a different kind of life, of travel and of the public stage. To be confined to this dreary room for much of every day, even on a temporary basis, must have been discouraging.

The sympathy died. Such discouragement might have given rise to desperation. She could have seen a quick way out of the trap brought on by her injury and taken it without consideration for the pain inflicted on others as a result.

"Let's go to that park," he ordered. "Take the exact route."

Rella needed no encouragement to get out of that office. Hurrying down the outside stairs, taking care to lock the door just as she'd done the day before, she walked slightly ahead of Cort through the side streets leading south from the business district. On Sunday morning they were deserted. With Cort close at her side, she didn't stop until she was on the pathway that wound through the city park.

"And you didn't see anybody you knew," Cort said.

"I know few people in town," she said. "I saw few people on the back route I took, certainly no one I recognized. Perhaps I ought to advertise in the *Daily News*. Someone might have recognized me."

"There was a story in this morning's paper about your arrest. No one has come forth."

Rella's spirits sank, but she rallied, reminding herself she really hadn't expected an eyewitness to support her story. With the way things had gone for her lately, it would have been a fruitless hope.

She found the bench, secluded in a bower of trees, where she'd eaten her small repast. With the overhead branches motionless in the heavy air, she listened to the distant sound of the ocean. Usually its muted regularity gave her assurance that there was continuity in the universe. This morning the beat of the waves seemed more a reminder she was a prisoner on this narrow stretch of land.

As had happened yesterday, she sat there unaccosted. Only this time she had a sharp-eyed marshal staring down at her.

"How long were you gone?" he asked.

"Half an hour, three quarters. I don't wear a watch."

From the corner of her eye she saw him nod, as if he had expected everything she had said. No witnesses, no proof that she wasn't telling a lie. How all knowing—and all powerful—he looked sitting beside her, his long legs stretched across the path. He didn't need that badge to give him the stamp of authority, or the gun strapped to that strong thigh. It was in his eyes, in the way he carried himself, in the way he seemed always to be thinking, analyzing, judging.

Rella realized with a start the importance of his understanding she was incapable of murder, and not because he held over her the power of life and death.

In other circumstances she might have respected him, might have wanted—

She pushed all foolish thoughts from her mind. He was more of a man than anyone she had ever known, but their paths had crossed at the wrong time. Suddenly the whole exercise seemed futile. She rose. "Let's go back and finish this up."

Her pace was quicker on the return trip as she tried without success to put distance between the two of them. Let him finish with his interrogation, she decided. Back at the jail she would hand over that ridiculous file, refusing of course to reveal where she'd gotten it, and await her fate. He hadn't any real proof against her. At least she kept telling herself he hadn't. With each repetition, however, the thought gave her less and less comfort.

She paused on the outside landing of the alleyway stairs. "The door was unlocked when I returned. It was secure when I left."

Cort made no comment, thinking to himself it was too bad she didn't have an eyewitness to anything she claimed.

Rella stepped inside the dimly lit office. The oppressiveness of outside had invaded the law office, sapping her last reservoirs of strength. As if in a dream, she walked past her desk and into the larger room. Her hand fluttered in front of her. "I saw him right away. I kneeled down. Then you came in."

To her everlasting shame, she felt her eyes blur. She swayed, then felt a pair of strong arms around her.

"Let's go into the other room," Cort said.

Guided into the smaller office, she continued to lean against the soothing strength of the marshal, her head nestled against the crook of his broad shoulder. What had come over her? She had no inclination to pull free.

When she became aware of Cort Ramsey as a man and not as a source of solace, she didn't know. But gradually the image of death faded from her mind, and she thought only of the arms that were holding her. Here was what she had wanted back in the park—for him to embrace her, to use his strength for comfort and, yes, for so much more. She breathed in the musky maleness of him and touched with tentative fingers the muscled sinews of his chest. She heard an intake of breath and looked up. She drowned in a pair of blue eyes.

Never in her twenty-one years had a man held her in such a way. Never had she encouraged one to do so. But when Cort Ramsey's head bent to hers and she felt his breath warm on her cheek, it seemed the most natural action on earth to meet his lips in a willing kiss.

Chapter Four

Soft lips moved against Cort's as he enveloped Rella in his arms. Regardless of what he'd meant to do when he offered her the comfort of his support, right now he wanted only to continue the very pleasurable act of kissing her. His hands rested against her back. He tightened his hold and felt the distinct pressure of her breasts against him.

Warm fingers touched his throat, and he knew she must surely feel the quickening beat of his heart. If he held her like this much longer—and he had no intention of doing otherwise—she would most likely feel more solid evidence of his sudden arousal. Like summer lightning, Rella Sandringham's kiss had ignited a spark in him that threatened to burst into full flame.

Rella was well aware of his reaction to her, for she matched it with sensations of her own. She felt her own rapid pulse and a new and wonderful warmth coursing throughout her body. Her mind reeled with the intensity of her response. Never had she responded to anything with such overpowering loss of will, and she found herself on the brink of complete submission.

But Rella hadn't spent a lifetime taking care of herself without instinctive reservations coming into play when she neared the edge of danger. Even as

Cort Ramsey held her tightly and pressed an incredibly provocative mouth against hers, somewhere in the recesses of her mind rippled a thought that no matter how caught up she was in his spell, all he wanted was a quick sexual release, a release he had been too willingly offered.

Warmth turned to chill. She'd been waiting for him to offer a deal, the same sort of offer she received on more than one occasion from her late employer, a suggestion for favors rendered on both sides. Cort couldn't feel the way she did about him, couldn't share the special attraction that had taken her by surprise, although, Lord help her, she must be weak in the head to feel such a way. Cort was a virile man; the spoken words that spelled out exactly what he wanted would soon follow this physical assault.

She stiffened but could detect no lessening of his ardor. Rather, he hastened his ravishment of her by moving insistent and expert hands lower down her back, pausing only momentarily at her waist before cupping her backside and pulling her hard against him. The folds of skirt and petticoat offered scant protection against his arousal. For a moment her resolve—and her stiffened spine—weakened. She was well aware of his intent, but with the way his body fit into the valley between her legs, she felt closer than ever to her downfall. She had been a fool to think of him in a special way, but at the same time she had to give him credit. He certainly knew how to proceed.

Her proclivity for self-preservation saved her. The marshal was a determined man. But no less determined was she. She parted her mouth, heard a guttural sound issue from deep inside him, and caught his lower lip firmly between her teeth. The guttural sound became a yelp, and he loosened his hold on her just as she loosened the grip she had on him. Freed from his embrace, she stared at the mark she had left, a scarlet bubble on his mouth. She had drawn first blood. She could not contain a smile of triumph.

His lip was fast increasing in size.

"Maybe," she said, holding her position close to him and her eyes steady on his, "you ought to put some ice on your wound. And whatever else is swollen."

Cort stepped away, disgusted with himself as much as he was with her. "Right now, lady, your coldness is doing the job just fine. What in hell was all that about?"

"I think, Marshal," she said, summoning the shreds of her dignity, "that I should be asking such a question. After all, you attacked me."

Cort shook his head in disbelief. How could he have let himself forget who he was dealing with? Rella was most likely a murderer and a thief, wrapped in the guise of a honey-skinned actress. He had realized yesterday she could play the part of innocent. Now he would add wanton to the list.

Many a man had been led astray by such a Jezebel. But not he.

"We see things differently," he said, gingerly touching his mouth. He remembered too late how, back at the jail, she'd reminded him of that West Texas wildcat. With the way his lip was throbbing, it wasn't likely he'd forget it again.

Cort's eyes trailed insolently down her body. "You must have some kind of switch in there. Turn on the heat. Turn on the indignation." He frowned and winced at the pain. "Turn on the mayhem."

Heart pounding, Rella felt hurt by his words. Yet how could she possibly let him wound her in such a way? He was no more than a narrow-minded, lusty lawman, a fact she had better not forget.

"How like a man to attempt an assault and blame

the woman," she threw back at him. "I suppose I enticed you so that you lost your head for a moment. Poor marshal."

Cort's temper boiled. How much time would he have to serve for attacking a prisoner under his care? Whatever amount would be worth the satisfaction he would receive.

"You're good," he said scornfully. "But not good enough. I would have eventually remembered my purpose in bringing you here. Which, I assume, you figured out. You shouldn't have stopped so soon, however. We could have both gotten a little release and then gone about our business: you lying to me, and me proving your guilt."

Rella's only regret at that moment was she hadn't bitten his lip in two. Until now, she hadn't realized the real danger she was in. Cort Ramsey was more than just narrow minded and lusty; he was a brutal lawman who was intent on clearing up a case and finding his money. Her only consolation, a scant one indeed, was that in concentrating on her as his suspect, he was losing his money to the real culprit. She would laugh all the way to the gallows on that thought.

Cort held out the bank statement he'd found in the home of Gerhardt Maas.

"Care to explain this?" he asked. "It's dated four days ago. Are you sure there's not another one dated yesterday?"

Rella recognized it immediately. The man was thorough. "Clutching at straws, aren't you, Marshal? Are private citizens not allowed bank accounts in Texas?"

Cort waved the paper. "It's a lot of money to save in a few weeks."

"I'm a frugal girl."

"Also too close-mouthed for your own good perhaps."

"I don't have to explain anything. Except to an attorney."

"You'll need a good one."

"I don't suppose there are any women practicing law in this state?"

Cort shuddered. His luscious little suspect might be part Texas wildcat, but she also carried a strong streak of Missouri mule. In open court, pairing someone like her with a similarly shrewish attorney could set the law back twenty years.

"You'll have adequate representation. Although you will have to depend on a man. I suggest you hold off on any kind of attack."

Rella counted to ten in Romany, the language of the Gypsies. Before this morning's disastrous sortie, she'd been planning to hand over Greta's ridiculous file to the marshal and ask that they discuss sensibly and without emotion the merits of the case against her. The Widow Welch had known immediately she was innocent. Surely a professional lawman, given time for reflection, could realize the same.

She'd planned to point out that Marcus Clapper could easily be lying about Tuttle's dying words. She'd planned to explain the way her parents had raised her to be honest and straightforward, even as she pursued her dreams. She'd planned to remind the marshal that even the victim's son knew she was incapable of such a horrible act.

Now, as she found herself escorted none too gently back toward the county jail, roiling thunderclouds and oyster-shell streets offering little distraction, all she planned was to find a way to escape.

The storm hit close to midnight and pushed for a time all worry about legal problems from Rella's mind. Wind and rain howled about the small brick enclosure. For hours the barred window at the end of the corridor rattled a frightening cadence, as though the storm gods themselves sought admittance to the jail.

The walls gave incomplete protection against such force, and the normally stale air was permeated with a cold wind that blew through the cracks around the window with such force it extinguished the few lanterns hung along the way. Darkness was as frightening as the swell of sound. Rella heard more than a few prayers sent heavenward by the men down the way. A few repented their sins, vowing abstention from drink and assorted other vices. The Widow Welch remained silent on her bunk, deep in communication with her late husband.

Sometime before dawn, a calm descended, and the jailer Ben made his first appearance beside the cells, a lantern held high in one hand.

"Thought you left us back here to die," one man said.

"It'd save the county some money, all right," Ben said, " 'ceptin' for the cost of a pauper's burial."

"Does a man's heart good"—came a sarcastic voice from another cell—"to hear such concern."

Rella peered down the corridor and saw Ernest Bowles standing in the shadows beside Ben. "This isn't the place for concern," the deputy said.

"That's for damned sure," the same prisoner said.

Taking the lantern from Ben, Bowles made his way back to Rella's cell and stood in a pool of water that had worked its way in around the window frame. "Looks like you two women are doing all right. Wouldn't want anything to happen to you while the marshal's out of town."

Rella decided that was probably when she was

safest, but she kept the thought to herself. "Where did he go?" she asked. "To find a hanging judge?"

Bowles scowled. "Left right after he brought you back yesterday. Went up to Houston to make sure some farm land he wants is still available. Damned Yankee. Taking advantage of hard times, he is, buying up people's property for taxes."

So that's what he wanted with the money. Still, she wondered how he had gathered such a sum. He'd questioned her paltry account, but that didn't put him above reproach.

He must be after that farm as an investment. Rella had a hard time picturing Cort Ramsey settling down in the country and working the land. Somehow it didn't figure into the picture of strutting arrogance he'd presented to her.

"Did he say when he would return?"

"Tomorrow, most likely," Bowles said, then added in disgust, "Still trying to gather evidence, he says. Seems to me we've got enough."

Rella's mind worked fast. If she were to gain her freedom, she would best do it when the marshal was far away. The problem was that she could see no way to accomplish the task.

"Anyway," Bowles continued, "just thought I'd let you know the storm's not through. A little calm here is all this is. The wind will be back stronger than ever."

Rather like the marshal, she thought. A day away from her wasn't likely to make him think more kindly of her, especially if he were asked about his fat lip.

Forgetting whatever tender thoughts she had once harbored concerning him, she wore a satisfied smile. He'd been fighting to hold his temper when he deposited her back at the jail. His already ruddy complexion had been tinged with more red than usual. He had a hard time controlling his anger. At least he did around her. Since he didn't frighten her, it was one of his characteristics she most enjoyed.

The calm lasted only a few minutes after Bowles and the jailer left. The back side of the storm seemed more savage than the front. Water that had pooled on the corridor floor from the first onslaught of wind and rain worked its way into the cell, and the two women huddled on their separate bunks.

Incredibly Rella found herself drifting off to sleep. The sound of a key in the cell door lock brought her quickly to wakefulness. She blinked her eyes and looked up from her bunk to see sunlight streaming through the window onto the bent form of Ben Woods. He stared at her for a moment before directing his attention to the Widow Welch. Rella thought he had an air of confusion about him. Most likely the storm was the cause.

"Let's go, widow," he said, opening the door. "Careful about the water. Got to get a mop back here."

Unmindful of her skirts, the Widow Welch stood docilely. Her black shawl lay forgotten on the bunk.

"Where's she going?" Rella asked.

"Been sent for from the hospital. Soon as the railroad tracks have been cleared of whatever the storm washed up, she'll be headin' out for Austin."

Rella watched as the widow moved slowly to the open cell door. The woman paused, turned and offered Rella a slight smile, then shuffled out toward her fate. Rella was overcome with sadness, both for the widow's unknown future and for her own loss of a friend.

She stared helplessly as Ben closed the cell door. Here she was, young and healthy. She should have thrown herself against the jailer in a surprise attack and bolted for freedom. In self-disgust she watched him lead the widow down the quiet corridor.

Too quiet. After the door banged shut, she heard nothing but the sound of their feet on the wooden floor, the widow's squeaking from the water that had soaked into her shoes, Ben's boots scraping slowly after. What should have assaulted her ears—and didn't—was the slam of a bolt. Ben had forgotten to lock the cell.

It simply couldn't be. She pushed against the bars. The truth came gloriously to her as she felt the door give way, heard the melodious sound of a creaking hinge, and prayed that what was music to her ears didn't echo harshly down the corridor. Here she'd been waiting to seize opportunity; incredibly, it had seized her.

She touched the brooch at her throat and wished for the stealth that was supposed to be a Gypsy trait. What she needed was a weapon, although even if she'd possessed a gun, she wouldn't have known what to do with it. She remembered the file and pulled it from beneath her mattress, then headed out on the long walk that would take her to the front office of the jail.

As she made her way toward the light at the end of the corridor, she felt the eyes of the other prisoners on her. None spoke, as though they were all in some kind of conspiracy to see that she got free—until she got to the cell housing the man Tom, who had issued a none too subtle invitation for her company the first day she'd been in the jail.

He leaned against the bars and grinned. "Comin' to see me?" he said in a slurred voice. She wondered how he could have remained drunk after two days in jail. Ben had called him pickled. It must be a permanent state.

"Shhh," she whispered. "I'll get us a bottle and be right back." Her lie brought a widened smile to his face.

She stood at the partially opened office door and listened for the sounds of occupants. All was quiet. Slowly she opened the door. Deputy Bowles was bending over a desk, his back to her. As she stepped up behind him, assuring herself all the while she was only acting a part, she thrust the tip of the metal file into the fat above the deputy's belt.

"I've got a gun," she said. Her words sounded like a shout in the still room. "And," she added, embellishing her tale, "I know how to use it."

Bowles pulled himself upright and glanced over his shoulder. She pushed the file deeper into his back. He raised his hands in surrender.

"I'll be damned! Where'd you get such a thing? And how did you get loose?"

Rella's mind raced. Why was she faced with questions at such a time?

"You'd better teach Ben to lock the cell doors," she advised. "And the marshal not to let a prisoner go through her own desk without searching her afterward." Rella took a deep breath. She liked placing blame on Cort, especially when it was undeserved.

She kept the file firmly in place. "I want you to head out for the cells," she said, carefully remaining behind him as he did what she asked. This time, as she made her way down the long corridor, she was met with words of encouragement and more than a few catcalls directed toward Bowles. Even Tom managed a garbled word of praise.

"You won't get away," the deputy muttered as he stepped into the last cell. "Ben will be back before long. He'll hear me yelling."

As might anyone else who ventured inside the jail office, Rella realized. She needed time to make her escape. Never in her life had she hurt another human being, but never had she been so desperate. Closing her eyes, she lifted the file and swung in the direction of the deputy's head. Whatever contact she managed seemed inadequate, but she opened surprised eyes to see him slumping onto the wet floor.

I've killed him, she thought in panic, then saw the infinitesimal movement of his breathing. Muttering an apology for the brutality that necessity had demanded, she stepped over Bowles' inert form and grabbed up two items which might prove beneficial: the widow's abandoned shawl and a mattress from one of the bunks. She dropped the file beside Bowles—no one else was liable to take it for a gun—and, rolling the mattress awkwardly beneath her arm, made her way once more to freedom. This time the men were silent, even Tom.

The grounds outside were littered with fallen limbs and leaves. Just as she had figured, the gate through the surrounding brick wall was locked. But she didn't plan to go through the front, anyway. Too many lawmen might be lurking around. The courthouse was only a block away.

Behind the jail she found what she was looking for: a split tree branch which would give her access to the top of the wall. Using the mattress as protection against the broken glass imbedded along the surface, she managed to reach her desired perch, only to notice with dismay that there was no handy tree available for descent to the other side. But there were also no witnesses to her escape, and lying at the base of the wall was a mound of wet leaves. Never one for cowardice, she gripped the widow's shawl around her and dropped to the alley ten feet below. Her backside broke the fall. She stood and wiped the damp leaves from her injured parts, glad that she would suffer no more than a bruise.

Reaching high, she flipped the mattress back onto

the jail grounds where it wouldn't be so readily seen and began the second part of her journey. On the street were the signs of destruction: more fallen leaves and trees, a few uprooted, and what appeared to be the stern of a small boat. With the black shawl effectively obscuring her face and tangled mass of hair, she bent her shoulders and joined the throng of people making their way through the aftermath of the nighttime storm. Some were scavengers, others merely curious. She paid them no heed. Her path was chosen. The only place of refuge for her was Gerhardt and Greta Maas.

She approached their home from the rear, slipping past the small shed that housed the Maas's old carriage and making sure as best she could none of the neighbors was peering over a back fence. Gerhardt and Greta welcomed her as she'd hoped they would. An awkward moment with Aaron was soon got over when he said, "The marshal's wrong. I don't know who killed my father, but no matter what anyone says, it wasn't you."

The marshal should have been so smart, she thought. He was foolish enough to believe he needed to consider the evidence.

After she had bathed and dressed in one of the gowns she'd left in the upstairs room, she took time to describe her escape.

"The file really helped, didn't it?" Greta said with a proud smile.

"It was essential," Rella said, then turned to Gerhardt. "Any suggestions about what I do now? I can't let any harm come to you."

"We're not worried about that," Greta interjected, handing her a cup of tea.

"I am," Rella said.

Gerhardt bent his bearlike head in thought, then

looked up at her. "The storm may delay departures. I noticed damage to some of the docks when I went out a while ago. But there's one that shouldn't be affected. Do you have any objections to travel on a trading ship? It has no facilities for passengers, I'm afraid."

"I'll swim alongside if it will guide me out of here."

Gerhardt smiled. "I think, *liebchen,* you have a trace of German blood in your veins."

"Your money is in my room," Greta said.

Rella nodded, remembering the bank slip that had so concerned Cort Ramsey. It should have. She'd withdrawn all her savings, and in cash, for her planned departure. Greta had kept it safe for her. Her only regret was that she had wasted some of her funds on a ticket that she would never use.

"The journey will be expensive," Gerhardt warned, "since it must of course be clandestine. The ship sails under a German flag; the captain I knew in the old country. The vessel did not seem to receive any damage from last night. My friend will no doubt keep to his schedule and leave before noon."

"Will I be crossing the ocean?" Rella asked.

"Not unless you choose. The captain has an initial destination of New Orleans."

Rella heaved a sigh of relief. The Gypsies were right. Both bad things and good did come in threes. The fire, the murder, and her arrest had all brought her great harm. But her luck had changed. She'd escaped from her incarceration and would soon set sail. For a third bit of good fortune, she just might book passage out of New Orleans and catch up with Templeton's Traveling Thespians before they left St. Louis.

Once she was out of the state, surely Cort Ramsey would turn his attention to finding his money and the real culprit. She felt not one twinge of guilt about running away. After all, she had done nothing worse than protest her innocence. For that she had spent two nights in jail.

And a few moments in the marshal's arms—she couldn't forget that, not when she'd come so close to bending her will to his. What a cruel irony that moment had been. She had never been tempted to submit to a man's ardor before, but then she had never before met anyone like Cort. Her lone experience, already a bitter memory, had been with the one man in the world who most wanted to do her harm.

Chapter Five

A breeze coming off the Illinois and Michigan Canal wafted across the heavily laden wagon carrying Rella into the part of Chicago known as the Levee. Sitting high on the seat by the youthful driver, she was trapped in a stench of sewage from the canal and the wagon's cargo of rotted vegetables—potatoes and carrots for the most part with just enough spoiled cabbage to turn even the strongest stomach. Food for the hogs, the young man had told her when he'd agreed back at the theatre to take her as passenger. Got at a good price at market, he'd added with pride.

Rella looked at the dingy street corner, already in shadows on this August afternoon, the sun having dipped behind a rundown brick building bearing a WAREHOUSE sign. Rows of dilapidated one- and two-story structures stretched out in separate direction. Equally worn were the bent-shouldered pedestrians who trudged, eyes directed downward, along the raised wooden walkway; Rella decided the load of refuse at her back was no more decayed than the streets through which it was borne.

She held back a sigh. What an ignominious arrival this was for the granddaughter of a queen on her way to join her people. But it was no more than she should have expected, considering the way things had gone throughout the weeks since she'd left New Orleans.

The driver pulled the sway-backed mare to a halt. "Not a very good part of Chicago, I'm thinkin', for a miss of your tender years. Sure you're wantin' me to leave you here?"

Rella smiled, thinking she and the driver must be close to the same age. But he did have a point about the district, although the conditions made no difference to her plans. She hadn't considered herself tender in a long time and had better not start such foolish weaknesses now.

"I'm sure," she said, smiling with a confidence she was far from feeling. Scrambling to the street, a small valise clutched to her side, she pulled out a coin and refused to think how few remained to separate her from destitution. "Thank you for your help. I have family meeting me here."

It wasn't an entirely accurate statement, she thought as she watched the wagon move slowly down the street. Her family—a rather liberal use of the term—had no plans to welcome her. How could they when they were unaware she was alive?

"Gypsies take care of their own," her mother had said. Rella prayed she'd not been speaking only with her heart.

As she had done all the days since she stood over Perry Tuttle's body, she refused to show the weakness of tears or fall into despair. So far, she'd escaped capture by the short-sighted Marshal Ramsey, but nothing else had gone as she'd hoped. She had been seeking refuge for almost two months and had been frustrated in almost every endeavor. Surely her luck was bound to change.

The journey had started out propitiously enough. Just as Gerhardt Maas had predicted, the captain of the German trading vessel headed out to sea only hours after accepting Rella aboard. Not that he'd wanted to, not with the eastward direction of the storm that had raged throughout Rella's last night in jail. But he was already a week behind his schedule, and he steered into the storm's wake all the way to New Orleans.

The quick exit from Texas was the last good fortune Rella was to encounter on her flight. It was followed by a week's delay in Louisiana until steamboat passage up the Mississippi could be purchased. Then the boat had broken down when one of the crewmen over-imbibed and let the fire in the boiler go out.

"Never happened before," the captain explained when she'd sought him out on the listing stern-wheeler and demanded an explanation.

He'd never had a bedeviled Gyspy actress on board, either, she almost retorted but held her tongue. She was supposed to be melting into her surroundings unseen and unremembered.

Causing a ruckus would leave for Cort a clear sign of her passage. That he would attempt to follow her she had no doubt. He was a man who never let a job go unfinished. To overcome his determination to haul her back to face trial, she would have to overcome all the blocks put in her path by unjust fate.

Throughout her journey she had seemed to feel his eyes on her. Always she felt him close on her heels. Whenever she gave in to her sense of foreboding and whirled around, heart pounding in her throat, he was never there. The curious part of this phenomenon was the depression of spirit that followed. He must be part Gypsy himself to have cast such a spell over her.

There had even been nights, usually those dark hours when the wind howled around wherever she had bedded down—a shipboard bunk or a second class inn—and she sought desperately for sleep, she felt a niggling doubt that she might be running the wrong way.

Daylight brought a return to sanity, however, and she knew what she must do: escape, no matter the obstacles she must conquer.

Her resolve was sorely tried when she arrived in St. Louis and found Templeton and his players had already left for the far-ranging western loop of their wanderings.

In Chicago she'd missed connections again and had to admit her funds were too limited to chase the troupe further. Rella had thought she was prepared to meet disappointment, but standing there in the dingy theatre office, she realized she was at the end of a very frayed rope. Weighed down by misfortune, she too timorously asked the manager if he knew of any work for her. He did not, and she retired to a coffee shop to spend a sorely needed coin for sustenance while she considered her options.

There were no choices left, she discovered. She was almost broke, and there seemed no place left to go, no one who would aid her. Cort Ramsey might not have appeared just yet, but he could show up any time. Once he started on the right trail, it wouldn't take him long to go from Galveston to Chicago.

The only reason she wasn't in chains right this minute was probably because of Aaron Tuttle, who had promised to misdirect the marshal into checking trains headed north. The medical student had an air of vulnerable innocence about him that would lend credence to whatever he said. Her one cheerful thought was Cort Ramsey following a false trail all the way to Denver.

Desperately she assessed her belongings for something to help her. There was nothing valuable enough to sell except the brooch of her Gypsy mother. She took it out and studied it. Intricate silver loops entwined around the polished moonstone. She had regarded it as a kind of talisman, symbol of her heritage, to be saved for emergencies that until now had never seemed dire enough to demand its sacrifice.

She resisted the idea. There had to be a better way. After all, she had a dual heritage on which to draw for strength: the acting blood which had flowed through her father's veins and the Gypsy blood of her mother. She had long known that Chicago had a large and fluctuating Gypsy population and grasped at the idea of seeking them out.

It took only a few questions after she left the theatre manager to learn the location of a Romany camp. She'd had to listen to disturbing complaints about their thieving ways, but this afternoon's foray was more than a last desperate attempt to find a hiding place from the law; she needed a bed and food.

She glanced ruefully at her neat blue gown with its high lace collar and full skirt that brushed the tops of her slippers. Gypsies didn't like outsiders. Gorgios they called them; her mother had said the term was used with scorn. When Nara had wed the gorgio actor Jonathan Sandringham, she'd felt unwelcome among the people with whom she'd been raised. Esmeralda was dead by then, the one person strong enough to demand her daughter Nara's continued acceptance in the tribe.

As much as she'd loved Jonathan, Nara had once confessed, she always regretted having to sever her Gypsy bonds. For that reason she'd filled Rella with Gypsy lore and language. Maybe, Rella thought, touching her moonstone brooch, she could find the shelter she needed and at the same time fulfill her mother's dream.

But not looking as she did, with her bleached curls and gorgio clothes. They wouldn't trust her any more than the Chicagoans back at the coffee shop placed faith in the goodness of a Romany tribe.

A swap shop down the block was the first stop in her transition. When she exited a half hour later, gone was the blue gown, as well as the clothing she'd carried in her valise, traded for layers of brightly colored cotton skirts and a drawstring white blouse. A small purse suspended beneath the skirts held her fast-dwindling funds; pinned to the low-cut blouse and prominently displayed in sight was the brooch she hoped would help her gain the respect of the Gypsies.

Fake golden hoops dangled from her ears, and around her neck she wore a half dozen necklaces of varying lengths. Bracelets and rings decorated her arms and fingers. The only place left unadorned, she thought, was her nose, but even given her flare for the dramatic, she decided against embedding a jewel in its side.

One last bit of transition remained. For that she needed the jar of a black coal tar powder which had cost her so dearly in the shop. After her long time on the road, the blond locks which had been so necessary for her ingenue roles were darkening, and the roots displayed their original raven hue. Slipping into an alleyway and using a sheet of discarded tin for a mirror, she proceeded to brush a light coating of the coal tar onto her curls.

She bound her head with a scarf the color of midnight and let the ends trail against her bare shoulder. No one seeing the dusky-skinned beauty who emerged onto the street would have taken her for the decorous young miss who had stepped down from the cart.

Proud of her sartorial accomplishment, she stretched her long legs into a healthy stride—and found out right away she'd completed her transformation almost too well.

A bleary-eyed man with dirty-blond hair stepped into her path. "Want me to tell your fortune, Gypsy wench?" he growled. "Spread those legs and I'll pump some good news into you."

With her progress so rudely and unexpectedly halted, Rella was too angry to be shocked. She should have known what to expect from gorgios. *Gorgios.* As though she wasn't one. The thought almost brought a smile to her lips. How quickly she was slipping into her new role.

But a pleasant expression definitely was not called for now. Pointing a finger at the crude suitor, she hissed, "Be gone before I cast the evil eye on you."

The man blinked, and Rella began to count in Romany, making the innocent numbers seem threatening as they rolled off her tongue. A waving finger punctuated each syllable. With the rasping inflection she put upon the words, they sounded frightening even to her ears.

Muttering something about most likely catching the pox anyway, the man pulled his threadbare coat tight across his chest and scurried across the street.

Rella didn't wait around for any more indecent proposals but turned her feet toward the canal. Somewhere along the north bank was supposed to be a field where the Gypsies were camped. She found out quickly enough that if she kept her eyes downward as the other pedestrians were doing, showing no interest in anyone or anything but her destination, she could move along without fear of being accosted.

The shadows were lengthening into early evening by the time she arrived. Chattering children played at the edge of a circle formed by a half dozen vardos, the carved and brightly painted wagons which served as the Gypsy home. In the center of the clearing an old woman stirred the contents of a large kettle, which hung suspended over a fire.

The woman glanced up and ceased her stirring. The muted sounds of talk and laughter which had echoed around the camp as Rella approached faded into a silence more chilling than the roar of a storm. From the shadows cast by the wagons emerged both men and women dressed in flamboyant Romany clothes: wide-sleeved shirts and kerchiefs at the neck for the men, and for the women garb not much different from Rella's. Even the barefooted children playing in the dirt grew still.

Her heart caught in her throat. The next few moments would spell disaster or success.

Fear gave a husky quality to her voice as she managed, "I come seeking my people."

More than any of the others, she felt the stare of the old woman at the kettle. Eyes like black buttons peered out from a weathered face as old as time.

"You have no people here," the woman said.

"Are not all Gypsies of one family?"

A shrill voice came from behind her. "Gypsies, yes. What gorgio trick brings you here?"

Rella whirled to face a middle-aged woman with fists placed defiantly on her ample hips. "I have no tricks. I have not come to do you harm but to ask for your help."

"Bah!" The woman spat upon the ground. "We barely help ourselves."

"Lucretia—" began a gray-haired, spare man who appeared beside her.

"Do not deny the truth, Torry John," the woman said. "We do not need another mouth to feed."

Pride pulled at Rella's tightly-held composure. "Then my mother was wrong. And her mother before her."

The old woman at the kettle drew nearer. "Who be they, child?"

Rella shrugged. "It matters not," she said tiredly. "Both are dead. You would have only my word that they ever walked among the trees and smelled the flowers growing wild in the fields."

"Take that," Lucretia said with a snap of her fingers, "for the word of a gorgio."

"The word of a Gypsy," Rella flung back.

"The child has the fire of our people," the old woman said.

"But Alepa—" Lucretia said.

"We will hear her story." The old woman's words carried a finality that brooked no argument, and Lucretia fell silent.

"My mother was called Nara," Rella said, deciding to omit mention of any family members without Gypsy blood. "Times grew hard in England, and she brought me to these shores. We traveled from town to town performing. When Nara died, I tried to travel on my own. But too many men wanted more than I was willing to give."

Nothing she'd said had been a lie, but in her heart she felt the weight of her deception.

"Our maidens are virtuous," Lucretia pronounced haughtily.

Rella's eyes flashed fire. "I will not taint them by my presence."

"You come penniless to our midst."

Rella dared to lift her skirts and pull loose the small purse which held her worldly goods. What the Gypsies might do, she hadn't the faintest notion. They had a reputation for duplicity, but somehow, with the commanding Alepa nearby, she felt she would come to no harm. It was an unreasoned feeling, but she hurried to act on it before she lost her nerve.

She held out the small purse. "I bring but a few coins, it is true, but surely these will help pay for my stay. Until I can earn my fair portion."

The throaty voice of a young woman sounded out in the stillness. "In what way would you earn your keep? I am the dancer here."

Rella turned to a wagon deeper in the shadows and saw that a voluptuous Gypsy girl had emerged into the firelight. From a mane of tousled black curls to the hem of a scarlet skirt brushing against her slim ankles, she held herself with graceful defiance.

"I challenge no one," Rella said. "I am not a dancer." Even as she spoke, she knew the girl would not be easily placated. Rella sensed trouble ahead.

"Our Serafina is quick to take offense," Alepa said to Rella, moving closer. "How would you bring in the money you speak of?"

Recitations from Shakespeare being decidedly inappropriate, Rella could think of only one answer. *"Dukkerin."*

"Fortune telling," Alepa said. "You are good at seeing into God's heart?"

Rella slipped into one of the untruths she had known were bound to come. "I am good at telling the gorgios what they want to hear." She sent a wish skyward that she could indeed do as she claimed, never having told anyone's fortune in her life.

"What are you called, child?"

Indeed, she did feel like a child as she gazed into the woman's probing eyes. "My name is unimportant. I call myself the Romany."

"There is perhaps someone who would find you, someone you do not wish to see."

For a brief moment Rella imagined a sharply-hewn face bending to hers, a strong, encircling arm, and a pair of lips pressing against hers. She also remembered that fact etched with scorn and staring implacably at her through a door of iron bars. "There is someone I do not wish to see."

"It is a man, of course." Alepa waved aside her protestations. "You mentioned a grandmother."

"Esmeralda Scamp. She is long since dead, buried beside an English stream."

"All dead!" It was the woman Lucretia who spoke with disgust. "All who would give testimony to your story."

Alepa spoke. "I am very much alive, although these old bones protest sometimes I have lived too long." She stepped close to Rella. With darkness descending and the fire at her back, her features were difficult to make out. Rella held her breath as Alepa reached out and touched the brooch.

"It was my grandmother's," Rella said. "And my mother's before it became mine."

"A curious piece, with its scrolls of silver. The moonstone glows with the opalescence of a pearl. I saw the brooch once. Perhaps it was the woman who wore it that made it memorable."

"You knew my grandmother?" Rella gasped.

"She mated with a gorgio."

"They wed in the Gypsy way, mingling their blood."

The two women stood in the flickering light and studied one another. Rella knew her fate lay in the hands of the old Gypsy. If the woman decided against her, she would lose this bid for a haven.

Alepa addressed the assembly which had gathered around the fire. "I say we let her prove herself tonight at the fair." Over the murmuring of the Gypsies, she declared, "The fortunes of Lucretia and Torry John have not gone well. Let her stay with them; if there is coin to be made tonight by the child who calls herself

Romany, then they will claim it. If not, then we can again challenge her right to stay."

The crowd moved restlessly, but Rella's attention was on Lucretia and Torry John, waiting to see their reaction to Alepa's high-handed assumption that the newcomer would be welcomed.

Gripping her husband's arm, Lucretia moistened her lips and gazed at Rella avidly, much as a dog would slaver over a juicy bone.

But her words were as skeptical as before. "She will probably do no more than feed herself," she said. "We shall see."

"Posh-rat," the young girl Serafina hissed.

Recognizing the hated term of half-breed, Rella ignored Lucretia to answer this new threat. She met the girl's stare straight on.

"Serafina," she announced in her full-throated, theatre voice, "you will not call me such a name after tonight!"

Chapter Six

Rella had hours to curse her braggadocio. Other than a small role as a seer in an unsuccessful play, she'd had no experience whatsoever in telling anyone's fortune. But her future, her freedom, and perhaps even her life depended on such nonexistent skills. How difficult could it be to predict with conviction that a person would meet love or riches or both and live a long and happy life?

The very simplicity of the thing immediately raised her suspicions. Lately everything that had seemed easy to accomplish had turned into a debacle.

From listening to the arguments of Lucretia and Torry John, she learned they were childless and the possessors of one of the smaller vardos in the camp. In recent weeks a dwindling number of gorgios had laid down coins to let Lucretia read their palms. If Rella did indeed prove as successful as she claimed, then they would, at great sacrifice, let her sleep on blankets beneath their wagon and share the stock of food brought with money Rella earned.

While hardly choked with gratitude, Rella was in no position to label the arrangements unacceptable, and she stifled any objections. It was her best offer of sanctuary since she'd left Galveston.

After the evening meal was done—a heavily seasoned stew whose ingredients Rella did not care to identify—the Gypsies prepared for their nightly trek across the canal to the fairgrounds a short walk away. With her host and hostess casting dark looks in her direction and sullen stares coming from Serafina, Rella received her only encouragement from Alepa, who walked beside her to the fair.

"The gorgios are foolish, would you not say?" the old woman observed.

"It is so," said Rella. "I have observed them in my travels." She intended to stay deliberately vague about her past. Even if she made good with these Gypsies, it wouldn't do to mention Galveston.

Alepa's faded old eyes remained directed to the trail. "They take our simple words and twist them as they want. If you tell each one who comes in that he has at one time suffered great trouble with a friend or family, or that he has faced death, he will nod and wonder how you knew."

Rella kept silent.

"And even more foolish, he hears you say he once was in trouble from the commission of a good act. He is astounded that you could be so wise."

Rella measured her stride carefully to match that of the older woman, afraid the slightest misstep would stop the discourse. She wondered if Alepa sensed her apprehension and was deliberately giving her hints about fortune telling. The thought warmed Rella's heart.

"No man—and few women—will deny that he has been in several love affairs," the old woman continued. "In each, of course, he has remained blameless. And then there is the simplest generalization of them all. He will meet a person who will have great influence on his life. This could be a carpenter who builds his house, or the drayman who delivers goods to his door, but they do not see so simple a thing. A man thinks you speak of riches. A woman thinks of love."

They came to a broad field where flames from dozens of lamp posts cast welcoming light. The sounds of laughter and music beckoned. Alepa stopped at the edge of the grounds, Rella close at her side. Crowds of people, strolling in small groups or alone, flowed past them like water around rocks in a stream.

"But of course," Alepa said with a shrug, "I tell you only what you already know."

Rella was positive she saw a hint of laughter in the old woman's eyes.

"Of course," she said, at the same time trying frantically to remember everything Alepa had said.

The music quickened. Alepa disappeared into the crowd, and Rella let herself be borne along toward the happy sound of a guitar. Standing near the musician in a pool of flickering light was the Gypsy Serafina.

A hush fell upon the crowd, many of whom were from the Gypsy camp. The music slowed as Serafina began to clap her hands and slap her bare heels against the hard-packed dirt of the field. She circled, her eyes never leaving the faces of the men who watched in silence.

Soon the beat quickened, and it was the men who clapped as the girl lifted her skirt to display well-rounded calves. Always her feet beat against the ground in the pulsating rhythm set by the guitar. Gypsies in the crowd began to stamp their feet faster and faster and clap their hands louder and louder. Shouts of encouragement echoed into the night. As the beat of the guitar grew more insistent, Serafina's movements became wild and free and seemingly uncontrolled, as though she knew not from one moment to the next what she would do. This air of abandon spread across the crowd. Even Rella felt the excitement; her heart pounded in time with the guitar.

Faster and faster Serafina twirled, her crimson skirt whirling to reveal a flash of thigh. Just as Rella thought the tension had become unbearable, the music ceased, and Serafina dropped to the ground. The sudden stillness was shattering.

The shouts were slow in coming, but when they did, they were accompanied by the tossing of coins. Serafina gathered in the money, dropping it in her upturned skirt. As the onlookers began to drift away toward other entertainment, she placed the bounty in a purse suspended from her waist and strolled over to Rella.

"Do this well, Romany," she said, jiggling the coins, "and I will accept you as one of us."

"What have we here?" queried a tall, swarthy young man behind Serafina.

Serafina whirled around. "Sandor!" She threw her arms around the young man's neck and gave him a loud kiss.

With her arm wrapped possessively around his waist, she said to Rella, "This is Sandor." Her eyes added that the handsome man belonged to her. "He buys and sells the horses for our people, and trains them as well." She smiled knowingly. "Sandor is very good with his hands." She turned her gaze up to him. "Did you see me dance?"

"I arrived only at the end." He pulled free of Serafina. "But I have not been answered. We have a guest in our camp?"

Rella nodded. "If I am allowed to remain."

"A Gypsy does not turn another Gypsy away."

"If that's what she is," Serafina said slyly. "First she must prove herself tonight by telling the fortunes of the gorgios."

Sandor studied Rella with friendly admiration. "This one will have no trouble." He grinned broadly, revealing a flash of white teeth against the darkness of his face.

"A fine horse I brought today," he added with a laugh. "The foolish gorgio believed his stallion was ill because he turned from his feed. If only he had looked closer, he would have seen the tallow I rubbed on the horse's teeth. Of course the animal would not eat." He strutted proudly before the two young women, his hands indicating the size of the horse.

Serafina scowled. "You talk too much, Sandor." She tugged at his shirt. "Come. You will tell me about your journey into the country. The one who calls herself Romany should get on with her trade. We must send our hopes upward that she does not bring shame upon us."

Rella stared after the departing couple. Obviously Serafina thought she posed some kind of threat to the dancer's relationship with Sandor, but her worries were indicative only of a jealous nature and a deep caring for the young man, not of his straying heart. He had welcomed Rella readily enough, but as a fellow Gypsy and nothing more. Something about him seemed familiar, something about the kind look in his eyes, but she couldn't think of what it might be.

Reluctantly, Rella turned her thoughts to the evening awaiting her. She had a strong urge to dive into the darkness that surrounded the fair, but she could see Torry John and his wife Lucretia directing very determined steps in her direction. Within minutes she found herself ensconced in a small tent at the edge of the field and listening to Torry John intone her talents to the crowd outside. Two chairs and a shawl-draped table came close to filling the small enclosure.

"The Romany sees all," Torry John proclaimed.

"Dare you to risk learning the truth?"

Rella settled into one of the chairs and tugged nervously at the scarf covering her hair. If the people learned the real truth—that the Romany had made a botch of her own circumstances and was the last person on earth to be listened to—then her stay in the Gypsy camp would be ended after one night.

A hoarse male voice responded to Torry John's exortations. "You talking about that old fake who told me last week I'd meet the woman of my dreams? If'n I did, I sure as hell hope my wife don't find out."

Laughter drowned Torry John's immediate reply.

"A new seer has come into our midst," he managed at last. "A young and beautiful mystic," he added to the quietening crowd, "one who has only to look at a man's palm to know what the fates have decreed."

At that moment Rella had an unadorned insight into her own future. If she didn't come up with some fast and smooth predictions right away, there was only misfortune ahead.

The flap lifted, and a young couple entered. Her heart sank. Two! She'd have a hard enough time talking to them one at a time.

The girl giggled. "The man outside said it would be all right if Robert came with me. I've never done this before."

That made a pair of them, Rella thought, but wisely kept silent. The girl settled into the other chair.

Rella reminded herself that she was an actress. "Give me your left hand," she said huskily.

The girl did as she was told. Remembering how her mother had held her own hand in their playful games of fortune telling, Rella held the girl's hand in a similar manner and stared. As best she recalled, a picture was supposed to appear at the base of the thumb. Rella saw only smooth skin the color of cream.

The girl stirred nervously. "What's taking so long? Do you see something bad?"

"What you ought to be asking, Elizabeth, is whether she sees anything at all," her companion opined from his post by the flap.

Rella slowly lifted her thick lashes to stare coldly at the man. "The Romany sees," she said, stalling. Robert was showing the unfortunate characteristics of a smart aleck, she thought. She fell back on the standby that had gotten her out of scrapes before: flattery of the male.

"The future of a young girl who is loved and cared for is sometimes difficult to envision. That of a worldly man like yourself would be far easier to predict."

What she said didn't make much sense, but then men seldom analyzed a compliment. Her theory proved right.

"Well," he said, clearing his throat and standing taller, "let's hear what you have to say."

She sifted through Alepa's scarcely concealed advice, seeking to find the approach that would best suit the wide-eyed Elizabeth. Talk about death and love affairs she ruled out right away.

She pulled the girl's hand closer to the lamp. "You have lived a simple life but not, I think, one without pain."

"Oh, yes," the girl whispered.

Rella wondered what pain the girl was remembering. From the feel of her soft skin, she'd never done a hard day's work in her life.

"You have tried to do good, but your goodness has gone unrewarded." The girl gasped, and Rella sent a silent thanks to Alepa.

Rella took a wild guess. "I see a suffering animal. Maybe more than one, but the image is dim."

"How did you know about the kittens?" the girl asked in wonderment. "What a cruel man he was trying to drown them. He . . . yelled at me when I begged him to stop."

So that was Elizabeth's idea of pain. Rella sincerely hoped the young woman would never experience worse.

"You must not, however, let such an experience turn you from goodness."

"How wise you are," the girl said.

Rella ignored a pang of guilt. "Through your caring, you have much to offer those around you."

"I help out sometimes at the hospital."

Rella nodded sagely. "It is here in your hand."

After a few more platitudes and a gush of thanks from the girl, her companion Robert plunked down a coin on the table and with a knowing smile guided her from the tent. Rella had never received a salary she enjoyed more or deserved less.

The night wore on, and a seemingly endless parade of gorgios passed through the canvas portal. Much to her surprise and pleasure, Rella found herself growing more at ease at her task. As an actress she'd played many roles; she tried putting herself into the place of the people who sat opposite her; she simply told them what they wanted to hear. After three hours she congratulated herself on a successful first outing as a seeress Romany.

Her sense of well being was short-lived. A discordant note was sounded back at the camp when Lucretia demanded the night's receipts. Sadly Rella watched her money disappear with the woman inside the vardo. Almost immediately Lucretia reappeared and tossed two blankets and Rella's small bag to the ground at her feet.

"You will sleep well with what I give you," she said

with the air of a too-generous benefactress.

Rella stood uncertainly, eyeing the sparsely grassed area beneath the wagon. It seemed poor pay for the job she had done. She looked around and saw others preparing for sleep in much the same way that faced her. None of them were removing any clothing.

Gypsies, she realized, did not change clothes for the night, but slept in what they already wore. In the case of the women with their multiple skirts, that meant virtually everything they owned.

Rella shrugged. She was a Gypsy now; she must accept the Gypsy ways. Depositing her jewelry and scarf in her valise, she crawled beneath the wagon and made a pallet out of the blankets. Somehow being fully dressed in her crude bed made her feel safer, less vulnerable. She wondered if perhaps others in the camp felt the same way.

She lay at the edge of the space beneath the wagon and for a moment let her herself think about tomorrow. What could it possibly hold? So much she had to learn. Making peace with Serafina came close to the top of her list, immediately after she talked with Alepa about the grandmother Rella had known only through stories.

And there was another, more practical, snippet of information she hoped to gain. Surely the old Gypsy could advise her on how to return her hair to its natural shade, most definitely a better method than the coal tar she had used. She wondered if she could ever remove all its oily traces.

But as she stared out into the starry night, all such pedestrian concerns faded from her mind. The air was cool and dry; she was sheltered and fed. Such conditions were no more or less than she had hoped for when she arrived in the city hours before.

Even without showing a monetary profit for the

night, she felt curiously euphoric. Gypsies owned no property except what would travel with them. Theirs was a carefree life. Something deep within her stirred. In truth, she must have always been a Romany; it was the reason she had liked traveling with the troupe.

Freedom was an opiate to her. More than ever, she knew she must not be caught by Cort Ramsey. She remembered the weakness she'd felt in his arms, the closeness of her capitulation to his desire. How far would she have gone? It was a question she had asked herself for weeks.

She'd finally come to one conclusion. Emotions could be a trap as much as any jail. Never could she be imprisoned by either one.

Chapter Seven

"Aiiaah!"

Rella's cry rose into the October air as she let her black mare race unimpeded across the grassy plain outside the western Chicago city limits. With her skirts tucked between her legs, she straddled the horse Gypsy-style, as naturally as if she'd always done so, her body cradled comfortably by a small leather saddle.

When she was on horseback like this, she was able to feel for a while the Gypsy spirit her mother had described. For this time she could let her spirits soar.

In truth, before coming to Chicago, she had never ridden a horse in her life. An onlooker would never have guessed, not with the way she rode seemingly without effort, eyes sparkling and dark hair blowing free in the wind. Rella had taken to riding the way she had so few other Gypsy ways.

Gypsies confined to the city were a sad lot, she had decided. They should have been camped beside a clear-running stream, not entrenched downwind of a sewage-laden canal. Never was she ashamed of her Gypsy heritage, but she was disheartened that they were no longer the proud people her mother had presented.

Still, there were moments—galloping across the prairie as she was now or listening to the cry of violins or watching the children at play—when she felt the ancient celebrated Romany freedom. Sometimes she could push aside her loneliness, especially during the evening meal when Alepa joined her and they talked of Esmeralda and the ways of life back in England.

Just as Rella had hoped, Alepa gave her a more permanent dye for her hair than the black coal tar; she'd also revealed other Gypsy secrets, strange cures for illness and injury, ways to survive in the wilderness, and even, on one balmy evening, the use of tarot cards. Rella had allowed herself to be the subject, but when talk turned to visions of a tall, steely-eyed stranger, she had claimed a headache and gone to an early bed.

She soon found out why Sandor looked familiar. He was Alepa's nephew, the only child of a much younger sister who had died giving him birth. The young man and his aunt were the only real friends she had made in the camp.

The food, she'd discovered, was passable, heavy and grease laden, although tasty. Usually it was rabbit or chicken stew seasoned with wild garlic and onions gathered by Rella and the children on forays into the country. Sometimes an unidentified rodent was thrown in; even then, she bravely downed it.

The clothing she accepted more readily than her other adopted ways. The loose-fitting skirts and blouse gave a freedom to her body that was sensual. Occasionally the feeling of sensuality communicated itself to one of the men entering her fortune-telling tent, resulting in blatant requests for more than just palmistry.

Rella had learned to deal with the situation. Dire predictions of sexual incapacity dampened even the most insistent ardor. She'd learned that fact concerning male vulnerability with the return of Robert, the cynical man who'd accompanied the wide-eyed Elizabeth that first night at the fair. Seated opposite her in the dimly lighted tent, he had fairly drooled in anticipation of what the night would hold. His hands hadn't been content to rest inactively on the table.

"You will meet with disappointment," she warned when his fingers stroked hers.

"Let me be the judge of that," he answered huskily.

"I do not mean with the woman you choose to honor." She feared she had gone too far, but a quick glance at Robert's smug visage changed her mind. "It is with yourself that the disappointment will occur."

He ceased the stroking that he'd apparently thought provocative.

She lifted her kohl-darkened lashes to look at him once again, then directed her attention to his now-open palm. "Such things are difficult to say with delicacy, gorgio. I read here an imminent laxity of . . . purpose. An inability to rise to your ultimate aims."

Having grown used to the back stage crudeness of actors, Rella could have put her prediction into even plainer words, but Robert had caught on quickly enough. He'd tossed down a coin and hurried through the tent opening. She hadn't seen him since.

But others came back, again and again, the women in fine silk, the men clad in evening dress. Alepa informed her she had become the darling of wealthy Chicago. It took her as much by surprise as it did Lucretia and Torry John, who gladly gathered in the coins each night before the Gypsies headed back for camp.

She chafed under the restrictions of the Gypsy pair. They were helping her—had even provided her with a tent as the nights grew cool—but they were helping themselves more by taking the money she earned. When she was satisfied that Torry John was pleased with the many coins she turned over to him, she began holding out one or two a night, telling herself she was not being a thief, but had the right to some of the money she earned.

She must prepare to move on and have the means to do so, whatever the reason. Her past could easily catch up to her. Cort Ramsey didn't strike her as the type to give up entirely; even if he'd lost her trail, unlikely as that seemed, or been interrupted by other concerns, wanted posters would be out.

Her dreams were haunted by those posters, always stark white with big black letters and nailed to a tree trunk. From a sturdy overhead limb a hangman's rope dangled; in the shadows nearby was a man she couldn't quite see. But she wasn't afraid of him, and for a time after waking from the vision, she couldn't help thinking of Cort's hypnotic gaze and his strong presence, could almost feel his hands pressed against her flesh, his mouth hot on hers. In the daylight hours, she forced herself to stay busy to keep from thinking of him in any way except as one who would steal her freedom.

Somewhere her troupe of actors was still performing, and as much as she had come to appreciate the Romany ways, she fastened her hopes on rejoining it. Her life would be as carefree as with the Gypsies, and she could put her acting skills to more exciting use than gulling foolish men and women who paid to hear her gratifying lies.

Rella had loved entertaining, finding pleasure in presenting even the silly melodramas American audiences preferred. Unlike some, Templeton's had been a prosperous troupe and, more importantly, was less likely than the Gypsies to draw the attention of a local sheriff.

Thus far, the coins she was appropriating were few, and she was able to keep them in the purse she wore beneath her skirts. Each time she added one, she counted the total, estimating how far they might take her should she be forced to leave suddenly. Knowing that her departure was inevitable, she found herself longing for the time she could go on alone.

Still, as each day went by, she felt safer from discovery and dreamed less often of hanging ropes and an unseen tormentor.

With her fears fading, she looked forward to the occasions when she could take a morning ride. Sometimes she rode in solitude; at other times, like today, Sandor joined her. She could hear pounding close behind her on this glorious Saturday morn the pinto that carried the swarthy young rider. Unasked, Sandor had anointed himself her friendly protector, much to Serafina's anger. Rella had been unable to make peace with the girl, no matter how hard she tried. Blinded by love, Serafina didn't understand.

With only a slight nudge of her knees, she directed her mount toward a stand of trees a hundred yards to the right. As if sensing her mistress's intentions, the fiesty mare stretched her long legs in a gallant effort to outrace the pinto to the trees. The horse succeeded, but only by a nose.

As she entered the grove, Rella reined to a halt.

"Romany," Sandor said, pulling up beside her in the shade, "you test me as no gorgio has ever done. You are truly a Gypsy."

"It's the horse I ride," she said with a laugh. "Anyone would appear skilled on such an animal. I assume you paid less than a fair price for her."

Sandor's dark eyes twinkled. "I paid what the gorgio

asked. It was not up to me to offer more. He should know better the quality of his stock."

Rella pushed aside the certainty that Sandor wasn't being entirely honest in his dealings. His boasting sounded childlike, certainly not larcenous. From the Gypsy point of view, it was up to the gorgios to protect themselves. Gypsies suffered the hate and distrust of outsiders; it seemed only just that in return they succeed with an occasional swindle.

The sound of running water caught her attention. Dropping to the ground, she led the mare through short grass and fallen leaves toward the stream. Sandor followed, rock tethering the horses where they could drink and nibble along the bank.

He glanced around the sylvan glade, broken ribbons of sunlight filtering through the thick branches of the trees.

"Gorgios are foolish in ways beyond the selling of animals," he said in disgust. "They have a natural stream, clean and pure, and must mar the land with the building of a canal, which now carries the stench of the city outward across the land. If they would play with God's work, they should plant trees and flowers as God has done."

Rella agreed.

"But who could ever understand the gorgio ways?" he added with a shrug.

Reaching down into his boot, Sandor pulled out a silver-handled knife, its blade long and narrow like a spear of wild grass. He placed the sharp tip between his fingers and thumb.

"You see a knot halfway up that oak?" he asked, gesturing toward a tree away from the stream. Rella's eyes were trained upon him as he raised his arm high. With an overhanded flick of his wrist, he sent the knife flying through the air to land precisely in the center of his target. Swaggering, he retrieved the weapon and twice more sped it on its way. Each time the result was the same.

Again Rella thought of a child's pleasure.

"You are very good, Sandor."

The Gypsy smiled broadly. "I could teach you my skill."

"I doubt it."

"It is true." He pointed the handle at Rella. "Hold it gently."

Gingerly she did so, gripping the silver handle and being careful to avoid the razor-thin blade.

"If you would be good, you must hold the blade as I have done, with the tip between your fingers."

"It's all right if I'm not so good."

Sandor laughed; nevertheless, he insisted on showing her how to hold the blade and flick it overhand in the direction of the tree. After a half dozen attempts, the closest she had come to the knot was a place on the tree trunk just above the ground.

When Sandor strolled back to her once again, the knife in his hand, she said, "Give up. You have too much patience with me. I am not a good student."

A hissing female voice interrupted his reply. "What is it the Gypsy tries to teach you? And what gorgio lies do you use to lay traps for our men?"

Rella stared past Sandor at a wild-eyed Serafina, who sat astride a white horse at the edge of the woods. Slowly the girl rode toward them, her skirt hiked high, her naked dancer's legs brown against the horse's flanks.

"Sandor was teaching me to use a knife," she said.

The girl's lips curled in an ugly smile. "And is the knife all that he unsheathed?"

"Serafina," Sandor growled, "you speak too boldly. Such talk is not fit for a maiden's ears."

"I, too, am a maiden," Serafina flung back.

Rella guessed that Serafina would have had it otherwise, but she also knew that Gypsies preferred their women to be untouched before their wedding day. Serafina had been saving herself for Sandor, and now she believed he had turned to another.

Rella sighed in exasperation. There was nothing she could say that the Gypsy girl would believe.

"I hope," Serafina said, glaring down at Rella, "that you have learned your lessons well today. I have great skill with the knife."

"You go too far," Sandor said, moving threateningly, fists clinched, toward Serafina.

The white mare bobbed her head, dark eyes rolling back in her proud head, as if she sensed the anger of the approaching Sandor.

"I do not go nearly far enough!" Serafina shot back. "There are things I could tell you. . . ."

Rella's heart caught in her throat. What *things* could Serafina possibly know? The coins she wore beneath her skirt? No witness had ever been with her in the tent when she secreted them in her hidden purse. Perhaps, Rella thought with a start, the dancer had learned of her reluctant rival's past. But how could she know anything other than what Rella had claimed? Was she lying to turn Sandor's affection back to her?

"I do not want to hear your lies," Sandor said, reaching out and grabbing her hand which held tightly to the reins.

"Once," the girl answered in a whisper, "you yearned to hear all that I said. You are a fool, Sandor, to turn from what I have to offer." Her voice strengthened as she spoke to Rella. "And do not think you can succeed so easily. I fight for what is mine."

She reined the horse around and in a flurry of leaves and dirt rode rapidly from the woods, leaving behind a dismayed Rella and an angry Gypsy man.

"She is too wild," Sandor said, his hands clinched at his sides. "She must be tamed."

Rella realized for the first time how much he cared for the fiery young beauty. He was the one who must tame her—if she didn't someday push him too far. Somehow Rella must figure out a way to bring the couple together. If she did not, trouble lay ahead.

Rella could easily brush aside Serafina's threats about the knife. What lay heavily on her mind was the secret that Serafina claimed to know. Whatever it was, she would not be content to keep it a secret long.

There was a crisp hint of fall in the air as Rella walked about the crowded fairgrounds that night. Little rain had fallen in Chicago throughout the summer, and the ground was hard-packed and cracked. She'd heard the fairgoers talking about the fires that had broken out across the city, sorely trying the highly touted fire department. They'd spoken of the loss of lives and the damages suffered.

Rella shuddered, unknowingly rubbing at her scarred hand. Ever since her boardinghouse accident back in Galveston, she'd been unable to think calmly about fire.

But she had more to worry about this October evening than faraway flames. Only a few hours ago a new danger to her safety had arisen. She could not rest until she found out exactly what it was.

In her first performance of the night, Serafina danced more wildly than Rella had ever seen her. The stillness after she had dropped to the ground at the close was broken by shouts and unbridled applause. Even the watching Sandor joined in. With breast heaving, the Gypsy girl stared triumphantly from her crouched position at her adversary.

He is mine, she seemed to proclaim. *You cannot have him.*

Rella turned thoughtfully from her. She had to let Serafina know she presented no threat, but she hadn't the vaguest idea how to do so. Perhaps she could find a way to discourage the persistent Sandor. Deciding she would have to come up with a plan, she entered her tent.

The evening moved quickly, and Rella found herself receiving more money than ever before. Each time she held back a coin for herself, she was especially careful that no one could see her slip it into the pouch. When Lucretia or Torry John entered, she read their faces for signs of suspicion that the Romany was holding something back; she saw only venal pleasure over the evening's take.

It was after she had closed for the night and was standing in front of her darkened tent that Serafina made her move. Sandor had already returned to the camp, but dozens of Chicagoans still strolled about the grounds. The sound of violins echoed in the cool air.

"Romany!" Serafina called to her, her voice edged with sarcasm. "Do you steal once again from those who would help you?"

Rella started. She knew Lucretia and Torry John stood and listened beside the tent.

She felt her face flush. "What are you talking about?" To her own ears her voice sounded weak.

"I mean the coins you hoard for yourself." Light from a lamp post flickered across Serafina's scornful face.

How could the girl have possibly known? Was she guessing? Or did she possess some Gypsy power to read the truth in Rella's eyes?

Rella felt curiously relieved. Serafina did not know about her life in the gorgio world or her flight from the law.

By this time a crowd of gorgios and Gypsies had gathered around the pair. Lucretia stepped closer. "Speak what you know, Serafina. What gold does the Romany withhold?"

Instinctively, Rella's hand moved toward the purse suspended beneath her skirt. No one could possibly know she wore it.

Serafina tossed a handful of coins onto the ground. "I found these hidden beneath the blanket in your tent."

Rella smiled. The little liar. She was willing to give up her own money to discredit the woman threatening her happiness.

"Look," Serafina hissed, gesturing toward Rella, "look how she laughs at us. Gypsies do not steal from one another. She does not belong."

The cracked voice of Alepa cut off Rella's response. "Serafina!"

The girl turned toward the old woman. "I speak only the truth."

"You speak where the gorgios can hear. In the English that they can understand. Gypsies do not display their troubles in such a way."

Color rose in the girl's cheeks. Rella knew she was embarrassed to be chastised before the crowd. Perhaps here was a chance to remove Serafina's enmity or at least to lessen it.

"Do not be too harsh with the girl," she said to Alepa, then turned to her accuser. "You are too smart for me, Serafina," she said, shrugging. "It is true I saved these few coins for myself. For that time when the gorgios no longer listen to me. For that time when Lucretia and Torry John no longer extend their kindness." She watched carefully for a sign of gratitude that she did not deny the crime.

Serafina's eyes narrowed. "You admit you are a thief?"

"You have found the proof against me."

Alepa's thoughtful eyes moved from one girl to the other. "All is not revealed, I think."

"Yes!" Serafina hissed, killing Rella's hopes for a sign of peace between them. "We must ask her what other perfidy she hides in her heart."

"We must," Alepa retorted, "inquire why she so quickly admitted to your accusations. Otherwise, it would have been only your word against hers. And the Romany has brought much to our coffers in her stay here. There are those who would have believed her. Perhaps it was to avoid such a scene as this."

Rage overcame the girl. "Always the Romany wins! Even when she admits she steals from us." She threw herself at Rella, hands pulling at her hair, thumbs seeking her eyes.

"Fight! Fight!"

The yells brought a larger crowd to the scene as Rella fell to the ground at the unexpected onslaught. She grabbed Serafina's thumbs, bending them backward, forcing the Gypsy to relinquish her painful hold on Rella's hair.

The two women rolled on the ground and landed weak blows on one another. Fingernails scratched across Rella's cheeks, drawing blood. In retaliation she drew back a fist and struck her opponent hard in the stomach. She heard a satisfying "Uumph!"

But Serafina was not undone, and she renewed with vigor her hold on her opponent's hair. Rella tried another stomach blow, but this time without effect. Serafina's hold was firm.

All was noise and confusion, shouts in the background, Serafina strong and relentless, Rella holding her own, barely aware of the pain. Round and round they rolled in the dirt, spurred on by bets coming from the crowd.

"A fin says the dancer wins!"

"I'll take that bet!"

Rella fought with all her might but was unable to dislodge Serafina, who had come out on top and was astride her, beating her head on the hard ground by jerking on long hanks of hair.

Dimly in the background came the sound of a police whistle, and Serafina immediately landed a blow on Rella's chin that momentarily stunned her. When she was able to get to her knees, it was to see the Gypsy girl disappearing into the crowd. The police whistle sounded louder, and Rella, struggling for breath, brushed tangled hair from her face. In the background, the bettors began to argue about whether police intervention meant neither girl had won.

She struggled to get up and follow Serafina, but crouched on the ground, she saw that her drawstring blouse had slipped low enough to expose the tip of one breast. Embarrassed, she jerked it back in place.

"A little late for modesty," a man said.

Rella's eyes focused on a pair of dusty boots, traveled up a long pair of legs, paused at the gun strapped to a powerful thigh, and studied for a minute the badge pinned to his chest.

Damnation, she thought, *I've done this before.*

By the time she made the journey all the way to his face, she knew exactly what to expect.

Staring down at her with keen interest, a hint of amusement in his piercing blue eyes, was Marshal Cort Ramsey.

Chapter Eight

Rella bent her head, dark curls forming a welcome curtain around her face, and waited for the inevitable. As much as her head and body pained her from the fight with Serafina, she was aware of only one sensation. Already she could feel the noose around her neck.

Cort extended a broad hand. "You all right?"

She shrugged. The police whistle sounded shrilly behind Cort, and pounding feet grew louder. The crowd that had moments ago enthusiastically goaded the two women scattered into the darkness surrounding the fairgrounds. By the time a blue-uniformed officer arrived, only Rella and Cort remained beside the fortune-telling tent.

"Here now! What's going on?" the red-faced policeman growled. "Damn Gypsies!"

Cort turned, exposing his badge to the officer. "Got things under control," he said. "Just a little argument, that's all. No harm done."

Rella held her breath. Public fighting must surely be against the law. She would rather the Chicago police take her in custody than the United States marshal who had come unexpectedly to her defense.

But for a Gypsy to suggest incarceration in a city jail would draw even more unwanted attention to herself than she had already managed. Unwilling to take the risk and fervently wishing for the clairvoyance she claimed each night, she held still and awaited her fate. Crouched as she was on the ground, she felt a little like a bug about to be squashed by the broad foot of the law.

The policeman kicked at the dirt. "There was enough caterwauling from around here to disturb a dozen city blocks."

"But no harm done," Cort said.

Rella silently observed that though he might be far from his usual haunts, the marshal liked to have his way. Slowly she began to scoot toward the beckoning darkness behind the tent. He had come upon her before she'd had a chance to flee. Maybe if the two officers kept each other occupied. . . .

"As you can see," he continued, "the crowd has dispersed for the night."

She was almost to the side of the tent. Only a few feet more. . . .

"Not at all," the policeman said, gesturing toward Rella and effectively bringing a pause to her escape attempt. "Need to run her in, I'm thinking. Show these rascals they can't bring their Gypsy ways to Chicago."

Rella looked at the officer in disgust but held her tongue. The stories she'd heard about gamblers and drunkards and thieves prowling the filthy city streets made her wonder who was safe from whom.

She had about decided she would spend the night in a Chicago jail when Cort said, "It was over by the time I got here. Too bad you don't have any witnesses."

She found herself looking at him with gratitude. He was actually trying to save her; most gorgios she'd observed since slipping into her Gypsy role would have thrown her to her fate. As much as she wanted to avoid Cort, she knew she didn't really want to be arrested by the policeman. She'd already spent two nights in a Texas jail. Incarceration was not a habit she cared to form.

The trick would be to avoid both men, and she gave a longing glance to the welcoming dark behind the tent.

Cort glanced sideways at her, his lip twitching when he saw how far she'd moved. He gave a slight shake of his head, as if warning her not to run away. With a sigh, Rella decided that for once he was right. The Gypsy camp was easy to find, and the law might decide to run them all off as troublemakers. And she would be blamed.

"I'll hang around awhile longer," Cort said to the officer, "although I imagine the trouble is over for the night."

Rella watched as Cort edged away from her, drawing the policeman with him. The men's voices grew faint, probably just congratulating themselves on what fine fellows they were and commiserating over their responsibilities as upholders of law and order.

As she slipped into the tent, she thought about the last time she'd seen the marshal. He'd been nursing a bloodied lip, and there had been fire in his eyes. Perhaps biting him had been a mistake. As satisfying as it had been, it also offered evidence of a violent nature. When it was added to the fight he'd just witnessed, there was little chance she could ever convince him that at heart she was a gentle creature.

No, it wouldn't do to let him recognize her as the fugitive from Texas. If that's what she still was. She felt a surge of hope. Maybe their meeting tonight was a coincidence. Maybe he wasn't after her any longer.

And just maybe the moon really was made of green cheese.

Positioning herself on the side of the table away from the tent opening, she used a small mirror from her pocket to study her appearance: tangled brown hair, dirt-streaked face, ropes of gaudy, cheap jewelry around her neck and a loop of gold dangling from one ear. The second earring must have been lost in the fight. One sleeve was torn, and her skirts were in disarray.

She started to straighten herself as best she could, then stopped. Disheveled, her skin darkened by the days she spent in the sun, her lashes darkened by more artificial means, she hardly resembled the fair-haired ingenue Cort had seen in the Galveston law office. Then she'd been gowned primly in a high-necked, blue cotton dress. Then she'd argued with him at every turn; except for that disastrous moment when he'd first embraced her, she'd been forced into the part of shrew.

It would take considerable acting skills to hold on to this earthy Gypsy role—more, perhaps, than she possessed once Cort turned those damnably penetrating eyes on her. She gripped the edge of the table, hoping he'd gone away with the policeman, wondering if he'd learned somehow that her trail led here.

The flap lifted and he entered. His tall, lanky frame seemed to fill the space as no other man had done. Surely he could hear her heart pounding. With great force of will, she kept her eyes down . . . and spied the burn scar at the base of her right thumb. She might as well have been wearing a sign that read CINDERELLA SANDRINGHAM. With an insouciance she was far from feeling, she dropped her arms to her side.

Cort thought the Gypsy looked beautiful in the

flickering lamplight that bounced against the canvas walls, even more than she had when he'd come across her kneeling on the ground. Did she have any idea the picture she had presented, with her blouse pulled low to reveal a dark-tipped breast? And that shy, startled look she had cast up at him when she heard his voice . . . even yet, the image lingered teasingly in the back of his mind. He admitted it was the reason he'd returned to the tent.

"The policeman is gone," he said.

Modulating her voice to a husky whisper, Rella said, "I offer you thanks." Not with a handshake, however. She placed both hands behind her.

Cort wanted a lot more than just thanks. He'd been on the road for a long time looking for a blond murderess and thief. He'd had no time for women, not since he'd started his search. One look at the Gypsy and he had realized just how long it had been.

Cort forced himself to slow down. If he kept thinking the way he was—and received the slightest encouragement—he'd be using his hands to discover if she wore as little under her skirts as she did under her blouse.

"No need to thank me," he said, moving around the table to stand beside her. "You seemed to be the victim out there more than the attacker."

Rella drew into the darkness away from the lamp. "Serafina took me by surprise."

"And what might your name be?"

"They call me Romany."

"You seem very shy, Romany. I've known a few Gypsies, and shyness is not one of their traits."

Rella was forced to put a halt to her retreat. "I am always shy around a gorgio who adorns his shirt as you do."

"The badge, you mean. I intend you no harm."

Rella almost laughed. How little he knew.

Instead, she said, "Then you will let me return to my people?"

"Not just yet."

Cort reached out and touched her cheek. "Your skin is warm. As though you carried the sun with you."

"I carry fear of what the gorgio plans to do. You wear a badge. It gives you unfair advantage."

"It saved you from arrest a minute ago. That was quite a fight you were in."

"A misunderstanding is all."

Cort laughed. "I'd hate to see you two have a real disagreement."

Rella realized with a start that this was the first time she had ever heard him laugh. The sound was warm and soothing—or at least would have been under other circumstances. Cort Ramsey filled the tent the way he had the small office back in Galveston. Ruefully she remembered how quickly she had fallen under his spell before. Once she was aroused by this particular man, it seemed her will faded into unimportance.

The trick was to stay away from him . . . far away.

"The hour grows late. I must leave."

"There is no one about to see you home. Is it far?"

She shook her head.

"Then I will escort you."

She thought of several retorts but knew they would all sound like Cinderella Sandringham. She settled for a simple, "As you will."

Rella had no fear that her walk would expose her identity. Back in Galveston, she'd held her tall body erect and her head high, as she'd been taught to do upon the stage. But during the past weeks with the Gypsies, riding across the open countryside or taking long walks, she'd developed a softening grace that was new to her. Her hips swayed gently with each stride. She was not so befuddled by Cort's presence that she didn't notice his appreciative glance as he strolled beside her.

The walk to the encampment was slow and quiet, Cort asking occasional questions and Rella answering as ambiguously as she dared.

"Is Chicago your home?"

"A Gypsy has no home but the open road."

"Have you been here long?"

"It is the gorgio who owns a calendar. My caravan has been here long enough for some among us to grow restless."

"Do you have a man?"

Rella paused at that one. She knew exactly what he meant. Most outsiders thought Gypsies had low morals and swapped sleeping partners whenever they chose. Gypsies might abscond with another man's cow or chicken to put food on the table, and they certainly couldn't be trusted in any livestock business deal; but they were loyal to their mates, a fact the marshal would no doubt find hard to believe.

"I am not wed," she said.

When they arrived at the edge of the circled wagons, Cort persisted. "You do not have a husband. But do you have a man?"

With the firelight at her back, Rella allowed herself to look directly into his eyes. "I have all the men I want, gorgio. I do not seek more outside the camp."

Cort watched as she disappeared into a tent away from the wagons. The camp appeared deserted, but he knew he was being watched. Somehow the other Gypsies had gotten wind that a lawman was about. He didn't know how they managed to communicate so efficiently, especially since they had no written language.

Reluctantly he turned away. The Romany had managed, for just a little while, to take his mind off the fair-haired killer who had so smoothly escaped his clutches. During the past months nothing or no one else had done so.

Slowly he headed toward the streetcar that would take him to his hotel. He'd been in Chicago only a few days, but it was already apparent that as in every place he'd tried, he would have to work hard for a clue.

Such wouldn't have been the problem if he had been able to follow a fresher trail. But he'd been tied up for two weeks working on a rustling case west of Houston, the authorities there assuring him it was more important to determine just who had taken a hundred head of cattle than it was to arrest the suspect in the killing of a lawyer.

Then there had been the time investigating Rella Sandringham's possible escape to Denver. He hadn't considered the possibility that mild-mannered Aaron Tuttle would purposefully mislead him away from his father's killer. But that's exactly what he'd done, weaving a story about how Rella planned to rejoin her acting friends in Colorado. Cort had made it halfway to Denver before receiving a reply to one of his telegrams that Templeton's Traveling Thespians was unknown in that part of the country.

Under his relentless questions, a befuddled Aaron had been forced to reveal the truth, at least part of it. Rella did indeed plan to join her friends, but instead of heading for Denver, she had sailed for the East. Deputy Bowles had been openly derisive concerning his chances of success, although why he had taken on a superior air, Cort couldn't fathom. It was the deputy who had been careless and allowed her to get away.

Cort knew exactly who had talked Aaron into his duplicitous behavior: Greta Maas. The French had a phrase for it. *Cherchez la femme.* Look for the woman. The young medical student, as different as he was from his late father, shared Perry's weakness for the feminine gender.

Cort had his own *femme* to look for—the beautiful, scheming Cinderella Sandringham. Until her escape, he'd harbored doubts about her guilt, but no more. Unfortunately, by the time he was turned in the right direction, Rella's trail had grown cold. It had taken him days to find someone who remembered seeing her around the New Orleans docks, and more time to locate the captain of the steamboat that had carried her up the Mississippi.

He'd tugged at his captain's hat. "Not hard to recall that one. Sharp-tongued miss with the look of an angel."

"She's the one all right," Cort had replied.

"Left her off in St. Louis. Hope the folks there fared all right with her in town."

They must have done well enough, he found, for again she seemed to have been swallowed up by the ground. No one at any theatre remembered her, but Templeton and his troupe was headed north for Chicago.

The journey up the Mississippi had been painful for Cort. His Missouri home was only a short distance west of the river, and a flood of memories had assailed him—of good times with Josiah Ramsey and of bad times looking in vain for his killers. But he couldn't dwell too much on the injustices of the past, not until he had settled Rella firmly in the Galveston jail.

Cort had become obsessed with finding her. He told himself that he was only after justice in solving Perry Tuttle's murder, that Rella's violently terminated kiss had nothing to do with his search. But she'd played him for a fool twice. First, she'd taken his money and successfully hidden it; second had been that painful bite. For both she would have to pay.

He'd found the Chicago theatre where the Thespians had performed. The manager had readily reported that several weeks ago Rella, too, had been there, but had missed connecting with that particular troupe. She had appeared close to destitution, but he'd had no work for her.

"Good looking blonde," he'd said, "but looked worn down to a nub." He would bet she'd found some kind of work in Chicago since it appeared her friends were well away on a long trek somewhere out West—Denver, they'd talked about, and then maybe San Francisco after that. The little lady didn't appear to have the means for traveling after them.

By the time Cort left the theatre, he had a lot to think about. She might be headed for Denver after all, provided she had come up with the money. But if she really was without funds, what had happened to his six thousand dollars? She couldn't have spent it all, not the way she'd been on the move. Maybe she'd had to leave it in Galveston when she broke jail.

He rejected any idea of going back toward Denver before he searched Chicago. Dividing the city into quadrants, he would continue his tedious search. Some of the local lawmen had promised to help; to aid them he'd provided a few wanted posters containing her fair-haired likeness.

The problem was the size of the place. There were many places to hide among Chicago's three hundred thousand people—if Rella had bothered to stay in town. With a woman of her looks and lack of morality, there were many options open to her. And she could work with figures in a business. She could be anywhere waiting for another six thousand dollars to fall into her lap.

The next day, just as Rella was figuring on how she could make another escape, she was subjected to a diatribe from Lucretia and Torry John. They'd provided her with a tent so that she didn't have to sleep on the open ground. And what had she done in payment? Taken what was rightfully theirs.

She'd pointed out that but for her, they would have much less. She'd made out before without them and could again. But could they do as well without her? The two seemed unimpressed by her unrefutable arguments.

In her tent she counted her secret hoard; it seemed enough for passage out of town. But she had no clothes, no disguise other than her flamboyant Gypsy attire. If, as she feared, Cort returned to find her gone, he would know for sure his search was close to an end. Looking as she did, she would be damnably easy to trace. Until she could come up with some kind of plan that was more than just a panicked fleeing, she must try to keep the peace. But between dodging Serafina and expecting any minute to feel a firm hand on her shoulder and the words "You're under arrest," she spent the long daylight hours jumping at shadows.

Dear Alepa was the only one who came to her defense. At supper, with the Gypsies gathered near the fire, she'd stood and made what amounted to the first speech Rella had heard in the camp.

"There is one among us who has added greatly to our coffers," she said, slowly circling and pinning her dark eyes on each of the men and women in turn. Even Serafina grew quiet.

"We will not make her feel unwelcome," she intoned.

No one spoke in opposition, but Rella knew there were those who sided with Serafina. No matter what was done against the gorgios, Gypsies did not steal from one another. And holding back what Lucretia and Torry John claimed as theirs was a grave breach of custom on Rella's part. The fact that Serafina had thought she was making up the story did not ease Rella's niggling feelings of guilt.

But necessity, she had found, was driving her to many desperate acts. It was time to move on.

She would have preferred consuming an entire kettle of rodent stew rather than go to the fairgrounds that night. But to stay away would only bring additional wrath down on her head. If Cort Ramsey did show up, she would simply have to fool him once again. As a precaution, she rubbed a diluted solution of hair dye on her pale burn scar.

She almost made it through the night. Many customers came and went; Cort was not among their number. She had begun to relax and think that the interest he'd shown in her yesterday had been no more than he would have for any woman suddenly appearing, alone and unarmed, at his feet.

He walked in, again seeming to fill the small tent, and she gave an involuntary gasp.

"I see you have not forgotten, Romany," he said, removing his hat and dropping it on the table.

She lowered her eyes. "You are difficult to forget, although I am surprised you remembered our small fair."

"After the fight last night, I figured the police might start watching the place more closely, as they are. Thought maybe I might be able to help you avoid trouble. In case someone still wanted to throw you in jail."

Rella bit at her lip. "I do not understand. Why

would you help a tribe of Gypsies?"

Cort shrugged. "You're outsiders here. Much the same as I am down in Texas. Maybe I just wanted to make sure you're treated right." He grinned. "But don't make me out a hero. It could be I just wanted my fortune told."

Rella took a deep breath. "You do not look like a man who would believe in such things."

He stared down at her. "What kind of a man do I look like?"

Rella had several answers for that one, none she could state aloud. She stalled. "Romany does not speak until she sees the coins."

"Spoken like a true Gypsy," he said with a laugh, tossing down a sum of money that surprised her. He settled into the chair opposite her and extended his hand, palm up. "Now tell me. What kind of a man do you think I am?"

Cort stared at the gracefully bent head. He shouldn't be here. A deadly serious business had brought him into town, and there was no justification for seeing the Gypsy again—except that he had wanted to make sure she wasn't bothered by an overzealous officer of the law. Despite her earthy beauty, there was something vulnerable about this Romany, something that reminded him he was a lonely man.

Rella could no longer postpone the inevitable. She took his hand in hers. He'd said her skin was warm, and so was his. Like her, he seemed to carry the sun.

Cort had a broad, callous palm and long fingers. Any other man she would have called hard working, strong, yet sensitive and gentle. But she knew the marshal too well to give him any such traits. If he seemed to possess them, it was only because he could play a role as easily as she.

"You have been long on the trail," she said, taking

care to keep her voice at a low pitch.

"Not hard to surmise," he said. "I must look road weary."

Rella glanced up. Perhaps he did, she thought, noticing the new lines around his eyes and mouth. But his lean, ruddy face also looked more ruggedly handsome than she remembered, and she fought an impulse to brush from his forehead a lock of copper hair.

She forced herself to concentrate on his palm. "You are a strong-willed man. One who does not take easily to unwanted advice."

"That would depend on what I am advised to do."

"You also are quick to anger."

"I'm quickly aroused in several ways."

Rella saw an unfortunate pattern had developed. She gave him a trait she knew all too well he possessed, and he turned it on her.

"You insult me," she said, her own temper flaring, "if you think I do not understand what you mean." She removed her hands from his. "I do not believe, gorgio, that you have faith in what I say."

He placed another coin on the table. "You're right that I've been long on the trail. Too long to remember how to treat a lovely young woman. Try me again."

What arrogance, she thought as she took his hand in hers once again. Pride moved her to incaution. She wanted him to believe in her Gypsy power.

"You seem to be on a great search," she said. "One that has met with failure."

She felt the muscles of his hand grow tense. "What else do you see?" he asked.

"That you look in the wrong place. The prize you seek is far, far away." Her words hung in the air. She waited for his response.

"Are you trying to send me on my way?"

In ferreting out her exact purpose, Cort sounded

sharper than he had before, and Rella attempted to mend whatever damage she had done.

"You were my friend last night. I try only to return the favor and give you a fair reading."

"So you don't want me to leave."

"I cannot give thought to what I want."

Deftly, Cort moved to capture both her hands in his. "Until last night, I thought I knew what I was after. Now, I'm not so sure."

Rella gave an ineffectual tug to free herself. "You must leave. There are others who await the Romany."

"Let them."

She gave a helpless shrug. "My people depend on me to do my work."

He freed her hands. "You do it very well." He stood and moved toward the opening of the tent. "So do I. I don't know whether you were just guessing, but you were right about my search. Only I don't think my quarry has gone in another direction. I'm not sure just why, but the longer I stay in Chicago, the more positive I become that at last I'm on the right track." He smiled down at her, and Rella's heart caught in her throat. "If you were wondering whether I planned to hang around for a while, the answer is definitely yes."

Rella watched in dismay as he left. He was her enemy! She must not forget that inescapable fact. No matter what approach she made toward Cort Ramsey, it turned out wrong. She was barely able to concentrate on the last few customers of the night. She knew very well who would be waiting for her outside when she was done.

"Ready to leave?" he asked as she stepped into the cool October air. He acted as though it were the most natural thing in the world for him to be waiting to escort her home.

Without answering, she fell in beside him, and the

walk was made in silence. When they neared the open field where the Gypsies camped, Cort halted. A cloud passed over the moon, and they stood side by side in the dark. She listened to his even breath.

"We must say good night," she said, facing him, intending to turn away. Their eyes met, and as the moon reappeared, he seemed to sway toward her. Unable to move, she felt his arms close around her.

He pulled her close. She tried to remember the clang of the jailhouse door as it slammed behind her, but when Cort's lips touched hers, she forgot all else but him. Just as she'd done back in Galveston, she curved her body against his and let him have his way.

His way was all that she could have wanted and more than she'd ever dreamed. The touch of his lips on hers sent unfamiliar tremblings coursing through her. Dizzy with exhilaration, she wrapped her arms around his neck and held on tight. His body was tautly muscled, hard and unyielding, a contrast to the warm lips that moved enticingly against hers. Each place that was touched by Cort seemed on fire.

Her lips opened to his demands, and her tongue moved with his. How sweet he tasted. He crushed her against him until she thought surely she would break. She welcomed his fearsome embrace.

Strong hands trailed down her spine and back again to entwine in her hair. He had such knowing hands that could melt her body into his.

Suddenly her lips were freed. He gripped her shoulders, or she might surely have fallen. Her breath came in a rush.

"Romany," he whispered into her hair, "what kind of spell have you cast on me?"

She could have put the same question to him. Her knees threatened to give way, and she leaned against him for support. She fought to catch her breath, to calm the pounding of her heart.

"Have I known you in another life?" He brushed his lips against her cheek. "I seem to have held you before—"

Rella trembled in a mingling of fear and longing.

"—and yet you affect me as no woman has ever done."

She had played a dangerous game long enough, and she pushed away, her fingers touching the sharp edges of his badge.

"Good-bye, gorgio," she managed. "You cannot . . . you must not see me again."

Without looking back, she hurried toward the Gypsy camp, toward the sanctuary of her lonely tent. With each step she cursed the weakness that consumed her each time the marshal took her in his arms. She must be several kinds of fool to risk her freedom and perhaps her life for his embrace.

Wrapped in her tormenting thoughts, she failed to see a figure standing in the shadows at the edge of the camp. Serafina had been waiting for the Romany to return. The wait had been worthwhile.

So the fortune teller liked gorgios as well as Gypsies, did she? In truth, she must have an insatiable desire for men.

Serafina shared that desire, but for her only one man would satisfy. Sandor must be hers. He was gone on another hunt for horses, but he would be back soon. When he returned, Serafina vowed to let him know how he had been played for a fool.

Chapter Nine

Rella took careful aim at the knot on the faraway oak and let the knife fly. It landed handle first against the rough bark and fell with a thud onto the ground.

Breaking the silence of the morning air with a Gypsy oath, she shuffled slowly across the shaded clearing to retrieve the weapon. Her sandals crunched against the leaves that had already fallen in this dry, cool October; her skirts swayed gently and caught against the tall, soft grass.

Everything she'd tried lately seemed to turn out wrong. She'd sought obscurity in a Gypsy camp and had become more of a celebrity than she'd ever been on the stage. She'd made enemies among the Gypsies when all she was after was to be among friends. And the one man in the world she should avoid at all costs she'd wanted to give herself to last night with no more provocation than a simple kiss.

Rella paused at the base of the oak. Simple? Perhaps that wasn't quite the right word. Nothing that involved Cort Ramsey could be described in such a way.

She picked up the knife and, heading back to her place twenty feet away, tried to picture the way Sandor had held the tip of the blade and the angle of the knife before he sent it like an arrow toward the tree. All she could conjure in her mind was Cort Ramsey bending his head to hers, his lips pressing down with demands that needed no words.

And his hands. . . . Those wonderful, damnable hands! He showed more skill with them on her body than she'd ever been able to manage with a deck of tarot cards.

Or with this blasted knife, she thought as she looked down in disgust at the carved wooden handle and stiletto blade resting in her hand. She'd borrowed it from Alepa early this morning before setting out alone on her ride for the isolated grove, grateful that Sandor had not returned to continue his lessons.

She'd spent a miserable night thinking about Cort and her reaction to him. She needed to be alone to sort out her feelings. Nothing about them made any sense. She should hate him for what he believed she had done. She should revile the way he refused to listen to reason. She should deplore her own weakness whenever his body neared hers.

Instead, she still felt the tingle of his touch hours after his departure. Cort read her body with his hands and lips the way she read palms. He knew just how to get the reaction he was after.

"You have need for a weapon?" Alepa had asked when she approached the old woman in her vardo after breakfast.

"I have a need to be by myself awhile," Rella answered bluntly. "And to get away from the city."

"Spoken like a true Gypsy."

Rella smiled. "I thought I might as well put my time to use. Sandor tried to teach me how to throw a knife, but I wasn't a very good student. Serafina interrupted us, and I'm afraid she misunderstood."

"She is foolish. Love does strange things to a

woman."

"Help me convince her I have no interest in him."

"I will try," said Alepa. "There could be much trouble over such a misunderstanding. Worse than the foolishness two nights ago."

Watching Alepa take the knife from a small trunk, Rella remembered her fight with Serafina. This was the first time it had been discussed between the two of them. "Of course it was foolish. But she came at me with such fury, I had no time to do more than defend myself."

"You must be glad that the lawman appeared to save you from jail. I saw that he returned last night and walked with you back to the camp."

Rella drew in a deep breath. There was no censure in the old woman's voice, but Rella knew she was curious. Playing with the strands of golden chain around her neck, she said, "He thinks I need an escort home."

"Do you encourage him?"

Rella pushed from her mind the memory of how she had let his lips and hands move at will about her body. Yes, she had encouraged him. Not only had she failed to assault him with her teeth as she had done before, she had responded readily to his every touch. But she could never tell Alepa such a thing.

"I can make my way back from thc fairgrounds alone or with other Gypsies," she had said, avoiding the woman's eyes. "I do not need the marshal."

"Perhaps you do not realize, Romany, how unusual it is for a gorgio lawman to defend a Gypsy against one of his own. He seems a good man." Alepa's wrinkled old face was broken by a smile. "This is a strange thing for me to admit, this admiration for such a one. Perhaps it is because I sense something between the two of you. More than is ordinary between a man and a woman who find each other of interest. Some day," she had said softly, handing over the knife, "you will tell me all. Perhaps you need him more than you know."

Here in the woods, with only the rustling leaves and an occasional songbird to break the stillness, Alepa's words rang in her ears.

Over and over she practiced, after each toss edging closer to the target. Sandor had told her such a Gypsy knife was specially honed to land point first; obviously it took a full-blooded Gypsy tossing it to accomplish the feat.

Still she persisted, forcing all else from her mind. It wasn't until she pictured a grim-faced marshal staring back at her from the tree trunk that she managed to land the knife point-first in the target, where it remained. True, she had halved her distance from the tree, but that didn't lessen her feeling of triumph.

Deciding to quit while she was ahead, she turned back toward the stream where she had tethered her mare. She was placing the weapon in its sheath tied to her saddle when she heard the sound of a horse's hooves striking the ground somewhere in the stand of trees. Supposing it was Sandor coming to renew the lessons, she peered around the rump of her horse. Galloping down the leaf-strewn path that wound through the oaks was Cort Ramsey.

Rella panicked. He must have asked at the camp where she would be. He was seeking her. And there were only a couple of things he could possibly want: her body beneath his or her body thrown in jail. Probably both, and he wouldn't care about the order in which he accomplished his goals.

He had never seen her in daylight, but that didn't mean he hadn't figured out who she was. She should have run . . . should have risked getting hauled off some stagecoach or train by a grim-eyed marshal. At least their moment of truth wouldn't have come in this out-of-the-way woods where he could wreak whatever revenge he chose.

She backed up, tripping over a rock. Clutching at the horse's mane, she managed to stay upright. On tiptoe she peered over the saddle, put her foot in the stirrup to mount, then withdrew it. He was coming too fast on a powerful stallion her mare could never outrun.

Heart racing, she concentrated on one crystallized thought. He must not see her in the shaft of bright sunlight that illuminated the spot where she stood. Abandoning her horse, she thrashed through a thick copse along the narrow stream and headed for the darkest part of the woods.

His deep, rich voice called after her, "Romany!"

Branches scratched at her face and arms and caught in her locks of dark hair, but she ran on. Suddenly she broke through the thick underbrush and into another clearing; she went sprawling onto the ground, Cort running only a few feet behind her.

He dropped to his knees beside her. "Are you all right?" he asked.

Trying to catch her breath, she could only nod mutely.

"You might have hurt yourself," he said. "And why did you run like some wild animal?" His voice softened. "I'm not a predator, you know."

Rella had a comeback for that, but she wisely swallowed it lest she make another stupid move. She berated herself for not behaving more casually. At least, as far as she could tell, he hadn't recognized her. He still thought her a Gypsy, most likely a particularly fuzzy-headed one. Or maybe he thought all Gypsies ran in panic from a gorgio. She relaxed a fraction, sure she was in as deep a shadow as trees in daylight afforded.

"Wind knocked out," he said, wanting to gather her into his arms, put her in front of him on his white stallion, and ride off like some knight of old. It was a crazy thought.

He reached to turn her toward him and saw a nasty scratch on her arm. He wanted to kiss away any pain the wound might have brought, but as frightened as the Romany seemed, he knew he would only add to that fright. That, he did not want. On the contrary, he had come because he couldn't stay away. The memory of her haunted him more than any call to duty. He'd seen the wild side of her in her fight with the dancer; he'd discovered the warm and tender side of her nature last night when he'd held her in his arms.

"If I leave for a few minutes, can I trust you to stay?"

Again, Rella could only nod, glancing around the secluded clearing. The trees grew thickly here, their branches forming an almost-solid roof overhead. It was as dark as a moonlit night.

True to his word, Cort returned shortly, his handkerchief dampened in the stream. He wiped at the scratch on her arm.

"The bleeding has stopped," he said. "It's too shallow to leave a scar."

Startled, she looked at her arm. She'd not even felt the wound. For one brief moment her gaze locked with Cort's. She looked away, her mind racing to find something she could say, some way to exit gracefully without arousing his suspicion even more. Nothing came to mind.

"Why did you run?" he asked for the second time.

As usual, Cort wouldn't let up on a point. She had

an answer for him, but it wasn't one she could reveal. She answered obliquely.

"I told you last night not to return," she said, daring to glance up at him once again. Even in the muted light she could see his blue eyes pinned to her, and she quickly dropped her kohl-darkened lashes.

"That's what you said, all right. Which, of course, doesn't tell me what I want to know."

"You frighten me," she whispered. She spoke from her heart. He held great power over her, not only because of the badge on his chest. He was a strong-willed man—and a good one, according to Alepa. Bathed in his gentle concern, she could only agree. The need to have him near, to touch her was proving irresistible. For the first time she admitted that when she wasn't trying to run away from Cort, she wanted to throw herself into his arms.

Cort had a number of impulses to fight, chief among them was to moisten those full red lips with his kiss and take up where he and the Romany had ended last night. There was something about this Gypsy girl that stirred his blood. He wanted her. With the way she had responded last night, he knew it was only a matter of time until she submitted to the inevitable.

Besides, she'd said she had all the men she wanted. She wasn't an innocent, despite the fear she exhibited now. She was a puzzle to him, a dark and beautiful puzzle he had to solve.

"Let's talk," he said, sitting and stretching his long legs on the ground beside her.

Rella inched away, but her tensed muscles began to relax. At least all he'd proposed—thus far—was conversation.

"What does the gorgio think I have to say?" she asked, tucking her heels under her full skirts.

"You looked at my palm last night and said I was on a great search. You were right. I am looking for a woman."

"Many men are," Rella managed.

"I seem to have found you. Not the one I set out looking for. The other is a shrew—"

Rella bit her lip.

"—and most likely a killer and thief."

"Do you hate this woman?"

Cort thought that one over. Hate Rella Sandringham? That innocent looking blond liar? She'd made his blood boil—with anger and for a fleeting moment with an entirely different emotion. She'd made a fool of him. If he didn't hate her, he'd certainly worked up a powerful lot of dislike.

"It was my money she stole," he said at last. "Down in Texas."

"You have come a long way looking for her."

"She's become an obsession with me. She won't get away."

Even in the muted light, Rella could see the firm set of his jaw as he spoke of his quarry. She shuddered and could think of nothing to say.

"As a matter of fact," Cort said, his voice softening, "she was all I could think of until the other night when I came upon this wild-eyed beauty in a most unlikely place." He sat up and moved closer until his breath stirred her hair. "Now it is the picture of another woman that fills my mind."

Rella swallowed. So he carried the images of two women in his head, did he? Once he discovered the truth—and he would—Cort Ramsey would be a terrifying enemy to behold.

"Are she and I so different?" she couldn't help but ask.

He reached out and stroked her hair. "Very different." Shifting until his thigh brushed against hers, he lifted a dark lock from her neck and brushed his lips across a sensitive spot behind her ear.

Rella trembled, strange sensations skittering across her skin, and her head rolled back.

"She is cold and calculating," he said.

No, she's not, Rella thought, her pulse hammering. Each breath she took was like a burning coal.

Again his lips brushed against her neck. "She would never have allowed me to do that," Cort whispered. "Or this." He kissed the pulse point at her throat. "Your heart beats wildly, Romany."

He pulled to his knees in front of her and held her shoulders lightly. His lips trailed feather kisses across her cheeks and eyes and at the corners of her mouth.

"You are all softness," he said as his mouth touched hers.

"No," she whispered, even as her hands clutched at his shirt. Behind her closed eyes a velvet blackness eddied. She felt lost in a mad world that had no time or space, no future or past. Reason fled. She could not understand the powerful urges gripping her, and yet she could not deny them. She could not deny Cort.

His hand caught at the drawstring of her blouse, a thumb stroking the rise of her breast and playing with the tip. Her flcsh swelled and hardened under his touch.

Rella struggled for the anger that should have been her defense. Cold and calculating, he'd said. She tried with all the power she had left to concentrate on those words; but a longing beyond anything she'd known swept through her, and all she could say was his name.

The whispered sound of *Cort* on her lips brought him to the edge of control. He'd wanted a woman, any woman, and then he'd wanted the Romany. She was warmth and comfort and excitement all in one. He would give her the pleasure she claimed she didn't need.

"Romany," he whispered in turn, lifting the golden chains from around her neck and tossing them aside. "I will love you as you have never been loved."

No, her mind screamed. *What we do has nothing to do with love.*

She tried to push away, but his hands became as iron bands on her shoulders. For one brief instant she felt the anger that had been denied her before. Here was the arrogant marshal who saw no way but his. She should scratch and bite him, should hurt him as he was about to hurt her. But to do so could too easily unveil Rella Sandringham, the woman he had not been able to find.

Her breath quickened. She must play the part of Gypsy. What would the Romany do?

When he pulled her beside him to lie on the soft grass, reason warred with desire until the two mingled and she lost all sense of self that was separate from Cort. Whoever she was, she wanted him to make love to her.

Boldly she fingered the drawstring of her blouse. "You brag about what you will do, gorgio. It is time for more than talk."

If Cort lived to be a thousand, he would never hear more inflaming words. The Romany was no longer a puzzle; she was a warm and willing woman who needed him as he needed her. He felt as though he'd come to the end of a long journey.

When he covered her hand with his and tugged at the drawstring, he felt her move as one with him. The cotton blouse fell loose, revealing in the dim light a subtle curve of breast. He slipped the blouse lower and caught his breath. He was lost in the beauty of her.

Unashamed, Rella watched the look of pleasure flicker across Cort's face and settle in his eyes. In a movement that was new and at once natural, she arched her body toward him, glorified as he bent his head to her. He caught one nipple between his teeth and played at her with his tongue. Her answer was a long and silken sigh.

All the while his hand stroked her hot skin. Rella caught her fingers in his hair and gave herself up to velvet desire. She felt herself flowing into a new and unreal world, her guide a tempter who was part apparition, part tautly muscled flesh.

Sensation after sensation washed over Rella as Cort moved his lips in a tantalizing trail toward her own moist, waiting mouth. Always his hand stroked her.

This time there was nothing gentle about his kiss. His mouth crushed against hers, and his tongue plundered inside in a desperate demand for her submission. Passion flared within her. Hunger intensified. Eager fingers roamed down his back and pulled him hard against her bare breasts. She felt the ripple of his muscles, knew his strength. For a fleeting moment she reveled in the power of the man she held in her arms.

Mindless, she was swept by a determination to feel her skin against his, to know the texture and heat of his body. She slipped her hands to the front of his shirt and worked at the buttons. She grew impatient. He helped her with the unfastening; then taking one breast in his hand, he rubbed her against his chest.

Rella became a wild thing, writhing against him, moaning his name, sucking at his tongue, tasting the moist, dark sweetness of him. When he lifted her skirts and placed his hand against the underclothing between her thighs, she was already close to ecstasy.

The feel of his intimately probing fingers was a pleasure distilled of all else but passion. She shuddered with jolts of rapture. Surely this was all. Surely there could be nothing more wonderful than this electrifying sensation that his touch brought.

But Colt knew far more than she. He had planned to undress her slowly, unveiling her dusky beauty before him in agonizing sweetness; but the Romany was a creature of passion, and he answered with a passion of his own that could not be held to design.

With her skirts bunched around her waist, he tugged impatiently at her undergarments until he could feel her warm skin and the downy softness between her thighs. Tossing the garments aside, he worked at the buckle of his belt. She reached up to help him, her fingers brushing against his swollen manhood. He caught his breath and with untold force of will held still.

Rella saw what she did to him. As eagerly as her body thrummed for him, he matched her desire. She had never touched a man before. Even through his trousers, she could feel the size of him, the pulsing need he had for her. Shivers of fright shot through her. She was wandering in a strange land of dark and sensual pleasures and had placed her very being in the hands of a man she knew little about. More than ever, she felt the power and strength of him.

But she also knew her own power. He trembled under her touch.

Cort could wait no longer. Stripping off his pants, he lay between her open thighs and plunged inside her.

Stunned by the momentary pain, Rella cried out. Cort swallowed her cry as his mouth covered hers. He knew all too well what that cry meant, what that resistance of her body gave evidence to. He was the first for his Gypsy beauty. She gave him what she had given no other man.

Shaken, he slowed his movements until he felt her own rhythmic response. Gradually the spirit of sweet madness returned. This time there was no pause, no slowing down, but rather an inexorable quickening of sensation, widening waves of passion which inundated them both.

They peaked together, Rella's fingers digging into his back, Cort holding her close, treasuring her, cradling her until the tremors subsided. They lay still in each other's arms, their quick, uneven breaths gradually slowing, the velvet blackness opening up to the ragged light which filtered into their hideaway.

The enormity of what she had done weakened Rella, but she could not pull away. For one last bittersweet moment she clung to Cort. Believing her to be a Gypsy, he had stalked her much as he did any other prey.

Did she regret so easily giving in? Maybe later, but not now—not when she still carried the thrill of his lovemaking. But Rella had sense enough to know this could not happen again. Whatever she felt for him—and she could not give in to what she already knew dwelt in her heart—she must flee.

"You lied to me," he said softly against her cheek.

Rella started. "Never," she said, adding another lie.

"You said you had all the men you needed in the camp. I know now there have been no other men."

She resorted to the truth. "I did not know I needed you."

"And now?"

"The gorgio talks too much." She pulled free of his arms. "I have given you proof of my need. It is enough without the words."

With that, Cort had to be content. He dressed, watching her in silhouette as she prepared to return to the camp.

"It is time for me to go," she said and added, "alone. You will do me harm if I am seen with you too much. It is wrong for a Gypsy and a gorgio to make love."

Cort stood beside her. "Do you think what we did was wrong?"

Without answer, Rella turned from him. It had been much worse than wrong. It had been insane. She started to leave, but Cort caught her arm.

"I'll answer if you won't," he said. "It wasn't wrong. And it won't be the last time. You know it as well as I."

Rella rode back to the camp as though she were fleeing the devil. Only she knew she carried the devil inside herself. Her weakness for Cort would lead her to damnation.

Alepa stopped her outside her tent. "You are changed."

Rella avoided her eyes. "I am still the Romany."

"The lawman found you."

"He . . . found me, yes."

"You do not have to tell me more. I must warn you. Serafina knows."

Rella looked at the old woman with widened eyes. "What does Serafina know?"

"How it goes with you and the gorgio. I must tell you this. Sandor has returned. And it is too late to reason with Serafina. The two of them had a terrible fight before I could try to talk to her."

"Surely not about me," Rella said. "You know there is nothing but friendship between me and Sandor."

"He tries to tell her this, but then grows stubborn with the foolish girl. He says she must believe what she will. I fear trouble lies in our midst. And it awaits you, too. It is a bad thing for an unmarried woman to give herself to a man." She reached out and touched Rella's arm. Her gray eyes flashed a warning as clear as her words.

"You play a dangerous game, Romany. The marshal is not a man that will take yes and then no."

As Rella entered her tent, she stifled a hysterical laugh. A dangerous game, Alepa had said. Dangerous it was, all right, but it wasn't a mere game that had caught her. It came closer to being a matter of life and death.

Chapter Ten

Rella sat on her heels in the narrow, half-filled washing tub she'd dragged into her tent and watched a rivulet of bath water trickle down her breast. It followed the same path Cort's lips had taken only hours before. She shut her eyes against the memory.

Do you think what we did was wrong?

Cort's question echoed in her mind. Asked with firm conviction, it had carried its own answer. In his view, there had been nothing but pleasure in their coupling. For Rella the pleasure had been tainted by a knowledge that Cort did not possess.

Then she relived the soaring wonder of his love-making. Nothing so glorious as that could be truly wrong.

She cupped a small amount of the cool water and splashed it against skin grown warm with the remembrance of him. Surely what they had done was right. Even as the thought flitted through her mind, she knew that the sweetness of a morning hour spent in Cort's arms had not eradicated one scintilla of the truth. Once he knew the identity of the woman he'd held so passionately, the marshal would not hesitate to throw her in jail.

The fact that he had as yet not recognized her was no assurance she was safe from him. Sooner or later, he would learn that she appeared to have no past and would begin to ask questions no one could answer. Or he would catch her in a bright light. She must disappear before that happened, no matter how reluctant to leave him she might become. To stay was playing with fire. She couldn't withstand his lovemaking. His every glance, every touch filled her with yearning for more glances, more touches.

It won't be the last time.

He'd stood tall and sure in that shadowed clearing and had spoken with determination. She pictured the shock of copper hair brushing close to a pair of blue eyes that seemed to stare into her soul. Even in the filtered light of morning, he'd looked as strong and unyielding as one of the oaks that surrounded them.

And just as likely to listen to reason, she thought. He was certain that the fair Cinderella Sandringham was a killer and a thief. And he was just as certain that the dusky-skinned Romany was a creature made for passion. If he wanted to make love to her once more, nothing she could say would cool his ardor.

But what of her own awakened desires? He'd taught her the secrets of rapture. Even now, knowing the danger he presented, how could she possibly hunger after him? Impatiently she scrubbed at her body, trying to wash away all memories of his touch. Nothing had changed about her. She was still the woman she had been before this morning. Two arms, two legs. Two breasts. . . .

Inventorying her various features was a wrong tack to take. Too quickly she remembered how Cort had aroused each part of her. Never again must she allow herself to be alone with him.

Drying herself, she dressed quickly and disposed of the water in the stream that ran behind the Gypsy camp. The long afternoon was spent trying to keep busy, but there was only so much she could help with in the preparation of dinner, only so many stitches she could practice with needle and thread.

Neither did the tarot cards hold any appeal for her. What little she had learned from Alepa about reading them only told her on every turn that her future was irrevocably linked with a tall, bold man—nothing about whether that future was happy or sad.

Throughout the long day she was surrounded by the usual rustling of activity, the laughter, an occasional song from one of the women as she worked, the play-fighting of the children, and the clang of hammer against metal as one of the men worked at a small forge.

Rella gave thought to the strange world in which she found herself. The Gypsies led a curious existence, one of innocent enjoyment even as they prepared for an evening at the fairgrounds where they would go about separating the gorgios from hard-earned coins.

As much as Rella needed the money skimmed from Torry John, the job of coping with her hopeful clients was one she relished even less than most times. A few more nights, she told herself, and then she would have enough gold. But she didn't *have* a few more nights. Cort would show up at the fairgrounds; she would expect nothing less. And what he would want was something more intimate than having his fortune told. That, after all, involved the touching of no more than hands.

She would have a good chance of avoiding him if she could devise an excuse for staying away from the fair. In the dark of night, when the Gypsies were either still away or fast asleep, she would run . . . maybe all the way across town to the lake. In the morning she would buy a simple gown and buy her way on the closest conveyance that she could afford. It was a foolish plan, maybe, but then so was staying in the camp.

After supper, she lay down in front of her tent. When she saw the light in the wagon dim and knew her benefactors were ready to go, she put her wrist on her brow and feigned being in the throes of a painful headache.

As Lucretia came to stand over her, she moaned softly.

"You are not ready. The time is late."

"I am often bothered by headaches," Rella said, "and this one is particularly bad. I will not be going with you tonight."

Lucretia's dark eyes narrowed. "The gorgios will be expecting you to tell them the secrets of the future."

"The gorgios"—at least one in particular, Rella thought—"will have to get along without me tonight."

Torry John came to stand beside his wife.

"This is the thanks we get," she told him, gesturing broadly with a beringed hand. "I do not think she is ill."

Torry John shrugged. "I have learned that when a woman decides to be ill, there is no way a man can reason it out."

"Just like a man to make such an excuse for *her,*" Lucretia muttered in disgust. "She has only to state her wishes, and they are granted. You are not so understanding of my illnesses, no matter what you say."

"Foolish talk!" he said, then turned away. "Come," he ordered without looking back. "After the rest you've had, you'll give good readings tonight."

Eyes trained on Rella, the Gypsy woman smoothed her brightly colored skirt over her broad hips. "He is right. Perhaps it is just as well that tonight the gorgios will hear what a woman of wise years has to say."

Swallowing a reminder that Lucretia had been willing enough, night after night, to give up her place in the fortune-telling tent to the more successful Romany, Rella watched her waddle off behind her husband. She felt no regret that someone else would take her place. After all, she could take no pride in what she had accomplished, resulting as it did from her ability to read characters and to assume another role. She had no more power to see into the future than she did to alter the past.

Gradually the camp settled down into quiet as Gypsies headed for the fairgrounds. A few of the women stayed behind to bed down with the youngest children, but they paid Rella no mind. She was about to slip into her tent and pack her few belongings when Alepa paused before setting out on the journey to the fair.

"You have been by yourself much of the day," she said. "Is it wise to stay alone tonight? Too much thinking can only bring confusion."

Hiding a pang of guilt, Rella said, "I fear the gorgios are figuring out that I am a fraud."

"It does not do to stay around them long," Alepa said, nodding. "Winter is coming on. It has been decided that we will leave this very night. Long before dawn, we will be gone. I see you are surprised. Lucretia should have told you, but she is a spiteful woman."

"Perhaps she is the cause of my headache," said Rella.

"It is the gorgio lawman who gives you a headache," said Alepa. "Wait here."

She went to her own wagon and returned quickly with a brown bottle. "Take a half cup of this. It is mostly alcohol, but I have added powerful herbs to cure aches and bring on sleep." Alepa smiled reassuringly. "I will call you in time to fold the tent away lest Lucretia try to leave you behind."

"Is this dangerous, then?"

"No, but the more you take, the longer you sleep. Remember, this night will be a short one. Take only the half cup." Alepa paused. "If you are sure you wish to stay alone tonight."

Rella shrugged. "I don't think I can face the gorgios."

"It is only the one who keeps you away."

"Sometimes one person is all that is necessary to bring trouble into a life."

"I am sure the marshal is such a man," Alepa said. "He can bring much trouble. But also, such a one as he can bring much joy. Enough to make the trouble worthwhile."

"For some, maybe," Rella said, "but not for me."

"And you are different from other women?"

Rella found herself smiling wryly. "Not so different, it would seem."

Alepa frowned. "And still you seek refuge from him? I think he is a good man. For a gorgio."

Rella longed to confess all, but she drew back from laying the sordid truth of her past before one of the few Gypsies in the camp she could call friend.

Alepa seemed to read her mind. "Perhaps someday we will talk," she said. "In the meantime, if you wish to avoid the gorgio, you can depend upon my help."

In a rare show of affection, she gave Rella a brief, hard hug before following the other Gypsies away from the camp.

Rella listened to the footsteps of the departing woman. The slap of sandals against the hard-packed dirt road was surprisingly strong, considering Alepa must be close to seventy years of age. When Rella could no longer hear their sound, she felt a wave of loneliness wash over her. Was this the last time she would see her? She fought the urge to call her back.

Minutes passed as the night settled around the widely circled vardos and tents. Overhead the moon and a million stars shone down from a cloudless October sky, illuminating the scene in a ghostly glow. Rella risked a few moments to watch the fire in the center clearing slowly burn its way down.

How peaceful it all seemed, and how settled. And yet she knew now the Gypsies would break camp and be gone before dawn. Her way seemed clear. She would go with them. She had no other real plan, only a decision to make a panicked flight. Once on the road, she would take her leave of the tribe. Cort would follow the caravan, of course, but there was one thing she knew about the Gypsies: rather than send him after her, they would use their infamous skills at artifice to throw him onto the wrong trail.

"Why does the Romany stay alone?" she heard a man ask.

Her reverie broken, she turned to face him. "Sandor," she said in surprise, "you return late. Do you not have horses you wish to trade at the fair?"

He smiled, and white teeth flashed in his dark face. "The trip was a poor one. The gorgios demand too much for their stock."

"You mean they demand what the stock is worth," Rella said, matching his smile.

Sandor lifted his hands, palm up. "It amounts to the same thing. There is no profit in paying the same for an animal as I will receive when I sell him."

"Perhaps you should join the others at the fair." She paused a moment. "Serafina is there."

"Bah! Why should I care?"

"Because you love her, that is why."

"The Romany can now read into the hearts of Gypsies as well as gorgios?"

"The Romany," Rella answered bitterly, "is having trouble with her own heart. But I understand how you feel."

From behind them a shrill, short laugh cut into the night. Rella glanced past Sandor to see Serafina glaring at her from out of the dark.

"And how does Sandor feel?" the dancer asked.

"What the Romany and I discuss does not concern you," Sandor growled. "Why must you forever creep around and listen where you are not wanted? First by the creek, and now here. You must leave."

"Not until I have finished my business of the other night." Serafina glanced around the quiet camp. "No policeman will bother us here."

She flicked a wrist toward Rella; moonlight reflected on the blade of a knife. "Sandor teaches you the use of a weapon. Let us see how well the lesson has been learned."

Rella stared wide-eyed at the shining blade. "I am unarmed," she said. Even to her own ears, her protest sounded feeble.

"Here," Sandor said, tossing his own knife at her feet. "Teach her that she cannot forever abuse you because of her foolish jealousy."

Rella was not in the least inclined to thank him. She didn't think she could teach Serafina anything in the way of combat. Only the intervention of the law had saved her from being beaten by Serafina the other night. A cold fist wrapped around her heart at the thought of what the Gypsy girl could do with a knife.

She tried ignoring the weapon that lay in the dirt. "I do not want to harm you," she said to the girl.

"Have no fear for me. Worry instead for yourself."

"We have no quarrel," Rella said, persisting.

"We will not after tonight." Serafina waved her knife through the air. "If you do not arm yourself, that is your choice."

Rella could see Serafina meant what she said. Jealousy was a terrible demon which had driven the fiery Gypsy dancer to unbelievable lengths. Rella had no choice but to stoop and pick up the knife. As her fingers wrapped around the wooden handle, she wondered what in the world she was supposed to do in such a fight. She had only learned to throw at a target, the broad trunk of a tree. She had no intention of harming another human being.

In movements as graceful as her dance, Serafina began to circle, always keeping her face toward her enemy. Rella had no choice but to do the same, arms raised at her sides, the knife held tightly in her right hand. She ignored the sweat trickling down the valley between her breasts, forcing herself to concentrate on Serafina's movements.

Suddenly Serafina lunged forward, blade taking a wide swipe. Like a cat, Rella arched her back and drew in her stomach. The tip of the knife cut a long gash in Rella's skirt an inch below her waist. Had she not moved as quickly as she did, the knife would have opened her up as she had seen the Gypsies open up a rabbit for the stew.

But Rella was no rabbit. Serafina meant business, and she would have to defend herself. She would not go down without a struggle, but she knew she could not win the particular battle that the Gypsy girl had begun. Words were Rella's weapon, not a razor-thin blade.

"How long has it been," she asked, "since Sandor has kissed you?" Her voice, forced as it was, came out little more than a whisper.

A low growl sounded in Serafina's throat. Again she slashed with the knife, and again Rella jerked away just in time.

"Do you think he will want you after tonight?"

"It is you he will not want," Serafina spat. "Not after I am done."

"But will Sandor want you? Even unscarred, you have not won him. He wants a gentler touch."

Rella saw the fury in the girl's eyes. From such fury she hoped to draw carelessness. And from carelessness . . . she hoped something would occur to her because she had not planned that far.

She was aware that Sandor was leaning against a tree watching the fight and understood he would not interfere with the quarrel between the two women. It was not the Gypsy way.

Rella's hand was sweaty where it held the knife. What a long way she had come from Cort Ramsey's passionate embrace of the morning. If the situation were less deadly, she would have laughed out loud at how ludicrous she and Serafina must look.

Rella again launched her own kind of attack. "I am sure that Sandor could be such a thrilling lover. Such wonderful hands. Such wonderful lips. Such—"

She heard the low cry, saw Serafina's knife pulled back, and knew what to expect. She hit the ground hard, and the blade flew over her head to land against the canvas tent and roll feebly onto the ground.

Serafina held her proud stance. "Now it is your turn. Surely even you cannot miss from such a distance."

Rella stepped back to pick up the Gypsy's knife. Holding both weapons in her hand, she tossed them inside her tent, then turned to face her adversary.

"We will never know if I could have missed or not.

I know only how to throw at trees. I do not think I could have taken steady aim at you."

Serafina planted fisted hands on her hips. "That is because you lack courage."

"It is you who lacks courage," Sandor said, stepping into the fray now that the battle was done.

"I fight for what is mine," Serafina hissed.

Rella started to speak but saw that the two Gypsies only had eyes for each other. It appeared the young man took pleasure in having a woman fight for him.

But the admiration was quickly gone. "You have much to learn about what a man looks for in a woman, Serafina," he said with scorn, as though he were goading her to see how far she would go. With those words, he turned on his heels and headed away from the camp in the direction of the fair.

"I know what a man wants," the girl said almost under her breath. She glanced sideways at Rella. "And not just Sandor. There are others who can be won."

With a toss of her head, shc followed in the direction that Sandor had taken, leaving Rella to wonder just what she was conjuring in that fertile, impassioned Gypsy brain.

Cort watched from a distance the entrance to the fortune-telling tent. In the hours he'd spent at his work away from the Romany, hours in which he tried to question street people and passersby in the quadrant of Chicago which included the Gypsy camp, a dark-eyed beauty kept supplanting the face he should have kept in his mind.

It was strange that thinking of her as he did, he could not recall her exact features. He'd seen her only in the diffused light of night and the shaded clearing in the woods. Far from distinct, the picture that haunted him was the essence of the Gypsy temptress, and not a sharply defined image of her face. She was a wild spirit, flitting away from him just when he thought he had captured her. Everything about her was dark and enticing and veiled in alluring mystery.

Cort raked impatient fingers through his hair. What in hell had come over him? He was a United States marshal, not some romantic fool given to flights of fantasy about the mysteries of womanhood. Until Chicago, he'd never mooned over a woman. And here he was, fast on a difficult and vital quest, letting himself pursue a raven-haired, exotic beauty who was quick to mclt into his arms when he kissed her and just as quick to fade away.

Reason told him to put distance between himself and the Romany. But it wasn't reason that had control of him. He imagined what she must look like in that tent, flickering lamplight bouncing against the dark, undisciplined tresses that lay against the gentle slope of her shoulders.

She'd gotten under his skin, in a way no woman ever had. A Gypsy! He'd always thought them a thieving lot, more given to deceit than loving ways. The minute he'd seen her crouched on the ground in front of her tent, her slender body curled in defense against the increasing shrillness of a police whistle, he'd begun to change his mind. She'd been frightened and vulnerable. The more he was around her, the more he realized she carried those two traits with her all the time.

Cort's body coiled tight at the memory of the morning. He was so far gone he wanted to go into that tent and tell her just what she was doing to him. And he wouldn't leave until she'd confessed that she felt the same.

He was certain she did. No one could fake the pleasure she'd taken from their lovemaking in the woods. Experience had nothing to do with what she felt. He'd been the first. A fury rose in him at the thought that some other man might someday sample the loving she'd shared with him.

Making his way across the crowded fairgrounds, Cort brushed past the middle-aged Gypsy man who stood at the entrance to the fortune-teller's tent. He entered, expecting to see the Romany's familiar, graceful face look up in surprise.

He was greeted by a strident voice he'd never heard before. "The gorgio is impatient," a woman said. "Sit down and I will tell you if you have cause."

Cort looked down at the broad, lined face of a Gypsy woman he'd seen outside the tent on his previous trips to the fair.

"Where is the Romany?" he asked.

"Bah!" the woman said, slapping at the table. "Is that all the gorgios can ask?"

"Where is she?" Cort repeated. A sudden worry gripped him. "Is she ill? Has something happened to her?"

"The Romany does not come tonight. Show me your palm, and I will reveal all that you wish to know."

Cort wheeled around and exited. Maybe she'd had second thoughts about the morning. His experience with innocent young women being nonexistent until today, he wondered if maybe she was now too embarrassed to face him. As wild as she'd been in his arms, as eagerly as she'd shared everything that passed between them, she might think that lack of inhibition was shameful.

He'd find her and tell her different. They had shared something special. And he'd meant it when he said it wouldn't be the last time.

"Lawman."

A husky voice called to Cort from out of the dark at the edge of the fairgrounds, and he turned toward the sound.

"Lawman," the voice repeated, "come here. I have that which you seek."

The first thing that sprang to Cort's mind concerned the Romany. Whoever the woman was, she must have news of the absent fortune teller, and he followed the sound of her voice.

He recognized the sultry dancer who entertained so effectively at the fair, the one who had fought with his Romany and in a way brought them together.

"Perhaps you can help me," he said, standing close beside her in the tall grass.

"Serafina understands. You are a man." The girl's long fingers traced the outlines of her breasts, sculpted her narrow waist, and rested provocatively against her hips. "All men are after the same."

In another time and place, Cort might have been intrigued by the obvious eroticism of the Gypsy, but he remembered too well someone else.

He reached into his pocket and pulled out a coin. "Here," he said. "My thoughts are elsewhere. I wouldn't do you much good tonight. It is only information that I need."

Serafina slapped at the money and sent it flying into the grass. "I am not a gorgio whore! Not like the other one."

Cort grew still. "What other one?"

"She who calls herself Romany. I sometimes call myself queen of the Gypsies, but it does not make me so. No more that she is a Romany."

Cort felt the hair prickle on the back of his neck. "What are you talking about?"

"I know what I say. You want a Gypsy in your bed, lawman? You have been played for a fool."

Serafina turned to go, but Cort reached out and grabbed her by the wrist. He pulled her hard beside him and ordered, "Tell me what you know."

Her dark eyes flashed in triumph. "The lawman shows interest in Serafina now."

Cort tightened his hold. "Talk. Or do you only speak lies?"

"No more than the Romany does. She comes to our camp and asks us to take her in." Serafina spat into the grass. "She plays the part of Gypsy well. She knows the words to say. She fools the old women, and of course the men. But Serafina is not deceived. More gorgio blood flows in her veins than Gypsy."

"She has not been in your camp long?"

The sharpness in Cort's voice seemed to frighten Serafina, for her voice turned to a whine.

"Already the leaves had begun to turn," she said, twisting her arm in vain. "Already the nights had grown cool when she appeared."

The Romany had led him to believe she had been with the Gypsies long, had shown herself as one of them. Yet the dancer claimed otherwise, and Cort's lawman instincts wouldn't let him discount what she said.

"And what about this gorgio blood you mention? Isn't she full Gypsy?"

"A grandmother from the old country is all she mentions. She has a brooch that some recognized, but it could have come to her in many ways. It is as I said. She has learned to play a part."

Cort's thoughts turned briefly to another woman who had learned to play a part, and the stirrings of uneasiness grew stronger in him.

"You speak harshly of the Romany," he said, watching her eyes, hoping to catch her in a lie. The dancer was steadily pulling veils from the mystery that surrounded his Romany, and he didn't like what she revealed.

"I speak only what I know," Serafina said.

Cort remembered the fight between the two women. A misunderstanding, the Romany had said. "Could it be jealousy that sent you looking for me?"

Dark Gypsy eyes flared, and he knew he had struck a nerve.

"Serafina jealous of a gorgio? Never!"

Twisting free, she hurried into the dark, but Cort paid her no need. He had a lot more on his mind than putting further questions to her. The dancer apparently still harbored such ill will that she would say anything to stir up trouble for the Romany, even calling her a gorgio whore. But that didn't mean everything she said was a lie.

A gorgio whore. Serafina's bitter words echoed in the cool air. He knew enough about Gypsies to realize that no other accusation could hold more reproach. The unthinkable ate into his mind, but he needed more evidence of what he suspected than just the dancer's word.

He had that something else—something that had been worrying the back of his mind since this morning. He'd thrust it aside, concentrating instead on the hunger the Romany had aroused in him.

The worry was a small thing. In the throes of passion, the Romany had whispered one word. *Cort.* Yet he'd never told her who he was. They'd been gorgio and Romany to one another, nothing more. How in hell could she possibly know his name?

Chapter Eleven

Staring at the darkness that had swallowed Serafina, Cort thought of the Rella Sandringham he'd known in Galveston. He could picture her blond hair and blue eyes and her softly sculpted face. He tried superimposing that angelic picture onto one of the Gypsy fortune teller he'd met in Chicago, the dusky-skinned Romany who always kept herself in hazy light around him, the mystery woman who had diverted his quest with her charms.

The picture just might fit. The idea hit him like a fist in his gut. If the Romany was Rella Sandringham, she was indeed an accomplished actress. And she was more than that. She was a woman who had used her body to elude punishment for her crimes.

In Galveston, she had allowed him to kiss her, no doubt hoping that was enough to put him off actually following through with her prosecution. That she'd ended the kiss with an attack gave testimony to her real nature. She was at heart *not* a loving woman.

Cort let his hot temper guide his imagination. If he really had found Rella in a Chicago Gypsy camp, maybe just when she thought herself safe from him forever, then the scene in the morning woods took on an ugly cast. She'd sacrificed her virginity to tempt him into letting her go again. He would erase that idea in a hurry! She wasn't going anywhere except back to Galveston.

With the crowds of fairgoers milling around him, he stood still and tried to think it all out, to hold back his anger at being played the fool. Nothing was for certain yet; he was too good a lawman to act without evidence, and he'd not gathered enough to condemn the Romany just yet. Serafina was jealous of her, that was clear. Her word didn't strike him as being entirely trustworthy.

Remembering the morning spent in the Romany's arms, he admitted to one sobering truth. As much as he wanted to end his search, he wanted her to be everything she professed to be. More was at stake here than his pride. How much more, he didn't care to think about. All he knew was that while he was with the Gypsy, the restlessness that always drove him disappeared.

And yet she'd whispered *Cort* . . . She'd said it more than once.

Slowly he made his way across the fairgrounds, too close once again to rage to heed the music of violins and the laughter around him. He should not see the Romany again until he'd cooled off and had asked a few more questions along the Levee to get all his facts straight. He would need them to prove to the local law who she was. He paused at the idea of calling the Cook County prosecutors who would arrange to send her back. There was no imperative reason to see her again, at least not for weeks until he had to face her in a Texas court.

That idea reeked of cowardice, and he started along the path to the Gypsy camp. There would be no rest for him until he put a few questions to her. If he got the answers that his lawman's mind told him to expect, he would take her to jail and make plans to get her back to Texas. No matter how temptingly she looked up at him . . . no matter how vulnerable she appeared.

He came up short at the edge of the moonlit camp and glanced around, picking out details he hadn't noticed when he visited there in the morning and asked for the Romany. He counted a half dozen wagons at the outer edges of the clearing to his left. From the rear overhang of most of the vehicles, a lantern was suspended, illuminating their bright colors and the carved geometric designs which graced the sides.

To his right he spied the isolated tent. Through the flap, a light flickered. If the Romany was not inside, perhaps he would find someone who could direct him to her.

As he moved closer, he made out, against the tent wall, the silhouette of a woman. She was seated, her head bent as she brushed her hair. He paused a moment, trying to determine whether it was Rella or Romany who presented such an enticing picture. Confronting her, would he find the sharp-tongued woman who had turned on him in Galveston or the passionate lover who had lain with him in an Illinois woods?

Slowly he lifted the opening to the tent and bent his tall frame to look inside. She was seated on a pile of blankets, her back to him, legs bent under a golden skirt which was splayed across the blankets like a pool of sunlight. An arched hand gripping a small hairbrush was still in the air, and he knew she was lost in contemplation.

"I looked for you at the fair," he said. "Why weren't you there?"

She whipped her head around and stared at him. A mane of tousled black hair partially obscured her visage. Her thick-lashed eyes flared in surprise. As she slowly lowered them, they looked darker and more languid than Rella Sandringham's; the soft cotton blouse, pulled tight across her twisted body, followed the curves of her breasts and gave her a more voluptuous look. Cort's own body began to tighten at the sight of her. With the lantern light glinting against the ropes of golden chain around her neck, she looked everything that she claimed.

She has learned to play a part.

Serafina's words came back to haunt him. If she had, she was playing it well.

He stood and moved inside, the tent flap falling into place behind him. Hunching his shoulders against the low, angled canvas roof, he took a quick survey of her home. One dim lantern sent out a flickering light from the rear of the enclosure. The pile of blankets on which she knelt almost covered the hard-packed dirt floor. There was no other furniture, only an incongruous small valise resting to the side and nearby a few woman-type objects: jars, combs, a small jewelry box. Whoever she was, the woman calling herself Romany didn't live well.

Rella slowly lowered the brush, instinctively hiding her scarred hand in the folds of her skirt and following his disapproving lawman's eyes as he looked around. She should have known that finding her absent from the fairgrounds, he would seek her out. The real surprise was that she was glad.

Here was one last time together . . . one last goodbye, although he must never realize it. She was several kinds of idiot to feel as she did, and she fought against her own desires.

"If we must talk, gorgio," she said, "then I suggest

we move to the outside."

Cort looked disconcertingly at her. "You can answer me here. Why weren't you telling fortunes tonight?"

Fighting panic, she touched a fingertip to her temple and said, "I have a headache. It would not do for me to face the public tonight."

"All the public . . . or just one man?"

Rella forced herself to breathe deeply. She'd made it thus far without breaking. If she could hold on to her control for just a while longer. . . .

She met and held his eyes with her own. "I told you this morning it was wrong for a gorgio and Gypsy to make love."

"Is that what happened?"

Rella's heart pounded. Something was different about Cort, something strained like a tightly-drawn wire about to break.

"Perhaps you would give another name to what happened in the woods." Try as she might to hide it, the hurt crept into her voice.

"You're purposefully misunderstanding," Cort said. "We made love, all right. The question is, are you really a Gypsy? I hear reports that you are not."

Rella swallowed her panic. Serafina had been at work. She was sure of it, and she shifted on the blanket to kneel in front of him, determined to be as cold and heartless as he. Her foolish expectation of a last good-bye had turned into a fight for her life, and with her route of retreat blocked off, she went on the attack.

"Bah!" she said, putting heart-felt disgust in the word. "You have talked to that fool of a dancer. She spreads lies, and you listen."

If she wasn't the Romany, Cort thought, she was good at playing the part. She'd almost sounded hurt a moment ago when he'd mentioned their lovemaking . . . and he'd almost forgotten his suspicions and pulled her into his arms.

"How do you know my name?" he asked.

Rella's mind raced. What in the devil was he talking about? She knew that with typical Cort Ramsey arrogance he had never bothered to introduce himself.

"You are a lawman, one who is on an important search," she said, waving an arm in the air. The jangle of her bracelets accented her words. "I read such in your palm when I told your fortune, and you said I was right. What else is there for me to know?"

Cort's eyes narrowed. "My name. You whispered it this morning. Again and again. I don't imagine you realized what you said."

Rella felt her cheeks redden. Damn him, standing there so smug and self-assured, confident he had caught her in a mistake. No doubt, in the throes of passion, she *had* said his name. It was Cort she had clung to, Cort who had awakened her slumbering desire. Until this morning she'd been an ignorant virgin, but he had changed all that. He had made himself a part of her, and she would never again be the same.

But that didn't mean she was blind to his faults. He was hot tempered, opinionated, short-sighted—the list could have gone on. Most of all she saw before her the same overbearing man she remembered from Galveston. She might have been so carried away this morning that she didn't know what she said. The far more experienced marshal had been in control.

In desperation, she stood, and with hands planted on her hips and hair brushing against the canvas roof, she purposefully taunted him with her body. He had been eyeing it closely enough ever since he came into the tent. Let him get a good look.

"Perhaps, gorgio," she said in her huskiest voice, "you heard what you wanted to hear. I have no idea what I said. I speak several languages." She ignored his bark of laughter. Her story was absurd and he knew it, but on such short notice she couldn't think of anything else. "There is no remembering what words I whispered. I was not thinking clearly at the time," she added, her eyes flaring in defiance. "And neither were you."

They stared at each other in the dim light, a few feet of wrinkled blankets separating them. Cort's solemn face looked carved out of granite, and his tall frame and broad shoulders blocked out the outside world. Sudden terror raged within Rella, both at the fear of discovery and at the understanding of just how much she wanted him. If he remained much longer where he was, she would either confess all or throw herself into his arms.

"Please leave," she managed, her defiance gone. "The others will be returning soon, and I wouldn't want them to find me with a gorgio."

She looked astonishingly beautiful to Cort at that moment, and he let himself forget his purpose. "I just came from the fairgrounds," he said in a low voice. "It is a crowded Saturday night. We won't be interrupted. Not for a long while."

Rella felt her control slip. "I did not invite you here," she said, as though mere words could hold him away.

"If I waited for invitations, we wouldn't have had this morning. And don't tell me you're sorry about what happened, because I won't believe you. I was thinking clearly enough to know you enjoyed it as much as I did. You've gotten under my skin, Romany. And I read in your eyes that you share the way I feel."

"If I scream, help will soon arrive. Not everyone is at the fair."

"Then scream."

Try as she might, Rella could make no sound other than a low cry. Curse him! *She* was the one who was supposed to cast spells, not Cort.

She drew in a deep and ragged breath. "I have answered all of your questions as best I could, lawman. Remaining here will gain you nothing."

In the small enclosure, Cort had only to reach out to grip her shoulders. His gaze locked onto her full lips. "You and I both know that's a lie." His voice was full of tenderness and a wanting that made her dizzy.

Rella raised her hands to push him away, but he caught her wrists and brushed his lips against one palm. He paused, and his gaze fell to the dye-darkened scar too clearly visible even in the flickering light. A cold stillness enfolded them, and she felt as though all air had been sucked from the tent. When he looked up, she realized that gone, too, was all the tenderness he had shown.

"And I wanted to be wrong," he said bitterly, his anger returning in a rush. He crushed her hard against him. "You've told a lot of lies. Let's see if we can make that headache you claimed go away."

Rella's fists pounded against him, and she struggled to get away; but her movements only set him on fire. Rage warred with desire, each feeding on the other, and he knew that he would not be denied. He wanted to burn out all of her resistance, to bend her will to his.

His lips were close to hers, his breath hot on her face, as he said, "You want me. Admit it."

Rella closed her eyes, and they burned with unshed tears. "No," she whispered, "no," knowing her words were a lie. Cort had learned the truth; once again they were captor and captive. She should have hated him, grappled for the gun strapped to his thigh, done whatever lay in her dubious power to deny the growing passion coursing through her veins. But he was right. She wanted him. No physical force could have devastated her defenses as completely as his insistent words.

When his lips took control of hers, she was lost. Whatever fears she harbored melted under the heat of desire. This was no part she played. She could no more deny what his lips demanded than she could cease to breathe.

They fell to their knees on the pile of blankets. Rella's hands clutched at his shirt, and she felt the warmth of his skin. Her fingers ached to rip aside the cloth, to tear the badge from him, to strip him of everything that came between them. For all the evil that he wanted to visit upon her, this taking of her body was only good.

Cort's anger melted under the compelling heat of passion. Whatever this woman called herself, she had truly gotten under his skin; in only two days she had become a part of him. Her tongue was sweet against his; the honeyed taste of her only made him want to sup deeper, to know with his lips and hands all the dark, moist secrets of her body. She had sucked him into a world of sensory mysteries and promised wonder, but he knew even the wildest of those promises would not go unfulfilled.

Their lips parted, and for the second time within the day Cort lifted the golden chains from around the Romany's neck. He set them aside, and with fingers coiled in thick, black curls of hair, he traced the edge of her throat with his thumbs.

"Your heart beats wildly," he said. Crazy shadows

played across her face and raven hair, and her lips were wet and swollen from his kiss. His own blood pounded in his veins. He had to fight the urge to raise her skirts and take her fast as they kneeled together.

Rella rested her forehead against his, and their breaths mingled. She pressed her fingers against his chest and said, "Mine is not the only one."

Slowly she felt Cort's hands move down her back and press against the flare of her hips, drawing her knees nearer to his. His erection nestled within the pulsating valley between her thighs. Dizzy, she closed her eyes and let the sweet sensations wash over her. All the long, lonely hours of recrimination that had eaten away at her life force throughout the day were forgotten as she gave herself up to his will.

If she had been desolate, it was not because she feared detection. In truth, she had believed he would never touch her again. The woman she had been before Cort—the reasoning, independent person who took care of herself—was gone, at least for this brief, wonderful while, replaced by a wild, unthinking creature who was guided by only the sensations that came from the heart. Now that their bodies were close to joining, the darkness of spirit that had enveloped her was lifted, and she was caught in the brilliance of imperative joy.

A low growl sounded in Cort's throat, and he pressed his lips against her temples, her eyes, and the corners of her mouth. If this morning had been gentle, tonight was a time for primal mating. His hands kneaded her buttocks and he felt her legs part, only slightly but enough for his body to fit tight within hers.

He trailed light kisses against her throat and down the swell of her breasts. It was Rella who pulled at the drawstrings of her blouse and bared her body to his questing lips. Arching her back, she lifted her hardened peaks to the tease of his tongue and teeth. Prickles of pleasure radiated across the surface of her skin, and within she felt the increasing beat of desire throbbing, throbbing. Unconsciously she moved herself against his body to the rhythm of its demands.

Her movements drove Cort crazy. With more strength of will than he'd known he possessed, he loosened his hold on her long enough to pull at the confining clothes which kept her body from his. His actions were awkward and hurried, but aided by her own hands working with his, the Gypsy garb slipped smoothly from her body. With a wanton cry, she threw her bracelets against the brightly colored fabrics which were mounded at the side of the tent, then set to helping him undress.

Gun and holster were tossed beside the bracelets. His shirt and trousers took longer, aroused impatience as well as heightened desire. His clothes joined hers and they stretched out beside each other.

Rella stared at the whorls of copper hair across Cort's chest, saw the muscles contract even under her gaze, then let her eyes move slowly down to the thickening hair at the base of his abdomen. She held her breath. Even in the flickering light, the power of him overwhelmed her.

Her eyes darted up and met his burning stare. Trembling, she watched as he took his own tortuous time to look at her. Resting one arm beneath her shoulders, he stroked her cheek and let his eyes move langorously downward. The shyness that should have been hers blossomed into a curious pride when she saw pleasure smoldering in his eyes.

The sight of her body had been denied Cort in the woods; he'd been too eager in his desire. Tonight he held tight to his impulses. She was a beautiful sight, her skin smooth and tawny in the lamplight, her curves gentle and taunting. She was made the way a woman ought to be.

A duplicitous woman. Try as he might, he couldn't completely forget who she was.

Cruel fingers pressed against the flesh at her waist. Rella cried out in surprise and tried to pull away, but Cort held fast to her body. Ignoring her protests, he moved one hand lower to stroke at the thatch of dark hair between her thighs. Relentlessly he sought the pulsating core of her womanhood. His eyes never left hers.

Cort knew what he was doing, knew exactly where to concentrate his massage. "Tell me to stop," he whispered, his lips inches from hers.

Rella's answer was the undulating motion of her hips as she moved in time with his strokes. She bit at her lip and her fingers pressed against the taut muscles of his upper arm, urging him on.

Incredible rushes of pleasure surged over her.

"Say my name," he demanded. "Say it!"

She bit at her lip and remained silent.

Cort bent his head and played at the peak of her breast with his tongue. "Say it," he whispered against her skin.

Rella submitted to his will. "Cort," she said with a sob. "Oh, Cort, don't stop." And then came a plaintive "Please."

Knowing who he held in his arms, Cort was no more able to control his passions than Rella had been. He, too, was a prisoner, as much as she. Raging thoughts of her had driven him a thousand miles on a frustrating search, but he did not exult in its end. Only the feel of her against his body excited him now.

He took a savage pleasure in the writhing of her under his touch. Her legs parted, and he plunged deep inside, drowning himself in the wonder of her, his hands caressing her buttocks and lifting her to meet him.

"Rella," he said as his lips moved to claim hers, "you are mine."

Only the edges of Rella's mind took in what he said as she gave herself to passion. This second lovemaking was even more glorious than the first; the realization filled her with wonder. Knowing what to expect, she was taken by surprise, and she let herself be carried away by the swirling, velvet darkness of reckless desire.

Quickening thrusts brought them both too soon to a shared peak of ecstasy. She clung to him until the trembling subsided, her face buried in the crook of his shoulder, her mind for one blessed moment free of all thought except how Cort made her feel.

If only she had the power to extend that moment forever. Just as Cort had heard his name on her lips in the woods, her blurred senses had picked out the sound of her name on his. The long struggle for escape was at an end.

Rella was too late wise. She'd have been much better off to have remained in Texas, for there she had experienced only Cort's kiss. Now she was caught in a far more imposing prison than the Galveston County jail. Emotions trapped her tighter than those bars had managed to. Maybe she was wrong to label what held her in thrall as love; maybe it was only aroused passion. But that didn't mean its grasp was any less weak.

She felt his embrace grow slack. Tired of skulking away from him, she pulled back to look into his eyes.

"You know."

"I know."

She could read nothing in the implacable set of his face. Even his damnably probing eyes were empty of expression.

He sat up, his muscled, naked back turned to her still supine figure, and raked a hand through his hair. He let out a long, slow breath and at last said, "I need a drink."

Never one to seek the comfort of alcohol, Rella shared the sentiment. She tugged at the edge of the top blanket and pulled it across her body. "Sorry," she said, "but I hadn't planned to entertain."

Cort's laugh was sharp and brief. "Is that what you call it?"

"I'd call it madness." She spoke from her heart. There was no other way to explain her wanting a man who could use her so. She shifted as far from him as she could. "You've taken your pleasure twice today, Cort. I assume your fun is not over."

He glanced down at her. "As tempting as the idea is, Rella, I'm not up to it quite so soon."

"I meant," she said, her voice laced with disgust, "that after taking me to bed, you still have to place me under arrest."

"I'm not proud of what I have to do. Or of what I've done."

Rella felt her old independence returning. With her arrest imminent, it seemed a most inappropriate time. "Surely you're not going to apologize."

Cort took note of the lifted chin, the wide, blazing eyes. Here was the woman he had been searching for. He might not have wanted the Romany and Rella to be one and the same, but they were. He'd been played for a fool; the thought was sharply painful.

"No, you'll get no apology. Of course I have to arrest you," he said. "I've got the warrant back at the hotel. What happened between us—"

"Was just a temporary interruption," Rella snapped. "A pause in the pursuit of duty. Pleasure first, and then it's back to business. How nice it was for you to find them so closely intermixed."

"I didn't plan this . . . or this morning, either."

"And neither did you deny yourself the opportunity."

"I must have been so overcome I missed your begging me to stop. Admit the truth for once."

The truth? She saw it in two parts. For her she'd fallen stupidly in love. But Cort wanted only one thing.

Freed from the lingering tentacles of rapture, she searched the tent for something with which to hit him. Something that would hurt him as much as he was hurting her. Her eye fell on the jar of sleeping potion.

She sat beside him, making sure the blanket covered all but her shoulders and arms. Locking the barn door, she thought, long after the horse was gone, but she wasn't so wanton that she could expose herself to him again. Even if he had offered her freedom for one more roll on the ground, she would have burned in hell first.

She shrugged casually. "I need that drink you mentioned. Too bad all I have is a Gypsy brew."

"Concocted by a real Gypsy."

Her fingers itched to slap him. "Of course. I guess we could try it." She reached for the jar which was hidden beneath the pile of their clothes. Unfastening the lid, she sniffed at its contents, then took a small sip. "A little stronger, maybe, than you're used to, gorgio."

"I'll decide that for myself." Cort pulled on his trousers, his movements smoothly graceful considering the narrow confines of the tent. He sat beside her once more and took the jar from her extended hand. The swallow went down more smoothly than he had expected. "What's in it?"

"Don't ask. I learned that soon after I got here. I never cared to know what was in the stew."

Rella held the blanket tight against her chest and watched as he took another long swallow. "I don't suppose," she said, "that it would do me any good to swear my innocence."

Her final word seemed to hang in the air between them. Innocent of what? Murder and robbery? Deceit? She certainly could no longer claim the innocence of a young virgin. But that had been Cort's fault as much as hers.

He'd said flatly he could not let her go; like the voice of fate, he'd declared she must return to jail. He'd had his way with her; for Cort that wasn't enough. His arrogance challenged her. She'd gotten away from him once before. Just maybe she could again.

"You might as well finish that off," she said, gesturing toward the jar. "I'll get dressed and you can run me in. That is the correct expression, isn't it? Run me in? There's so much about this business I have to learn."

Cort was only dimly aware of her movements away from the protecting blanket. He took a long swig from the jar and, finding the taste more and more to his liking, finished off the brew. He tried to focus on Rella and wondered how long two women had been inside the tent. Two with silken, tawny skin. Two with wonderfully provocative curves. He'd thought there was only one such as her in the world.

Two Rellas. . . . The image stirred in his mind. One was more than a man could handle. And all that a man could want. . . .

The next clear thought penetrating his mind was that he'd like to lop off his head and thus remove all traces of unbearable, throbbing pain. But he'd have to move in order to execute such a wish, and he didn't have the vaguest idea where he could find a knife.

Indeed, he didn't even know where he was—or for that matter, *who* he was. He lay still and forced his eyes open. He was in some kind of tent, lying beneath a light blanket. The ground beneath him was hard and cold. The natural light told him it was day.

He risked turning his head and saw a shirt lying close beside him. Something was wrong. There should have been other clothes. Gaudy Gypsy garb. And there should have been a woman beside him.

Reality came in with a rush. He sat up and forced himself to ignore the viselike grip of pain. Where was she? He thought back to last night. There had been a lantern in the tent, and a small valise. Both were gone, as well as all signs that Rella Sandringham had ever been there.

Quickly he pulled on his boots, grabbed up his shirt, and rushed outside. It was noontime; the sun was directly overhead. He stood still and cast unbelieving eyes around the clearing. As if by magic, the Gypsy wagons and tents had disappeared. Only the cold ashes of a fire remained in the center as proof that they had ever been there.

Ashes and the tent where Rella had once more played him for a fool, Cort thought. He slapped in disgust at his leg. She was only postponing the inevitable, but by God in the doing she was certainly making a pest of herself.

He brushed aside the idea that she'd done a great deal more than that. His long stride took him to the abandoned fire. He found the buried ashes as cold as those exposed to the October air. The Gypsies had left hours ago, taking his prisoner with them.

She'd managed to elude capture for a long time, but a traveling band of Gypsies should be easy to trace. He glanced up at the sun and wished for the hat and protective kerchief he'd left last night at his hotel. The wagons couldn't go far in a day. Once he found their direction, he'd go pack his belongings.

He turned his stiff body toward the road. Everything about his situation rankled . . . everything but the thought of having Rella once more under his control.

Chapter Twelve

The crack of a rifle echoed from behind the stalled Gypsy caravan and down the dry dirt road that wound across the brown prairie on the western outskirts of Chicago. Rella, standing amidst a group of women near Torry John's disabled wagon, flinched at the loud report.

Of course it had been necessary to shoot the milk cow, she told herself. As soon as they had gotten out of town, the animal had broken loose from the last wagon and headed for the grass in the field. Chased by one of the young men, she'd taken off at a run, had fallen and snapped one of her forelegs.

Almost immediately Torry John's wagon had hit the rut; there was no choice but to halt and fix the broken axle that resulted. With the rifle shot still ringing in her ears, she watched the men brace the awkwardly angled vehicle. Delay was piled on top of delay. Rella could see the bad luck that had stalked her all the way from Galveston to Chicago had caught up with her again. Here she was, at high noon, not far past the edge of town. She had planned to leave the caravan long before now, but heading out across a dry meadow hardly seemed like the thing to do.

She shouldn't have set out with them . . . shouldn't have lingered after the wagon came to a halt in the rut. Each day she was fast adding to the list of things she shouldn't have done. She hated to think what else could happen to slow her escape.

She shook her head slowly. Escape? The idea was beginning to seem more and more farfetched, especially when she was surrounded by some two dozen Gypsies and, suspended in cages beneath the wagons, twice as many chickens and an assortment of rabbits.

There was no doubt about it. Her nerves were on edge. All morning, through the loading of the wagons and their slow progress out of the city, she'd been expecting to hear the pounding of hooves, to feel a strong hand on her shoulder, followed by those dreaded words *you're under arrest.* Not that Cort would say anything so ordinary. The sarcastic lawman would be far more inventive.

And what would she do when she saw him? Want him. Love him. Try to get away. In a perfect world, he would put his arms around her and say he knew in his heart she was innocent; together they would prove he was right. In a perfect world, she would be free to tell him how he made her feel. . . .

The jarring voice of Lucretia interrupted Rella's musings about perfection. "We never should have left that tent behind," she grumbled to the women around her. "And with a gorgio inside!"

The other women muttered their agreement, and Rella stirred nervously under Lucretia's malevolent stare. It had been hard enough for the Gypsies to accept a gorgio hanging around a stranger whom they accepted as their own—especially a gorgio lawman. But to find him at dawn passed out in her tent had been truly a disgrace! Only Alepa's intervention had stayed a decision to leave Rella behind.

"She has brought much money into our coffers," the old Gypsy had reminded them. "And it was she who outwitted the lawman in giving him the potion. What more could we ask?"

As presented by the respected matriarch of the clan, the argument had finally been accepted, but Rella had known her already tenuous standing among the Gypsies was hurt. It was then that she had presented her plan to leave them somewhere out on the trail whenever she could manage alternate transportation. A passing hay wagon would do. The only thing she asked in return for all the coins she had earned was that they cover her departure. Let the lawman believe she had never accompanied them, that she'd caught a stagecoach out of Chicago, or that she'd run away from them, too. Tell him anything they could to send him heading another way.

She didn't explain about the money pouch hidden next to her skin, nor about why she was desperate to escape; with their Gypsy respect for privacy, they hadn't asked. Alepa had looked at her curiously, but the others had quickly agreed. Now that the journey had been delayed, the critical Lucretia was proving all too eager to be disagreeable again.

"Never do we leave valuable goods behind," the woman whined, kicking at the dirt road. "It was a bad way to begin. Needless waste. No good will come on this trip."

"What would you have had us do?" Alepa asked. "Fold the tent and drag the lawman into a field, leaving him for the muggers and thieves?"

"The idea is not without merit," Lucretia said.

"Such an act would only bring trouble. If the Romany is correct when she says the marshal will be pursuing us, he would want to extract punishment from us. And we want no trouble with the law."

The other women mumbled their disagreement, but Alepa paid them no mind. "What's done is done. You sound like a gorgio, Lucretia, worrying over things you cannot change. Predicting the future! You've listened to your own voice too long in that fortune teller's tent."

The scowl on Lucretia's face said louder than words that she did not agree.

Weary of argument and praying for a passing hay wagon, Rella moved away from the women and watched the children playing chase in the field. The traffic was light on this Sunday morning. Serafina was nowhere in sight, most likely sulking somewhere in one of the vardos. As far as the dancer was concerned, she'd lost both the knife fight and her man to a gorgio. Even worse must be the loss of her pride.

But there were a lot worse things to lose besides pride. Rella glanced back at the buildings of the city, a sight that was far too close for comfort. A black cloud of smoke hung over what she decided was the business area, signaling another of the many fires that had been plaguing Chicago throughout the arid autumn. This time it was a big one.

She shuddered, remembering the burning boardinghouse in Galveston where her troubles had begun—not that she hadn't added to them with her own unanticipated weakness. For someone who always handled her business with calm efficiency, she'd shown a strangely perverse inclination lately to do herself harm. Just because that harm had come in the form of a tall, enticing man with magical hands didn't make it any less serious.

Nervously she began to pace along the rutted road, casting anxious eyes at the sun hanging over the city. Somewhere beneath those golden rays Cort was stalking her, questioning where the Gypsies had gone.

It was westward she must scurry, toward Templeton or any other acting group in need of a somewhat soiled ingenue. If she'd ever been tempted to surrender in the hope that justice would be done, that temptation had died last night when, after she'd given herself to Cort for the second time, she'd looked into his eyes. What she'd seen had come as a shock. She'd expected rage; instead, she'd found disappointment, as though somehow she had let him down. The hurt had been the timing of that flat, accusatory look. He'd been condemning when she'd been filled with feelings of love.

Rella sighed. How bitter now was the memory of their time together. Lovemaking, she'd called it; for Cort it had been simply a trap in which to ensnare her, a trap that had too easily worked.

Funny how innocent he'd looked lying there asleep. Not innocent at first, she remembered. He'd passed out so quickly, and so deeply, that when he collapsed on the blankets, she'd thought he was dead.

She had no idea what Alepa had put in the potion. Alcohol and herbs, the old Gypsy had said, but there were plants that had to be taken in moderation. And moderation wasn't one of Cort's strongest traits. He'd drunk the entire jar.

As she had stared down at Cort, the hard lines of his face softening by stillness, she'd panicked. Maybe he had had some kind of reaction. A feeling of utter despair had washed over her. Nothing was as important as his life—not even her freedom.

Kneeling beside him, she had placed an ear against his bare chest, but all she'd heard was the sound of her own shallow breath. Cort had been proven right. She really was a murderess!

Then had come a startling grunt and the ragged sound of his snoring. She was torn between kissing him because he was alive and hitting him because he had frightened her so. Either course might have awakened him, and she settled for a silent lecture about how, even in his sleep, he had gotten in the last word.

Leaving him had been harder than she would have believed. As she'd helped the Gypsies break camp under their censuring glares, she'd found herself brushing tears from her face. What in the world was she doing crying? He wanted to throw her in jail!

But, oh, he'd wanted more of her than that. Even thinking she was someone else, he had been captivated by her. She would always have the memory of his desire.

"Does the Romany have regrets?" Alepa asked from behind her, startling her out of her reverie.

She turned and tried to smile. "I guess everyone does. But I'm not sorry we left so suddenly. I'm just grateful—"

Alepa hushed her with a wave of her hand. "I could not abandon the granddaughter of Esmeralda Scamp." Her pale old eyes sparkled. "Especially one with a United States marshal drugged in her tent. In felling such a man, you have accomplished what others should envy, not deplore."

"Don't give me too much credit for heroics. Do you know why he was there?" Rella blushed. "I don't mean what we had done . . ." She stumbled over her words. "What I mean is, he'd been looking for me for a long time." Somehow, she thought, she wasn't making anything clearer with her rambling.

"It is not necessary to tell me why."

Rella ran fingers through her loose-flowing hair. "It is necessary for me. I realize your . . . our people do not pry into the concerns of others, but you have been my friend. The marshal believes I killed someone back in Texas and stole some money."

"The marshal is a fool."

The surety in the woman's voice reminded Rella of Greta Maas. Her young Galveston friend had been equally positive Rella had committed no crime.

"Thank you for everything," Rella said from her heart and for a moment let herself back in the warmth of Alepa's acceptance. "My real name—" she began.

"Is Romany," Alepa said firmly. "For me that is all I need to know. But there is something I must tell you. This marshal has a special feeling for you."

Rella felt a pang of remorse. "For a while he had a special feeling for a mysterious Gypsy who proved all too susceptible to his charms. For *me,* he has only contempt."

Alepa brushed her fingers against Rella's hand. "Do not think you are two people, my dear. What the marshal sees in the Romany is part of your true spirit."

"I used to understand what that spirit was, but I'm not sure anymore."

At the sound of hoofbeats, Rella whirled around, half expecting to see the spectre of a rope-wielding Cort Ramsey running her down. It was Sandor who, in a swirl of dirt, pulled to a halt beside her.

"Careful, young fool," Alepa said with a scowl, but there was affection in her voice.

"We are in need of a new milk cow," Sandor said, smiling down at Rella and his aunt. "We passed a grazing herd only a short way back."

Rella knew the manner in which the cow would be obtained. No money would exchange hands. As much as she loved many of the Gypsy ways, she could never grow accustomed to this habit of appropriating the property of others as it was needed.

"Sandor, you must stay here," Torry John barked from his position beside his wagon. "Our work will soon be done, and we must put more miles behind us before the sun has set. We will take care of our needs then."

It was the wrong tack to take with the proud young Gypsy. "The children will be wanting milk," Sandor said to no one in particular. "I will return in time."

He motioned toward another young man standing by the broken wagon. "Come, Michael," he said, "get your horse. We go on a hunt." He grinned down at the gathered Gypsies. "You will have cream for your supper. I swear it."

Torry John ordered him back, but he took off down the road toward town. In a moment another horseman, the young Michael, followed in his dusty wake. Muttering under his breath, Torry John returned to work.

Rella sighed in exasperation and said to Alepa, "Sandor will get into trouble someday."

"Do not worry," Alepa said. "He is grown. He knows what he should do."

Rella disagreed. For all the larceny in his heart, Sandor seemed like more of a child than a man.

"What he ought to do," she said, "is pay more attention to Serafina. She would keep him busy and out of trouble."

Alepa laughed. "The dancer has not handled him well, but it is in her direction that his true affections lie."

The old Gypsy turned to join the other women, leaving Rella to take up her pacing once more. The repair work took less time than she had figured; Sandor and Michael had not yet returned by the time the wagon was once more upright and the dray horse hitched in its yoke.

"We will leave without them," Torry John announced. "Our pace is slow. Even with a milk cow in tow, they will soon catch up, if not by afternoon, sometime during the night."

Rella chose to walk for a while beside the wagon instead of riding inside with the surly Lucretia. As she trod along, she glanced over her shoulder often in hopes of seeing the two would-be rustlers of a dairy cow. A town lay not far ahead, a place where she would try to take her long-delayed leave, and she hoped Sandor would return so that she might tell him good-bye. After an hour of looking and worrying she spied a lone Michael racing down the road behind the caravan. He pulled to a halt beside the wagon of Torry John.

"Sandor has been arrested!" he proclaimed, fighting for breath.

Torry John spat in the dirt. "The fool!"

"The farmer caught us, but I was able to escape. He sent his son for the law."

"Sandor is wily," Torry John said. "How do you know he has not escaped as you have done?"

Michael drew himself up tall in the saddle. "I did not abandon him but hid and waited for an opportunity to aid him. When the lawmen came, I saw there was little I could do but report what had happened," he said; then in answer to Rella's hastily asked question, said, "Two men in uniform." She breathed a sigh of relief.

With the wagons pulled to a halt once more, the Gypsies quickly gathered together around the horseman and listened to him as he spoke.

"Where is Sandor now?" Rella asked, ignoring the scowls of both the men and women that she should have such effrontery.

"They were to take him to the jail in the city."

"We will leave our signs along the way, and he can find us when he is free," Torry John proclaimed. "I warned him not to go."

A wail went up from amongst the women, and Serafina pushed her way to Torry John. "It is because of *her* that he has been caught. He wishes to prove his daring."

Rella had no doubt to whom Serafina referred with such scorn. The dancer was wrong, but she didn't try to refute her. Sandor was her friend, and he was in trouble. Nothing else was important. Too well she remembered the sound of a cell door closing behind her. The police would be hard on a Gypsy transient caught stealing a cow. He would be in jail for a long, long time.

Turning away from Serafina, she looked up at Torry John. "We can't leave him," she said.

"This is none of your concern," he replied.

Rella glanced at Alepa and saw the worry in the old Gypsy's eyes. What if Greta and Aaron Tuttle had not helped her get away? She would be languishing yet in a faraway jail. They had risked much in aiding her escape. Realizing she could do no less for the young Gypsy who seemed like a brother to her, she looked defiantly at Torry John.

"It is my concern," she insisted. "I know as much of gorgio jails, perhaps, as you. Enough to know that Sandor cannot be left in such a place." She turned to Michael. "Perhaps I can gain his freedom. Will you take me back into town?" The words chilled her as she said them.

She felt a hand on her arm and turned to face Alepa.

"Is what you propose wise?" the old woman asked. "You know who looks for you there."

"I've been thinking of nothing but my own safety,"

she said, covering Alepa's hand with her own. "It's time I thought of someone else. I can hire transportation in town as easily as I can out on the road. Easier, it would seem, since in half a day I've been unsuccessful in locating so much as a suitable cart."

"If you go after him, so do I," Serafina hissed.

"No," Rella said. "You were right, Serafina. I am more gorgio than Gypsy. Perhaps I can deal better with the law."

Rella very much doubted she knew what she was talking about, her recent experiences with the law having been decidedly unsuccessful in their outcome, but she didn't care to think about that now.

She turned to Torry John. "You and the others go on if you must. I will do what I can."

As she rode away on the horse Michael had saddled for her, Rella was glad she'd had little time for goodbyes. Alepa had given her a parting gift—the knife she had lent her once before. She wore it sheathed and strapped to her leg beneath her several skirts. There was nothing else for Rella to take. She wore all that she owned. Her only security was the pouch of coins hidden at her waist.

It seemed like a pitiful defense against Cort Ramsey. She expected at any minute to come upon him. Unable to give up completely her gorgio ways, Rella had kept up with the date. It was Sunday, October 8, 1871. In the years to come she might well remember it as the day she returned to a cell.

With hungry eyes she took in the sights and sounds of all that she and Michael rode by, ignoring the curious, unfriendly stares sent their way. Even the factory district through which they rode looked beautiful to a woman who expected soon to gaze on nothing but four ugly walls.

The fire that she had seen from a distance had died

down, the smoke no longer visible against the horizon, but as the two of them moved through the city streets toward the jail, she could still smell the cinders in the air. They passed a steam fire engine being drawn slowly by a team of worn horses, their heads hanging low, their coats matted with sweat. From the tired, soot-streaked faces of the firemen, she knew they'd been battling the blaze. At least, she thought, their work was done.

She rode beside Michael in silence. The young Gypsy seemed to know just where to go. She didn't inquire how, figuring knowledge about jails and lawmen were part of what every Gypsy was expected to acquire.

By the time they arrived at their destination, the afternoon was almost gone. Rella dismounted and stared at the structure provided by Cook County for the incarceration of its prisoners. It was wider and taller than the Galveston jail, and situated on a more crowded street, but the cold, forbidding aura surrounding it was the same. Rella realized with a start she was terrified to go inside.

It took all of her thespian skills to turn to Michael and say, "Wait out here. I'll let you know if I need help." She was especially proud that the fluttering in her stomach was not reflected by a weakness in her voice.

To freshen herself was impossible, and probably unwise. She could picture a wanted poster of the fair-haired Cinderella Sandringham hanging on every wall. Surely no one would recognize her in her current state of dishabille—no one except Cort, of course—and she hurried through the door before she could decide otherwise.

As she stepped inside, the thought came to her that all jails smelled alike—damp and stale, as though the despair of incarcerated men and women had an odor that hung in the air. She stood in the shadows by the door and watched the policemen pass by, some in uniform, others in civilian dress. No matter what they wore, she recognized them as officers of the law. It was something about the set of their jaws or the arrogant way they carried themselves. Maybe, she thought with a curious pride, this ability to spot a policeman was a skill inherent in her Gypsy blood.

The talk she heard was of prisoners and crime and an occasional mention of the fire. During the night and early morning four city blocks had been destroyed, she learned. "This town is like a kindling box waiting to go up," one of the men said as he passed her at the door. "Not much rain since July. And the whole damned place is built of wood."

Rella shuddered. She'd heard more comforting talk from her jailer back in Galveston.

She stepped out of the shadows toward the front desk.

"What's the likes of you doing in here? First time I ever saw a Gypsy walk though that door on her own."

She stared straight on at the uniformed man behind the desk. "I have come about one of your prisoners. I know him only by the name Sandor."

"Don't have to tell me who you want. He was brought in a few hours ago. Stealing, as I recall. Somebody's cow."

"Can I see him?"

"Not likely. Probably want to sneak him a knife."

Rella sent out a silent prayer that she wouldn't be searched. Passing Sandor the weapon strapped to her leg had not occurred to her, but the chances of her being believed were nil.

Abandoning her Gypsy stance, Rella stood tall and commanding, just as she'd done often on the stage.

"Then let me talk to someone in charge," she ordered, taking pleasure in the surprise on the officer's face.

"Trouble, officer?" asked a black-suited man who had walked up to the desk. Rella took him to be another policeman.

"No, Captain. One of the men brought in a Gypsy thief. This woman wants to see him. Of course I told her no."

Starting with her tousled hair and ending with her dusty, sandaled feet, the captain appraised Rella rather more thoroughly than she thought necessary. She didn't care at all for the supercilious curl of his lip when he was done.

"Maybe I better talk to her." He gestured toward a hallway to his right. "Down here," he said and, turning his back to her, headed toward an open door. She had no choice but to follow. Stepping inside, she closed the door behind her as he instructed.

When she exited through that same door a half hour later, she could only hope she had done the right thing. The first request—no, demand—made by the captain she had found impossible to fill. Such a suggestion! And in his office! Even Cort had never mentioned anything like that. And she let him know it in no uncertain terms, going so far as to tell him she was personal friends with a United States marshal who would take offense at anyone laying a hand on someone he considered his. The lie had fallen easily from her lips.

But then she'd offered a counterplan. Figuring the captain was no stranger to either greed or lust, she decided if she couldn't satisfy the second, she would concentrate on the first. She had figured right. Unfortunately she'd had to leave her entire cache of coins to satisfy that greed. Sandor was to be released within the hour. She had only to wait outside.

The captain made her wait longer than he had promised, but she was not surprised. Lawmen were not particularly honorable, she had learned.

Michael grew impatient long before she. "I say Sandor will never be let loose," he growled just after sunset.

"I say we have no choice but to wait," Rella said. Certainly she did not. The coins that had offered her a chance to get away were in the captain's pocket. Besides, she had vowed to save Sandor. Despondent though she was becoming, she had to see her promise through to the end.

Too often she could feel a pair of eyes watching her, but every time she looked around she saw only strangers, most of them only too willing to ignore a pair of disreputable looking Gypsies now that the sun had gone down. When Sandor finally emerged through the jail door, both Rella and Michael were half asleep as they leaned against their horses.

Sandor grinned at the pair. "I knew you would not desert me," he said, startling them awake.

Rella heaved a sigh of relief. "Let's get out of here. We've a long way to go to catch up with the others."

"How did you manage this?" He directed his question to Michael, who immediately gestured toward Rella.

"Don't ask," she said. "Let's just mount up and go."

"You work miracles," Sandor said as he positioned himself behind Rella on her horse. "The gorgio jail is a terrible place."

With that, Rella was in complete agreement, but she kept her opinion to herself.

They headed out west through the factory district where she and Michael had ridden during the day. Maybe, she thought with foolish optimism, Cort had talked to Torry John and Alepa while she was gone, and they had steered him away from town. Maybe in her sacrificial act of freeing Sandor, she had freed herself. And maybe she could just sprout wings and fly away. Any of the choices that occurred to her seemed equally possible.

She was surprised when Sandor reined the horse toward the south in the direction of a residential section of the city. The way was dark here, without the streetlights of the more traveled parts of town. Only the stars and a sliver of moon lighted their path.

"Where are we going, Sandor?"

"My mission is not yet done."

"Now that's the—" She started to add *dumbest* but hesitated. Sandor was already embarrassed by his failure to steal a cow. He was a decidedly stubborn young man. He wouldn't listen to any discouraging advice she might offer now.

"If you land in jail again," she said flatly, "I won't be able to get you out."

"I plan to use caution. This morning the farmer was out in the field. I grew careless. But all is quiet here. The people are settled indoors."

He turned onto another street, this one narrower and darker than the first, and she was barely able to make out a street sign at the corner. De Koven Street, it read. A row of small houses extended down each side. Sandor stopped halfway down the block and said, "There is a barn behind this one, I believe. Let us see what it holds."

Both he and Michael dropped to the ground, and Rella had no choice but to follow. She was not about to remain alone in the dark. She paused.

"What is wrong?" Sandor whispered.

"I thought I heard someone behind us." The three stood silently and listened, but they heard only the sound of a barking dog somewhere in a neighboring alley. She tried to shake off her fear. "Sorry," she apologized.

Tethering the horses to a tree which grew close to the street, the three slipped past the darkened house and stood in the small backyard. Just as Sandor had predicted, a small barn loomed in the dark at the back of the lot. Suddenly the back door of the house opened, and a shaft of light fell across their path. As if their movements had been rehearsed, they edged deeper into the shadows. A woman shuffled across the yard toward the barn, a lamp held high in her hand.

Sandor gestured toward the street, and they retraced their steps toward the horses. But this time a third animal had joined their mounts. Rella knew who was astride that horse as surely as she knew her name. The thought came to her that this whole evening was like a bad melodrama, one that could have no happy end.

Cort heard them approach. "I've been tracking you for some time now," he said in that familiar, sarcastic voice she knew so well. "Your friends sent me on a fast trail for a while, but you should have known it would be only a delay." He dismounted and looked toward the barn behind the house. "Can't give up your thieving ways, can you?" Rella knew the words were directed at her.

"My friends?" was all she could manage.

"The Gypsies." He moved close to her side, and she edged away. "By the time I found you, you were already at the jail. A curious place, I told myself, and decided to see what you were up to."

"I suppose you're carrying the warrant you mentioned."

Cort nodded. "May add the drugging of an officer to the charges."

"I didn't force anything on you," she threw back at him.

Sandor listened, wide-eyed, to the exchange. "Let's get out of here," he said, lighting out down the street. Michael was close on his heels.

Rella panicked. Instead of following them, she could think only of putting as much distance between herself and Cort as possible, and she ran for the back of the house. Her rush to freedom took her into a trap; all she could see was the barn door. Just as she shoved against it, a woman's scream came from inside. "Help! Come quick!"

Cort slammed into the barn right behind her, and they both took in the scene quickly. The kerosene lamp lay broken on the wooden floor, which was now engulfed in flames. A bundle of hay against the wall was likewise ablaze, and a billow of fire was headed for the loft, where more bundles of hay were stacked.

From the rear of the barn came the whinney of a terrified horse, and the bay of cattle. The woman was flapping her arms at the animals, but they refused to move toward the fire.

"Get out of here," Cort ordered, then moved quickly to help the frantic woman.

Paralyzed with fright, Rella found herself unable to move. All around her the fire crackled, and the smoke curled thick and black and suffocating. She was back in that boardinghouse, trapped in her locked room, unable to find the door, unable to save herself from impending death. *Make it go away,* was all she could think. *Make it go away.*

Her slender figure blended into the impenetrable curtain of smoke, and Cort hurried past her to try to save the animals. He was dimly aware that someone else had run into the barn, a man who grabbed at a calf in one of the stalls. Cort turned his attention to the woman, and wrapping his arms around her, he led her to safety. He was confident Rella was already outdoors, was hoping she had called for additional help. As dry as this city was, Cort knew the fire must be contained.

In the fire-heated night air, he searched frantically for Rella, needing to know she was safe. A scream issued from inside the barn. Only then did he remember she was terrified of fire. She'd been unable to leave.

A fear unlike anything he'd ever felt overcame him. Even as he heard the pounding of feet heading toward the backyard and the shouts for more assistance, he grabbed at the handle to the barn door. The heat seared his skin. Flinging the door open, he threw himself into the smoke-filled enclosure.

He found her huddled close to the door, unaware how close she was to safety. He cradled her in his arms and stumbled out of the barn, hurrying as fast as he could toward the sweet air in the street. "Say something," he ordered as he loosened his hold.

Gradually Rella's heart slowed. She allowed herself the luxury of a moment resting against the strength of him, but only a moment. With the passing of her panic, she remembered he had saved her in order to throw her in jail.

Her eyes burned more than her throat—she'd been too frightened in that hell to breathe—and she was able to say with startling clarity, "Please put me down. The last time you ordered me to speak, you wanted to hear your name."

His eyes glittered down at her. "Always the smart answer," he said, ignoring the sounds of running and shouted warnings around him.

"I could say the same about you."

From somewhere in the troubled night came the

cry of a child. Cort realized he must give his help, even at the risk of losing his prey. "If I put you on your horse, do you think you can find your way out of town?"

"What about you?"

He glanced around the night that was fast becoming light as day. People were beginning to tumble out of their houses, and the sounds of panic grew.

"This whole street could go up in flames," said Cort. "I imagine somebody has already sounded the alarm, but the wind is gusting tonight. A lot of damage could result before a fire engine arrives. These people are going to need help."

Rella pulled free of his touch. "Then I suggest we get started doing what we can. I won't put out the fire, but I can certainly help the people as well as you. I'm not the she-devil you think I am, Cort. Besides, I'd rather be working beside you than running and wondering when you're going to find me again."

Chapter Thirteen

"Here you go, dearie. A nice cup of coffee is just the thing."

Rella shifted her gaze from the open doorway of the Aurora Tavern and smiled in appreciation at the proprietress standing beside her. Brushing a stray wisp of gray hair from her cheek, Flossie Pruitt returned the smile.

It was mid-morning Tuesday, a day and a half after Rella had arrived at the tavern, which bordered on a roadway leading southwest out of the city. When the barn had exploded Sunday night—in spite of frantic efforts to extinguish the burning hay—Cort decided Rella had given all the side-by-side help he could deal with. Firebrands were spreading flames faster than the firefighters could contain them; insisting she would only be in the way, he'd hustled her out of town to the Aurora.

By the time they made their way to the tavern, it was already beginning to fill up with displaced Chicagoans fleeing from the city, and Cort had insisted on paying Flossie in advance to insure Rella a room.

"We'll find some place to put her, Marshal," the proprietress said, eyeing Rella with cold speculation.

Rella could read her mind. What was such a ragtag woman doing in the company of a United States marshal? Thank heavens she hadn't asked.

Cort nodded, then took Rella's hand to guide her outside. "You're worn out," he told her. "Rest awhile and then there'll be plenty of ways to help here."

"How do you know I'll be here when you get back?"

His eyes caught hers. "I don't."

How like Cort not to embellish his opinion with softening pleas. Both of them knew the truth. If she had gone, he would come after her.

He promised to return as soon as he could—it was the one promise she would have believed—and disappeared into the stream of people, his course firmly set against the tide of exhausted humanity pouring out of Chicago. She thought about joining that stream—considered it long and hard—but Cort was right. There were plenty of refugees to help out here.

Besides, she knew the danger waiting for him back in the city. No matter how much he scorned her and wished her harm, she could not leave until she knew he was all right. Once she knew he was alive, she didn't care if she never saw him again.

The someplace Flossie had promised turned out to be a little, musty attic space. The woman had continued to regard Rella with suspicion, but as Monday stretched into Tuesday and Rella made herself tirelessly useful, she had thawed.

Wiping her hands against her soiled skirt, Rella thanked Flossie and took the proffered cup of coffee.

"Now come over here to the table." Flossie gestured across the crowded, noisy room. "We'll find another chair, and you can take some weight off your feet. Not that you carry much," she said as she rested her hands on the apron covering her ample stomach, "not like me. But you've been pacing all morning and half the night. Must be worn to a frazzle."

Rella thought of the hundreds of people she'd seen

come through the Aurora, refugees from the fire carrying whatever they'd been able to salvage from their homes, parcels mostly, bundles of clothes, occasionally a chair or table—as though that one piece of furniture could compensate for all they had lost. One glassy-eyed man had stumbled past clutching only a small, gilded cage holding a parrot. The bird seemed his most valued, indeed his only surviving possession.

Even now, as she stood in the crowded tavern serving room, the people continued to edge along the roadway looking for shelter. Many had collapsed in the surrounding fields, too tired to move on and too frightened to go back, grateful only that they were still alive. Studying them from her upstairs window shortly after dawn, she'd thought some horrendous wind must have ripped them from their homes and scattered them across the countryside during the night.

The mighty conflagration that had begun Sunday night was at last dead, its final embers doused during a Monday night rain after twenty-nine hours of destruction. For many Chicagoans, she knew, the suffering had just begun.

"I'll be all right," Rella assured Flossie. "You've done a great deal more than I have, trying to come up with space for these people to rest, and finding them food."

Flossie waved away Rella's praise. "The Lord somehow provides. Especially when we've got good country folk around. They've been bringing what was needed. Blankets and bandages and such, as well as food. And coffee. Now you drink up. You've done your share of helping. Your man will be along right soon."

Rella turned away quickly. No need to show the tears that sprang to her eyes. At that dark hour early Monday, Flossie had been right to assume something was suspicious about a lawman arranging quarters for an unkempt woman in Gypsy garb. Cort was Rella's man. And just maybe he wouldn't be back. The thought, which before last week would have delighted her, now cast her in despair. If only there were some way to find out for sure he was all right without facing him again.

"If you don't mind," she said, directing her words to the open door, "I'll take the coffee outside and get some fresh air."

Under the cloudy morning sky she found no respite from her thoughts, and she pressed her untouched cup of coffee into the hands of a surprised and grateful passerby. Seeking a moment of solitude, she circled the tavern and made her way past the resting mass of people to a low hill where she could watch the road. To the east she could make out the smoldering remains of what had been the city of Chicago.

Not all had been lost, but reports from the refugees indicated the entire business district and thousands of homes, including some of the finest in town, were gone. According to them, they'd been lucky to escape, and they'd proceeded to describe the horror of their experience.

She'd been a part of that horror when the flames leaped at her in the barn. Never would she forget Cort running in to save her. For a brief moment he'd been the loving man who held her in the woods.

Staring down at the crowded road, Rella cursed the sense of duty that had thrust him once again in the midst of that danger, cursed him for being so foolhardy and brave, and cursed herself equally for caring. Overcome by weariness, she sank to the ground. Already the moisture from the night rain had soaked into the parched earth, and under a westerly wind the grass was dry. Once again she took up the vigil she'd held in the doorway of the tavern, forcing herself to concentrate on the sad parade playing itself out across the land. Most of the people were making their way west on foot down the winding dirt road, but occasionally she saw a wagon or a man on horseback.

She passed the time by counting the horsemen. The hours passed, and she grew drowsy. It was mid-afternoon when a pair of horsemen galloping at the edge of the crowd roused her to wakefulness. From the graceful manner in which they sat, they appeared to be young men. Something about the natural way they rode set them apart from the crowd. As they drew nearer, she felt a jolt of recognition. Exhaustion forgotten, she stood and waved her arms excitedly.

"Sandor! Michael! Over here!"

She waved frantically, calling again. At last she got their attention, and the two Gypsies reined their mounts in her direction. At the crest of the hill Sandor dropped to the ground beside her and took her hands in his.

"Hello, Romany," he said. His soot-stained face was darker than ever, and there were lines of fatigue etched around his eyes. Still, his flashing white smile was like a glimpse of sunshine on the cloudy day.

"What are you two doing here?" she asked, looking from one to the other.

"We went looking for you," Michael said from his position on horseback.

Sandor's face grew solemn. "You did not follow us down the street, and I had to know you were all right." His eyes drifted down her disheveled person. "I am glad to see you are not hurt, but it is God's truth that you look a mess."

His description was accurate enough, Rella knew. She'd given no time to brushing her hair or bathing, and her limp clothes, as stained with soot as Sandor's face, appeared beyond repair.

"Still," the Gypsy added warmly, "you are the most beautiful sight I have seen."

His mount, a sway-backed nag long past her prime, snorted as if in agreement.

"How on earth did you get the horses?" she asked. "They aren't the ones we were riding before."

"A Gypsy can always find a horse," Sandor answered with a grin. "Even such a one as this."

Rella laughed, and the feeling was good. "Don't give me any details." She grew solemn. "And thank you for returning to find me. That was a bad time back there."

"True," Michael said. "All was confusion. Sandor was very brave for someone who has been unable to steal so much as a slow-moving milk cow."

At Sandor's expression of chagrin, Rella couldn't resist throwing her arms around him and giving him a hug. "How glad I am to see you are all right," she said, holding tight. She pulled back and gave him a careful look. The smile remained on his dark countenance, but something in the depths of his dark eyes told her he'd grown older. She saw no sign of an impetuous child.

"Come," he said, tugging at her arm. "The mare will hold us both. If not, I will walk beside you. We will find Torry John and tell him all that he missed."

Sandor spoke so innocently, but she knew what he really meant. Having heard Cort mention a warrant for her arrest, he wanted to lead her to safety. This time, in the confusion after the fire with so many homeless seeking shelter, so many on the roads, this time she might get away. The fire had made Gypsies of thousands. Cort might never find her, if he were left with the energy to try. If he were still alive.

"What is wrong, Romany?" Sandor asked.

"I can't go with you. I wait for someone."

"The lawman?"

Rella nodded. "I'm not waiting exactly. I just want to know that he's all right."

"And where is this lawman now?"

She glanced briefly toward the east. "He went back to help. As did you. There is not, it would seem, much difference in the gorgio and the Gypsy." She forced a brightness in her voice. "Will you have trouble finding the caravan?"

"Gypsies have their own signs to mark the trail. A bent twig or a branch off one kind of tree placed in another. Such things tell me the wagons have been that way. We will find them."

"Then this is good-bye. I promise you I will be all right," she lied, ignoring his scowl of protest.

"I am not sure I should leave you like this. After all, you came after me."

"I have taken care of myself a long time. Trust me, Sandor, the way a Gypsy should trust another Gypsy. I know what I am doing." It was another lie, and she forced herself to smile. "Think about how much Serafina will enjoy listening to your tales of heroism. Don't be shy. Tell her all that you did."

"I will see that he does," Michael said.

Sandor grinned. Already he was thinking of the reception he would receive.

Unfastening the brooch pinned to her blouse, she pressed it into his hand. "Do me a favor, please. Give this to Alepa. She has a special affection for my grandmother. I would like her to have it."

The decision to send the gift had been impetuous. Perhaps, she thought as she watched the two young men make their way back down to the road, each time Alepa looked at the brooch, she would think of the Romany.

Rella kept to her post on the hill. The sun was low on the horizon behind her when she spied a tall, broad-shouldered man making his way toward the tavern. The crowd had thinned, a few turning back toward the city, and he was easily visible on the road. She blinked and wondered if the shadows of late afternoon were playing tricks on her. She dared herself to believe it was Cort. Of course it was. He might be moving slower than usual, but she would know the tilt of his head and that long-legged gait anywhere.

She began to walk down the hill toward him. The closer she got, the faster became her pace. Her spirit soared at the sight of him, torn shirt, dirty face, and all. The first impulse that struck her was to rush into his arms, but she held back, stricken by an unexpected shyness. He had left abruptly, without much of a farewell. She had no way of knowing how he would regard a welcoming embrace.

They met at the side of the road. "You're back," she said, cursing herself for the inanity, wishing she could have joyfully shouted the words.

"Sorry to take so long." Blue eyes dulled by fatigue studied her face.

"Have you been fighting fires all this time?"

"Mostly trying to find drinking water and food. There are thousands of homeless back there, Rella. The whole heart of the city is gone."

"It doesn't look as though you took care of yourself. Let's go see about getting something to eat," she said, linking her arm into his. "Flossie can work wonders with a few beef bones and some beans."

When he didn't respond, she studied his face. Food was not what he needed first. He needed sleep.

"On second thought," she said, "we'll put you on my cot."

"I'll be all right." He stared across the distance to

the destroyed city. The two of them stood silent for a few minutes, and she could only guess the images tearing at his mind. At last, he set the pace as they went into the tavern.

Flossie took one look at him and said, "Marshal, you got to get some sleep. You look like death walking."

Cort nodded. "Maybe that's what I am. Hard to tell."

Rella followed him upstairs, extra blankets over her arm. He fell onto the hard cot, and she bent to pull his boots from his feet.

She leaned over him, making sure the covers were in place. "I'll be here when you wake up," she whispered, knowing he couldn't hear, and settled on the blankets beside the cot.

Confident he would be out for hours, she allowed her head to nod. Only a few minutes had gone by when he started a restless turning, crying out at some remembered horror which disturbed his sleep. The restlessness grew until he sat up in bed with a start.

Immediately she was at his side. "You're all right, Cort," she assured him. "It's all over. Go back to sleep."

"Can't," he said, reaching for his boots. "I'm going for a walk."

"Now that's—" She started to add *stupid*, but demon memories ate at him. He had to rid himself of them as best he could. "I'm going with you," she said, and hurried after him down the stairs.

His stride was long as he headed for the hill behind the Aurora. Rella had to run to keep up. For a man beset with exhaustion, he was demonstrating a powerful lot of reserved strength. The clouds had departed, leaving a rosy hue in the west where the sun was setting. To the west all seemed at peace, but he kept his eyes turned on the city. At this early evening hour, little of the destruction was visible. Still, they both knew what the dusk obscured.

"Would you like to talk?" she asked when he came to a halt.

He raked fingers through his hair. "There's nothing to say." He sounded impatient, as though she should have understood without hearing the details of what his time had been like. "You want to hear about people running everywhere, frightened out of their wits? You saw some of that for yourself. A lot of them died. Hundreds, they say. Probably never know how many."

He fell silent, and Rella waited for the time when he wanted to talk some more.

"So many bad things," he said at last, lost in memory. "Fire engines sent to the wrong neighborhoods. Bastard carriage drivers charging up to sixty dollars to carry people across the bridges."

Rella took his hand, and he held on tightly. "We freed the prisoners before firebrands landed on the courthouse. Damned if they didn't start looting. And they weren't the only ones."

On and on he went, as though once he'd started, he was unable to stop his description of the misery, the thousands of homeless gathered on a stretch of lakeshore, some buried in sand to avoid the flames. Mostly he came back to the feeling of helplessness as fire engines broke down and pumps ran dry.

She longed to wrap him in her arms and let the weariness pass from his body to hers, but she doubted he would find comfort from her embrace. Then he took her by surprise. "But there were good moments, too," he said, the sharp edge gone from his voice. "People helping others the way you did. A jeweler started giving away his stock when he saw the store would soon be lost. A fellow by the name of Marshall Field has put up a sign telling his workers they'll get their wages. Even though he doesn't have a business anymore. And would you believe a real estate office is already in business. 'All gone but wife, children and energy,' the sign reads."

"Maybe you better forget the bad things, Cort," she said. "You've got enough good memories to take away with you."

"Maybe so." He grinned, but it was a feeble effort, and she could see the fatigue he'd been fighting was finally taking over. She felt much the same way, and the two of them barely made it back to the upstairs room of the tavern before collapsing, Cort on the narrow bed and Rella on her pallet of blankets. It was fifteen hours before either of them opened their eyes again.

It was the familiar, outspoken marshal who arose the next day and scolded her for sleeping on the floor.

"Gypsies are used to such accommodations," she responded without thinking her answer through. "I would hardly know what to do in a bed."

She wished she could take back her ill-thought words. He let them go with only a glint in his eyes to let her know he heard. Rested, Rella realized the war between them had once more begun.

"I don't suppose you misplaced that warrant," she said.

"You know me better than that."

"If you do manage to get me back to Galveston—and don't be too confident you'll manage it—please remember I waited for you here."

Cort's eyes warmed. "I've been thinking about that. Want to tell me why?"

"You wouldn't believe me if I did. Just tell the judge, will you? It might help in my defense."

She flounced past him, and they descended to wash at an outside pump as best they could. After a healthy meal with Flossie in the tavern kitchen, he set out to make the arrangements for their journey back to Texas, leaving her to think about the back door to the tavern. If only she hadn't been so tired last night . . . if only she hadn't needed to know he was all right. But there she went again, speculating about things that had not been.

Cort returned in a very short time, a confident look in his eye, and a briskness to his step. "Cinderella," he said, "I've got your carriage outside."

Something about his tone of voice aroused her suspicion. "A carriage?"

"A wagon, actually. It'll take us to Joliet. We'll need to get from there to La Salle for a steamboat to St. Louis. We're leaving immediately."

Rella was left unable to swallow another bite of what she regarded as her final meal in freedom. From St. Louis they would be going on to New Orleans. And then Galveston. "I'm ready," she managed.

Flossie regarded her silently, speculation again in her eyes, only this time it was softer. Why, why, *why* was Cort so stubbornly insistent on hauling her back? She ought to be grateful he hadn't placed her in handcuffs to let everyone know she was under arrest.

Flossie had called Cort her man and had shown no surprise that they shared a room; but since his return he'd shown no signs of affection, just efficient concern. Did they look like brother and sister? Or maybe a long-time married couple whose passions had long since died? Probably neither of these. Sisters didn't start every time a brother walked into the room, and disinterested wives didn't rest longing eyes on husbands who no longer cared.

A sobering thought struck Rella as she rose to take her leave. She and Cort would be meeting a lot of people who would wonder about their relationship before this journey was through. She brushed the thought from her mind. It was as well not to worry about what they might think or what he told anyone.

Rella bid a hasty good-bye to Flossie and hurried outside to see exactly what Cort had arranged. The only vehicle on the roadway was a farmer's wagon loaded with a dozen squealing pigs. Or piglets, she amended. She didn't know much about the beasts, but they didn't look very old.

"Takin' em to market down at Joliet," said a lanky man in overalls standing by the wagon. Cort introduced him as Josiah Pair.

"Ma'am," Pair said graciously, "sorry to hear you got separated from your family. Musicians, right?" He cast a quick glance at her Gypsy blouse and skirt. "The marshal here was tellin' me how you played the violin while ridin' on a horse. Now that's an act I'd like to see."

Me, too, Rella thought, refusing to give Cort the satisfaction of a sharp denial.

"You can ride up here with us," the farmer continued, "or take a place in the back."

"How nice," Rella muttered, casting a dark glance at the pigs. "If you don't mind, I'll sit up front." She eyed Cort's disheveled appearance. Neither had done more than wash their hands and faces. "The pigs might object."

The farmer cackled, then said, "Suit yourself. We'll be goin' kinda slow all night, don't want to push the horses too much."

Rella settled between the two men on the narrow

seat, and they were under way.

"So you folks was in that fire," Pair said; then added with a shake of his head, "Bad business that was."

Rella could see Cort tense. "Nice pigs you've got, Mr. Pair," she said. "What kind are they?" As if she would understand the answer.

"Mixed," the farmer said with pride. "Me and my brother have been doing some experimenting and got us several fine litters. Guess you city folks don't know much about breeding."

She felt Cort's eyes on her for a brief moment.

"Guess we don't," he said.

Pair needed no more encouragement to provide the education they lacked. Two hours later, back sore and ears weary from listening to the men discuss the problems of breeding hogs—and from Cort asking rather more questions as to the exact process than Rella thought necessary—she came to the uncomfortable conclusion that she couldn't be worse off with the porcine passengers.

She glanced over her shoulder at the critters. Several returned the look with eyes surprisingly similar to humans.

"Here, ma'am," said Pair, reaching under the seat. "Curl up with this blanket. It's gettin' a mite chilly."

Rella climbed over the seat and stretched out, surrounded by a surprisingly well-behaved bunch of fellow travelers. The pigs had an endearing, pixie look about them as they rooted about making new burrows. A good breeze wafting across the wagon bed carried away most of the odor.

She awoke sometime later to find the pigs nestled around her and the wagon pulled to the side of the road so that the horses could feed and rest. The men's voices droned in unintelligible conversation; she snuggled back down with her companions and didn't awaken again until they reached the river town of Joliet.

Cort tried to pay the farmer for the ride.

"No, thankee," he said. "There's lots of folks givin' free rides to those havin' to leave Chicago. Guess I can do the same. Besides, I got to get the little lady here back to her violin and horse."

Rella offered him heartfelt thanks for his generosity and concern for her comfort. What she wanted to add was gratitude for his belief in Cort's outlandish story. Except for that first cursory glance, not once had he cast a curious look at her soiled Gypsy clothes; not once had he given any sign that he wondered what kind of woman was traveling with a lawman without either a ring on her finger or a chaperone.

The river was too low at Joliet to hold much boat traffic, and Cort arranged for a more orthodox mode of transportation—a stagecoach to La Salle, where the Illinois River began.

"We won't be leaving for a while, and I've got to take care of a few things," he said at the stagecoach office. "You'll be all right here."

"Don't be too sure."

"I can handcuff you to a hitching post, if you prefer. Or maybe buy you a little rotgut whiskey and get you too drunk to run. It'll also give you a headache like the one you gave me."

"I was wondering when you would get around to mentioning that. What was I supposed to do? Let you carry me off to a Chicago jail?"

"That's exactly what you were supposed to do. If you had been a man, I never would have taken that drink."

"If I were a man, you wouldn't have dallied so long in my tent."

She knew she had gone too far. In a flash she found herself dragged to the sheriff's office down the street and deposited in one of the cells. The sheriff had seemed amused that he would house such a prisoner for even a short while. It was an amusement she didn't share.

"I'll be back as soon as I can," Cort said, a wicked smile on his lips as he looked at her through the bars. "Try to stay out of trouble. Although maybe it's the sheriff I should be warning."

Rella turned her back on him and listened as he walked away. If only she hadn't given up her savings, she could maybe buy her escape. But those horded coins had gone to free Sandor, a sacrifice Rella didn't regret. She was learning fast not to look back in regret.

It was almost two hours before Cort returned, clean-shaven and wearing a blue shirt under a brown leather vest. Tan trousers looked brightly new against his well-worn holster. When he led her outside, his badge glinted in the noonday sun.

He thrust a portmanteau at her. "Thought you might need some of the things in here. Sorry it took so long, but I had to clean up some before presenting myself at the bank. Had to arrange for some money. If we're to get very far, we'll need more cash than I had."

Rella remembered the stolen six thousand dollars had been his and wondered anew just how rich he might be. Certainly, no matter how spruced up she was, if she'd gone into a bank and asked for unsecured money, she would have been laughed out of the bank.

Cort led her to a public bath down the street, one he assured her had no back door. "Normally they don't cater to women, but I convinced them to make an exception this time."

"How thoughtful of you," she said curtly.

He grinned. "I was thinking of me, too. Those stages are awfully enclosed."

Without answering, Rella hurried inside. She immersed herself in a tub of warm water, scrubbed skin and hair, and slipped into the blue cotton dress that had been in the portmanteau. The thought occurred to her that Cort had made a fine-fitting choice of dress for her. Had he purposefully picked out the color and style of the one she'd worn in Galveston? It seemed a subtle touch to remind her just who she was. Maybe too subtle for Cort. He had a more direct approach.

She studied the stained blouse and skirt, and the golden necklaces which had been part of her costume. As filthy as they were, she wrapped them in a towel before thrusting them into the bottom of the portmanteau to wash later.

She found Cort waiting for her outside and caught the gleam of appreciation in his eyes. If he thought for one minute . . .

"I prefer your hair dark like that," he said.

She started. It was the lone comment he'd made on her changed appearance, but she couldn't take his words as a compliment. He'd made love to the dark-haired Rella. Naturally he would prefer her that way.

"I feel a little like those pigs being taken to market," she said. "Why don't you just leave me in Joliet? There's a prison here, isn't there, in addition to that little jail? It would save you a lot of time and effort."

The gleam in his eye quickly died. "As a matter of fact, the town has a pretty good prison. The idea isn't all that farfetched."

He took the portmanteau from her hand. "The stage is about to leave. We'd better hurry."

Rella forgot the people hurrying past them on the street and waiting stage. "You really believe it, don't you? That I'm a murderess and a thief."

"You want to discuss this now?"

"I want to hear you say it." Rella's voice almost broke. He looked so strong, so invincible, with his lean, tough face and hat pulled low on his forehead. Even now, with so much separating them, she had to fight reaching out and touching him. "After all that's happened since you came to Chicago, I want to know for sure."

Cort's eyes were flat and unreadable. "All the evidence pointed to you, but I still found it hard to believe. But then you knocked out that fool Ernest Bowles and ran, and I knew for sure. Maybe you didn't kill Tuttle on purpose. Maybe he made a pass and you tried to defend yourself. And there was all that money. . . ."

It was the lone concession he'd made, this offering of an excuse, but it wasn't enough.

"Of course," she said. "It could have happened that way."

"All you have to do is tell the truth."

"The truth?" Every drop of bitterness in her heart she put in her words. "You wouldn't recognize the truth if you heard it, Cort. Believe what you will."

She pushed past him and hurried toward the crowded stage. Before he'd strolled onto that Chicago fairgrounds, what he believed had been important only concerning whether she'd be thrown in jail. But now. . . . Rella felt cold and alone. She might be able to count on Cort in an emergency, like a burning barn, but in the long run he would let her down. Knowing she was being too harsh on him and too quickly ignoring his sense of duty, she couldn't feel otherwise.

The journey to La Salle proved monotonous and long. She tried to concentrate on the other passengers; but they were a complaining lot, and she found herself thinking back with longing to the pigs. When they arrived, Cort hustled her down to the dock.

He kept her in sight as he talked to the clerk at the riverboat office, then led her outside. "We're in luck. I got us passage on a boat that's leaving right away."

"How nice," she said. If he noticed the sarcasm in her voice, he gave no sign.

On board the steamboat an hour later, they listened as the whistle gave evidence the journey was under way, then he led her to a narrow stateroom on the upper deck. A single bed took up most of the space.

"Where will you be staying?" she asked.

"There's lots of river traffic just now, Rella."

"That doesn't answer—" She stopped and stared at him in disbelief.

Cort shrugged. "We'll have to share a room. I had to show the captain my warrant to get on at all."

"I'm your prisoner, Cort, not your . . . paramour. We'll get off somehow and wait for the next boat."

"They don't come along like trolley cars. I'm trying to make connections in St. Louis, remember. We'll have to make the best of what we can get."

"And what do you mean by that? Another quick tumble? I won't give in this time without a struggle. Now that I understand exactly how things are between us."

"I'm not in the habit of abusing my prisoners." Cort's temper flared. "And don't be so damned sure it would be either quick or a struggle."

With an anger that matched his, Rella exploded. "I know what you really think. You're angry I managed to trick you for even a little while, and you think I used your lust."

"That's putting it bluntly enough."

"I've always spoken that way. Except when I was the Romany. You'll have to forgive me for that deception. I was trying to save my life."

Cort pulled her hard against him, his lips hovering close to hers. "Is that all you were doing? You claim I was the one who wanted the sex, but your remembrance is different from mine. You're a good little actress, but nobody's that good."

The force of him took her breath away, and she squeezed her eyes shut. She had craved his caresses not only then; she wanted them right now.

"Go ahead," she taunted. "Kiss me. Take what you will. After all, I'm your prisoner. Only don't be surprised if I bite you again. You'll have to gag me to make sure you'll be safe."

He thrust her from him. "Now here's the Rella Sandringham I've been looking for. Couldn't play the gentle role all the way back, could you? It's just as well. At least let's be honest with one another. As the Romany, you had me going for a while. I won't deny it, but I can promise it won't happen again."

He took only two steps to be standing at the door. "There's bound to be some whiskey on this boat. I'll see if I can have some food sent up here. Don't do anything foolish, Rella, like trying to jump overboard and swim to shore. If you managed not to drown, I'd only catch you again."

He slammed the door behind him, barely avoiding the pillow she threw with all her might. In the little space allowed her, she began a furious pacing and even more furious pondering.

How could she have ever thought she loved him? She knew the answer to that. She'd been raised with a strong moral code. Women didn't give themselves to men wantonly; they had to be in love and, idiotic creatures, to expect marriage. She was twice a fool. He offered neither love nor a permanent attachment. She'd only been deceiving herself, trying to make acceptable excuses.

She might not be a murderess or a thief, but she was a lustful creature, God forgive her. She was almost grateful that Cort was being so arrogant. His attitude made him easier to resist.

Oh, he was right. He wanted her at least as much as she wanted him. She would have to fight it, this weakness when he was near. It would be a cold day in hell before she ever gave herself to him again.

Chapter Fourteen

When Cort entered the saloon on the steamboat's main deck, he had his badge tucked inside a shirt pocket under his vest. There were two occasions when he didn't feel comfortable wearing it: the times he sought out female companionship and the rare times he was doing some serious drinking.

This afternoon he wasn't after a woman; just the opposite, he was trying to get away from one. And he had drinking on his mind. Rella was a fever in his blood; he would burn her out with alcohol.

He ordered a bottle and glass, then settled down at a table away from the door, his back to the small room to discourage company. The whiskey went down neat, burning its way into his stomach. Unwise, he thought, to drink without any food, but hell, when had he been smart lately?

Now that he knew the truth, he couldn't believe his stupidity. When he'd first seen her in Galveston, Cinderella Sandringham had been fair and fragile in appearance, but her sharp tongue had given her away. That façade of fragility was a steel wire that could bend and reform despite tremendous pressures put to it. She'd reformed all right—as the sensuous, willing Romany who had ensnared him.

He could see both women in that splendor, provocative figure she'd presented in the cabin. Uplifted chin, lips firmly set, breasts heaving with indignation. It was a picture he remembered from Perry Tuttle's law office when she'd denied her guilt. Only now, instead of blond curls, she had a mass of dark hair tumbling about her shoulders. Since she'd left Galveston, her ivory skin had turned golden under the sun. And she'd developed a different way of holding herself, a more womanly, graceful way. Hell, he didn't know exactly what it was, but even in memory it could cause a familiar tightening in his loins.

Cort sighed in disgust. What was it that traveling preacher had shouted over his bent head when he was a boy in Missouri? *The truth shall set ye free.* He poured another drink. He didn't feel free. Not yet, at least, but he was working on it.

The whiskey was going down smoother now, and he felt his muscles begin to relax. Maybe he had left the cabin too soon. Rella's blazing eyes burned into his mind. She'd stood close to him, hands on hips, and dared him to kiss her. She'd wanted him to. But if he'd accepted that dare, if he'd claimed the lips she so tauntingly offered him, he would have done a lot more than stop with a kiss. She didn't know how close she had come to having her skirt lifted. A few minutes would have provided a quick release for them both. And she could bite him all she wanted.

I'm your prisoner, she had said. If that were no more than the simple truth, then why was he the one driven to drink?

"Mind if I join you?"

Jolted out of his musings, Cort sent a warning look at the speaker, a spare, pasty-faced man with a pencil moustache. A string tie at the neck of his white shirt matched his black gabardine suit.

Gambler, Cort thought. The saloon pallor and delicate, almost feminine, hands gave him away, as did that friendly smile that was at odds with his dark, assessing eyes. Cort was not surprised when the man ignored the warning look and settled into a chair across the table, the glass of whiskey he'd brought with him resting beside Cort's bottle. Riverboat gamblers tended to have leather hides.

"Looks to be a quiet ride down to Peoria. Odom's the name. Ralph Odom. What might you be called?"

"Ramsey," Cort answered briefly.

"Ramsey, is it? Knew a family by that name in Detroit. Ever been there?"

"Never been there," Cort said. "Now if you don't mind . . ."

Odom raised a hand in protest. "Sorry. Shouldn't be asking too much about a man's past. Just passing the time, which is hanging heavy on my hands right now, I don't mind telling you." He smiled, but Cort noticed the man's narrow eyes remained speculative. "Hey," Odom continued, "you suppose the barkeep has some dominoes or cards?"

"I wouldn't be at all surprised."

"Well, you just sit here and have your whiskey, and I'll go see. Might as well do something to kill an hour or two. A friendly game, nothing more. While I'm at it, I'll see about some chips."

Cort figured he must look stupid, which he'd already decided for himself, or drunk, which he was working on. He wondered what Odom would do if he returned to see Cort wearing his badge. Maybe later he'd pull it out. For now, he agreed with the gambler. Card playing was a way to pass the time.

They started with twenty-one, but neither man was able to gain the advantage. A traveling salesman working the river towns joined them when they switched to poker, and then a store clerk from La Salle who said he was going to visit his sister in Peoria.

The game turned more serious as chips began to multiply in front of the gambler. Most of them came from the newcomers. Cort held his own.

Odom was good. Cort could see nothing amiss, at least not for a while. He started to cash in his chips and take a stroll on the deck, but something about the look in the gambler's eyes aroused his lawman's instincts and kept him at the table.

"Never had such a run of bad luck," the salesman said as Odom dealt another hand.

"Just maybe," Cort said, his eyes on Odom's supple fingers, "your luck's about to change." He reached inside the leather vest for his badge and placed it on the table. A flash of understanding in Odom's eyes was gone in an instant, supplanted by the friendly look. The bottom card of the deck, the one the gambler had been fooling with, remained in place.

"A United States marshal, eh?" he said. "Guess we can all feel safe with you aboard."

Cort shrugged. Whatever respite from duty he'd sought in the saloon was impossible now, and he turned to the salesman and clerk. "You men have a nice, friendly game. Odom here will see that you do. I'm cashing in my chips now, but I'll be around." He glanced at Odom. "You can count on it."

Outside, Cort took as deep breath of smoke-free air and put the glambler from his mind. He stood a long time on the deck watching the sun set. Around him passengers were heading for the dining room, but he paid them no attention. The river was low and meandering, and silently he congratulated the skill of the captain for maneuvering the steamboat past the shoals. He hoped the man knew his job well enough to avoid all the snares dragged up by the ever-changing river currents.

He would have to be vigilant—the way a U.S. marshal had to be vigilant against evil doers. Sometimes Cort grew weary of the burden. It seemed he'd been on duty ever since that anguishing day years ago when he returned from the war and learned about his father's death, the day he decided to join the forces of the law. In Texas he had given time to horses and cattle, making sure he wouldn't wind up poverty stricken like so many other retired lawmen he'd met, but basically his allegiance had been to the enforcement of justice. There were men like Ralph Odom—and some far worse—wherever he went.

The steady slap of the stern wheel drifted across the deck. On this part of the river, trees grew close to the riverbanks, and he thought about the lush East Texas plantation he'd bought. He'd seen it only once, but the solitude of the peaceful setting had impressed him. There were neighbors around, all right, enough to give a man all the friends he could want—even a Missourian, although he knew he'd have to prove himself in that insular part of the state which still was more Old South than West. A man had to fight for anything worthwhile.

He hadn't purchased the land with any idea of living on it; an investment it had been, along with the cattle and horses he owned. But lately he'd been giving thoughts to settling down. He was thirty-five years old. Hell, did he want to be traveling a lonely river somewhere in another thirty years, protecting naive young men from cardsharks? A man had to have a cause. A reason for being. And working the fertile land, bringing it back from the destitution brought on by the war, might be cause enough.

If he had a woman to work beside him. Strange, but he'd never given thought to settling down. Since his mother had died when he was young, he and his father had lived without a woman around. As he looked back on those growing-up years, he saw that at times they'd been lonely.

He would need a wife, all right. Someone loving and gentle, yet strong and with a will of her own. Someone who shared his passion, someone who would stand by him during the bad times and rejoice in the good, someone who wanted children.

She ought to be broad hipped and have a determined chin and tight corkscrew curls over her ears. She would be the terror of her offspring and the servants.

Try as he might to picture such a woman, he kept getting the vision of a supple, rounded woman with silky black tresses, rousting the families out of homes which lay in the path of a spreading fire. He saw her comforting a lost young boy as she searched the panicked crowds for his mother. He smiled as he pictured her blanket-wrapped figure snuggled down amidst a wagonload of pigs.

Strongest of all was the image of her lying in his arms, her lips swollen from his kisses, her eyes hot with desire.

His smile died. Damn Rella! She had woven a spell over him no amount of whiskey had erased. Maybe just as well. Look at the fool he'd made of himself by drinking Gypsy moonshine. But she had offered that. Always his thoughts returned to how that woman could complicate his life.

Cort began to pace. Here he was, tired and restless, and she was no doubt sleeping comfortably in their shared cabin and dreaming away. She had no conscience. At the tavern he'd given her another chance to explain what had happened in the Galveston law office, even prompted her with a story about Tuttle making advances and forcing her to defend herself. She had refused to respond.

By damn, she wouldn't keep him from getting a few hours of much-needed rest, and he set his course for the cabin. He found her as he had expected, lying on the bunk and sleeping. A blanket was pulled to her waist, but he could see she still wore the blue dress, as though if she'd taken off so much as a collar she would have invited his attack. Foolish woman. She didn't know how inviting she looked lying there with her dark hair spread across the pillow, dark lashes resting against her golden cheeks.

But she was his prisoner—and off limits. He'd fallen for that innocent yet sensual look before. He'd be damned if he would again.

Cort never slept in his clothes, and he wasn't about to start now. Not bothering to lock the door—she'd have a hard time getting away from him tonight—he stripped and maneuvered his long frame next to the wall to lie down beside her. There was no room for any space between them, and he pulled the cover over them both. If she wanted to use the bed, she would damn well have to share it. He slipped an arm around her waist and nestled her back against him. She fit just fine. Too fine, he decided as his body grew uncomfortably warm.

She shifted slightly, and he caught his breath at the sweet torture. But he refused to abandon the bed. Lying beside her and not doing what came naturally would be a penance for him, a punishment for having allowed her to fool him, a cruel yet not unwelcome sentence for having been so dumb.

* * *

Rella opened her eyes to the early morning sunlight streaming through a small porthole beside the cabin door. Nestling down into the comfort of the bunk, she followed the path of the narrow beam. Like a stage-light, it fell across a brown hand at her waist. No wonder she had, at first awakening, imagined herself resting in a cocoon. She was snuggled in Cort's arms. Cort's naked arms, she realized and darted out of her chrysalis like a startled butterfly.

She stood as far from the bunk as possible in the narrow cabin. With the blanket thrown back, she saw that far more than his arm was naked, and she edged near to cover him once again.

He cocked one eye open, then shut it fast. "Do you always get up so wide awake?" he said sleepily.

"How dare you!" she sputtered, knowing full well how he dared. He was Cort, after all. Despite his caustic assurances that he would leave her alone, he could dare anything he pleased.

This time he opened both eyes and took a long, leisurely tour of her wrinkled clothes and tousled hair. "I only bought you the one dress. You better take care of it. At least take it off at night."

In frustration, she picked at the pile of men's clothes at her feet. "I don't intend to share a bed with you. Dressed or otherwise."

"I thought we settled that yesterday. We don't have a choice." He propped himself up on one arm, and the blanket fell to his waist. His chest was broad and taut and dusted with wiry curls of golden hair; his well-muscled arms looked as though they could snap her in two.

After a while, Rella bit at her lower lip and looked away. "We can sleep at different times," she managed, hating the break in her voice.

"Won't work," he said. "Look at it this way. I'll be

like a pair of handcuffs making sure you don't run away."

She looked back at him in desperation. "And if I promise not to?" She would promise anything to keep from sharing close quarters with an undressed Cort.

His eyes narrowed. "I imagine you know the answer to that."

She would not mention the tavern again. Already she had decided her refusal to leave with Sandor had been a mistake. Cort couldn't possibly have been hurt in that fire. He was simply too mean. In her frustration, she lashed out at him. "You actually enjoy this power you have over me!"

"I'm only doing my duty."

She was surprised at the edge in his voice. "Of course," she said, then added bitterly, "Marshal Ramsey." She plucked the leather vest from the pile of clothes and ripped free his badge of office. "This proves you are an honorable man," she said, brandishing it aloft. "Whatever you decide is right." She squeezed at the sharp metal until it cut into her fingers.

Cort sat up in the bed. "Drop the badge."

"Yes, sir!" she snapped. "I'll drop it all right." Flinging open the door, she ran onto the deck and lofted the brass star as far as she could into the slow-moving Illinois River. It floated for an undulating moment on the waves, then sank from sight. She whirled in time to see Cort rise from the bed and head for the door. Coming at her in his naked manliness, he was an awesome sight.

Her eyes rounded. "You can't come out here like that!"

"Then come back in here." His voice was deceptively soft.

Her chin tilted in defiance. "I won't!"

He stepped onto the deck. "Oh, you will. If I have to run after you and drag you back."

"I doubt that. There are people up and about already."

"Most of whom have seen a naked man. Don't be coy, Rella. So have you."

She got a clear picture of Cort catching her halfway down the deck and slinging her over his shoulder to bring her back. Deciding to act on the side of discretion, she pulled herself up tall. She might have to give in to the inevitable, but she refused to cower. "You, sir," she said as she edged past him through the door, "are no gentleman." His only reply was a laugh.

Knowing nothing else to do, she went to the basin and washed her face and hands while he dressed. As best she could, she arranged her hair into a knot at the back of her neck. In those days with Templeton's Traveling Thespians, days which now seemed so long ago, she had managed in quarters less spacious than this, and without the mirror that hung on the cabin wall—except on those occasions, she hadn't shared the room, and she hadn't caught the eye of a man appraising her when he thought she wasn't aware.

"Throwing that badge away won't do you any good," he said to her reflection in the mirror. "I've still got the warrant and papers to show who I am."

She smiled in satisfaction. "Oh, it did me good, all right, although you probably wouldn't understand."

She turned to face him and announced, "I'm starving. Never having traveled in custody before, I can only assume food comes with the journey, but I have to warn you I'm broke. My alleged life of crime had proven to be singularly unprofitable."

"Unless you have six thousand dollars stashed away somewhere on Galveston island."

"Of course," said Rella, snapping her fingers. "I

forgot about that. Just add the expenses to my bill. Once you find the money, you can take out what's owed. Although I imagine whoever really took it has little left by now."

Giving him no chance to answer, she exited the cabin once again, this time a neatly clad but badgeless marshal at her heels.

After breakfast, she attempted to wash her Gypsy garb in the small cabin sink and managed to get out most of the pig smells. The rest of the day was spent idly, with Rella pacing in the shuttered ladies' cabin in the stern and Cort sequestered in the adjoining cabin with the men.

"The sexes are segregated," he said as he left her at the door, "to protect the virtues of the women. You know how lusty we men can be."

She had hours to remember just exactly what he meant. A knot formed in the pit of her stomach that she knew would remain there as long as he was near.

Once she tried to leave the ladies' cabin for a stroll on the deck, but when she was no more than few feet from the door, Cort joined her. She gave up and returned to her genteel jail.

Cort excused himself again that night to go to the saloon, muttering something about watching some man named Odom. Again she heard the hated turn of the key in the lock. Using her training as improvisor of costumes—Templeton's never having been a very prosperous troupe—she fashioned a nightgown from a cotton sheet. Unfortunately, harking back to that performance in New Orleans when she'd played a part in *Julius Caesar,* the garment resembled a Roman toga and revealed rather more of one shoulder than she would have liked.

She climbed into the bed and pulled the blanket close around her neck. When Cort joined her some-

time in the wee hours, she kept her eyes firmly shut and ignored the feel of his body as he applied what he had called his handcuff hold. At least she tried to ignore him, instead working on a plan to coax him into a toga like hers.

The image that the plan conjured did little to relax her, and with the sibilance of his soft snore telling her he was asleep, she spent a long while reciting to herself Calpurnia's speeches to her husband Julius.

The next morning she slipped more quietly out of bed and was dressed and ready for breakfast by the time he awoke. And so began another day of routine. The monotony of the journey was broken when they landed in Peoria. She stood on the main deck and watched a number of passengers debark. Always she was aware Cort stood tall beside her, the auburn glint of his hair a brighter contrast to his brown vest.

"Maybe," she said, "we can get another cabin now."

"Not likely. The captain says we'll be taking on an entire circus troupe."

"With elephants?" she asked, amazed.

"Trained horses, and a few cats. These folks are mostly acrobats, not wild animal trainers. Although they do have one man I hear can put his head into the mouth of a lion."

"He'd make a good marshal."

"He might at that," said Cort.

Just then as colorful a parade of people as Rella had ever seen made their way up the gangplank, complete with a small marching band at the rear. A tall, graceful man in top hat and tails led the procession as they wended their way past the boxes and supplies loaded on the main deck.

He tipped his hat as he came to Rella and handed her a small paper embellished with black headlines.

"AMUSEMENTS," it read, "Smythe and Sargent's

European Circus," and proceeded to list performers from France, Germany, England, Spain, and even America.

Halting in front of Cort, a flamboyant redhead in a spangled green cape and matching skirt which revealed her ankles gave him a copy of the advertisement. "I am Fifi," she said in a strong French accent. "A contortionist. Oohlala! the things I can do." Her eyes twinkled. "You do understand me, do you not, monsieur?"

"He understands you, all right," Rella said, cutting off his reply. "And he likes exotic women. I can assure you of that."

She brushed past the two of them and climbed the stairs to the upper deck, where she could watch the loading of the animals and avoid seeing Cort pursued by the beautiful circus contortionist. Just wait until Fifi is escorted to the ladies' cabin, she thought with glee. To protect her virtue. Then Rella sobered. She remembered a secluded woods and a Gypsy tent—and the thoughts that had kept her awake last night—and admitted that where Cort was concerned, she and the circus performer were not really so different.

But Fifi could come and go as she pleased. Rella looked down on the crowded Peoria wharf. Somewhere, surely, there would be transportation out of the town. If only she had some money . . . Maybe she could enliven the ladies' cabin with a little fortune telling. Or a knife-throwing demonstration. She still had Alepa's gift tucked inside the portmanteau. Perhaps she would try something like that the next morning, there being no reason she could think of to be circumspect in her behavior when she was on her way to jail.

Whether she could have worked up enough nerve to do as she planned, she never got the chance to find out. Early the next morning, after another sleepless night, a time when she and Cort took once more to sniping at one another and she wondered how things could go on as they were, they left the cabin to go to breakfast. The boat was rounding a sharp bend and suddenly lurched to the right.

Rella fell against Cort, and he put out his arms to steady her.

"What happened?" she asked as she heard the frightened horses whinny below. Then came the ominous roar of a wild cat. She hoped the cage was secure.

"Run aground on a sandbar, I'd say. Damn it! I don't want any more delays. We've got to make connections in St. Louis."

Rella was as upset as he was. As much as she dreaded going back to Texas, she wanted the frustrating nights to end.

Warning her to stay where she was, Cort took off for the pilothouse. He returned shortly. "We're aground, all right," he explained. "The captain was trying to avoid snags. Those big logs lurk just below the surface of the river and can tear at a boat and sink her. With so little rain lately, the river's low. They're a big problem along here."

"So what do we do now?"

"Just stand back and watch. The procedure is called grasshoppering. I've never seen it, but I've heard it described. It should be quite a show."

Which it was. A pair of long spars were raised on either side of the boat, one end set in the river bottom and the other high in the sky leaning toward the bow. The riverboatmen then rigged each spar with a tackle-block, over which a cable was passed. The cable was attached to the gunwale of the boat and to the capstan. The process took close to an hour, but neither Rella nor Cort mentioned leaving their observation post on the deck.

"Hold on," Cort said at last. "Here we go."

Rella watched in amazement as the capstan was turned and the paddle wheel rotated. The boat was lifted from the bar and edged forward toward the navigable part of the river. The spars were reset, and the procedure repeated. Ralph Odom circulated among the onlookers taking bets as to how long the procedure would take. It was mid afternoon by the time the job was done, but Cort didn't like the angle of the boat in the water.

As the passengers assembled in the dining room, the captain explained what was wrong. "We've got to head back to Peoria. Suffered some bilge damage."

"Are we going to sink?" a woman cried out.

"We're not taking on more'n we can pump out," the captain said in assurance, "but that's not saying we could make it all the way to St. Looey."

"How long will repairs take?" asked Cort.

The captain shrugged. "Wouldn't want to make any promises. A day. Maybe two. Can't take a chance on losing this old tub. We've been together too long."

Fifi sidled up beside Cort. "Perhaps, monsieur, we will have that demonstration after all."

"Be my guest," Rella said. "He's all yours."

He caught up with her back in the cabin. "You'll not get rid of me that easily," he said. "We have a change of plans."

Curiosity ate at her, but she refused to give him the satisfaction of asking what he meant. When they eased back into Peoria early the next morning, she found out.

"Pack everything," he said. "The river will be low all the way to St. Louis. The captain's a good man, but this could happen again." He glanced at the bunk.

"And I don't like these arrangements any more than you do. We're going by land."

Foolishly Rella expected he meant stagecoach or train. Or even, she thought with regret, another pig wagon. To her surprise he directed her to a stable in the middle of town. They would make better time cutting across southern Illinois, he explained. Besides, he was ready to work out a few kinks and get back on a horse, and he rented two bay horses, a stallion and a mare, both fully outfitted. Rella was glad he hadn't insisted on a sidesaddle for her; when she'd been with the Gypsies, she'd ridden astride.

Next it was on to a general store, where Cort again purchased her clothes. He didn't ask her what she wanted; it was his money, he was no doubt thinking, and he could buy what he chose. She didn't have any more say in her outfitting than did her mare.

In La Salle he'd purchased the blue dress. This time, to the surprise of the clerk, he bought a pair of boy's denim pants and a green cotton shirt, along with a leather jacket in case the nights were cool. And, of course, gloves, a pair of boots and a hat. He thought of everything.

Nothing that he did surprised Rella anymore, and she changed into the unusual garb in a room at the back of the store. She drew a few stares as she made her way to the street to join Cort. Cort's lips twitched, but otherwise he gave no indication he noticed anything out of the ordinary in the way she looked. Maybe nothing about her surprised him, either.

It should have. She was more determined than ever to make good her escape. After another stop for supplies, they were on the road south of town, on their way to St. Louis and the steamboat awaiting them there.

Cort surprised her by wearing a black silk kerchief suspended from a forage-style hat to shade the back of his neck. "No use adding sunburn to all the other miseries on the trail," he said. She thought it gave him a romantic air, like a desert nomad. Well, not romantic, exactly. She didn't want her thoughts to stray down that particular, winding path.

Cort directed her to tie a large bandanna around her neck and to wear gloves. They traveled fast the first day, stopping only to feed and water the horses and chew at a piece of jerky. Rella thought longingly of the food that would be spread on the tables of the steamboat, but she wouldn't have complained for the world.

For a while she felt a release of the tension that seemed always to be with her. The freedom that she'd tasted riding across the prairie out of Chicago returned to her now, and she could pretend that the freedom was real. She let the hat ride against her back, and the wind rippled through her hair. Oh, to be able to turn the mare away from the road they followed and head cross-country over the rolling fields. And as long as she was dreaming, she could imagine a man at her side. A man willing to accept her as an equal. A man who would love her at night.

She jerked away from the dream. By the time they made camp beside a narrow stream away from the road, the knot in her stomach had returned. She was proud of one thing. She'd kept up with him during the long ride. Her major source of discomfort—if she discounted his unnerving presence—was the boots. They'd rubbed a blister on her inner ankles, and she gave in to the urge to remove them before they ate.

They dined on a supper of fresh meat and beans that Cort had bought back in town. The food tasted delicious after the hard day's ride, and even with Cort sitting unnervingly close to her beside the fire, Rella found it possible to eat. She washed the plates in the stream and, stepping carefully in her bare feet, returned to the fire to accept the cup of coffee he extended to her.

An uneasy peace settled between them.

"I'm tired," she announced, setting down her cup. "I'll spread my bedroll under that tree."

"You'll sleep beside me."

Rella turned to him in surprise. "You don't mean. . . ."

"That's right. Unless you prefer real handcuffs."

She stood and with hands on hips stared down at him. "That's exactly what I prefer." She watched in amazement as he walked over to his saddlebags and returned with the handcuffs.

"Are you going to sleep in your clothes?" asked Cort, a gleam in his eyes. "Maybe I should have bought a sheet back in Peoria."

Fuming, Rella whirled and, blanket under her arm, headed for the grassy place she'd picked for her bedroom. All the while she was scouring the ground to free it of stones and sticks that might poke her in the night, she looked for something substantial enough to do him harm. Her mind raced. She would knock him out, turn his stallion loose, then head out on the mare. In which direction, she didn't know, but for the first night it mattered little as long as it was away from him.

When she found a good-sized rock, she tucked it near to hand and spread her blanket beside it, then fetched her saddle for use as a pillow. From the corner of her eye she saw Cort likewise occupied, the handcuffs dangling prominently from his rear pocket.

She shifted the saddle more to her satisfaction, having to take her eyes off him to arrange the hard stirrups under it. After one last pat, her hand stole from the saddle to close over the rock. She shifted weight to her feet, squatting, preparing to rise and turn smoothly, concealing the weapon behind her hip. Seconds ago she had seen Cort bending over his own bedroll. She had plenty of time to approach, to hit him from behind—just the way she had attacked Deputy Ernest Bowles in the jail.

A twig snapped, but before Rella could react, could finish her turn, a hand closed tightly over her wrist.

"Drop it, Rella!" he ordered.

She was no match for his strength as he bent her arm up behind her, the rock falling to the ground. Before he could immobilize her other arm, she flailed out at his head with her fist. He dodged back, grabbing at her arm, and Rella found herself pinned against him, both wrists gripped behind her with one hand. With the other he cupped her face close to his. "I knew you'd try something. You don't learn easily, do you, Romany?"

The bitterness in his voice hit her hard. "Romany, is it? Is it convenient for you to call me that?" she asked, then added with a bitterness equal to his, "Lawman!"

His lips twitched into a smile. "You threw the badge away, remember? Whether you know it or not, you were asking for this to happen. We're man and woman tonight."

His hand lowered, and he began to unbutton her shirt, his fingers hot against the rise of her breasts. The night was overcast, but the flickering fire cast shadows across her creamy skin.

"Let go of my hands," she whispered huskily, and for once he did as she bid. In a last desperate denial of her need for him, she pushed with all her might. She caught him by surprise and was able to stumble away from him. He tackled her, and they landed hard on the blanket.

Gasping for air, she struck out wildly, twisted and turned on the ground in a desperate attempt to get away. He paid no mind to her struggles. Abandoning all gentleness, he tore the shirt from her body and tossed it aside. Rough hands unfastened her pants and raked them down her hips, baring her womanhood to his hungry eyes.

His hands moved slowly up her naked body, feeling each soft curve of her flesh, pinning her against the ground. "I only meant to stop your attack," he said huskily, "but I want more than that now. And so do you. Admit it!"

With his fingers biting cruelly into her shoulders, she felt the rising heat of his body invade hers.

"Admit it!" he repeated.

The tips of her breasts brushed against his rough shirt, and she inhaled the smell of him. "I want you," she said in a rush, forsaking all shame.

Cort unwound his tall frame and stood over her. Naked and lying at his feet, powerless to move, she watched him undress. Her eyes devoured his tall, muscled strength as greedily as he had stared at her. When he dropped beside her, they kissed with avid mouths, tongues darting, teeth nipping at desire-ripened lips. She became acutely aware of her backbone, an anatomical area she'd scarcely ever reckoned with before. Hot tremors followed by cold ones went from her neck to her tailbone, left there and finally centered in the pit of her stomach only to be lost in the searing scorch of his kiss.

The earth seemed to move as quakes of passion shuddered through her. She was swallowed up by him, lost in his ravaging assault. His kiss deepened, seeming to draw all energy from her, then his lips burned a trail from her cheeks to the hollow of her throat.

"You torment me, Gypsy," Cort whispered huskily, words she barely comprehended, knowing only they came on his hot breath.

The beat of her heart grew large in her ears, and she was dizzy as if from too much wine, her wits slipping away so she could not think, only feel.

His lips claimed hers again, and his hands began to rove over her heated flesh, arousing mindless ecstasy. Her body molded itself to his, then seemed to meld into him. The fluttering pulse in the hollow of her throat beat strongly as Rella offered the slender column up to Cort, her head thrown back in abandonment to his desire, its graceful length bare for his taking. With delight, she trembled under his mouth as it traveled moistly, heatedly down the length of her throat, teeth nipping gently at her flesh, one hand tightening possessively at the back of her neck.

"Mine, you are mine," he said between kisses, and Rella shivered at the words, feeling the power that lay with him, power as ruthless as that of any prairie predator that might end by tearing her to shreds.

But she was powerless to repulse him. Her hands crept up to smooth his hair, and she gazed into his blue eyes. Fire was reflected in their depths, not only from the dying flames nearby, but from his very soul. She twined her arms around his neck, drawing him nearer until his lips once again found the sensitive spot at the base of her throat. Torrid waves of renewed ecstasy swept through her body, making her nipples harden against his chest.

He drew back and cupped her breasts, admiring the twin mounds of perfection he'd longed to see every night he'd lain beside her on that narrow bunk. Their translucent paleness and creamy expanses were topped by two blushing crests, grown hard from the touch of his body. He caressed them, nipped at them and brushed his palms over them sensuously, moving in slow circles.

Their eyes met, and Rella's whole soul seemed to rush to the twin centers of her universe. They throbbed, then the heat of sensation spun away only to come back in a shower of sparking pleasure that left her weak, to be energized once more under the onslaught of his tongue which circled first one nipple, then the other. The warm flutterings within her were gradually replaced with a primitive longing as Cort's fingers massaged the rigid buds, teasing them to greater hardness.

He licked the valley between her breasts, then fed on them with deepening avidity. Rella arched against him, and her hands grasped his back, feeling the muscles bunch beneath her questing fingers. They dug into his flesh, and her nails raked him. His breath seared against her as he moved to the other breast. It swelled within his mouth, and he made a mighty effort to consume all of her in the heat of his furious need. His hand cupped the other breast, and it flowered as a rose opens to the sun that feeds it.

An ever-growing ache deep within the dark, secret center of her womanhood began to grow into a fierce, overwhelming desire. She was a prisoner to him, complete and unresisting. She clutched him to her, knowing that only he could assuage her pain. Her nails dug deeper, telling him of her urgent need.

His hands rushed down her belly, paused to tantalize the thrusting vee, then fluttered on down her legs to caress the calves of her legs, then up again, inexorable as the wind rushing across the hot land. She moaned in animal madness and writhed wantonly under him, spurring him on until finally he plunged his fingers between her legs to rub along the insides of her thighs.

In an agony of longing, she parted her legs, and he laughed huskily as he found the luscious, swollen folds of her womanhood. Tantalizing her, he explored the moist edges of the chasm that beckoned him inside, pausing to find the tiny button of desire before plunging questing fingers inside her, plunging again and again in rhythmic abandon. Rella instinctively grasped his pulsating manhood and matched the age-old motion that would lead to assuagement of their mutual need.

Cort caught his breath at her touch, and his muscles constricted as mingled pleasure and pain exploded in his loins. He rose over her, guiding the tip of his manhood to thrust into her. Impatiently, she grasped his shoulder, seeking to draw him closer.

He guided her legs to lock around him, and his hands moved to lift her buttocks to meet him. Again and again he drove his shaft deep into the burning crevass faster and faster, until they both panted for air. Her nails scraped furrows down his back, but he was too caught up in her passionate response to care. Each time he thrust into her, she arched her hips frantically to meet the lunges of his body.

Suddenly, she stiffened and cried out at the moment of climax, and Cort felt himself burst within her. Two more thrusts and he collapsed, his cries of pleasure mixing with hers.

Their breath rasped in unison until gradually the wild beating of their hearts slowed to a steady pace. The unbridled vent of their desires left them spent and yet bound together by a shared sense of fulfillment more powerful than steel. A sense of rightness settled over them, and Cort slipped his body sideways to lie beside her and cradle her head on his shoulder, the clean fragrance of her hair soothing him into further lassitude.

This time as they lay together, there was no bitter longing, no passion denied. Cort pulled at the corner of the blanket and enfolded them both in its warmth. Nestled together, they gave themselves up to the comforts of night.

Chapter Fifteen

When Rella awakened the next morning, the sun was already showing over the edge of the eastern horizon. Squinting into the daylight, she stretched, and every muscle in her unclad body protested.

The discomfort—and the realization of her nakedness—brought a shocking remembrance of everything that had happened before she drifted off to sleep in Cort's arms.

The smell of coffee drifted toward her on the cold morning air, but she remained still beneath her blanket, caught in a private censure for wanting to see his long-legged figure moving about the campsite. She should be wishing him in hell, this man who planned to throw her in jail. Rella wasn't a fool. Murderers were hanged. If she was found guilty—the thought brought a rising of the panic that was always with her—it would matter not that she'd lain with the man who brought her to justice.

Justice, she thought bitterly, would hardly be met by her death. No, justice had little to do with her situation now. Of course she was a fool. Otherwise, she would not be drawn so irresistibly to the one man who could do her harm. She'd better find a way, and soon, to get away. Once back in Galveston, all hope for her freedom would be gone.

Rella reached for her clothes lying in a crumpled heap beside the makeshift bed. Struggling into the shirt and trousers, she thought that blessed though she was with friends like Greta Maas and Aaron Tuttle, Alepa and Sandor, the curse of Cort's intrusion into her life had more than compensated.

You torment me, Gypsy.

Cort's whispered words of last night came back to haunt her. As best she could, she slammed her feet into the boots, then tied back her hair. So she tormented him, did she? It was scant comfort, but she would take whatever amount of that commodity she could find.

Cort kept his back to her as he rustled up breakfast. He wore the shirt and trousers and leather vest from yesterday; already he'd strapped on his gun. His head was bare, revealing the thick copper hair that curled against his neck. She knew that if he turned to face her, a lock of that hair would rest across his forehead; his eyes would reflect the blue of the clear sky and the coolness of the air.

After last night, he should have greeted her with more than his backside. Where was the *good morning, dearest one? Thank you for last night. You have made me a complete man.* In the fantasy world of the stage, the leading man would have uttered such words to his love.

Rella might have toiled on the stage, but she lived in the real world. Here the ground was hard and the morning air biting. Here the passions of the night, even with their ultimate tenderness, did not carry over to the day. Few were the happy endings in this world—at least for her. She should be grateful that Cort wasn't so hypocritical as to greet her with false sentimentality. He'd made her no promises, even in their moments of greatest passion.

And why should she think of such a thing with regret? She'd been independent for most of her life, long before the untimely deaths of her romantic, impractical parents. The answer to her question struck with tremendous force. What she really wanted was to be cherished. Maybe Cort could bring such a feeling to another woman. But not to her. Never to her. Between them there were only the lustful urges that neither had been able to deny. If she felt a heaviness of heart at the thought, she assured herself it was only temporary.

At least she would let him know the woman he was fooling with; grabbing up the jacket he'd bought her in Peoria, she joined him by the fire.

Cort turned the thin slab of bacon frying in the pan, well aware of every movement Rella made. Purposefully he had allowed her to gather her thoughts, to determine just how she wanted to face him. A great deal had passed between them last night, everything they'd sworn to resist. Even with his back to her, he felt the air crackle with the tension that hung between them. His anger was directed inward. She was in his care; he ought to be able to find another way to subdue her than the methods he'd used last night, but somehow he couldn't summon real regrets for what had happened. And he didn't care to speculate whether it would happen again.

What would Rella expect him to do, apologize for tackling her? Thank her for how she'd met his demands with equally passionate demands of her own?

The thoughts surprised him and were followed by the realization of what he would like to do—take her in his arms, kiss her good morning, and tell her that last night had been better for him than with any other woman. He would ask if she was all right. He would tell her about himself, about his past, about his dreams. Hell, he might even talk about how a woman could be a part of those dreams. The right woman.

Cort shook off the thoughts. When it came to showing his feelings, he was no freer than Rella to express himself. He didn't like himself very much this morning. Didn't like what he had to do. She'd once accused him of being too close to the murder and robbery since it was his money that was gone. He was too close to the case, all right, but the money was the least of his concerns.

Pouring another cup of coffee, he held it out to her as she knelt beside him. She'd tied her hair back with the bandanna, giving her a little-girl appearance that was in its way as endearing as the fiery woman's look she had presented last night.

Rella took the drink as casually as though he served her every morning. "I really am a Gypsy," she said, her eyes flashing with pride.

Cort looked at her in surprise. The woman had a way with her, that was for sure, a habit of doing and saying the unexpected that threw him constantly off guard.

"At least I have Gypsy blood in my veins," she added, giving him no chance to respond. Her gaze was now trained on the campfire. "My mother's mother was a full-blooded Romany. She married an English earl, but unfortunately his family didn't approve."

"Why are you telling me this?"

She lifted her eyes to look at him straight on. "You seem inordinately interested in Gypsies. In the way of most gorgios. My grandmother was considered worthy only to take to bed, not to take to wife. The marriage, performed according to the Gypsy ways, was not recognized, and my less than noble grandfather went back to the protective folds of his family, leaving a disgraced woman with a baby on the way. Through the years Esmeralda won back the respect of her people. My mother was raised as a Gypsy. She taught me their ways."

How proud she looked as she held his gaze, and Cort found himself admiring her. "Is that why you went back for Sandor and risked arrest again? Because he was a Gypsy?"

"I went back because he was a friend. Except for him and Alepa, even the Gypsies didn't welcome me. They are very much like the earl's family—a closed society. Most of them could not overlook my gorgio blood. Except, of course, when I was earning money in that fortune-telling tent."

"You seem to have a way with gorgio jails," Cort said. "Just how did you manage to free Sandor?"

Rella reached for the plate of bacon and bread that Cort had prepared for her, careful to keep her hand from touching his. "One just has to know what a lawman is after. The captain settled for all the money I had managed to save." Her voice turned sharp. "Do you plan to add bribery to my list of crimes?"

Cort rose to his feet in frustration. "Rella, this situation is as uncomfortable for me as it is for you."

"I doubt that."

She stared into the dying fire, her delicate profile turned to him. He longed to reach down and lift her into his arms. With her hair tied back like a child's and her slender body bent away from him, she looked vulnerable and needful of consolation—no matter what charges had been brought against her.

"The first time I saw you," he said quietly, "I thought you looked lonely and isolated. I still do."

Rella stood to face him, hands white knuckled against the edge of her plate, and answered his soft words with prideful scorn. "Poor lonely little murderess, am I? Was that why you kissed me not twenty feet from where Perry's body was found? Was that the reason for last night? Or are you only using such an absurd assumption to justify all that you've done?"

"If you think I plan what happens between us, you don't know me very well."

Her gaze locked with his. "No more than you know me."

She turned her back on him and did her best to swallow the food, but it went down dry. She heard him head for the horses, his booted feet hitting the ground hard and quick. Sighing, she thought about how hard she had tried to get through the morning without acrimony, and how much she had failed. The only consolation she could draw was that at least those awkward moments were past.

Hastily finishing the meal and turning her attentions to breaking camp, she wondered how many more such occasions there might be. She could swear that she would never go into his arms again—she'd made such vows before—but she knew how little they meant.

Her worries proved unnecessary. On the ensuing two nights as they made their way southeast toward St. Louis, Cort made no overtures to lovemaking, and Rella assured herself she was glad. Nor did he give her an opportunity to escape. The handcuffs he'd so often brandished threateningly were placed firmly on her wrists each night, and he was always by her side during the day.

At the steamboat office in the bustling Mississippi River city of St. Louis, they were told they had missed a New Orleans bound vessel by only one day. With Rella kept close by his side, Cort left their horses and rigs at a stable near the docks and took her to a stagecoach office where he made arrangements for a journey across southern Missouri. If everything went accordingly to plan, he assured her, they could catch up with the riverboat at Cape Girardeau.

Another trip to a public bath—this one wonderfully welcome after days on the trail—and Rella was once more in her blue dress, the boys' garb tucked into the portmanteau along with her Gypsy skirt and blouse. And Alepa's knife. Cort still didn't know it was there, or that she knew how to use it.

She sensed something different about him as they headed toward an eating establishment near the stage office—something intense, unusually alert, an awareness of his environment . . . or maybe an anticipation of the journey waiting them. Was he that eager to get to Galveston? That eager to get her off his hands?

They found a back table in the large cafe. After their order had been given, she leaned forward in her chair and put her question to him without embellishment. "Getting eager for the trip to end? We could have awaited for another steamboat."

Cort looked at her thoughtfully, wondered how much he ought to say, and found he wanted to tell her what had excited his mind ever since they'd crossed the Mississippi.

"Missouri is home," he said simply. "We'll be going near the farm where I was born and raised. One of the overnight stops is in the town where I went to school. Startzville, it's called. My father and I used to bring our crops there before the war."

Cort a country boy? She would never have guessed it. And yet as she gave thought to the idea, it seemed perhaps not so preposterous after all. No matter where she'd observed him—in a city or out on the trail—he seemed to know what he was doing. Her heart warmed at the image of a carrot-topped lad riding beside his father along a country road.

"Where are your parents now?"

"My mother died from the fever when I was twelve. I hardly remember her."

"And your father?"

As soon as she'd asked the question, Rella sensed that his mood had changed. Gone was the gentle nostalgia that had overtaken him; in its place was the hard edge that she recognized only too well.

"My father was killed while I was fighting Rebs." Whatever anguish he was feeling lay hidden beneath his short, clipped words. "Night marauders," he said, continuing without pause. "They still ravage the countryside. These particular bastards were never brought to trial."

Rella let out a long breath. "And you became a lawman."

"That's right."

"And eventually came to Texas. Ready to fight for the cause of justice." If her tone was ironic, he chose to ignore it, and Rella grew silent as their food was delivered. When the waiter departed, she took up her spoken thoughts. "Ready to apprehend all those who break the law."

"I've never pretended to be anything other than myself."

"Meaning I have, of course." She looked past him, directing her words to the empty air. "Please save me from zealots with a cause."

Cort gave no answer. The chasm between them widened. There was nothing he could say that would explain his behavior, any more than he could understand what had driven her to that terrible crime. For driven she must have been. If she were guilty. . . . He'd been eaten with nagging doubts since Chicago, and she'd insisted on her innocence for so long. But then she was part Gypsy, and traveling woman, too, determined to be free.

They ate their meal in silence, as far apart as two people could be who sat so close together, then made their way along the busy walkway toward the stage. The coach was crowded as they left St. Louis, but on the journey south across the lush Mississippi Valley, several of the passengers departed. By the time the stagecoach arrived in Startzville late in the evening of the second day, there remained aboard only Rella, Cort, and a grandfatherly man who smiled beatifically at them as though blessing their union, a coupling that existed only in his mind. Somehow, when Cort made brief introductions, the man had gotten the idea they were betrothed, and she hadn't bothered to correct him.

William Matthews was his name—Will to his friends, and he'd insisted they call him Will. Pale, merry eyes rested in a laughter-crinkled face. He wore a vested brown suit, and a watch chain rested across his ample belly. Like them, he was headed for Cape Girardeau, only in his case the journey was a joyous one; on a small farm outside the river town a new grandson awaited. Rella wondered how friendly Will, positive as he was that he faced a loving young couple, would have reacted to the truth about his fellow travelers.

If Rella had entertained hopes of getting away from Cort at Startzville, he quickly dimmed them. The small inn used by the stage riders for their overnight stop had one particular feature that he admired. The upstairs room he picked for his prisoner had a single, sturdy door and an even sturdier lock. The lone window was high and narrow; far below it was a hedge of thorn bushes. Even Rella could see her chances of escape were nil.

She chose to have supper in her room. When Cort was relatively certain she had retired for the night—with Rella he could never be absolutely sure of anything—he headed for Startzville's only saloon. Not that he planned on serious drinking, but a whiskey surely would taste good after days on the road.

Inside The Saloon—Startzville residents were not given to fancy names—he could imagine he'd never left. Here were the same scarred tables and chairs, the same small bar at the side, and even the same buxom, gray-haired woman serving up drinks.

"Cort Ramsey!" she called out in greeting. "As I live and breathe. What brings you back here? Thought we'd seen the last of you after your old man got killed."

Folks in Startzville also didn't put soft names to hard facts. Cort appreciated the direct approach, and he reached out to shake the woman's hand.

"Katie Flynn, you're still the prettiest girl in town."

Katie laughed. "The prettiest one in the saloon, you mean. And the only one." She poured him a whiskey without his asking. "Now drink that down and answer my question, boy. What brings you back? You're not wearing a badge, I see. Quit the law?"

"You're just as sharp-eyed as ever. Let's just say I misplaced my badge, but the law is still my trade. Just traveling through. I'll be catching the stage tomorrow."

"Speaking of catching, hasn't some gal caught up with you yet?"

Cort pushed thoughts of Rella from his mind. "I'm holding out for you, Katie. Just say when."

"Seems to me you're a might quick with that answer. You sure there ain't someone waiting for you to say the right words? Can't imagine any woman taking a good look at you and not wanting what she was seeing."

"I'm *damned* sure," Cort said more emphatically than he had intended; then added in a lighter tone, "As I said, I'm waiting for you."

Katie studied him for a moment, then shrugged. "I always said there was Irish blood in your veins. Still as full of blarney as you ever were." She poured Cort another whiskey. "At least the way you were before the war. Lots of folks came out of that ugliness different. We may not have had any battles here in Missouri, but there's still hard feelings."

"We'll be paying a high price for that conflict a long time," Cort said in agreement. "I can see the deep resentments everywhere I go in Texas. They look on me as a Yankee down there."

"Truth to tell, you are here, at least by some. Never did forgive you for taking up arms with the Federals."

"Josiah never owned slaves in his life. Joining up seemed the thing to do."

"You never did know when to run away from a fight. That temper of yours, no doubt. The ones that stayed behind, they sided with that bastard Quantrill. Even after he and his killers ran down all those folks in Lawrence, Kansas, they made excuses for him. The Union boys didn't help matters any, raiding the away they did and taking folks' food and stock. It's easy to see why people around here haven't forgotten."

"They're going to have to someday."

"Guess they will, but not right away. Couldn't if they wanted to, not with those no-good outlaws still terrorizing this part of the state. Of course I don't have to tell you about them. With your pa and all."

Cort downed the small glass and let the whiskey's warmth spread through him. "No, you don't have to tell me about them. Still having trouble?"

Katie shrugged. "It comes and goes. So many men come out of the war hard and mean. Kansas, Missouri, Illinois—they get around. Keeps old Sheriff Alcorn busy. Must eat at you that no one ever did catch the murderers that got your pa."

"I try not to think about it too much. I've taken my share of bastards to the noose. Maybe it all balances out. Somewhere some sheriff or marshal has done the same with those men."

"Maybe." Katie hesitated, wiping the bar slowly with a rag. "Don't know as to whether I should mention it or not, but there's rumors that some of the gang that killed Josiah have been operating around here lately."

Cort felt a knot in his gut. "Anybody got proof?"

"Just talk as far as I know." She lifted the bottle, then replaced it on the bar when Cort shook his head. "But whoever they are, they're causin' lots of trouble right now. That's why the stage is leavin' before daylight tomorrow. So's it can get by a spot that's become notorious for being robbed. Seth over at the stage office says things have been quiet lately, but he isn't takin' any chances if he don't have to."

Cort knew all hope for relaxing was gone. Half listening to Katie's talk about old neighbors and friends, he could concentrate on only one thing. Somewhere in the hills of southern Missouri lurked a band of robbers preying on the people; among those bastards just might be the killer of his father.

But there were too many somewheres and maybes. And he had responsibilities to a woman back at the inn. Already a plan formed in his mind. He'd been thinking lately of quitting the law, of settling down on a place of his own, of— He brushed all thoughts of a woman from his mind. One thing at a time. And that one thing was not farming now. Someday he would have to come back to Missouri and take care of the job he'd been unable to finish six years before.

Bidding Katie farewell, he walked slowly down the main street of the town and took time to look around. He'd spent the greater part of his life in this country; but the place seemed no more like home than anywhere else he'd traveled, and the old restlessness ate at him.

He climbed the stairs of the inn and stopped before Rella's door. The key was heavy in his pocket. He ought to check on her, make sure she was all right, make sure she was still there. Hell, the truth was he wanted to see her. She'd gotten into his blood, no matter who or what she was, and no amount of whiskey would take her place.

Even when he hadn't held her in his arms, she'd been near him every night since the Chicago fire. His room was down the hall—not close enough to suit him, too close to let him forget she was near. Rella was a habit he better not get too used to. Even as he warned himself away from her, he realized the words came too late.

Rella heard the key turning in the lock. She'd been lying awake in the dark wondering where Cort was, wondering if he was having a drink and a laugh, maybe meeting some woman from the past in that saloon.

"I'm still here," she said softly, directing her words to the broad-shouldered silhouette standing in the open doorway. The light from the hall behind him cast a shadow across his face, but she could tell by the way he stood, or the slant of his head, or maybe the sound of his shallow breathing, that something was wrong. With all of the differences between them, and with all of their talk to the contrary, she was getting to know Cort Ramsey very well.

He stood silent, then said, "Decided to take advantage of a soft mattress, did you, and hang around? After those nights on the trail."

Oh, the mattress was soft, all right, but the solitude she thought would be welcome, the chance to be away from him for a while, had turned into a lost feeling that was closely akin to loneliness. She'd been giving a lot of thought to the irony of her plight.

"Those nights weren't so bad," she whispered into the dark. "Even the handcuffs." At least, she thought, she hadn't been alone. But the words wouldn't form on her lips.

"Would you feel better if you had them on now?"

Against all logic, Rella knew that at this moment there was only one thing that would make her feel better—to lie in Cort's arms. The handcuff hold, he'd called it back on the steamboat. How surprised he would be if she offered herself to him now.

"I guess not," she said, then hesitated. "What's bothering you, Cort? Don't lie. I know something is." Leaning over, she struck a match and lit the bedside light, then turned back to look into his face. Beneath the covers her chemise-clad body rested still and warm and wanting.

Cort stepped into the room and closed the door behind him. "It's just tough to come home again. Especially when I realize it isn't really home anymore. And then all the troubles about my father's death came back. Hints that maybe the killer was still nearby. Fool's talk, maybe, but it can destroy a man's peace of mind."

Rella sat up, unmindful that the covers came only to her waist. Cort seemed not to notice that her underclothing barely covered her breasts. "Then stay awhile. There's no need for either of us to be alone if we don't want to."

"You're right. If we don't want to."

The tenderness in his voice warmed her heart. During the past hour, alone in her bed, she had done a lot of thinking about Cort's past. Much had fallen into place: his sense of duty, his strong feelings of right and wrong. What she had once taken for arrogance had really been a sense of purpose. He'd made a terrible mistake about her, one that he had to realize, but she couldn't think of her own troubles now.

Rella knew exactly what she wanted to do. Practical, independent woman that she was, she knew that neither of them should be alone tonight.

She folded the covers aside and stood, her bare feet against a rag rug, black curls of hair resting loosely against almost bare shoulders, the light at her back outlining her slender body through the thin underclothes. Cort caught his breath.

"Don't try to figure out if I'm up to something," she said, her gaze locked with his. "We once said we didn't really know each other. That's no longer true, at least in one case. You're not the man I thought you were back in Galveston. I've learned I was wrong about you, Cort. And you have been wrong about me. I told you I was part Gypsy. That's the side of me you've made love to, the side that's on the edge of wildness."

He took a step closer, but she stopped him with a raised hand. "But there's a lot more to me than that. I can be tender and gentle, the way any woman can, and practical, too. There's a lot more Cinderella in me than there is Romany. I don't have to be forced into making love, or taken unawares. I know that about myself, even though I've never given myself to another man."

Slowly her fingers worked at the ribbons of her

chemise. She pulled the undergarment from her body to reveal breasts already swollen and hard-tipped, waiting for the touch of his hands and mouth. The petticoat soon joined the chemise on the rag rug at her feet, and she stood before him naked and unashamed.

Moving slowly toward her, Cort removed his gun and wrapped the belt around the holster. As he laid the bundle on a table, his eyes roved the fullness of her breasts, her narrow waist and gentle curve of her hips, and the fine, dark down between her thighs. Her legs were long and slender and gracefully curved. His body hardened. Rella was beautiful, a creature of wonder and surprise, full of promise and mystery that encircled him with tender tentacles he could not, would not break.

She reached out and brushed a lock of hair from his forehead. Catching her hand in his, he pressed a warm kiss against her wrist. Her pulse pounded under his lips. Her fingers stroked his bristled cheek. He drew her against him and kissed her hair, the delicate spot behind her ear, the corner of her eye that crinkled so delightfully when she laughed. At last he brushed a feather kiss against her lips and felt her tremble in his arms.

The texture of Cort's leather vest felt pleasurable against her skin, and she rubbed the tips of her breasts across its softness. Her fingers cut into his shoulders. Desire spread like wine in her veins.

"Rella," he whispered huskily, his breath mingling with hers. She treasured the sound of her name on his lips.

Her hands slipped beneath the vest to press against his shirt and feel the finely sinewed wall of his chest. "I'm not very good at undressing you," she said shakily. "I may need some help."

His lips curved into a smile. "Practice is what you need. But I don't think I can wait for you right now."

She caught her breath, her fingers moving inexorably across his taut muscles and around the flat nipples she could feel beneath the rough-textured shirt.

He laughed raggedly. "Keep that up and I know I can't."

She slipped her hands behind his back and drew him tight against her. His embrace grew stronger as he kissed her once again, this time deeper, this time with tongue and lips, invading her mouth and tasting the dark warmth she offered with an almost desperate eagerness. Insistent hands drifted low on her back, gripped her buttocks, and held her hard against his arousal. Rella drowned in a bath of fiery need.

Cort raised his head. Even in the dim light from the bedside lamp, she could read the raw desire in his eyes. His hands moved caressingly, tauntingly against her hips; in answer she thrust her body against him, feeling the hard tumescence of his need pressing between her thighs.

With a low cry, he claimed one last, lingering kiss, then lifted her in his arms and placed her lovingly on the bed. She watched with avid eyes his undressing, and followed those wonderful hands as they tossed aside vest and shirt, then stripped the trousers from his muscled legs. Sometime he must have removed his boots, for he was completely naked when he lay beside her. But her attention was caught by the size and wonder of him, the power of his man's body, a glorious, ultimate work of nature. The miracle was that such a magnificence should fit so well within her own slender frame without rending her in two.

As he nestled an arm beneath her shoulders, his free hand caressed her face, his thumb brushing across her open lips. With long, sure strokes, Rella explored the length of his body, learned to read the flare of pleasure in his eyes, and reveled in the catch of his breath when she touched him in vulnerable spots: the distended nipples, the lean buttocks, and especially the taut muscles of his inner thigh.

Cort cupped her hand in his and showed her the rapture that a woman could bring to a man. He was huge and pulsating beneath her massaging fingers. His skin was pulled tight, smooth and slick, and she longed to enfold it within her body, to make them one, to make her complete.

Holding her close, he gave her the same pleasure, his hand stroking her breasts and hips, teasing her inner thighs, and at last working its incredible magic on the folds and crevices of her womanhood.

"I want to be inside you," he whispered, then parted her legs with his thigh and laid his body on top of hers, pressing her down into the soft bed with the weight of his flesh.

He covered her mouth with his own as their bodies joined. In wordless response, she embraced him with her arms and legs, holding on tightly, returning the slow, even movements of his hips and thighs.

With a deep sigh Cort quickened his thrusts, faster and faster. The mystery of womanhood was his to know; the wonder of Rella with the enflaming gentleness she offered him tonight, her soft yet untamed passion was his to claim. His mind was filled with fragmented images of her flesh pressed against his. Wrapped in her embrace, he was possessed by her, heart and soul.

Rella felt the same electric thrills of their previous moments together, only this time she knew that the two of them were truly joined as one. Her glory was as boundless as her desire; she clung to him in rapturous surrender as he took her with him to the edge of ecstasy and beyond.

Her head reeling, Rella held his body tightly against her, clinging to the solid strength he offered her, protecting herself against the words that were sure to come. Gradually her heartbeat slowed, and she felt the ragged whisper of his breath against her cheek dissolve to a moderate cadence.

In the afterglow of spent passion, Cort lifted his head and stared down into velvet eyes that were deep and sated.

He opened his mouth to speak, but Rella placed a finger against his lips. As little as she knew of love, she sensed that anything he might say now, any words of affection that he might feel compelled to utter would be more the result of passion than of thought. He had been troubled, and he had come to her. Somehow his needing her had made them equals . . . for the first time since they had met.

For Rella this night had been of far greater import. Alepa had once said that eventually she would know how much she needed Cort. That time was now. She loved him, loved the determination, the dedication, the stubbornness of him. And more, she loved the gentleness, the vulnerability she'd felt when he first came into the room. He might not realize it yet, but in ways more than physical, he needed her as much as she needed him. Every instinct told her she was right; if only he realized the truth of that need before it was too late.

She looked deep into his eyes. "I want you to listen to me, Cort. My timing may be off. It usually is around you."

"Rella—"

"Please. Something in me would die if you believed that what I am about say is because of what we just shared. That I lured you into some passionate state where you couldn't tell truth from lie. I didn't plan tonight. But I couldn't turn from it, either."

She blinked once, drew a deep breath, and spoke slowly, giving each word the emphasis it deserved. "I didn't kill Perry Tuttle. I didn't steal the money from the safe. I ran because I suddenly found escape ridiculously simple . . . and defending myself against you incredibly hard."

She pulled free of his embrace to lie beside him. "I've said what I had to say. I'll understand if you want to leave." Her eyes flashed with spirit. "Just don't say anything to me now that you don't feel in your heart. I'll know it's a lie."

Cort had no intention of saying other than the truth. He reached out and stroked her tangled hair, pulling the sweat-dampened strands away from her face.

"We're a fine match, aren't we, Rella? Me the righteous lawman and you my prisoner. God knows it's hard enough to sort out the truth in this world. It's apparent I haven't done a very good job."

Her heart quickened. "Does that mean—"

"It means I believe you." He drew her once more into his arms. "I can't think right now beyond that. Too many coils go along with that belief."

She held back the joy that welled within her. "So what happens tomorrow? At least tell me that."

"We keep on south. You'll just have to trust me, Rella, to keep you from harm."

As usual, Cort proved to be a man of his word. Early the next morning, portmanteau in hand, Rella found herself at the stagecoach office with him close by her side. Dressed in her blue dress with her hair tied neatly back in a bun, she looked very much like the woman who had arrived in Startzville yesterday evening. Only the reassuring looks she got from Cort told her anything had changed.

Seth, the driver, explained they would have to wait for a passenger who had already paid his fare but who hadn't yet made an appearance. "Came into town last week and plunked down the fare. Curly haired fellow with a mean look about him, but his money was good. Company don't like makin' refunds," he explained laconically, "and we was trying to get away ahead of schedule. We'll have to hold up a bit."

When they departed an hour later, the passenger still had not shown up; only Rella, Cort, and the grandfather Will were aboard. Seth had one man riding shotgun beside him.

Rella settled back to make herself as comfortable as possible on the hard seat and stared out the window. Thick groves of oak and hackberry lined part of the trail; in other parts the grass-covered land stretched out in rolling hills. Sensing Cort watching her, she said, "Pretty country. You don't think you'll return someday?"

"It's not likely. I've bought a place in Texas. Been thinking lately of settling down there."

Rella's heart quickened, but she rushed on, not waiting for the awkward silence that would tell her she was not part of his plans.

"A farmer again?"

"That's right. There's forests there, too, for lumber. Ought to make a good home."

Across from them, Will Matthew stared perplexedly. Rella knew exactly what he was thinking. For a fiancée, she certainly didn't know much about the plans of her husband-to-be. Nodding to Cort, she closed her eyes and took refuge in pretended rest.

When the stagecoach was about ten miles south of town, disaster struck. They were on a winding section of the narrow road that crossed the low Missouri hills, both Rella and Will rocked into sleep by the undulating motion of the coach. Trees grew close, and boulders blocked what view might remain. Cort sat next to the open window, choked back the dust, and kept unwavering eyes on the passing scene. His fingers rested on his thigh, close to his gun. He was ready for trouble . . . but he had no way of stopping what happened when the stage slowed to round a sharp bend.

A rifle shot split the peaceful morning, and then in quick succession another and another. Seth yelled out one word—"Robbers!"—and the man who was riding shotgun beside him answered with a crack from his own weapon.

"Get down," Cort ordered Rella and Will as they were jerked into wakefulness. The stage picked up dangerous speed; a body fell to the ground outside the coach. Cort barely had time to realize it was the man Seth had hired.

Rage and frustration warred within Cort as he shifted to the other window. The coach careened wildly. More shots, the terrified whinnying of the horses, and the coach dipped crazily to one side, bounced, then with Cort reaching out to support Rella came to a sharp halt, resting at an angle in a deep ditch at the side of the road. The team of horses thrashed wildly for a moment, then continued to stamp their feet nervously.

Thrown against the down side of the coach, Rella stared up at Cort from a tangle of arms, legs, and blue cotton. "I'm all right," she said hastily. "What happened?"

"See about him," Cort ordered, gesturing toward

Will, who lay with eyes closed, chest heaving irregularly.

Gun in hand, Cort took off his hat and cautiously raised his head through the window to venture a quick look around. From a clump of brush on the opposite side of the road came gunfire. It echoed loudly over his head. Ducking, he heard answering fire from the front of the coach, more shots from the road, then the cry of a man who'd been hit. Seth's cry. The sound burned into his mind.

Cort heard the beat of hoofs against the dirt road. "Come on out of there," yelled a gruff voice. "Throw out your weapons first." Helpless rage washed over Cort; he had no choice but to do as he was ordered—not with Rella and the old man under his charge.

"Follow my lead," he mouthed to Rella, and wide-eyed, she nodded. "I've got some hurt people in here," he called out, throwing his gun through the portal over his head.

"Out!"

Cort reached for the handle of the door and heaved it open. Nodding encouragement to Rella, he maneuvered Will to an awkward stance. The old man stirred, then came awake. "Trouble," Cort told him. Will didn't need to be told more. "Hold on," Cort said, wrapping an arm around him.

"I can take care of myself," Will said proudly, and proved it by heaving his portly body through the open door and climbing out to sit shakily on the tilted side of the stage, his bottom protruding through the window.

Cort followed, then reached back to lift Rella by her arms into the nightmare that awaited them on the road. He set her down close to Will. Somehow the heel of her shoe had disappeared, and the sole had been torn loose; when she attempted to walk, it dragged in the roadside gravel. Three men on horseback, hats pulled low, their faces half covered by kerchiefs, watched as he lifted her back in his arms.

Without seeming to, Cort took in the details. Two of the bandits with the slender bodies of youth rested insolently in their saddles, rifles sheathed, revolvers in hand; one of them wore his pale hair long and greasy, the other showed no more than a few dark curls against the back of his neck. The latter's eyes stared down at the passengers with mingled hate and scorn, reminding Cort of the mean-looking stranger Seth said booked passage on the stage. The early departure had been delayed, and they'd ridden into a trap.

Cort turned his attention to the third gunman, who gripped gloved fingers around his thigh, the trousers torn and stained dark red with blood. Seth lay still in the road close to the carriage. The subdued team of horses, traces tangled, bent passive heads to the grass at the side of the road.

The stage was only half on its side, the ditch having a steep incline on the side close to the trees. He noticed all this as he settled Rella at the edge of the road, then turned to face the robbers, his body between them and her. He looked past the two young men to the wounded rider. Cold black eyes stared at him. Cort noted the blood and hoped the robber had been mortally wounded. But he continued to sit erect in the saddle.

"We'll take your valuables," the man said, identifying himself as the leader. The pale-haired young man—Blondie, Cort had mentally tagged him—dropped to the ground and began to search the coach, throwing the contents of the passengers' baggage over his shoulder as he progressed. The bandit Cort labeled Mean Eyes took the money from Cort and Will, then headed for Rella.

"She doesn't have any jewelry or money," Cort said. "She's with me."

"She's got valuables, all right," Blondie said flatly from his position by the coach.

"Sure does," Mean Eyes agreed.

Somehow Blondie's cold assessment was more chilling than the insinuating voice of Mean Eyes, and Cort thought of the gun he'd tossed from the coach, wondering where it had landed. Better to have gone down shooting than let anything happen to her. He might have taken one or two.

The leader swayed in the saddle. He'd lost a lot of blood, but there was a trail-hardened wariness in his eyes that told Cort he would still be dangerous.

"No gold," Blondie reported after finishing a hurried search. "You don't look so good, boss."

The leader blinked once, close to passing out; but he was mean enough to rally, and he gestured toward Rella.

"Don't feel so good, neither. Not sure I can make much time, and someone'll be coming along pretty soon. Only chance we got is to take a hostage." His eyes flared briefly in triumph at Cort. "The woman ain't with you anymore. She's coming with me."

Chapter Sixteen

Cort swallowed the bitter bile of fury and put his mind to work. Flying at the man as he wanted to do would only get him killed, a point he wasn't much worried about right now, except that his death wouldn't do Rella any good.

"See here," Will muttered behind him, and Cort gestured impatiently for him to be quiet.

"Get up, woman," Mean Eyes ordered.

"She can't," said Cort. "She got hurt in the accident." Mentally he directed a message to Rella, praying she wouldn't do something stupid that she mistook for bravery.

"It's my ankle," she said in a fluttery, helpless way as she waved toward her damaged shoe. For once he was grateful she'd learned her acting craft well.

"I could try to stand if you want—" she sighed helplessly—"but I don't imagine I'd get very far."

Cort kept his attention turned on the wounded leader. Was he buying her invalid state? It was hard to tell when all that were visible were those narrow, dark eyes that shifted so rapidly back and forth.

"Listen, Slade—" Blondie stopped at the warning

look.

"Shut up, fool." Slade's voice was harsh, but Cort thought he detected a weakening that wasn't there before. The red stain on his trousers leg continued to spread. "Let me have your kerchief," he said. "Got to have a tourniquet of some kind."

The dark cloth was reluctantly removed, revealing the cold, sallow face of a young man not much out of his teens. No way had he been around six years ago. He bound the kerchief tightly around Slade's upper thigh, then stood back, awaiting orders.

"The old man's ticker'd probably give out." The leader's gaze shifted to Cort. "Looks like it'll be you. Search him," he barked at Mean Eyes. "Make sure he's not packing iron somewhere that don't show."

The papers identifying him as marshal rested inside his vest, but there was nothing that Cort could to to hide them. He wondered if the bandits might be illiterate. Half of the desperadoes that Cort had arrested were.

His luck continued to be bad.

"Looky here," Mean Eyes said, pulling out the papers and giving them a quick glance. He waved the documents in the air. "Unless he stole these somewheres, it looks like we got us a U.S. marshal." His black button eyes reflected a grin Cort imagined on his face, and he glanced back at Slade. "And the little lady he's got with him must be the prisoner he's supposed to have. Cinderella something. Can't make out the last name."

Cort knew that beneath the protective bandanna, wily old Slade was grinning, too.

"Where's your badge, Marshal?" Slade asked sneeringly. "Traveling incogneeto?" He dragged every syllable of the word.

Cort shrugged. "No need to advertise. Looks like

you found me out."

"And me, too," Rella sighed from behind him. "Not that I'm not injured, but the mean old marshal insists I've done something dreadful. Which I haven't."

"Maybe we ought to take a look at the lady's leg," Slade said.

"Maybe we better," Blondie agreed, his passive expression broken by a leer.

"And maybe you better start thinking before you pass out," Cort warned Slade. "You want a hostage, but what lawman is going to stay clear of you when your only prisoner is a murderer and a thief? If you harmed her, all you'd be doing is saving the state of Texas the cost of a trial. That innocent looking 'lady' as you called her poisoned the gentlest man in Galveston for a gold watch."

"I did not!"

Shut up, Rella, Cort thought. *Let me handle this.*

"Take me," Will piped up. "Nobody's trying to put me in jail."

Slade shook his head in disgust. "Damndest bunch I've ever seen. Everybody wants to be a hero. We'll take the marshal. What's his name?"

Mean Eyes glanced down at the papers. "Ramsey, it says here."

"Tie Marshal Ramsey's hands behind him and give him your horse. You can ride with me. Don't know how long I'll stay awake."

Cort allowed himself one warning look at Rella. Huddled at the side of the road, she looked close to panic. But she fought it and kept her head. The toughness that she'd so often demonstrated in her battles against him was helping her now. The trouble was, she had too much toughness. There was something in her eyes that said she would go with him—

or in his place, if she could manage. Under his quick glare, she seemed to settle down, but with Rella, he could never be sure.

There was nothing he could do but let Blondie bind his arms behind him. The rope cut cruelly into his wrists. Awkwardly he mounted, boosted from behind by the boy who then scooped up Cort's gun and shoved it into his own waistband.

Slade ordered the second young man, the curly-headed Mean Eyes, to mount and take the reins of Cort's horse, then lead out. He glanced at Will. "Tell that sheriff not to come after us. The marshal is dead if he does."

No sooner were they out of sight around the bend of the road than Rella was on her feet, hissing to Will that they had to do something to rescue Cort. She might have controlled her panic while guns had been trained on them, but now she felt the full force of the situation. A sick feeling grew in the pit of her stomach, and she fought against the horrible images that forced their way into her mind. She hadn't given in to womanly vapors before, and she refused to start now.

She knew exactly what Cort had been doing when he made up that story about her ankle. He'd sacrificed his freedom for her, and by God she would see that he got it back.

"Settle down, Miss Sandringham," Will said, still the courtly gentleman. "There's no way the two of us on foot can do what must be done. We need professional help."

He knelt beside the still body of the stage driver Seth and bent his head to the man's chest. Rella, her shoe dragging in the dirt, headed for the front of the stage.

"What you doing?" Will asked.

"I'm going to try to untangle these horses and ride after Cort."

"A brave but foolish gesture, my dear. In the first place you can't ride far bareback if you're not used to it, and we have neither bridle nor saddle—not even a blanket."

"I can manage that if I have to. I've got to get started so I'll have some idea about where they've taken him."

Will removed his coat and placed it under the driver's head. "Have you ever tried to track anyone on horseback? It takes a skill I daresay you don't have. You don't even know this country."

"We're wasting time talking," said Rella, turning her back to stroke one of the drays. A trembling of her hand gave lone testimony to her distress as she said flatly, "I have to do something to save him."

"I know how anxious you are, but more than likely you would just get yourself and the marshal killed, even if you could find and keep up with them until you learned the lay of the land. Which you couldn't do anyway. Let me help you."

Rella didn't say anything. She was busy fighting a hopeless frustration the man's words had brought.

"He is a marshal, isn't he, and you his prisoner?"

Rella nodded, waiting for the man's censure. Instead, he bent to peer into Seth's face, then pulled a handkerchief from his pocket.

"He isn't dead, as I at first feared," Will announced with relief. "The bullet went cleanly through. And I detect a faint heartbeat, but he's lost a lot of blood."

He placed the cloth against Seth's bloodied shoulder, then looked around for something in the scattered contents of the luggage to bind it. Rella breathed deeply, then picked up a shirt to hand to him. They worked together in silence, quickly and efficiently despite her trembling hands. When Will tied the last knot, Rella said, "You're right, of course. I couldn't rescue him alone. And just to set the record straight, I may be his prisoner, but I didn't poison any kindly old man. Cort made that up."

"No need to explain. I figured he did. Somehow you don't have the look of a killer about you, my dear."

Rella waited for a question about the charges that really were leveled against her, but again Will proved decidedly understanding as he added, "Now, if we're to do anything about those robbers, and your young man, we've got to get this stage upright."

Rella cast a doubtful look at the angled coach. "Is that possible?"

"We have no choice. This is a lonely part of the country along here. We might have to wait awhile for help. See if there's rope in that stagecoach somewhere. I'll do what I can about the horses."

In a rush of gratitude toward him, Rella hurried to the boot on the rear, already opened by the highwaymen. Finding a coil of rope, she tossed it onto the ground before going to help with the horses. After untangling the lines, he unhitched the calmest animal, leaving the harness in place on both.

Next he turned his attention to the rope Rella had found. For a corpulent man, he demonstrated himself to be quite agile as he kneeled at the front of the overturned coach and tied one end of the rope firmly around the raised end of the forward axle.

"That ought to hold," he said, trailing the rope to the far side of the road. He selected a sturdy tree some distance in front of the horses and wrapped the rope once around the trunk, then spent some time tying the end to the harness still on the loose horse.

"Now," he said, "if my engineering skills are what they're supposed to be, we need only one more item and we're in business."

Rella followed him back across the road and stared doubtfully at the stage wheels sticking in the air.

"Good thing the ditch is as steep as it is. Kept the coach from turning completely on its side," said Will. "Now look around for a sturdy log. Big enough not to snap in two when a little weight is put on it, but not so big we can't start to wedge it under the up side of the stage. If it falls too hard, there's a good chance of breaking a wheel or axle or both. Just hope one of the off wheels isn't broken. I'm no wheelwright."

Rella was beginning to see the man's plan, and she scurried to her appointed task. She had learned to manage the flapping sole and didn't let the awkward gait it caused bother her. In keeping the robbers from taking her, it had done its part to bring about the present situation. She decided it was the little things that controlled most situations in life.

She looked for the log that Will wanted, but luck wasn't with them; nothing that could be used as a wedge was lying in the proximity of the ambush scene.

"Probably too heavy for us to angle it right, anyway, to pull it gradually and let the thing down easy," said Will. "We'll just have to pull her over and hope the fall doesn't break anything. Stand by the horse that's still attached and keep him calm. He could still crack something vital on that coach if he stamps around.

"Better yet," he added when Rella started toward

the horse, "put a blinder on the brute."

She picked up another garment from the emptied luggage and put it over the horse's eyes, talking soothingly, trying not to show her own impatience and panic.

Will had gone to the horse tied to the rope. "Now, slowly, slowly," he crooned to the animal, urging him to move forward toward the stage. Rella watched the rope tauten around the tree.

The coach gave a moan of protest as it inched away from its resting place in the ditch, then settled back again. Will encouraged the straining animal with a tug on the bit and the rope tightened again.

"A little more," he said, and the horse responded as though he understood.

With a lurch the stage came to an almost upright position at the edge of the road, then fell downward with a crash and clatter and great bouncing of its springs. The horse under Rella's supervision shivered but held steady as the vehicle settled upright.

Will ran to inspect the wheels of the stage that had landed hard on the packed earth of the road, passing his hand over them and inspecting the iron rims, then each spoke. He did the same on the other side, brushing off the dirt gathered while they were wedged into the ditch.

"They're okay," he pronounced, and Rella drew her first good breath in several minutes.

She kneeled beside Seth to check his breathing, then began gathering up the belongings spread along the deserted road. Her own and Cort's that she recognized, she stuffed into the portmanteau he'd bought her a long way back in their journey—La Salle, the place where they'd left the pig wagon.

As she tucked the clothes carelessly inside, her fingers brushed against something hard wedged beneath a flap of lining in the bottom. In his greedy haste, the bandit had overlooked the knife Apela had given her. Rella took it as a favorable sign.

After she helped Will gather his belongings, the two of them went back up the road to the slain guard and carried him and his rifle to the stage to stow him in the baggage compartment. By then, a feeling of numbness had settled on Rella, as though the sudden catastrophe was too horrible to be real, but she went doggedly on, reminding herself that the body she helped carry might well have been Cort's. She had no room to wonder about the guard's loved ones and sought to atone for her neglectful thoughts by arranging him so that he lay comfortably, his head on a coat. She shut the boot cover on him and helped Will lift Seth into the coach.

Seth moaned in pain as they lifted him; Will said it was a healthy sign. A man feeling pain was a man still alive. Rella sat inside the coach, the driver's head in her lap, as they got under way.

Somehow Will managed to maneuver the vehicle in a circle, and they were soon heading back toward Startzville. Away from Cort. But Rella knew Will was right. They needed help, and so did Seth.

On the outskirts of Startzville they encountered a young man on horseback; he rode ahead to signal they were coming.

"No need to say anything about those papers the marshal was carrying, is there? It just might muddy the situation even more," Will declared with a smile. "I don't know the sheriff, but he could feel obligated to throw you in jail."

Rella shuddered. Another incarceration was a possibility she hadn't even considered, and she thanked Will with a matching smile.

In town, Will helped the proprietor of the inn

carry Seth, pale and once again unconscious, into a downstairs room. A gray-haired woman introducing herself as Katie Flynn met Rella in front of the sheriff's office.

Her sharp eyes quickly assessed Rella. "Alcorn's not here," she explained. "Doc, neither. At least the sheriff will be returning before long. Rode into St. Louis a few days ago; he's supposed to be back by now."

The rider who had met them interrupted. "I'll just ride to meet the sheriff, hurry him up a bit." He was still mounted and without waiting for an answer wheeled away and pounded down the dusty street.

"He's a good man," Katie said. "Doc's tending a new mother with a sick babe out in the country. We'll have to help Seth best as we can till he gets back."

"And what about Cort?" Rella snapped.

Katie reached out a wrinkled hand and touched Rella's arm. "Alcorn will be here before long. He knows about those bastards that have Cort. He'll know what to do. Best thing for us is to help Seth here. You wouldn't happen to know anything about gunshot wounds, would you?"

Rella fought back a wave of despondency. Katie was right. "As a matter of fact," she said, "I just might. A woman named Apela told me a few remedies for infection and fever. Crushed beetles and brandy, I believe, and if that doesn't work, we can try pitch and fried onions."

Katie eyed her in amazement. "I don't know where you come from or what your relationship is to Cort, but I think maybe I might have to take over the nursing chores. Seth's a tough old coot, but I doubt he's tough enough to survive your cures."

* * *

Not long after the robbers left the site of the ambush, Slade was passed out and leaning against Blondie, mounted behind him. The trail was narrow and twisted through brush and thick trees. They crossed several narrow streams, always moving upward into the hills, Cort memorizing the way. Unfortunately, before slipping into unconsciousness, the Slade had ordered the front rider to blindfold Cort.

The thongs on his wrists were tight, and he'd already given up trying to loosen them. He continued to jounce along, concentrating on keeping his seat with no hands or sense of sight to steady him. The muscles in his thighs cramped from the effort.

Cort figured they were climbing; it wasn't a comforting conclusion. He pictured a chasm he might fall into where he would lie blindfolded and tied—and helpless.

They rode hard for what Cort estimated to be a couple of hours before coming to a halt. His arms were stiff and pained from the awkward way he had ridden.

The sounds of human voices came when they stopped.

"Slade!" The voice was deep and rough. "What the hell happened to you?"

Apparently Slade was in no condition to answer, for Cort heard only Blondie's flat, cold voice. "Bad luck today. He got hit. And for damned little cash. No gold."

"And who's this?"

Cort refrained from introducing himself, letting Mean Eyes perform the task.

"We got us a genuine U.S. marshal as hostage," Mean Eyes bragged. "Don't reckon anybody'll be coming after us now."

Cort picked up the sounds of dismounting, of footsteps, and suddenly he was jerked from his horse and shoved forward. He stumbled, almost fell, but managed to maintain his footing. When the blindfold was removed from his eyes, he blinked at the sudden shaft of piercing daylight that struck him. Slowly he got his bearings. The camp was on the side of a hill. A run-down building, more a lean-to than a cabin, was at the edge, and he spied the black mouth of a cave close by. His keen ears picked up the sound of moving water.

Shaking his head as though overcome from the ride—and in truth, he just about was—Cort cast quick glances around the camp. Slade was nowhere to be seen, but with the way the two young bandits were hovering around the mouth of the cave, he figured he knew the leader's whereabouts.

He took a tentative step in that direction. The click of a trigger brought him to a halt.

"Wouldn't go anywhere if I was you," said a man behind him. A different voice from whoever had greeted them. That made five men thus far, one being the wounded Slade. Cort would be looking for more. He'd need to know how many he had to take down.

Cort cast a glance back at the outlaw watching him. He was older than Slade, lean and mean although there was something about the lines of his face and the set of his lips that hinted he might have once been a gentler man. Hard times had worn away all the softness in him. He would pull that trigger if Cort so much as blinked wrong.

"Any chance I can get untethered?" he asked.

"None. Not until Sade comes to and tells us what to do with you."

"And if he doesn't?"

"Then I'd say you're going to your maker with hands tied behind your back."

Cort wasn't sure whether that meant the man would shoot him or just let him wither away. He didn't ask.

"Mind if I walk some, then? Need to get the kinks out."

"Marshal, I mind if you breathe. Especially if Slade don't make it."

"I didn't shoot him."

"That don't mean you wouldn't have. Somebody just beat you to it."

Conversation with his captor was getting him nowhere, except maybe dead, and he decided to shut up. He would learn more by watching and waiting. At least Rella hadn't come riding after him on one of the horses from the stage. He'd half expected her to. Will must have put on the brakes and convinced her she would do more harm than good.

She was some woman. For a change he didn't try to brush her from his mind. If he lived to be a hundred—a chance that was growing decidedly dim—he would never forget the way she'd stood before him last night, the way she'd reached out and touched him. And then the way she'd loved him in bed. She'd been gentle and sweet, the way he wanted his woman to be, yet passionate and unafraid to show that passion. If he could pick his last thought on this earth, he would just as soon it be about her.

The figure of a man, legs bowed and pants riding under a fat gut, emerged from the cave, and Cort pushed her from his mind.

"Ace," the man called.

"How's he doing, Jack?" asked Cort's captor.

"Not so good."

Cort recognized the voice as the speaker who'd

greeted them when they first rode up. His count of bandits was still five.

Jack drew nearer. "Bullet's buried deep. It's already festering, and the fever's settin' in."

"Damn!" Ace pulled a flat-bladed knife from a scabbard at his waist and ran his thumb across the tip. "Looks like there's only one thing to do. Fill him up with rotgut and cut it out."

Jack shook his grizzled head. "We been together a long time. Eight, nine years, I guess. Can't believe it's going to end this way. We shoulda gone with him. But he wanted to give those new boys some practice. Said it was an easy job today. Problem with Slade is he's overconfident."

Ace shrugged, then nodded toward Cort. "Take over here for a while. We'll put the boys on watch during the night." He made a move toward the cave, then paused. He spat into the dirt. "I know what I'm doing if Slade don't make it," he growled. "I'm takin' down the first lawman I see."

Cort didn't wonder who that might be. He needed his hands free. And he needed a gun. His eyes drifted toward the holster against Jack's thigh. He froze.

Beneath his paunch the bandit was wearing a belt with a fancy buckle, silver with a turquoise the size of a poker chip in its middle. He hadn't given any thought to that buckle since he'd marched off to war, but he recognized it, all right. He'd first seen it in a silversmith shop in St. Louis; he'd been a young man, proud to be in the city on his own, proud of the little cash in his pockets. He'd bought it for his pa.

Cort let his eyes move on without so much as a blink, then slowly raised his gaze to the wearer's face. Jack, he was called. Jack had said the three of them had been together a long time—longer than the robbery of the Ramsey farm six years ago.

Thoughts for escape passed from his mind, replaced by the need for revenge. Back in Startzville, when Katie had mentioned the possibility of these bastards being in the neighborhood, he hadn't allowed himself the luxury of going after them.

But they had come to him. He'd made a vow a long time ago that he hadn't been able to keep; it looked like now he would be able to. Not that he would be stupid about it. If Rella was able to get help to him, he would sure as hell take it. If not, he prayed she would have sense enough to keep out of the way.

Chapter Seventeen

"Glad we used something besides those crushed beetles," Katie said in a low voice, staring down at the sleeping man. "Looks like Seth's gonna be all right."

Rella moved from her post beside the front window of the inn's downstairs room and joined the woman beside the bed. Other than Seth, only she and Katie were present, Will having agreed to seek a little sustenance in the inn's dining room and the proprietor seeing to his other guests. The stagecoach driver lay still against the white sheets, a brush of color returned to his weathered cheeks, his breath coming regularly after a fitful while.

Since being brought in, he'd regained consciousness only briefly while Katie was bathing the wound with lye soap and water and dousing the area liberally with the carbolic acid that the enterprising Will had rummaged from the doctor's empty office.

Katie had ignored the colorful names Seth tossed at her as she bound the wound in a clean cloth. "Hush, you old coot. You're too mean to die from just one bullet, especially one that cut clean through."

Rella had sworn she saw a brief smile flit across his face before he slipped back into the balm of sleep. His brief, initial murmurings had told the two women and Will that his unrest came from remembrances of the robbery rather than any fever that was setting in.

Now that their concern about his safety could be set aside, Rella gave thought to the real worry that ate at her; panic bubbled like acid just beneath the surface of her calm; she was close to losing control.

Never had she felt like this—not when her parents had died and left her to fend for herself; not when she heard that cell door close on her down in Galveston; not even when she'd looked into Cort's eyes back in that Gypsy tent and realized he knew who she was. Those times had been bad, but they had been bad only for her. Now she was thinking of someone else. Now she prayed for the man she loved.

Katie reached out and touched Rella's hands twisted tightly at her waist. "Whatever color Seth got musta come from you. Pale as a ghost, you are. Like I said, Sheriff Alcorn will be coming along soon. He's a man to travel when he says he will."

Rella darted a quick look at the woman. "What can he do? Is this sheriff some kind of miracle worker? We don't know if Cort's—" The words died on her lips.

"Tell me what good a dead hostage is," Katie said bluntly. "Those bastards have got themselves a real problem, takin' a marshal and all. When they're caught up with, they got to show proof he's still alive. If anything has happened to Cort, not a lawman within three states is gonna let 'em get away."

If anything has happened to Cort. . . .

Whatever comfort Katie's reasoning should have brought was lost in the horror of those words, and Rella whirled away to take up her post once more by the window. Surely the torturous waiting would end before long, and she would spot this magician sheriff riding down the dusty main street of Startzville.

The door creaked open, and Will walked softly into the room. "You two get some food and sit a spell," he ordered. "I'll watch our patient here and let you know if there's any change."

Rella protested, but Katie somehow managed to maneuver her into the nearby dining room and to order them each a plate of hot food, a hardy stew that sat tasteless on Rella's tongue. Try as she might, she couldn't force down more than one bite.

Katie glanced around the small room where a dozen townspeople had gathered to talk and keep at the edge of what was happening. They kept their distance, giving the women a chance to rest.

"I was thinking," Katie said from her place across the corner table, "you needed some quiet, but it seems to me you need to talk. Brooding won't do you or Cort any good. You known him long?"

A few months or a lifetime, Rella couldn't decide, and she settled for a shake of her head. Besides, she lacked the strength to explain just where she and Cort stood, not being entirely clear on the point herself.

"You can bet he's not feeling sorry for himself right now," Katie averred. "More than likely, he's figuring out a plan for getting away. At least that's what he's doing if he's like the way he was as a boy." Her voice softened. "Full of vinegar he was."

Rella pulled herself from the vacuum of despair and to concentrated on what Katie was saying. All she knew about the gray-haired woman was that she worked at The Saloon and had a way with a gunshot wound.

"Then you're the one who's known him for a long time," said Rella.

"Sure have. Lived in Startzville most of my life. Saw him grow up into the fine man he is. Sure was sorry to see him ride out of here after his pa died, but there was no keeping him here. Folks were divided about the war—still are, as a matter of fact—and he was too restless to hang around. He needed more than this place offered and thought he might find it hunting down killers like the ones that got Josiah."

"And all it did was get him taken hostage," Rella muttered bitterly.

"Try to picture the way things were," Katie said, her voice calm and reasoning. "When he was no taller than a bar rail, Cort loved to ride that horse of his up and down the street. Rag tag look about him; half the widow women in town set their sights on his pa. Claimed the boy needed a mother to wash him up and mend his clothes and all, but they were really after that handsome father of his. Looked a lot like Cort does now, tall and handsome with that special way about him. Kinda tough and boyish at the same time."

Rella knew exactly what she meant.

"Unfortunately for the widows," Katie said with a shake of her head, "Josiah Ramsey was a one-woman man. Never looked at another female before or after his wife died, not that any of us could tell."

So Cort had inherited his father's looks, had he? No wonder the women in town had been after him, especially if he'd smiled crookedly at them, or if ever in some lonely, dark hour he'd approached one of them with a worried look and a need for companionship that communicated itself without words. The way his son had approached her last night. She couldn't help wondering if Cort, like his widower father, would ever be a one-woman man.

"His father's death must have hit Cort hard," Rella said.

"I'm glad I wasn't the one to tell him. Cort came back from the war changed. Lean and kinda haunted by what he'd been through. And then to hear that some night-skulking guerrillas had destroyed everything he was coming back to. . . . Well, it like to drove him crazy. He hunted the countryside for them, but it was too late. They were long gone."

Rella felt his anguish and frustration, suffered his helplessness at being unable to change the course of events.

"I love him," she said in a rush, the words spoken before she could give them thought. Even as they startled her, the sound of them was sweet on the air.

Katie smiled in satisfaction. "Thought as much. Saw it in your eyes."

There was still a question in Katie's voice, but Rella found that honesty could go only so far. "We really haven't known each other long," she said, then hesitated. "We're going back to Galveston on business." Her voice trembled. "At least we were."

"I'm thinking you better tell that marshal how you feel."

"What makes you think I haven't?"

"Saw him in the saloon last night. He looked kinda restless, like the way he used to with his unsettled thoughts. Joked a little, the way he always did, but I'm thinking now he was concentrating more on you. We talked about the trouble we'd been having with bandits, and that seemed to stir his mind. Still, that wasn't the only burr he had under his saddle."

For the first time since dawn, Rella smiled. "A burr, am I? You might call me that. Cort certainly would."

"Don't know what this business is between you two, but soon as you can get it settled, my advice is to work on what really matters between a man and a woman."

Rella shuddered. The business between her and

Cort was of little importance right now when she didn't know if she would ever see him alive again. What if she lost him before she had a chance to tell him how she felt?

"Are you married?" she asked.

Katie shook her head slowly, and her eyes took on a faraway look. "Fever took my man a long time ago. Never saw another one I'd take to bed."

"Not even Seth?"

"Rella, you're as plain spoken as me. That old fool in there has blabbered some about taking a wife. I always figured it was just saloon talk."

"He seemed glad enough to get your ministrations."

Katie's answer was lost in the sound of horses riding up outside the inn, and the shouting of men. Rella abandoned the table and, pushing past the townsfolk headed in the same direction, was outside in a flash. Milling about the street were a half dozen riders, dusty and red-faced from a fast gallop as they sat astride their sweating mounts. The man wearing a badge was exactly as she would have cast him: broad-shouldered and barrel-chested, his square face hard-bitten, his eyes cold and hard.

Sheriff Alcorn spied Rella right away. "You the woman from the stage?" Tossing his reins to one of the men, he dropped to the ground. "Let's go into my office and you tell me what happened."

Rella matched him stride for stride, the words spilling from her in a torrent as she walked. Alcorn listened, nodding, asking a question from time to time about what the robbers looked like, about the leader's wound.

"Most likely the one in charge is Monty Slade. He's been causing trouble around here for years. Got more luck than sense. Most of his gang is dead now, only a couple besides him left. Ace Pendley and Jack Murphy."

Inside the small office, he dropped a dusty, misshapen hat on his cluttered desk. "From your description of the two that joined in on the stage robbery, I'd say they were a couple of troublemakers who rode through town a month back. Drank a little too much, argued amongst themselves, and Katie had to ask 'em to leave. Had an eye for a few ladies walkin' by, and when they caused a ruckus I had to convince 'em the ladies didn't return the interest. Heard the dark-haired one came back last week while I was in the county. Good thing for him I was."

"How did they end up with this Slade?"

Alcorn shrugged. "Like turns to like, maybe. Or it could be they just smelled each other out. Now I guess it's time I did a little sniffing around. They've killed once. The guard riding shotgun was a good man."

"You're not going by yourself, are you?"

He wiped an arm across his brow. "Shouldn't have a hard time getting up a posse. Folks in these parts are slow to rile, but there's many that remember Josiah Ramsey and his boy. That was before my time, but I've heard talk about Ramsey's death. No one would want the same thing to happen to the son, even if, according to some, he fought on the wrong side. And I can tell you for damned sure, no marshal is going to lose his life in my domain."

Rella prayed he knew what he was saying. "When do we leave?"

"There's no *we* to talk about, miss. It's men's work now."

She let the words slide by without argument. "How do you know where to ride?"

"I pretty much know the area where they are holed up. Haven't pinpointed it exactly, but with Slade injured, they may be wanting help. And we want to be there to give it."

"Why wouldn't they ride on out of this area and leave Slade if he's apt to die?" Rella asked. "They could leave Cort tied up."

"Don't get your hopes up. Those compadres of his have been with him since before the war. They're not likely to leave him now."

"Perhaps not," Rella said, still doubtful, "if this Slade needs medical attention. But Katie said the doctor is out of town."

"Then maybe I'll just have to volunteer to ride into their camp." He slapped at the revolver strapped to his thigh. "Maybe do a little amputation. Take off Slade's head. That way he won't worry about that leg."

"But those two men who were in town know what you look like," Rella protested. "You can't fool them into thinking you're a doctor."

Again, Alcorn touched his gun. "I'll have to think of a way to persuade 'em, then. Or come up with some other trick." He strode to the gun rack against the back wall and began checking the rifles. "You go on back to the inn and stay with Katie. I'll be swearing in the posse, and we'll ride out for the place where the stage was held up. Good a spot as any to start, seeing as how the camp I'm thinking of is in that direction. A genuine robber's roost, it is. I'll let you know as soon as we get back."

Rella had no intention of doing what she was told. The past two hours had been the most miserable of her life—and she'd had several unhappy times since her path had crossed Cort's. Sheriff Alcorn was tough and trail-hardened, but she somehow doubted he had the subtlety of thought to carry off any subterfuge that could fool Monty Slade.

But Rella did. Already a desperate plan, born of this desperate time, was forming in the back of her mind. She stopped by the stage office to grab her portmanteau, then sought out Katie, finding her talking to some of the men on the street in front of the inn.

She motioned her aside. "I need help, and I don't have any money. You'll have to trust me."

Katie studied her sharply, then nodded once. "What is it you want?"

"A horse, outfitted and ready to ride."

"You going with the posse?" Katie asked in surprise.

"I'm not going to be left behind. Sheriff Alcorn may be tough as nails and brave enough for most situations, but I'm not sure he won't do something foolish that could get Cort killed. I plan to see he doesn't."

"I'm not sure I can get a sidesaddle this quick."

Rella slapped at the portmanteau. "I don't want one. You might see if you can get me a hat. Not a fancy chapeau, mind you, but one made for a boy. I left mine back in St. Louis."

Shaking her head, Katie left to do as she was told. Rella realized that somehow their roles had been changed. Katie had been in charge in tending to Seth and in passing out some unsolicited advice to the worried young woman. But now Rella was telling her what to do.

While Alcorn was busy putting out word for volunteers to join the posse, Rella slipped into a room at the inn and dressed once again in her shirt and trousers, hair tucked up under the broad-brimmed hat Katie had brought her. At the livery stable, she took possession of the mount Katie was providing, a sorrel mare, spirited but not so much that Rella feared she couldn't maintain control. With hat pulled low, she looked like a youth joining up with all the excitement.

"You'd fool your own mother," Katie said as she looked her over with admiration in the shadows behind the stable. "Here," she said, extending her hand, "I thought you might could use this."

The object she offered was a small gun which fit into Rella's hand. It felt cold and hard, like the eyes of those bandits yesterday.

"You know much about using it?" Katie asked.

"No." She was promptly treated to a quick course in the loading and discharging of firearms. She tucked the gun into her boot, just above the sheathed knife that she'd hidden back at the inn. In dealing with the likes of Monty Slade, a woman couldn't be overprepared.

Rella doubted that any of the townspeople would recognize her, at least if she didn't hold still long enough for them to get a good look at the unknown youth in their midst; nevertheless, she didn't care to test Alcorn's powers of observation, and with a few belongings wrapped in a bedroll behind her saddle, she rode out ahead of the posse toward the scene of the crime.

She selected a hiding place uphill from the road where she could get a good look at the men when they arrived. She didn't have long to wait. Alcorn was riding in front, a dozen armed men strung out behind him. Farmers and townfolk for the most part, Rella figured, the kind who showed up with wives and children to see Templeton's Traveling Thespians when the troupe made one of its rare stops in a smaller town. Only a couple of the men looked as though they'd done much riding out on the trail.

"We'll leave the road here," Alcorn yelled over his

shoulder.

From her hidden perch, Rella nodded silent approval. The sheriff was following the same route Monty Slade had taken when he abducted Cort. Maybe Alcorn knew what he was doing after all. Slowly she guided the sorrel down a winding path to take her place behind the men who were riding single file into the brush beside the road.

"Didn't know we was bringing kids along," said a ruddy-faced man at the rear. "Ain't seen you around these parts."

Rella merely shrugged.

Muttering under his breath about such a ragtag outfit hardly being tolerable, the man turned his attention back to the narrow trail.

The way was rough going part of the time, then wide and clear as the posse steadily wound its way through woods and brush up into the hills. It wasn't until they stopped at a shallow stream to water the horses that Alcorn realized he had acquired another hand.

Attempting to sequester herself on the far side of the mare away from the man, she heard footsteps stalking in her direction. She knew exactly who came to halt behind her, sensing that once he got a look at her she wouldn't fool him for a minute.

"I ought to turn you over my knee and spank you good," Alcorn snarled at her back.

She whirled to face him. "Save your energy for Monty Slade. Don't worry about my getting in the way. I wouldn't do anything to endanger Cort." The sorrel bobbed her head in agreement.

"We got a dadblasted woman here!" one of the trail-hardened men exclaimed, kicking at the damp grass beside the stream, and the others grumbled their discontent.

Rella held her attention on Alcorn, knowing he was the one she had to convince. "I'm not going back to Startzville," she said. "You don't let me ride along, then I'll go separately. And I'll keep riding until I find him."

"You'd starve first."

"I know a little about berries and leaves. Which to eat and which to leave alone. I've had an unusual education lately, Sheriff Alcorn. You might even find that I can help."

Alcorn shook his head in disgust. "About the only thing I believe is that you won't quit. Like as not, wandering around up in these hills, you'd get caught in the crossfire. Can't say what'll happen in the next day or two."

"Day or two! How far do you think Slade went? He looked bad when he rode off."

"Woman, back off. Don't try to hold me accountable for everything I say. Just speculating, is all. We've got to look at all the possibilities."

"And one of them is that I can help. Don't ask me how just yet, because I'm still thinking. I'll let you know."

Rella thought she detected a brief sign of admiration in the sheriff's hard eyes, but it was gone too quickly for her to know for sure.

"You ride in the middle," he said gruffly. "Can't take a chance on your lagging behind and holding us up if you take a notion to primp or some such. And if there's any trouble caused because you're here, I'll tie you up in a tree, stuff a gag in your mouth, and collect you again when we're done. Clear?"

"Clear."

Rella scrambled onto the mare and did exactly as she had been directed, ignoring all the while the comments of the men about bad luck and interfering females and work meant only for men. The days on the trail with Cort had prepared her well, and she saw to it she didn't hold them up for so much as a second. After another hour's hard riding, she noticed that Alcorn had slowed the pace. At last he came to a halt in a shallow, tree-shaded valley, in other circumstances a lovely place in the Missouri wilderness. Ignoring the scenery, Rella concentrated on the circle of men.

"Make camp here," Alcorn said. "Be night soon, and there's water. I'm not so sure of the way exactly. Need to do a little scouting. You men see to your horses."

Rella wanted to protest. Even in mid October, there was at least another hour of daylight left. But she'd promised not to cause any trouble, and at great cost to her short store of patience she kept her mouth shut. If Sheriff Alcorn said he needed to do a little scouting, she would have to let him.

It was no chore to keep to herself as she unsaddled the mare and spread a blanket onto the grass. She knew she was unwelcome, but she hadn't come along to make friends. She was here to save Cort. The sheriff might be skeptical and the others in the posse certain she was in the way, but then they didn't know her very well. Anyone who'd fought the Chicago fire and managed to fool Cort Ramsey, if only for a little while, stood at least a small chance against Monty Slade.

Alcorn returned after dark on a dead run. Reining in his slathering horse, he dropped to the ground to face the men and Rella who gathered around him.

"Found the camp, all right. More to the truth, it was the other way around."

"You've seen Cort?" Rella asked hurriedly. "Is he all right?"

"Hold up, woman. I haven't seen him. Just had a report he's all right."

"What do you mean, a report?" one of the men asked.

"One of those young men I remembered from town came at me waving a white flag. Blond fellow. Eyes cold as ice. Must have heard me thrashing around."

"If he did," said another, "it was because you wanted him to."

"Be that as it may," Alcorn said, "he heard me. Said the marshal was all right. They promised to keep him that way if we'll get a doctor to Slade. The old bastard's afraid gangrene is setting in and he'll lose his leg."

"But Doc's a long way away," protested one of the townsmen.

"Then we'll just have to come up with someone to take his place. If we're to save the marshal, we need someone inside that camp. He'll meet whoever we send back up the trail noon tomorrow. They know who I am. Any of you care to volunteer?"

"Take a cool eye and a steady hand to fool 'em," one of the townsfolk said.

The men stared silently at Alcorn, a few of them dropping their gazes to the ground.

It was Rella who stepped forward to speak. "Excuse me, gentlemen," she said in an authoritative stage voice. "I realize I'm a mere woman and just in the way. But I think it's about time you considered what contribution I can make to this search."

Early the next morning, Cort awakened after a restless night on the ground, surprised he'd been able to sleep at all without even a saddle for a pillow and with his arms still bound behind his back. Opening his eyes to the early morning sun, he saw the pale-haired thief Blondie was wrapped in a blanket under the next tree, his head on his saddle. Cort could put another name to him now—Danny Bade. The one he'd labeled Mean Eyes was called simply Cain.

"Morning," Cort called.

Danny sat up and yawned, then flicked Cort an incurious look, his eyes flat and expressionless, the color of water. Cort decided he'd never smiled in his life.

"Don't suppose a man could relieve himself," he said.

Danny shrugged. "Ain't had no instructions either way."

"I'm getting mighty uncomfortable."

"Not my concern."

"Then maybe you better ask someone to tell you what is your concern. Wouldn't want Danny Bade to get in trouble on my account."

At last Cort saw a sign of life in Danny's eyes, a flicker of indecision. He played on what he had been given. "Unless it would disturb one of the men to have a boy bother them with such an obvious question. If they plan to use me as a hostage, they'll have to keep me in relatively fair shape. I'll need to eat and drink. You planning on holding the cup to my mouth?"

"I ain't planning on doin' nothing but shooting you if you try to get away."

"Then I'll call out, see if I can rouse someone to give you permission to cut me loose for a minute."

Danny shot to his feet. "Stand up, lawman. Don't need permission from no one."

Cort swayed as he pulled himself upright. He hadn't eaten or drank anything in twenty-four hours, but mostly he wanted water. His lips felt cracked and his throat dry, as though he'd been swallowing sand.

Danny cut the ropes loose. In his weakened state, Cort had no chance to turn on him.

"Now take care of yourself, lawman. There's water and a hunk of bread," he snarled, gesturing toward his saddle.

Cort forced himself to move slowly, relieving himself behind the tree. When at last he turned up the canteen to his parched mouth, he gulped twice, then let the cool elixir trickle slowly down his throat.

He'd gulped down the bread and had more water when Danny abruptly jerked the canteen from his hands. "That's enough. Now turn around."

Cort's hands balled into fists, but there was no time to try for freedom. Ace and Jack came out of the cave toward them, and he slowly turned around.

The gun butt came down hard on his head. When he awoke, he knew it was about noon. Once more his hands were bound behind him, this time around the trunk of a small oak. His head had a thousand hammers pounding away inside his skull.

This time he saw the curly headed young bully who went by the name of Cain. Where Danny Bade's eyes had been flat and expressionless, Cain's were filled with hate.

"Danny had to go on an errand," he said. "Get a little medical help for the old man."

"Have to go far?" Cort asked, his tone casual. He knew Rella would sound a warning and send the law. Maybe this meant a posse had shown up.

"Naw. 'Count of Slade, we're more than likely sittin' ducks. Good thing we got you since that fool was stupid enough to get hisself shot."

Nothing that Cain said gave him any clue as to what was happening outside the camp, but he saw there was trouble enough close at hand.

"No respect for your elders?" he asked, managing a smile. "What would Slade say?"

"He ain't saying much except he don't want to lose his leg. Plumb scared, he is." Cain seemed to draw pleasure from the thought.

It was just as Cort had figured. Cain and Bade would turn on the older men in a flash if they thought it would do them any good—or if they thought they could get away with it. He filed the information away in his mind. Maybe he could use it later even while his saviors sat out there like cats besieging a mouse hole.

His attention was drawn to the sound of a horse's hooves striking the ground nearby. From his position at the edge of the camp, Cort could see only one rider, Danny Bade, as he came into the clearing. He dropped to the ground and hurried inside the cave, only to reappear a minute later with a pair of very angry men at his side. Cain moved away from Cort to join the men.

"Sheriff said to tell you he done the best he could," Danny said. "If this don't pan out, he'll try to get the doc. But we was to try this way first. Swears he's seen stranger things than this work."

"If he don't know what he's talking about," Jack hissed, "then we've got one dead marshal on our hands."

Without having the least idea what the sheriff had conjured up in place of a doctor, Cort shared the gunman Jack's sentiments. He wanted the eyes of the bandits turned toward the trail from where Danny had emerged.

The proud head and spindly legs of a sorrel were all Cort could see at first, then a pair of hands gripping the reins—graceful hands attached to bare and slender arms. Dread became the bitter taste of certainty in his mouth, but he managed to arrange his expression into one of interest, showing nothing of the surprise and consternation he felt.

Sitting astride the horse, skirt hiked between her legs, booted feet resting in the stirrups, was Rella. Only she was dressed once more as the Romany, drawstring blouse, golden skirt, and all. Her wind-combed black hair hung loose about her shoulders, and she let her dark eyes trail slowly around the camp, passing over him with not so much as a blink, then settling first on Ace and then on Jack.

"Where is the man who is hurt?" she asked in a throaty voice. "The Romany has come with the cure."

Chapter Eighteen

Without warning, the caw of a crow cut through the stillness of the afternoon. Like a precursor of doom, he flapped his wings and deserted the branch over Rella's head, casting a black shadow across her path.

The sorrel shied, but Rella kept her tight grip on the reins, willing her face to remain as impassive as Cort's. He had taken in her whole appearance, then looked down to hide any revealing expression in his eyes. Her gaze lingered on him long enough to see that he was indeed in one piece. She realized he was tied ignominiously to the tree where he lay. It was hard not to run to him, to comfort him.

She pushed the thought from her mind, knowing she must relax and play this scene better than any she ever had. If only her heart didn't beat so. . . . Surely these men could see the pounding through her cotton blouse.

Murmuring to the horse as much to take her mind from Cort as to soothe the animal, she surveyed the clearing, the lone, ramshackle building, and not far away from it the dark entrance to what looked like a cave.

She counted four men in all, not including Cort:

the curly headed, mean-eyed one who'd been in on the stage robbery; two older, more seasoned thieves she'd never seen before; and, of course, Danny, the pale, cold-blooded bandit who'd escorted her into camp. Each was wearing a gun. They were a sorry lot with their hard, bristled faces and clothes that looked as though they'd have stood alone. She would bet no other woman had ever set foot in that camp.

Never had she played before a more important audience . . . or a more critical one, judging from the way the men stared up at her. She'd done a lot of fast talking back with the posse about what she would be able to do here in the camp, but it all hinged on the opening scene—or on the reactions of Cort and the two young hoodlums who had seen her at the stage yesterday looking neat and prim. She took a deep breath, grateful they were the kind of men who seldom really looked at a woman's face.

She sat tall in the saddle, eyeing the men coolly. "I have come to do what I can." She nodded at Cort. "Is that the injured man?"

One of the older men hiked an arm under his protruding stomach and barked, "No, it ain't. He's in the cave. What kind of a fool does the sheriff think we are to send a woman?"

"You heard what Danny said when he was getting us to come out here, Jack," the other pointed out impatiently.

With his sharp cheekbones and narrow, deep-set eyes, he looked lean and mean, Rella thought, rather like a hungry wolf. If the sheriff was right, he must be Ace Pendley; the other would be Jack Murphy.

"Sheriff says she's the best he can come up with on short notice," Ace continued. "She's been in the area telling fortunes and offering to heal the sick. All for money, of course."

"That may be," the pot-bellied Jack replied, as though she couldn't understand a word he said. "That don't mean she knows what she's talking about. All Gypsies lie. You know that as well as I do."

The sharp-faced Ace aimed a shot of spittle at the bare, hard-packed ground. "The sheriff'll still be trying to get the doc. At least that's what Danny reported." His narrow eyes focused on the glimpse of leg between Rella's boot and skirt. "Hope Alcorn finds him, for Slade's sake. Only one thing wrong with a man this Romany can cure, and it sure ain't a gun wound."

The curly headed bandit slapped a hand against his groin. "I'm thinking I got such an ache," he said with a smile that failed to reach his eyes.

"Shut up, Cain," said Ace. "You want a woman, you ride on into town."

"I seen her first," Danny said flatly. "If anybody gets a poke at her, it'll be me."

She saw there could be trouble between the two young men that could be used by her and Cort. Carefully she studied them. Cain had a meaner look about him than she'd ever seen before, even when he'd stared at her yesterday by the stage; Danny would have brought a chill to hell. Ace glanced at the two of them as though they'd crawled from beneath a rock.

"Gorgios," she sneered. "Always you think the same thing of Gypsies. I have come to help the injured man, and nothing more."

"Why?" asked Ace, squinting up at her in the sunlight afternoon. "We don't intend to pay you no money. And I never seen no Gypsy ever wanted to help any marshal of these United States just out of the goodness of her heart."

Rella was ready for the question. "The marshal is

of no consequence. I do this for myself. Sheriff Alcorn has said he will put me behind bars if I do not help. He says I steal." She managed to keep a hold on Ace's glare. "I do not want to be in jail. This is a sentiment you share, is it not?"

"Maybe," Ace drawled, the look of wariness not quite gone from his eyes.

Dismounting, Rella glanced from man to man and, remembering the way Ace had done most of the talking, picked him as the leader. She gestured toward the dark entrance to the cave. "Take me to this Slade."

"I'm not gonna let you just walk in there," said Ace. "For all I know you've got a gun tucked up somewhere under that skirt. Or in those boots. Come to think of it, I never seen a Gypsy wearing boots before."

"There is much you do not know of my people," Rella hissed.

Cain reached out and grabbed a handful of hair, pulling her off balance. She fell backward against his chest, then jerked her body away from his, her neck and head twisted awkwardly toward him. She would as soon have cuddled a rattlesnake.

"I'll search her," the mean-eyed young bandit said.

Cort's voice drawled almost lazily across the taut circle. "No wonder you fools are holed up like this, arguing among yourselves, broke most likely, sheriff waiting out there for you. You can't seem to concentrate on the business at hand."

"Shut up, Ramsey," Ace snarled over his shoulder. "Cain, get your hands off the Gypsy."

Cain muttered an obscenity, but he did as he was told. Rella let out a long, low sigh.

"I'll do the searching," Ace added, bringing a quick end to her relief.

She went on the attack. "I did not come to play

games," she said, lifting the hem of her skirt. "A Gypsy wears boots for many reasons, the same as a gorgio." She leaned down and pulled out the small gun that the bartender Katie had given her.

"Drop it!" ordered Jack.

She tossed it at his feet. "Now that I am no longer armed and dangerous"—she glanced insolently from man to man—"perhaps you can trust me."

Insolence was definitely one of her defenses, as much as the gun had been. At best, even if she had managed to get off one shot, she would have stopped one of the four. Even Cort could not have done much better.

But if she stood up to them, unafraid, she might lull them into complacency. And she still had another weapon tucked inside that same boot—Alepa's knife.

Ace gestured toward the cave. "Slade's in there. But I'm warning you. He may not take kindly to your presence."

"A Romany does not expect kindness," Rella said with a shrug, then dared a glance in Cort's direction. She caught him in profile straining against his bonds, and she noticed for the first time a trickle of dried blood at the base of his neck. Of course one of the bastards had hit him from the rear. It was the only way of assuring he could be subdued.

"Lawman," she warned, "you had best pray these men accept what I do."

His eyes locked with hers. "I'm praying for a lot of things," he answered.

They stared at one another a moment longer than was perhaps wise, sending signals of encouragement before she turned to follow Ace into the cool, dank cave. Inside, her eyes slowly adjusted to the dim light. A still form lay atop a pile of blankets toward the rear; on the opposite side of the shallow cave was a banked fire, its embers glowing like the eyes of a watchful animal. A thin ribbon of smoke curled upwards toward some unseen outlet in the roof of the cave.

She knelt beside Slade, who lay stretched out on his back, eyes closed, breathing uneven. Venturing to feel his brow, she found him hot to her touch. His shirt was unbuttoned and open to his waist; she could make out a sweat-dampened chest crisscrossed with the ugly scars of a dozen wounds. A fetid odor rose from the exposed, jagged thigh wound where his trouser leg had been torn away.

Bile rose in her throat. Swallowing, she looked back at Ace, who stood near Slade's bare feet. "Has the bullet been removed?"

"Did it myself. None too easy. It was buried deep right up against the bone."

Rella swallowed again. "I will need water and brandy."

Ace laughed shortly. "We've been wanting a little of that ourselves. Not the water, of course."

"You have no liquor of any kind?"

"Rotgut is all."

"It will have to do. Look for a willow tree near the stream, take the bark and boil it in water, then bring me the solution. I will also need a handful of crushed beetles mixed in this rotgut. And last, a portion of moss. Please see that it is free of the droppings of birds."

Ace hesitated a moment, muttered something about Alcorn getting all of the so-called Gypsy medicines crammed down his throat if they didn't work, then disappeared from the cave. Jack quickly took his place as guard.

Slade moaned in his sleep, then settled again into stillness. As the minutes went by slowly, Rella kept reminding herself that the wounded man in her charge had been the one to kidnap Cort. He deserved to have the hole in his leg packed with bugs and whiskey and moss. Still, she was reluctant to apply the mess, and it proved a difficult job. Both Ace and Jack had to hold Slade down when the whiskey touched the wound.

Alepa had claimed that every step Rella was taking would cure almost any wound. At the time, her response had been an incredulous laugh, but as she packed a wad of dry moss on top of the beetles, she couldn't summon up so much as a smile.

And neither could Ace and Jack, who watched her movements with hard eyes until she had finished the loathsome task and sat back on her heels, overcome by the closeness of the cave. "I have a need for fresh air. One of you should remain with him," she ordered. "Call me when the fever leaves."

Outside, the first sight to catch her eye was Cort, once more sitting on the ground, his eyes pinned to the opening of the cave. Danny Bade stood watch over him near the base of the tree. She blinked once to tell him everything was all right inside the cave. It was poor contact but all she could manage right now. Somehow she must talk to him.

Glancing around the camp, she saw that the sorrel mare had been unsaddled and put to pasture in a grassy area with a small band of horses in the direction of the running water. The entire site was surrounded by thick trees and brush. With the sun low on the horizon to the west, the sky had taken on a paler hue, and mottled shadows played across the ground, softening the austerity of the camp. Under other circumstances, the scene would have looked inviting, almost peaceful in its pastoral simplicity.

Briefly she considered openly going to Cort's side.

They were both prisoners in a way and joining him might be accepted. But it might just as well start a fight.

She glanced back at the cave. Ace stood in the entrance, eyeing her.

"I would like to rest now," she said, hoping he would tell her to sit by Cort. "The day has been long."

A rustling in the brush to the rear caught her attention, and she whirled around to see the young bandit Cain staring at her. She was caught by his hot, beady eyes.

"Days are real long around here," he said. "Got to find some way to pass the time. And I don't favor resting alone."

Rella looked back at Ace. "I came to take care of Slade. If I am harmed in any way, I will put such a curse on him that he will die. It does not matter one way or the other to me. There are some things that are worse than jail, even to a Gypsy."

"Back off, Cain," Ace snarled. "I've come too far with Slade to take chances. This Gypsy seems the only help for him now." He turned to Rella. "You Gypsies live off the land. Rustle us up some stew. Ain't had nothin' much but beans since we come back to this country."

Hope rose. Here was an opportunity to get near Cort. "Can you lay traps for an animal? A squirrel perhaps, or a bird?" she asked.

"See what we can do," Jack replied with a shrug. "Not much on eating crows."

"Sparrows will do," she said. At least she'd heard back in Chicago that they were good in stew. If she'd actually ever eaten one, she didn't want to know it.

"I must be free to forage," she added. "For herbs and wild onion and garlic."

Jack shrugged. "Just don't get too far."

"I'll go with her," Danny said from his post near the watchful Cort. He gestured toward his prisoner. "He ain't going nowhere, that's for sure."

"You and that young compadre of yours put yourselves to use," Jack said. "See if you can't get us a bird or two. Don't use no gun. No need to signal where we are, in case anyone's out there watching."

"Rocks'll do," Danny said. "What I used when I was growing up."

Rella got a clear picture of a pale young boy killing songbirds just to pull off their wings.

She headed for the stream and for a few minutes put her mind to finding the onions and garlic that she'd learned grew near the damp banks. The search took longer than she had expected, but Sandor and Alepa had taught her well. To her small storehouse she added a few berries and roots to throw into the pot, all the while circling around the camp in the direction of the tree where Cort was bound.

Occasionally she heard a thrashing nearby and took it to be the bird hunters Cain and Bade. Never did they approach her, but she made sure she crouched low and kept to the thick brush. At last she managed to get where she'd been headed, hidden behind a large boulder close to Cort. As she peered over the edge, she saw that no one was close to him. The sun was cooperating nicely as it sank behind the trees on the far side of the camp. Twilight shadows were already deepening. A fire was burning near the cave entrance to her right; standing nearby was Jack, his back to her. She assumed Ace must be inside caring for Slade.

Removing her knife from her boot, she slipped away from her sanctuary and crept across the ground to crouch behind the tree, using Cort's broad shoulders to block herself from Jack's view should he glance her way.

Cort's head raised slightly, and she knew he was aware of the movement behind him. She thought of them fleeing together on one horse, her skirts trailing in the wind of their passage, a bright moon lighting their way.

"It's me," she whispered, her fingers pressing against his shoulder. His muscles tensed, and she could feel the heat of his skin.

"You shouldn't have come. Get out as soon as you can."

"Not without you." She began to saw at the thick rope that bound his hands, ignoring the raw skin at his wrists. She gave only a quick glance at the blood-encrusted knot at the base of his neck. There were many things she was having to ignore.

A lifetime crept by before the rope parted and Cort was able to flex his wrists. He turned his head, letting it slump to the side as though he had fallen asleep. "Leave the knife," he whispered out of the side of his mouth. "And get the hell away!"

"Forget any such nonsense," she whispered to his back. "I'll leave the knife, but I'm staying." Gathering her skirts around her, she made herself as small as possible and edged her lips close to his ear. With Cort so close, she drew strength from him—and heart.

"The posse is supposed to be waiting for a signal," she whispered. "I've got gunpowder."

"When?"

"Tomorrow. At dawn. Or whenever we . . . you decide."

Cort pictured the scene and found he didn't like it. Too much could go wrong, too much chance of cross-fire with so many men around.

"We better improve the odds," he said. "If you won't leave, get Jack and Ace in the cave tonight. Then follow my lead." He lowered his voice even further. "And we'll talk about your stubbornness later. I'm not forgetting it."

A dozen questions about his plans rushed to mind, but she swallowed her words. As she slipped back into the woods, she thought how they could talk later about a lot of things.

Cain and Bade managed to bring back a half dozen birds, which they cleaned and threw into the boiling herbs and onions Rella had rounded up.

They all gathered around the pot where Jack gallantly loaned Rella a cup for her stew. As she ate, she felt Cort's eyes on her. She could barely see him through the gloom and could hardly eat her meager supper for worrying about his condition. He hadn't looked at all well.

When she'd scraped the last bit of stew from the cup, she leaned over and refilled it. "For the prisoner. The sheriff will demand to see a live hostage. He will not last if you continue this treatment of him," she said. No one stopped her as she strode to Cort and knelt beside him.

Pretending to be still tied up, Cort swallowed hungrily each bite she fed him. She wiped his mouth on her skirt and was sorely tempted to lean closer and kiss him. She couldn't risk even talking to him, not with the close way she was being observed. After a long look into his eyes, she left hastily and disappeared inside the cave.

She soon emerged and walked slowly over to the campfire. "The patient shows signs of restlessness," she announced. "I need to clean the wound again and will need help. It is also best if someone is with him tonight."

Cort saw she was maneuvering Jack and Ace as she'd been instructed. The firelight flickered across her face and highlighted the slender curves of her body beneath her soft-fitting skirt and blouse. He had to give her credit. She knew just what weapons to use.

Ace glanced at the two younger men who were sprawled on the ground near the fire. "I'll be inside," he said. "You two been bickering all evening. Try not to kill each other tonight. We got enough to worry about."

As he and Jack followed Rella inside the cave, Cort directed his attention to the two younger men, who were stretched out on the ground near the fire. They'd been watching every move that Rella made. For all the good it did, Ace might as well have swallowed his warning. Cort figured that while Rella was relatively safe inside the cave, this was the best chance he was going to get to take out two of his captors.

"Which one of you is going to get her?" he called out. "Or are you going to give her a choice?"

Cain sat up and glared at him. "Ain't up to her."

"Danny might have other thoughts," Cort said.

Danny nodded and said softly, "I just might."

"One of you boys is going to have a good night, and the other one. . . . Maybe you'll hear about it in the morning."

Cain leered at Danny across the fire. "I tell tales right well. Almost as good as the genuine thing."

"You're all talk," Danny said coolly. "A real man don't have to brag."

Cain sprang to his feet. "You sayin' I ain't a real man?"

Danny pulled himself up to stand close to Cain. "I already said what I mean. You ain't nothing but talk."

Cain's blow caught Danny in the stomach, and he

staggered backward. Cain pressed forward, punching at Danny's face and chest, but his target managed to dodge and dart. Cain's blows missed as often as they found their mark.

Danny launched his body into Cain's and the two went down, rolling around on the ground, grunting, punching, stirring up the dirt around the fire.

The sounds of the fight brought Ace and Jack from the cave. Behind them was Rella, round-eyed with fright.

"Stop it!" Jack yelled, but he was ignored.

"Let 'em go at it," Ace said. "They've been itching for this a long time."

Cort knew only one of the young men would survive the fight. Which one, he couldn't tell, but if he had to choose, he would put his money on Danny Bade.

He guessed right. Cain lashed and punched wildly; Danny answered with methodical sureness, dodging and striking, gradually wearing Cain down. For all his spareness, Danny was the stronger of the two. At last he got an arm around his opponent's neck. One quick squeeze and the fight was done. The snap of Cain's neck was audible above the crackle of the fire. When he fell to the ground, Cort knew the mean-eyed young man was dead.

Danny looked down with contempt at the body of his former friend. "All talk," he managed, breathing heavily, and without a backward glance moved slowly off into the woods.

Ace watched him leave, then walked over to the fallen bandit. "Bound to happen," Ace said, nudging the body with his boot. "Guess we'll have to bury him tomorrow." He dragged the body behind a bush not far from the fire.

Rella allowed herself one look at Cort, then turned

to hurry back inside the cave.

Four, Cort thought. Down to four men. Ace, Jack, Danny, and the injured Slade. And all of them gone right now. He felt the knife close to his hands and flexed his knees, preparing his stiff legs to stay under him long enough to get to the cave. He would wait there to ambush whoever came out first.

Before he was committed to leaving the tree, Jack reappeared, and Cort was forced to subside back into seeming captivity. Impatience ate at him as the time passed slowly, Jack stirring the fire and staring off into the dark. Ace joined him, and at last Rella emerged to announce that Slade showed improvement and she was going to get some needed rest in the privacy of the lean-to shed near the entrance to the cave.

Cort set about figuring how to take down at least one more of the men before he tried to spirit Rella away. Or before the posse stormed in. He pictured her alone in the rude hovel, surrounded by moonbeams.

Danny Bade returned during the night to relieve Jack as his guard. Cort watched him through narrowed eyes, noting that he showed more interest in the lean-to where Rella slept than in his post. With both Jack and Ace inside the cave, Cort knew the young bandit wouldn't wait long to make a move in her direction. It was easy to figure the way a cold-eyed bastard like Danny Bade would think. He would be after a reward for an evening well spent.

Cort knew his man well. Shortly before dawn, Danny slunk across the bare ground to the door of the lean-to. Cort's fingers reached for Rella's knife and curled around the slender handle. He hadn't carried such a weapon often, but he knew how to use it—as Danny was about to find out.

Cort would have preferred arresting the young thief and murderer and hauling him to jail, but in the present situation, justice called for a different kind of trial . . . and a sentence swiftly and silently carried out. He watched as Danny slipped inside the shack, then crept quickly across the space to listen at the door.

"Get out of here!" he heard Rella hiss.

He opened the door and in the gloom was able to pick out Rella lying on the floor, a bent form standing over her. The creak of the rusted hinges caused Danny to jerk his head around. His hand went for his gun. Cort sent the knife flying, and the young man slumped soundlessly to the ground, the weapon having burrowed hilt-deep precisely in the center of his chest.

Rella scrambled to her feet and stepped over the body to fling herself into Cort's arms. He held her tight.

"Let's get out of here," he whispered against her hair.

She pushed back and looked up at him. "What about the posse?" she managed.

"No need to stir them up if we don't need to."

He reached down and loosened the belt of Danny Bade's holster, then strapped it on. "He won't be needing this anymore," he said, checking the gun to make sure each chamber was loaded. Satisfied, he slipped it back into place.

Rella shuddered, then forced herself to speak. "What about the knife? I . . . know how to use it, if I have to."

"Seems to me you've done more than your share."

"Not quite. You're not out of here yet."

Cort hesitated, then reached down to grab the handle of the knife. With a heave, he pulled it from the dead bandit's body; blood, black in the muted light, gushed from the fatal wound.

He wiped the blade against Danny Bade's shirt, then handed the weapon to Rella. "Better not put it away in your boot just yet. Might prove a little unhandy in an emergency."

Rella felt a momentary dizziness. She wasn't feeling nearly as tough nor as brave as she told herself she'd become.

Cort opened the door slowly, wincing at the creak. A dozen brawling cats couldn't have made more noise. With the moon behind a cloud, the clearing was quiet and dark. A hint of light on the eastern horizon gave proof that day would be coming up soon. He stepped outside, pulling Rella behind him.

Two things happened at once. The cloud moved, and Jack walked out of the cave.

In the sudden bath of moonlight, the bandit's eyes fell on Rella and Cort standing directly in front of him. He went for his gun, but Cort was too quick. The Colt he'd taken from Danny thundered, and Jack slumped to the ground, but not before he'd got off a wild shot of his own. The charge struck a boulder close by the dead campfire and ricocheted harmlessly into the early morning dark.

Cort stared down at him. His gaze lingered a minute on the silver and turquoise buckle that had been stolen a long time ago. The old hates rushed back on him. Jack's death had made him want the business completed all the more. He glanced toward the cave—

A single shot came from the dark outside the camp, and then another. All hell broke loose around them; gunfire seemed to come indiscriminately from behind every bush; Ace came running out of the cave and threw himself behind the lean-to, his gun barking.

Cort elbowed Rella to the ground and threw himself on top of her. He muttered a curse. Without waiting for a signal, someone in the posse had thrown himself into the attack and the others had followed; just as Cort had feared, he and Rella were caught in the crossfire.

Chapter Nineteen

"Into the cave," Cort ordered. With his body still covering Rella's, he wrapped one arm around her waist and half crawled, half crept across the clearing to the dark entrance.

She gave him no argument but scurried into the depths. The knife in her hand would do little good now against the unseen Ace. Let the posse take care of him. She breathed a sigh of relief. Except for keeping an eye on Slade, her work was done.

For himself, Cort wanted to make sure that Ace would wreak no more havoc on innocent people. He positioned himself at the mouth of the cave.

"Hold up!" he yelled toward the brush, hoping the posse would listen. With a bunch of volunteers, it was hard to know what they would do. Most of them were firing just to scare what was now mostly an imagined enemy, but they stood a chance of hitting each other. Cort had seen it happen when citizens decided to help the law.

He yelled again, "Only one man left! Hold up!"

One by one the men held their fire until an eerie quiet descended on the camp. Cort ventured one foot out of the cave; a gunshot bit the dirt inches away.

Only twenty yards separated him from Ace, bare

ground softened by the light of the moon—bare, that is, except for the still form of the gunman Jack close to the entrance of the cave. The camp was no less a battlefield than Cort had fought on during the war.

"You won't make it out of here alive, Ace," he called. "Throw out your gun."

"You'll have to come and get me, Marshal" came a growled reply from the dark behind the small shed.

"Don't be a fool. All we have to do is wait. You've got a dozen men surrounding you."

Cort's argument met with silence. At last he heard Ace's voice, which was edged with resignation as he said, "Always figured it would end this way." With a roar he came from behind the shed, gun blazing.

Cort stepped into the clearing and shot him clean through the heart.

He moved slowly toward the shed and stood looking over the still body, waiting for the relief of a settled vengeance; he was met with only a hollow disappointment that such a final and irrevocable immensity as death could leave him so unmoved. Josiah Ramsey was still buried in his grave; the death of his killers could never change that.

Cort paid no mind to the rustling in the brush and was barely aware when Sheriff Alcorn appeared beside him.

"All dead?" asked Alcorn.

"Not quite." Cort glanced toward the cave. Maybe once Monty Slade was taken care of, he would find the comfort he was looking for.

A sudden fear ate at him. Where was Rella? She should have heard what was going on, should have known it was safe to come outside.

He moved fast, gun in hand, not bothering to muffle the sound of his boots striking the ground. He found the two of them in the back of the cave, Rella standing with her back to him, Slade propped up on a blanket close to the fire and gripping a Navy Colt aimed directly at her heart.

"Move any closer and she's dead," warned Slade. "Drop the gun."

Rella ventured a quick, helpless look over her shoulder at Cort as he dropped his gun. Burying his rage, he stopped his forward movement; instead, he edged sideways until she was out of his direct path to the wounded bandit.

Slade's gun clicked like the warning of a snake.

"I'm holding still," said Cort, his hands in the air.

Shifting on the blanket, Slade grinned as he held the Colt steady on his target. "Looks like I got me two hostages now."

"And no backup men. They're all dead."

Slade's eyes darted to him. "Ace? And Jack, too?"

Cort nodded. "And the two punks as well. Give it up, Slade. You've been riding hard for a long while. It's time to quit."

The gunman shook his head as if in disbelief. "The three of us started with Quantrill over in Kansas. After the trouble at Lawrence, took out on our own."

"So you moved east," Cort said, all the while thinking of the gun that lay on the floor of the cave between him and Rella. He shifted his weight and lowered his hands as he added, "To do your shooting and robbing in this part of Missouri."

"Sure hate to see those boys go." Slade's face hardened. "You kill 'em both?"

"They as much as killed themselves. Didn't know when to lay down their guns. And they both could walk." Cort gestured toward the bandaged leg resting on top of the blanket. "How far do you think you'll get like that?"

"I can ride."

Rella could be silent no longer. "No you can't."

"Shut up, Gypsy," said Slade.

"I'm not a Gypsy," she said, desperate to distract him from Cort. "I was on the stage the other day."

Slade eyed her carefully. A gleam of recognition lit his eyes. "I'll be damned. Whatever you are, you sure helped me out. A real handy woman to have around."

Rella found it hard to feel proud.

Slade let his eyes rake her body, then turned the gun on Cort. "Maybe you're right, Marshal. Too much for me to keep up with two of you. They already got me for the killing at the stage. Can't hang me more than once. And the little lady'll come in a lot handier than you. Not nearly as dangerous, either."

With a low growl, Cort gave up on the gun and headed for him.

Rella acted without thinking, raising the knife which she'd gripped within the folds of her skirt and sending it flying through the air just as she'd been taught back in Illinois.

The grizzled old bandit let out a grunt, and his eyes widened in surprise. He looked down at the knife buried in his gut.

"I'll be damned," he managed, then slumped to his back and stared sightlessly at the roof of the cave.

With blood pounding in her ears, Rella felt the cave begin to whirl around her. She reached out for Cort. He caught her in his arms before she could hit the ground.

The first thing Rella did when she got back to the inn in Startzville was to take a hot bath. Maybe if she scrubbed long and hard enough, she could wash away the memories of the past few days. She should be rejoicing that Cort and she had escaped unharmed. All she could think of was the look on Monty Slade's face as he stared at the knife.

It was night. They'd been back a couple of hours, and there was celebrating below. Through the narrow window she could hear the sounds of loud talk and laughter from the nearby saloon. Let the men drink and brag. She wanted no part of any such activity. A woman was supposed to bring life into the world, not end it.

Never would she forget that long ride out of the hills into town. To the rear had been the blanket-wrapped bodies of five men tossed across their horses. She'd felt weak from her foolish collapse in the cave, but she hadn't once faltered, knowing that if she did the bandits' horses would pass her by and she would have to look at the results of her attempt to rescue Cort.

She shouldn't regard the deaths as her fault. Of course she shouldn't. Slade and his men had invited their demise when they chose to rob the stage. But Rella had found she wasn't as self-possessed as she'd always assumed. Since meeting Cort, she'd experienced a number of emotions that were not wise, not the least of them useless regret.

Cort rode beside her, silent for the most part. She saw him holding the silver buckle that Jack had worn, and he'd explained that it had been his father's. He didn't put it away until they arrived back in town.

Cort. What a change he'd brought into her life, and on many different levels. First had come fear for her freedom and her life, and then had been the bondage of her heart. What a gloriously brave man he was, and she thought for the hundredth time what a difficult man he was to ignore.

She was still waiting for the explosion over her

Gypsy ruse among the bandits. He'd been gentlemanly and considerate out at the camp, but she knew his mind had been on gathering up the bodies of the men who had killed his father. She hoped that when they were buried, so too would be the demon ghosts that had haunted him all these years.

She moved restlessly about the small room. The tub had been removed long ago, and still she debated what to do. She'd turned down the lamp and considered trying to sleep, but she'd quickly brushed aside the idea, not wanting to be alone, even though she'd told Cort she did. Even less did she want to dress and join him and Katie and the proud posse for a celebratory drink.

A knock at the door aroused her from thought, and she looked down at her undergarments. The tips of her breasts were visible through the thin cotton chemise, and beneath her petticoat her legs and feet were bare. With not so much as a wrapper to cover herself, she asked, "Who is it?"

"Me."

Her heart caught in her throat. Strange how one syllable could arouse a person.

Barefoot, she pattered to the door, turned the lock, and moved back to her place by the window, the moonlight streaming about her. "Come in."

Cort moved silently into the room and shut the door behind him. Hatless, he stood tall and lean, his presence filling the air with an electrical anticipation that robbed her of breath. She was relieved to see he wasn't wearing his gun.

"You may want to be alone," he said, "but I don't."

His voice caressed her in the dark.

"What about Katie and the other men?" she asked.

"Tried that." He hesitated. "I was more alone with them than I can remember ever being."

If at first she'd worried that he had come to lecture her, she pushed all such thoughts from her mind.

"Oh, Cort!" she cried and flew across the room to wrap herself in his arms. She had so much to forget—and so much to remember: the way his lips felt on hers, the touch of his hand as it stroked her naked skin and aroused her to madness, the feel of him within her body.

With his warmth enveloping her, she pressed her lips against his neck, desperate for the release that would come with loving him. He tasted of salt and the musky maleness that she had come to crave. Cort was alive; she could feel the beat of his heart against her breast, feel his hot breath whispering across her cheek. Nothing else mattered; nothing she had done would she undo, even if such a power lay within her grasp.

The two of them had passed through hours of hell, of darkness and pain and fear; but now as they clung together in this unlit room, the lightness of life was upon them. The soaring wonder of being together swept them along toward the inescapable melding of their bodies and the joining of their spirits. Cort had come to her in this lonely room—twice—and each time she had met him unashamed. Physical need was transcended by the desire to pleasure him, to welcome him under her skin, in her heart and mind, in her soul.

Closing her eyes, she let her other senses take over and breathed deeply of his manly odor, an aura that evoked memories of days on the trail and nights spent in his arms. His breathing was ragged in her ears, and she delighted in his low moan of pleasure as she circled his ear with her tongue.

Searching fingers tore at his shirt and stroked against the hard warmth of his chest, entwining in the mat of hair, circling and manipulating the hard nipples, pressing against his pounding heart. Each tactile realization brought her new delights, new satisfactions even as she hungered for more.

Cort's lips were hot and demanding everywhere they touched—her eyes, her throat, the rise of her breasts above her chemise. His tongue licked at her nipples, dampening the cotton, and she writhed under his every touch. A trail of kisses led back to her mouth; he invaded her, claiming her submission, proclaiming his right to do with her whatever he would.

It was a right she gladly gave—and one she claimed in kind. She met his tongue with her own and entered the dark, moist interior of his mouth. As their lips and teeth and tongues met in an erotic dance, he strengthened his hold on her, running his hands down her back, gripping her buttocks, pulling her hard against him. Frenzied, she ripped at her chemise and rubbed her breasts against his chest. She needed him more than she ever had, loved him more than life itself.

The sheer joy of being alive and able to love him coursed through her. Unthinking, she tugged frantically at the waistband of his trousers, pressed her fingers against the rough denim, in sweet exasperation moved lower to feel his swelling manhood, massaged him, and listened to the low, encouraging sounds in his throat.

Cort felt he would explode with passion before he was ready, and he thrust her hands from him, swept her into his arms, and placed her on the bed to tear at her clothes and toss them aside. Quickly he stripped himself naked and lay down beside her to drink in her moon-bathed body with his eyes, the silken skin and beckoning curves, the high, firm breasts with their hardened tips, the patch of hair between her thighs, her long, slender legs which were parted to receive him.

He wasn't ready to seek the ultimate end to this delightful torture. He let his hands and lips explore where his eyes had touched. She trembled as he stroked her breasts, played at their tips with his tongue, and ran his fingers through the triangle of coarse hair until he found the hardened bud of her womanhood. She lifted her hips to pulsate against him.

He felt her pleasure and took it as his own. Still massaging in answer to her quickening need, he probed deep within her moist valley with his finger. It was Rella's turn to utter low, guttural sounds in her throat.

Her climax was violent, and she shivered against him, squeezing his hand between her thighs. She opened her eyes to stare up at him.

"I wanted you with me," she whispered hoarsely.

He smiled, his eyes dark and glittering and full of promise. "We're not done. You have a great capacity, Rella. Let me show you how much."

Again came the sweet torture of his fingers against her, the tightening tentacles of pleasure, the pin-pricks of rapture that centered where he was caressing her, and at last the splintering peak of passion that she could not deny—not just once this time, but again and again.

Giving herself completely to sensation, Rella was filled with new and incredible urgings. Far from sated, she craved more, wished for nothing less than an endless night of such erotic wonder. Her hands groped for his manhood, feeling the hard, hot shaft beneath her fingers.

She caressed and stroked him, pressing her open mouth against his throat, counted his heartbeats, and listened to his ragged breath. Everything about Cort was a marvel to her. With no more than a look or a whisper of her name, he could render her helpless, yet her own delicate touch could make her master of him. Such was the way she felt at this moment, and she thought of the size of his manhood, the wild pleasure it could bring, the same wild pleasure that she brought to him.

She spread her legs wide and welcomed his invasion, shivering with pleasure against the length of him. Stretched on top of her, he felt lean and strong and sleek, like velvet-encased steel.

Her body closed around him, accepting the full length of his shaft, muscles tightening, each nerve ending tingling with erotic sensations. He was hard driving and yet gentle; it was another wonderment that such opposites could exist in one man.

He thrust deep inside her, over and over. Her fingers raked across his back and then she clung to him, swept up by the urgency of his need and of her own. They exploded into passion as one, her body arched, hips raised to meet his, lips pressed against the crook of his shoulder.

She trembled in his arms. With the gradual cessation of movement, she was able to catch her breath. He lay still for a long moment, pressing her against the soft down mattress, but for all his strength, his weight was of no matter. When at last their heartbeats slowed and he shifted to rest beside her, his head propped in one hand, she kept an arm around him, unwilling to let him go.

He stroked the dark strands of hair from her face and leaned down to feather a kiss across her lips.

"You have a great capacity, indeed," he said.

She opened her eyes to gaze up at him. She had half expected a lecture from him about her appearance at the outlaw camp—as ill timed as it would have been—but there was nothing censorious in his expression, nothing critical at all. "And is such a capacity wrong?" she teased.

His thumb outlined her mouth. "Unusual."

"Freakish, probably."

He smiled. "Desirable."

"Wanton," she threw back at him.

He shrugged. "I give up. Wanton it is."

She struck him in the chest with her fist. "It is you who have made me so."

"It's one of my better accomplishments."

"Admit the truth. I make you horny."

He began to stroke her leg with his foot. "As a matter of fact. . . ." His eyes glittered with a look she quickly recognized.

"And you say *I* have a great capacity."

Cort's hand drifted down to cup her breast. "I don't promise the same . . . enthusiasm."

She matched his smile. "I'll bet I get it anyway."

Once again Cort pulled her into his arms and pressed his lips to hers, and Rella found to the satisfaction of them both that she was right.

The lecture she'd been expecting didn't come until the next morning when they were dressed and prepared to descend to try the stagecoach once again.

"I talked to Sheriff Alcorn last night," Cort began innocently.

"You did?" she asked, tucking the Gypsy garb into her portmanteau. No longer were the skirt and blouse wrapped around Alepa's knife. Alcorn had removed the weapon from Monty Slade's body, but she'd had no heart to claim it.

"The sheriff says you presented quite an argument

about riding to my rescue."

Rella forgot about the knife. "There was no one who could refute anything I had to say," she said, her chin lifted defiantly. "Then or now."

"It was a foolish thing to do."

"It was necessary, Cort. For all your bravery, you couldn't have freed yourself. You needed me for that."

He stood in the open doorway and eyed her carefully. "Maybe. That's something we'll never know."

Her eyes flashed angrily. "Are you waiting for me to promise I'll never do it again? All right. If someone named Monty Slade takes you hostage after a stagecoach robbery, I promise to let him keep you."

Cort grinned. "And I thought I was the one with a temper."

"Maybe it's contagious."

"Along with a few other habits." He glanced at the rumpled bed.

Rella found herself blushing. "We'll miss the stage," she said, grabbing for her portmanteau.

Cort grew solemn. "Are you so eager to get back to Galveston?"

She met his gaze straight on. "Are you?"

"I told you I believe you, Rella. That wasn't a lie."

"I know." She felt a sudden rush of sadness. No words of love had ever passed between them. No matter what he believed about her, he still carried a warrant for her arrest.

Maybe, she told herself, he was waiting until she was completely free to declare himself. Maybe. Until then she would have to accept his trust in her. For now it should be enough. So why, when she could still feel his loving touch upon her from the night before, did she feel such despair?

She hurried past him and down the stairs. On the way to the stagecoach office a dozen townspeople waved at them, one or two stopping to shake Cort's hand and exclaim he had quite a fiancée there. True to his word, Will Matthews hadn't spread the true story about Rella, instead letting the people believe what he had at first. Not even Sheriff Alcorn was aware of her true status. Still, she stirred nervously at each compliment. She wasn't Cort's betrothed and doubted she ever would be.

At the office they were greeted by Katie and Will.

"Thought I'd try the stage again," the kindly grandfather said with a smile, "before that grandson of mine in Cape Girardeau starts school. I'm gathering lots of stories to tell him, that's for sure. Might even start as soon as I see him. Not that he'll know what I'm talking about, but that's the best kind of audience. One that doesn't ask questions or try to leave the room."

Katie gave Cort a brief kiss on the cheek. "Take care and don't stay away so long."

Cort shook his head. "I'm not sure I can stand the excitement around here."

Katie laughed. "We've had more going on since you rode in on the stage than in the previous five years. Things just seem to happen around you."

Silently Rella agreed.

Katie turned to her with a hug. "And you take care of him. We think a powerful lot of him in these parts."

"I'll do the best I can," Rella said, avoiding Cort's eyes. With a guilty start, she remembered the injured stagecoach driver. "How is Seth?"

"He's coming along just fine. Arguing with everything I say, the old coot."

"You take care of him," Rella said with a smile.

"Think I might do just that."

Good-byes were completed, and the journey begun. This time the stage made the trip to Cape Girardeau and the Mississippi River without incident, arriving at midmorning the next day. Cort was able to book passage on an afternoon sidewheeler to New Orleans.

While he was tending to the tickets, Rella stood on the dock near the steamboat office, a crowd of passengers milling around them and the chilled wind off the Mississippi ruffling her carefully pinned-up hair. A similar chill gripped her heart. Throughout much of the journey from Startzville, Cort had looked at her with that familiar gleam in his eye—the man really was insatiable—but what did he really want? Other than the obvious, of course. And what did he really believe?

As much as she loved and needed him, she knew exactly what she had to do—allow the fires of passion to die so that they could both know for sure if he still harbored doubts.

When he joined her outside, she looked him straight in the eye and said, "Did you get separate staterooms?"

Cort looked at her long and hard. "No," he said flatly. "I didn't know they were needed. If they are, then you'll have to tell me why."

She didn't mince words. "We're getting nearer and nearer to Galveston. Whether or not you believe in my innocence, I'm still your prisoner."

Cort's temper flared. "You were back in Startzville, too."

"Don't ask me to be logical, Cort. You ought to know women better than that."

"And don't you be coy. It doesn't become you."

"All right, then believe this. I didn't feel like your prisoner back there. I do now."

Cort reached out and touched a lock of hair that had blown free from the chignon at her neck. His fingers felt cold against her skin, and she pulled free.

"I don't know women at all," he said in disgust. "I thought you'd lost those sharp-tongued ways."

Rella was close to tears. This wasn't going at all as she had expected. She was suddenly aware of the stillness around them. She dared a sideways glance, only to see the bonneted head of a woman turn hastily away.

"I don't want to fight," she said softly. "We argued once before over this same topic. That time we were angry. Believe me, I understand—or I'm trying to understand—why we need to return. In legal matters, I'll do just what you say." She ignored his sharp laugh. "You can do me this one favor."

Cort didn't look at all pleased. "So keeping away from you is a favor, is it?" he asked.

Rella found herself grinning. "Frankly it will be torture. Would you try not to look at me that way?"

Cort shook his head and, incredibly, returned the grin. "You certainly know how to test a man. But if you'll feel better sleeping alone, then so be it. It's damned sure I won't," he added before turning to reenter the office.

Two hours later, as she stood beside him on the upper deck of the steamboat and watched Cape Girardeau disappear around a bend in the river, she saw him pull from his pocket the silver and turquoise buckle that had been a gift to his father. Studying his eyes, she detected the signs of pain she feared . . . but there was more, an affectionate touch of nostalgia as he remembered the past.

At last he was able to handle his loss. With the past no longer haunting him, perhaps he could look to the future. A future that just might include her.

But there was much to do, first. A law clerk was waiting in Galveston to testify that Perry Tuttle had used his dying breath to whisper her name. A deputy sheriff was waiting to describe how she'd hit him on the head and escaped from county jail. Both men were from families long respected on the island. She was a newcomer from England, an actress and working woman . . . as well as a Gypsy. Whatever judge and jury awaited her would probably find that out, too.

As for Cort, his word wouldn't be much good. He was still considered a Yankee, and they had traveled a thousand miles together. Even if proof were not easily found, there would be rumors aplenty that she had shared his bed.

Rella could hear the stories now. She had tricked him just as she had Tuttle and the law clerk Marcus Clapper and Deputy Ernest Bowles.

A dangerous woman, Cinderella Sandringham. Unless Cort were to pull off a miracle and find clues that had evaded him when they were fresh, she would be buried so deep in prison that she would never see the light of day until they hanged her.

Chapter Twenty

"All hands above board! All hands above board!"

Backed by the thrumming of rigging and sails, the singsong cry echoed across the crowded deck of the *Flying Cloud.* Rella's heart quickened at the sound.

If someone had told her last June that she would one day welcome a return to Galveston, she would have called him crazy. But gripping the railing of the clipper ship on this cold Monday in mid November, the sky leaden and a stinging northwest wind blowing hard enough to ruffle the usually calm waters of the Gulf of Mexico, welcome it she did.

She'd last seen the island, ravaged by a summer hurricane, from the porthole of a German trading vessel bound for New Orleans. Docks had been collapsed, ships damaged, all traffic in and out of the port virtually at a standstill. Except for the intrepid German captain that Gerhardt Maas had found for her, no one had been setting out to sea. Huddled below deck, she'd been alone and frightened, certain that if she stayed on the island she would soon be feeling a noose around her neck.

That feeling hadn't left her completely. Despite Cort's assurances that he would find out the truth and her faith that he would do what he said, she could still feel a fluttering in her stomach when she considered the danger to which she was submitting herself.

One thing gave her heart. Instead of Cort stalking her, he stood by her side, his hand warm against his elbow; instead of accusations of guilt, he was assuring her, with his presence and his smile, that all would be right. Not once since Cape Girardeau had he brought up the subject of their separate staterooms. A perfect gentleman—so much so that on several lonely nights she would have welcomed an arrogant pounding on her door.

Cort had an idea of the worry that ate at Rella. It was there to read in the clouded depths of her normally bright eyes and in the solemn set of her lips. He was proud of the brave way she stood on the deck and watched the approaching land. With the chilling mist blowing off of the water, droplets of moisture dampened her skin and caught in the tendrils of dark hair outlining her face, but she would no more have sought refuge inside her cabin than she would have jumped into the gray, undulating water through which the clipper sailed.

With his help she was coming back to Galveston to clear her name. After so doing, if she chose to leave, he would have another purpose in mind—to see that she stayed, if not on the island then certainly with him.

The last weeks had been hell, with her near and yet as far away as she'd been during the first months of her escape. Never a patient man, Cort had been hard pressed to keep from invading her cabin and convincing her with tactics he knew she couldn't resist that there were better ways to spend the time than brooding about the past and worrying over what lay ahead.

But he'd given his word. It meant a great deal to them both that he keep it.

A great hullabaloo went up as the *Cloud,* her sails flapping, took a cautious route up the channel leading from the Gulf along the northeast side of the island. Rope wielding sailors moved hurriedly about in a curious kind of order, and passengers, many of them immigrants, gathered their belongings about them on the desk, one couple even tying pots and pans to their children. A polyglot of excited exclamations swirled in the cold air.

"We'll be landing shortly," Cort yelled over the noise.

Rella nodded. The fluttering in her stomach tightened into a knot. The people around them would be startled if they knew the truth. The immigrants were seeking a home; Rella was fighting for her life.

How different this was from her first sailing into the port in those innocent days when she'd toiled with Templeton's Traveling Thespians. She had thought herself contented with a traveling life, but now she knew different. She thought of Cort's presence, of the strong appearance he made standing next to her. Even if all went as he'd said and her innocence was quickly proved, she had lost something that could not be easily recaptured—a contentment with her lot. For that if nothing else, she could blame him.

Ignoring the fine salt spray that covered them both, she glanced up at him. Hatless in the gray afternoon, the stiff breeze tousling his hair, he returned her stare. There was so much she didn't understand about him, so much she wanted to know. How she wanted to reach up and brush the dampened curls from his face, to feel the warm texture of his skin, to trace the outline of his lips. . . .

She looked away, directing her attention to their destination, to the narrow space along the wharf that awaited the *Flying Cloud,* and to the dockworkers scurrying about like ants. The busy port reminded her of one thing she'd forgotten during her journeys. Greta had talked about trouble on the wharfs, threats to the workers and possible payments made *sub rosa* to local officials. At one time she'd wondered if Cort had been in on those payments. There had been his unexplained six thousand dollars stolen from Perry Tuttle's safe, a great deal of money for a lawman.

She might not know what was in Cort's heart, but she knew something else with certainty. He'd already told her how he made his money by investing in cattle and land. He wasn't a thief or an extortionist.

It wasn't until they were ensconced in a rented carriage and wending their way through the crowded streets that she brought up the subject that had been eating at her.

"I suppose we're going to the jail right away."

"I wired back in New Orleans we were coming." At Rella's look of dismay, he added, "You're the one who wanted me to treat you like any other prisoner. I'll arrange bail as soon as I can, but it may be in the morning."

Rella stared at the passing traffic, but the carriages and people seemed a blur. "I keep going over the evidence against me. The steamship ticket and money I had saved can be explained. I really was planning to leave Galveston and rejoin the troupe. The most damaging pieces of evidence are Marcus Clapper's testimony and my escape."

"My thoughts exactly."

She turned to face Cort. "That jail cell was left open. It was a temptation I couldn't resist."

"I thought you were pretty strong about resisting temptation."

Rella looked away. Little he knew.

She pulled the woolen cloak he'd bought her in New Orleans tight around her body. "I'm not strong at all, just desperate. I want to get all this settled. There was a lot of ugliness I ran away from. Accusations about my relations with men, as well as the more serious charges."

"All of which I know are unfounded," he said.

If Rella refused to accept a more physical kind of comfort from him, she could certainly welcome his words, and she smiled up at him. "Without any more proof than my declaration of innocence?"

He ventured a brief look at her. "I've got all the proof I need about you and men."

"Meaning?"

"You want me to say it? I know for damned sure there's been no one else but me. And you're no more capable of killing anyone than my father was."

"You've forgotten Monty Slade."

"No, I haven't. You're also brave and willing to do what is necessary under trying circumstances."

Rella settled back in the carriage and wished that she could accept Cort's assessment of her, praying she could have as much faith in herself as she did in him. Trusting Cort was essential if she was ever to quit running from the charges against her, but all his belief in the world wouldn't erase the papers filed in a Texas court, the ones that carried her name in connection with murder and theft.

When they arrived at the jail, she couldn't see that

the building had changed much. Far off the street behind the wall which was still topped with broken glass, it crouched squat and ominous, its narrow windows striped with iron bars.

"I don't know if I'm brave enough to face that cell again," she said as they made their way slowly up the long walk. "Couldn't I stay at Greta's tonight? I know she and her father would welcome me."

She gave him no chance to answer. "Forget I asked," she said brusquely, squaring her shoulders. "You said we had to do this right. I'll do what you say."

Inside the stone building one difference was obvious. Gone was Ben Woods, the old jail guard who had left the cell unlocked when he left to escort the Widow Welch to the train bound for Austin. In his place was a burly young man whose face seemed set in a perpetual scowl.

The deputy Ernest Bowles bustled into the jail office shortly after Cort and Rella had entered.

"Someone over at the courthouse said he saw you riding by," Bowles said, casting a sharp look at Rella. "Had to see for myself if you brought her back the way the telegram said. It seems to me, though, she was blond when she left. I knew it was an unnatural color." He rubbed his left hand against the back of his head. "Still remember how she attacked me. A vicious woman is what she is."

Vicious was exactly how Rella felt as she stared contemptuously at the pot-bellied deputy. Cort steadied her with a hand on her arm.

"Good thing that old fool Woods is gone," Bowles continued. "He's the one who let her escape. Now Bubba here"—he gestured to the surly jailer—"won't let anything like that happen. Used to work down on the docks for Rip Griffin and knows how to handle trouble."

"Sure as hell do," Bubba said, giving Cort a hard stare to show he wasn't afraid of anything.

Rella shuddered, instinctively fearing the jailer. In his care, she could suffer almost anything. All he had to do was claim he was trying to restrain her from another escape.

"What happened to Ben?" asked Cort.

"Went to live with his sister out in El Paso," Bowles said. "Happened shortly after you left. He got to feeling bad about letting a murderer free to harm someone else."

"Too bad. I had a few questions I wanted to put to him." Old Ben might have been inept and a little on the venal side, but he wasn't mean or stupid. The inmates at the jail hadn't suffered from his ministrations, but Cort wasn't at all sure of this new jailer. He had a definite hooligan look about him, mixed with a slack-jawed admiration whenever he eyed his new prisoner.

"Jail seems crowded," Cort observed. "Must be a real job for you."

"Harder 'n I thought," Bubba responded with a shrug, "and every cell full to overflowing with riff-raff."

Bowles raised his hand, about to rebut what Bubba had said, but Cort cut him off.

"I think I'll just keep Miss Sandringham in my custody. I know how crowded the jail usually is."

Bowles scowled. "Highly irregular," he said. "We got some whores in the back that didn't have money to pay their fines. We can put her in with them. Being an actress, she'd feel right at home."

"She'd just be another one to feed," Cort said

evenly. If Bowles had an ounce of sense, he would have realized Cort was struggling to contain his temper. If he hoped to help Rella, he couldn't pursue this into a fight.

But that didn't mean he was going to leave her with charmless Bubba nor the insulting Bowles. "She stays with me. I'll see if I can round up a judge and have him set bail. Just so your fine legal sensibilities won't be insulted. And, too, doing it this way will save the county some money."

Everybody present knew Cort wasn't usually so keen on government frugality. He waited for Bowles to speak, but when he didn't, prodded him. "If you have any complaints about my keeping the prisoner in custody where she's been several weeks already, then I suggest you take them up with Governor Davis."

Cort was relieved when Bowles put up only token objection. "That Reconstruction bastard has other things on his mind," the deputy growled. "Too much to worry about an insignificant woman like that."

"Ernest, don't ever try to run for public office. You have a way about you that tends to rile a man." Without waiting for a response, Cort took Rella's arm and guided her out of the jail. With a great show of courtliness, he helped her into the carriage.

"You realize," she said as she welcomed his arm, "that he's probably back there itching to fire a round of shots at me."

"He's lucky I didn't fire some of my own. Old Southern gentleman is what he calls himself. Lowlife is closer to the truth." As Cort settled beside Rella and took up the reins, he cast one last look at the jail. "But then, as far as he's concerned, I'm just a damned Yankee interloper. He's not the only one around here who feels that way."

"When I left here, I thought the same thing, and I'm not even an American."

"And how do you feel now?"

"Depends on where you're taking me."

"The safest place would be to my hotel."

Rella caught her breath. "Not if we're to keep our distance," she managed. "Wouldn't I be safe enough at Greta's?"

"At least you're having as much trouble as I am keeping to this bargain," Cort said ruefully. When his mouth twisted into a half smile, Rella almost capitulated to whatever arrangements he wanted to make.

"Let's find that judge," he continued, "and we'll see. Don't know why it couldn't be arranged—if she promises not to put you on another boat."

It took some searching, all the justices having left early on this Monday afternoon, but Cort was able to find one of them in an eating place near the courthouse. He put up the bail himself, pledging the deed to his East Texas plantation in case Rella managed to escape again.

"That property means a great deal to you," Rella commented when they were once more in the carriage.

"I told you, I've been thinking about maybe settling there."

"I remember. It took me by surprise."

"There's lots of things about me that might take you by surprise, Rella."

Or a great deal he hadn't bothered to tell her, Rella came close to retorting. Obviously he didn't think it important that she know. She shivered, as though the chill wind had reached her heart, and concentrated on the ride to the Maas home near the docks.

The small frame house sat white and neat and welcoming in the gloom of the cloudy afternoon. The oleanders, which had been in bloom the last time she'd seen them, were now shorn of their pink and white blossoms, but in the November breeze they brushed noisily against the stilts on which the house rested.

Unfortunately it was closed up tight, and no amount of knocking brought a response. A visit by the medical school turned up neither Greta nor Aaron Tuttle.

"So much for that idea," Rella said with a sigh as they sat in the carriage in front of the school. "We have no idea where Greta is or even if she's in town. And she always said trying to talk to her father when he was at work was impossible."

"If you don't mind an unorthodox suggestion—"

"As long as it's not your hotel. I haven't done anything orthodox in so long, I wouldn't recognize it if it hit me in the face."

"Mollie Bigheart owes me a favor or two. I've stopped some fights at her place on Postoffice Street."

Rella cocked an eye at him. "I've heard about her. Doesn't she operate a brothel? Your plan doesn't sound much different from the deputy's. He wanted to put me back with some whores."

"You and Mollie's girls won't be watched over by Bubba."

"A good point," Rella said, but she wasn't at all sure she liked Cort's idea. He had said unorthodox, but this particular suggestion went all the way to bizarre. Did he plan to visit her in one of the rooms? Or maybe, since she was determined to stay away from him, he could check on her when he availed himself of the services Mollie provided. Cort had a great capacity for making love, and he'd been celibate a long time.

She seethed at the idea, even as she realized how absurd it was. If Cort wanted a woman for the night, he could no doubt find one who was willing to stay with him for free. Or maybe do the paying herself.

Never having been inside a brothel, Rella found her mental image of such a place far grander than the actuality. No stage director would have designed such a plain setting. In the dimly lighted parlor of Mollie's establishment, she looked in vain for red satin draperies and gaudily dressed damsels of the night stretched out provocatively on velvet settees. Instead, she was met by a half dozen young women standing around in various poses of nonchalance. Each wore a thin gauze wrapper and little else.

A half dozen high-backed chairs and a settee were scattered about a worn rag rug, reminding Rella of a rather faded but genteel parlor. The room looked clean, and it featured one bright spot—a feathered Indian headdress which hung on a nail near the front door.

"Mollie claims to be part Indian," Cort explained, then turned to one of the girls. "Is the boss around?"

"In her office," she answered, gesturing toward a second door at the rear of the small room.

Cort nodded and took Rella by the arm. He hadn't gone two steps before a customer came in behind him.

"Hold up there," the man said in a slurred voice, and Cort turned to stare coldly at him. The newcomer wore a pea jacket and carried with him the salt and fish odor of the sea.

"Been without a woman for six months," he said. "Scrawny looking bunch here. I'm taking that one you got. Hard to tell under all those blasted clothes, but I figure she's got a little meat on her bones. Don't look like she'd fall asleep, neither, once we got a-going."

Rella realized with a start the sailor was looking in her direction.

"How—" she began.

"I'll handle this," Cort said, and then to the sailor, "The lady's taken."

"Lady!" the sailor barked. "Not likely in here."

The rear door of the parlor opened, and Mollie Bigheart stepped into the room. A large proportioned woman with a mass of unnaturally bright red curls piled atop her head, she wore a plain black dress and a diamond brooch at her throat. Her face was smooth, and her cheekbones were high and tinged with rouge, as were her full lips. Rella estimated her age to be around fifty. The hardness around her mouth was offset by a kindness in her eyes that Rella found comforting.

"What's all the commotion out here?" she asked, then her eyes fell on Cort. A worried frown flashed across her face, but it was quickly gone. "Why, Marshal Ramsey. Haven't seen you around in quite a while."

"Had out of town business," he answered. "I came by to ask a favor of you."

Mollie studied Rella for a moment, then looked back at Cort. "I owe you, that's for sure," she said, her broad face broken by a forced smile. "Without charge, and you know how hard it is for me to say that. Almost catches in my throat, even with you."

To Rella's mind, debt or no debt, the woman sounded decidedly unenthusiastic about whatever Cort was about to ask.

"Hell's fire!" the sailor exclaimed. "I got more than money burning in my pants. Ain't anybody interested in a paying customer?"

Mollie gestured to one of the girls, who moved without enthusiasm to rest a hand on the pea jacket sleeve and guide the man from the room.

"Let's go back here," Mollie said.

Inside her office, she settled behind a wide desk and gestured for Cort and Rella to take a seat. "Now what's the favor?" she asked. "Never known you to use one of the girls, but could be you got something unusual in mind, maybe taking on more than one at a time." She glanced briefly at Rella. "Never can tell what a white man will do."

"You run a clean place here, Mollie," Cort said. "I was hoping you could find a room for Miss Sandringham. I'd pay for her keep."

The worried frown returned, and this time it stayed. "I'm full up. Don't need no more girls. Got some upstairs at work right now."

"You're not explaining this very well, Cort," Rella said, then turned to the madam. "I'm not here for employment."

"Miss Sandringham needs a place to stay, out of the way."

Mollie studied her thoughtfully. "She in trouble of some kind?"

"You might say that," Rella said in answer for herself. "I've been charged with murder and theft. Both of which I did not commit."

Mollie sat very still, her eyes trained on Rella. "You're that actress, aren't you? The one they said killed Perry Tuttle."

"How did you know?" asked Rella, startled.

"I hear lots of things here. Galveston ain't that big a place, and you want to know the truth, Perry made more than one visit here."

"Maybe you and I ought to have a talk about him," said Cort.

"Nothing I could say that would help," she said with finality, then stood. "And if you're looking for somewhere to stash the lady, this isn't the place. We got more people passing through here than some of the docks. Like to help you, but I got a business to run."

"Everything all right, Mollie?" Cort said.

Mollie avoided his eyes. "Couldn't be better."

Cort tried a few more questions but was met with the same firmness and forced smile. At last he guided Rella out to the carriage. Evening was settling on the island city; while they had been in Mollie Bigheart's establishment, most of the lamplights had been lit. Caught in their golden glow was the fine mist that had been falling since Rella and Cort had landed, and she pulled the hood of her cloak over her head.

"Let's try the Maas home again," Cort said. "If they're not home this time, we're heading for the hotel."

Rella had no opportunity to find out just what accommodations he had in mind. As they mounted the front steps of the house, Greta flung open the front door and hurried onto the porch. "I saw you from the window," she said in a rush, her round brown eyes brimming with tears. She threw her arms around Rella.

Greta was as blond and plump and softly cuddlesome as she'd ever been, and in returning the hug Rella felt for the first time welcomed back to the island.

The hood of her cloak fell back, and Greta stared up in astonishment.

"This way is natural," Rella explained, brushing one hand through her black hair.

"I like it," the young woman replied.

Bustling about to serve her guests tea, Greta waited until the three of them were seated in the parlor before adding, "I suppose this nonsense about Perry Tuttle is settled."

"Not quite," Rella said. "I can tell you the details later, but for now I need a place to stay. We came by earlier, but you weren't home."

"You poor dear," Greta said, reaching out to pat her hand. "I was at the market. You room is still waiting at the top of the stairs." Greta glanced worriedly at Cort. "Do you still think she's guilty?"

In answering, he looked for a long, warm moment at Rella. "No, I don't. But mine, unfortunately, isn't the only opinion that counts. She's still charged with the crimes." He smiled at Greta. "I was afraid, however, that if I put her in the jail, you would bring another file and we'd all be off and running again."

"And so I would," Greta said. She studied Rella and Cort thoughtfully. "Papa is still working at the dock. He keeps long hours now, but I know he'll be as happy as I am to learn that Rella is staying with us. Since it seems you caught her and dragged her back, at least we can see that she isn't bothered more than necessary."

"I wasn't dragged back," Rella said. When Greta seemed about to question her, she added hurriedly, "We'll have a chance to talk later about all that's happened."

Cort knew when he wasn't wanted—or at least he was fast learning. "I'll be back sometime tomorrow," he said. "It would be best if you didn't leave until I got here," he advised Rella, and then to Greta added, "Don't bother to show me out. I know you two women have much to talk about."

Not as much as he thought, Rella knew as she watched him leave the parlor. For a moment she remembered what it had been like to be on Galveston Island without his support. A feeling of desolation washed over her, an unexpected sense of abandonment, but she brushed it aside. Cort had given her the choice of staying with him, and she hadn't taken it. Oh, how she wanted him right now, the comfort of his strong arms, the balm of his reassuring words.

But Greta was watching her much too closely, and Rella had spent too many years on her own to give in to confession now. She hurriedly gave her friend a sharply expurgated version of the past few months.

"We read about that Chicago fire in the *Daily News*." Greta shuddered. "We've had some bad fires down here, but nothing like that. *Mein Gott!* Imagine your being there when it started. And disguised as a Gypsy!"

"The disguise didn't fool Cort."

"I should think not. Please excuse me if I go too far, but it seems to me he looked at you different. As if you two had become . . . close."

"He feels protective," Rella said hurriedly. "After all, we've been together a long time."

"Papa says two things can happen when people are together a great deal. They either like each other more, or less."

"He must have been talking about you and Aaron," Rella responded, turning aside the unsettling turn of the conversation.

Greta's pale, Teutonic skin was colored by a rosy blush. "As a matter of fact, he was."

"Have things become serious?"

A frown darkened the young woman's face. "Yes . . . and no. Aaron is a deep thinking person. More like Papa than me, really. Only unlike Papa, he can't take care of himself very well. Forgets to eat and things like that. He broods. Lately, he's taken to spending even more of his time than he used to deep in study at the medical school. He needs me to take care of him, but he won't think of anything more serious between us than just friendship. At least not until the culprit who killed his father is found. It still pains him, I guess because he and Herr Tuttle were not close at the end."

"Cort will find out the truth."

"You seem awfully sure."

"I am," Rella affirmed, and realized she meant what she said.

Before Greta could respond, they were interrupted by the slamming of the front door. Rella looked up at Gerhardt Maas as he paused at the parlor door. She was shocked at the change in him. When she left, he'd been a robust and hearty man who sported a fine head of gray hair and a full beard. More, he had carried himself with dignity. There was no light in the eyes of the man who stood before her now, no pride in his bearing. Even his hair lay lax against his bent head, and his arms hung limp at his sides. He'd lost weight, and the suit coat rested in loose folds against his body.

Recognizing her, he smiled. "*Liebchen,* you have

returned."

Not waiting for an invitation, Rella hurried across the parlor and kissed Gerhardt on the cheek. "I have returned."

For a moment, the old twinkle was in the man's eyes. "And without the handcuffs, I see."

Rella settled back and looked directly into his lined face, which was on a level with hers. "I've been released on bail. Cort . . . Marshal Ramsey agreed I could stay here."

Gerhardt's eyes widened for a moment, and he studied her thoughtfully. "You have changed, my little *fraulein*. There is not the worry about you. At least not as I remember it."

The response that came to Rella's mind died on her lips. Why tell him all that he, too, had changed? That the same kind of sick worry she once had carried now rested in his eyes?

"Are you hungry, Papa?" Greta asked from behind her.

He shook his head. "Please excuse me. The day has been long."

With a nod, he headed down the hallway toward his room at the back of the house. Rella remembered a sharp step against the hardwood floor, but all she heard now was a kind of slow shuffle. The sound was as worrisome as anything she had witnessed since his return.

She turned to face Greta. "What's wrong?"

"It is not your trouble. You have enough of your own."

"You helped me once, and are helping me now. We share our worries."

Reluctantly, Greta began to speak, slowly at first, and then the words came out in a rush. "Remember the trouble down at the dock? Papa won't tell me what is happening, but it is enough to make him stay away long hours and return as you have seen him, sick with private thoughts he won't share. There is bad trouble there, I know it. We left Germany because Papa did not like being told to do things with which he disagreed. Here, I am afraid he has found the same thing."

"Is there anyone who can help him?"

"Who could there be? I suggested he talk to someone in authority, but he told me to leave him alone. He has never"—Greta's voice broke—"spoken to me in such a way."

"There is someone now to help him."

"You?" Greta asked in wonderment.

"Hardly. I can't keep myself out of trouble, much less help anyone else." She started to add that she couldn't without posing as a Gypsy and carrying a knife in her boot. But she had left out the incident of the stagecoach robbery and Cort's abduction. Such a tale could be saved for later, a long time later when Rella had accepted how the incident had ended in so much death.

"I meant Cort," she said firmly. "Believe me, Greta, you can trust him. We will seek him out tomorrow and tell him that you know."

"But he is busy already, is he not?"

"Investigating Perry's death? Yes, he is. But," Rella said, admitting privately to her prideful love of him, "there's not much Marshal Ramsey can't do. Once he sets his mind to it."

Gerhardt left early, before the two women had risen from bed. After breakfast, Rella helped Greta hitch a swaybacked pony to the Maas carriage, a shabby affair that Greta said had been abandoned on the edge of town.

"Papa fixed it up and bought the pony, for me. He walks to his work. I use it mainly for journeys to the medical school."

The day dawned cool and crisp. It was the kind of weather that showed off the island to its best. There were few flowers anywhere; but the first frost had not yet arrived, and the island was still green. Maybe they should have waited for Cort to come by, she thought, but on such a beautiful morning he would understand that she was eager to be outside.

They made a quick trip to the jail, the only place where Rella knew to look for Cort. Since he obviously didn't think she would seek him out at his hotel room, he hadn't bothered to tell her where it was.

Walking up the long pathway that led from the street, Rella could hear angry voices from inside the jail office. Cort's, she recognized right away, having heard it often enough before. With Greta close behind, she quickened her step.

"You're a fool, Bowles," Cort was saying. "Ben Woods might have left in shame, but he wasn't the only one who let her get away. You were here, too."

As she neared the open door, Rella slowed her step.

"She caught me from behind," the unseen Bowles growled.

"Then I'm protecting you by keeping her away. So she can't assault you again."

"That's a lie," Bowles said, his voice raised in anger. "No way the bitch could catch me again. And there's no way a murderer like her should be let loose on the town. Why not admit the truth? You've been poking her all the way from wherever it was you caught up with her. You just don't want to give it up."

"Uh, oh," said Rella. "Bowles is up to his old insulting ways."

She arrived in the doorway in time to see Cort grab the deputy by the collar of his shirt, jerk him across the desk, and wipe the startled look from his face with a fist planted firmly against his jaw.

Chapter Twenty-one

"Cort!" Rella cried out.

Turning to the cry, he failed to see the blow coming from the rallying Bowles. It caught him from behind and landed hard against the base of his skull. His head jerked from the force of the deputy's punch, and he staggered forward. Bowles moved in fast, rounding to come head first at Cort and smashing a fist into his jaw.

Cort stumbled, caught himself, then with a quick jab sank his elbow into the deputy's belly. Bowles let out a sharp breath of air, clutching at his stomach, and Cort finished him off with a hard right and a left to the jaw. Bowles crumpled to the jailhouse floor.

It all happened fast. Taking a deep breath, Cort glanced sideways to see the jailer Bubba hurrying into the office from the back, a growl forming in his throat.

"Take care of your boss," Cort said, gesturing to the fallen deputy. He leaned down to pick up his hat, slapped it against his thigh, and turned to Rella. "Let's get out of here."

"That was the . . . most *courteous* thing I've ever seen," Greta said from her place of safety at the edge of the doorway.

Rella stepped deeper into the room, took one look at the cut on the back of Cort's head, and said, "Or the dumbest." She stared at him in disgust. "My honor didn't need defending. We both knew Bowles was bound to draw his own conclusions about what's been going on." Taking a handkerchief from her purse, she daubed gingerly at the flow of blood in the matted hair at his neck. "You're just too hot tempered for your own good."

Cort caught her hand in his. "Probably. But you have no idea how much satisfaction that gave me."

Their gazes locked, and Rella felt herself sway closer to him, taking his strength as her own. The restlessness she'd felt since he left her the evening before slowly warmed into a familiar feeling of rightness now that they were together again.

Bowles moaned as Bubba helped him to his feet and into the chair behind the desk. Cort let go of her hand. "When he comes to," he said to the jailer, "tell him we'll talk later. If he can mind his manners better."

With an arm at Rella's waist, he directed the two women down the walk. They were met at the street by Alderman Abner Hayes. Dressed in black suit and string tie, a bowler hat resting on neatly trimmed gray hair, he looked every inch the upright businessman.

Rella remembered him from that time long ago when she'd waited in a downstairs restaurant on the Strand for Cort to search her room at the boardinghouse. The alderman had been ready to hang her then, and from the grim look about him, she decided he hadn't changed his mind. Instinctively she pulled her cloak close against her body.

"Where you taking her, Marshal?" Hayes asked without preliminaries.

Cort lifted his hat in greeting, then settled it back low on his forehead. "Good morning, Alderman Hayes. The citizens of Galveston must be resting easy on this Tuesday morning, knowing you're up and about and seeing that all is right with the world."

"Yes, yes," Hayes said impatiently with a tug at his hat. "Good morning. Now answer my question. Shouldn't this culprit be in jail?"

Deciding she'd been called *culprit* one time too many, Rella said in exasperation, "I'm far too vicious to be housed in there. The marshal has a special place picked out for me where I can't escape."

Hayes frowned at Cort. "That true?"

"That's one way of looking at it, I suppose," Cort said. "You might want to run on inside and talk to Bowles. When he's able. I'm sure he'll have another version. I wouldn't put too much stock in what he says, however. The man woke up this morning in a terrible temper."

So saying, Cort guided the women to their carriage, then unhitched a bay gelding from a nearby post. Mounting, he pulled the bay to a halt close to Rella. "We're going back to the house," he said, "and remember I'll be riding behind you."

As usual, Rella thought, and with a flick of the reins worked the horse and carriage into the passing morning traffic.

Cort saved the rest of his comments until they were settled once again in the parlor of the Maas home.

"Care to tell me what brought you out?"

"For a change, it wasn't me or my troubles. Greta,

tell him what you've told me about the trouble on the wharves."

Cort listened quietly, then said, "That's not much to go on. Lots of men let long hours at work change them. Maybe he's just worried about money."

"We brought that with us," Greta said. "Not much, but we don't starve, and we were able to buy this house."

"Wasn't your father a professor back in Germany? He's not used to working on the docks."

"He doesn't load cotton, Marshal Ramsey. He keeps the books. Are you saying you haven't heard anything about any kind of trouble he might have come across?"

"Just rumors. The only sure thing I know is that the wharf company charges entirely too much for shipping goods out of here, but the owners won't listen. That's hardly enough to upset your father the way you claim."

"Have you ever heard of a man named Rip Griffin? Papa mentioned his name once. A big brute and bully, he called him, who came from someplace in the South. He's one of the labor leaders among the screwmen. Papa says he's powerful, since it's his crew that increases the load of goods on the ships."

Cort listened carefully. Only yesterday he'd heard Griffin's name for the first time. Bowles had said the new jailer Bubba had worked for him on the docks. It seemed a curious coincidence. And Cort didn't care for coincidences.

"So what has Griffin got to do with your father?"

Greta bit at her lower lip. "I don't know. It's just that Papa mentioned him, and he's not said any other names. He was talking more to himself than he was to me, but I got the feeling he didn't like the man. And with the way he's been worrying lately, I thought you ought to know. Rella said you were the one who could help."

"She did?" he asked casually, casting a brief look at Rella, who promptly blushed.

"I did," Rella said in defense. "I decided that since you were so sure you could solve my problems all by yourself, you might as well work on Maas's at the same time."

Cort stood. "Then I better get to work."

Rella stood. "How can I help?"

"By doing what I ask and staying out of the way."

"I'm good for more than that."

"I'm glad to hear you say it," Cort said softly.

"I meant in the investigation," Rella shot back.

Cort shrugged innocently. "So did I. Put your mind to work. You've got a good one. Try to remember back to the days before Tuttle was killed. Write down anything that seemed out of the ordinary, any new business he might have been involved in." He turned to Greta. "And you do the same with your father. I'll be back later for a report."

As Cort headed down the front walk, he turned back to Rella and Greta, who stood on the porch. "I'm going to find Marcus Clapper. Be back as soon as I can."

As he rode toward the small house Clapper rented on the west side of the island, Cort held the picture of Rella, hands on hips and a firm look of disapproval on that lovely face, long in his mind. She'd been a beautiful sight, an inspiration for a man to do the best he could not to disappoint her—ever. Damn. Here he was getting hot and bothered just thinking about her. There was one way he hadn't disappointed her, nor the other way around. She'd been everything a man could want. By God, he would see to it that this piss-ant of a clerk confessed the truth about Perry Tuttle's dying words.

Not knowing whether Clapper had sought and found employment since the murder, he hoped the clerk would be at home. A neighbor told him Clapper was working at an office on the dock, and Cort retraced his ride, coming close to the Maas home before turning toward the wharf.

When he entered the dingy, one-room office at the end of one of the warehouses, he found it empty and had to content himself with a visit to Perry Tuttle's office on the Strand.

"Most everything's been cleaned out," said the real estate man who let him in. "That son of his gathered up the papers. Been trying to rent the place, but folks don't want no part of a room where a man was killed. Maybe if I could rent it to some fortune teller or such, it might have the right atmosphere. But not for anyone respectable."

Remembering the times he'd visited Rella, or more correctly the Romany, in a Chicago fairgrounds tent, Cort decided this was one conversation he was better off not repeating.

Late in the afternoon, when he returned to the wharf, he found Marcus Clapper at work in his dingy office. He was in shirt sleeves and sat bent over a stack of papers, a green eyeshade protecting him from the glare of a nearby lamp. He looked up, startled, when Cort flung open the door.

"When did you get back in town?" he whined. "Don't know what you're doing here. I already told you all I know."

"Not under oath."

"I will, when the time comes. You got that bitch

thrown in jail, I take it. It's where she belongs."

Cort settled his long frame into a cane-bottomed chair opposite Clapper's neat desk and contented himself with a clinched fist. He'd hit one man in defense of her already today; for his efforts, she'd insisted her honor didn't need defending. This time he figured she was right. "I want to hear it all again," he said.

Clapper's thin lips settled into a grimace of distaste. "That was all a long time ago, but I remember it clearly. In case you're worried my testimony has changed."

Cort's worry was that it hadn't, but he kept silent, waiting for the clerk to continue.

"I heard a shot from downstairs, rushed up, and found Mr. Tuttle the way you found him. Of course I tried to help, but it was too late. All he managed to say was that woman's name."

"You couldn't have been mistaken."

"I know what I heard."

"What exactly did you hear?"

Clapper cleared his throat. "Rella, he said. Rella Sandringham."

"Are you sure it wasn't Cinderella?"

Using the cuff of his shirt, Clapper blotted beads of sweat from his upper lip. "He didn't have time to say much, not with a hole in his chest. What difference does it make?"

Cort felt sure the pasty faced young man was lying and wondered how he could ever have believed him. Rella had accused him of being too close to the case; he hadn't realized it at the time, but she'd been right.

"It makes a difference," he said. "Now tell me again."

Clapper did as he was instructed, and this time he insisted his late employer had whispered the name Rella. "She led him on, you know," he added maliciously. "The poor man was stunned that she could have done such a thing. Even with him stretched out the way he was and so near death, I could read it in his eyes."

Cort tried a wild shot. "What was Perry involved in?" he asked. "What didn't he want people to know?"

Clapper's eyes flared for a moment. "Don't have any idea what you're getting at."

Success, Cort thought, or at least the hint of it. "I think you do. He was an ambitious man. You might almost say greedy."

For a moment Clapper let his guard down. "Tight-fisted, was more like it."

"You mean he didn't pass on to you much of the profits he was taking in."

"It wasn't any of my business what he was up to," the clerk said warily, like a cornered animal. "He thought he was getting to be a bigwig around town. Even considered running for public office."

"Did he ever mention any office in particular?"

Clapper shook his head. "I don't think he cared. Just wanted to be important. If anything illegal was going on, I didn't know it. You might ask Cinderella. She handled more of the business than I did. Imagine she could tell you a thing or two."

"I prefer to ask you."

"I've told you all I know."

"Take some time to remember. See if you can't come up with something else. I'll be back to question you later," said Cort, rising.

"You better take my deposition soon in case I'm

not here by the time she comes to trial."

"And where might you be?"

Clapper seemed to draw strength from whatever he was thinking, and he smiled smugly up at Cort. "I'm supposed to come into some money. If everything works out, I'm leaving."

"Hasn't your family lived on the island a long time?"

"It's not the same place it was before the war. Too many Yankees coming down and taking over. Nothing to keep me here."

"And if I refuse to take a statement from you?"

"Then I'll have to talk to someone else."

"Deputy Bowles, perhaps."

Clapper started. "Could be he's the only one who will listen. I plan to talk to him, yes."

"Just don't leave town until we've talked. I'd hate to have to go after you, but if necessary, I will."

By the time Cort got out of the musty office, he was in need of some fresh air. And he figured Rella would feel the same. An evening ride along the beach was very much in order. The air was cool, but not yet cold the way it would be back in Missouri. It was a clear November, the first stars were breaking out overhead—he thought of a million reasons for such a ride. But the most important one was simply that he wanted to be alone with her.

He made a quick stop by a livery to rent another horse, then made his way to the Maas home. Gerhardt had not yet returned from work.

"Thought you might like a ride along the beach," he said when he met Rella in the parlor. "Got a horse saddled and waiting outside." He glanced down at the soft green dress that she wore, the one that brought out the rich color of her skin. He almost regretted that he hadn't got her a sidesaddle, but then he also liked seeing her in pants.

"I'll change and be right down," she said. She was true to her word. When she returned, she was wearing the trousers he'd bought her back in Illinois, along with the boots, shirt, and coat. Her black hair hung shining about her shoulders, and there was a sparkle in her blue eyes he hadn't seen since back in Startzville.

His loins tightened. Back then, she hadn't been wearing anything at all. He liked that picture even better than the one of her in pants.

"Would you care to join us?" Rella said to Greta in a last minute gesture of courtesy.

"That old carriage of mine wouldn't make it through the sand," she said, "and I don't know how to ride. Besides, I imagine you two want to be alone. To talk over the case."

Cort figured he owed the girl a bouquet of flowers for declining so graciously.

He guided Rella to a stretch of beach on the east end of the island where he knew there was little development and even less chance of their being interrupted in their talk. On the way, he reported his conversation with the former law clerk.

"He says Perry was thinking of running for office? I'm not surprised. He was getting very sure of himself. Once he bragged that he just might become a social and civic leader. After the Yankees got out of town."

Cort ignored the sly look she cast him. "Were you and Greta able to come up with anything that might help? Either with Tuttle or the trouble on the dock."

"Nothing we haven't already discussed. I'm sure Marcus is the one we ought to be working on," she said contemptuously, thinking of several things to call the clerk, all terms she'd picked up since being on the road with Cort. She contented herself with a shake of her head. "I'm sure he's lying."

"He sure seemed it today."

"Then how do we prove it?" she asked, guiding her horse across the low lying dunes toward the hard-packed sand close to the water's edge.

"*We* don't. Leave it to me."

Before she could argue, Cort dug his boots into the bay's flanks and yelled over his shoulder, "Let's see if you've forgotten how to ride."

Rella's protest was lost in the night air. Following Cort's lead, she set the mare in motion in his wake and was surprised at how easily she was able to put Marcus Clapper from her mind.

With the wind flowing freely through her unbound hair, she gave herself up to the glory of the ride. Unable to catch up with the bay, she managed to keep the distance between them even. What a glorious night it was, with myriad stars twinkling overhead, and a sliver of a moon casting down its silver light. The only sounds were the constant, irregular lap of the surf as it met the land and the pounding of horses' hoofs.

And then came her deep gulps for air when they reined to a halt two hundred yards down the beach.

Cort dismounted, and Rella yelled, "Catch me!" She fell from the saddle and into his arms. "Good man," she said, laughing up at him. "That was wonderful."

"It still is," he answered huskily, and Rella pulled herself from his arms. While he ground tethered the horses near a clump of marsh grass in the dunes, she caught her breath. Cort had an amazing effect on her. Just a touch, or the sound of his voice, and she melted inside.

Gradually her heartbeat slowed until it matched the soothing whisper of the waves. She stared out at the dark reach of the sea. What if she and Cort could catch a passing vessel and just ride away? They were both inventive enough. Somehow they could lose themselves and find a living out there.

"A penny for your thoughts," Cort whispered against her ear.

Lost in her dream, Rella said. "I was thinking about sailing away."

The silence behind her was broken at last by one sharp word. "Again?"

With a start, Rella realized Cort had misunderstood. She parted her lips to tell him that she hadn't been planning to leave alone. She didn't get the chance.

Cort whirled her around and clasped strong hands to her shoulders. Anger flared in the depths in his eyes. "I've always thought you could know a person by the kind of wishes he makes. You obviously want to get away."

"You always jump to conclusions, Cort," she said with an anger of her own.

"I just always give you too much rope," he said, his thumbs stroking her throat. "Somehow, you manage to hang yourself. If you're pretending you're leaving, then I'll pretend I'm telling you good-bye."

He pulled her tight against him, the anger in his eyes darkened to desire. Rella struck her fists against his chest. "No, Cort, no. Not this way."

"You won't fight long. You never do."

He caught her chin in one hand, and hard lips pressed against hers. Weakened, she tried to pound her fists against him once again; but her blows landed ineffectually, and she found herself spreading wide her fingers to hold tight to his shoulders. His muscles flexed tightly beneath her grip.

He loosened his hold for one second, and in a flash she was out of his arms and running down the beach. A narrow path of silver moonlight marked the way.

He caught her by the wrist and again whirled her around.

"Cort—" she managed.

His eyes burned down on her. "I'll stop if you want."

"I—"

"If you *really* want." He pulled her close. "But you'll have to convince me. And running when you know I'll catch you isn't good enough."

He brushed his lips against hers, softly, his kiss as gentle as the breeze blowing off the Gulf. With one hand still holding her wrist, he stroked her face, outlined her lips with one finger, then trailed down the column of her neck. Resting his hand against her throat, he felt her quickening heartbeat and smiled.

His fingers continued their silken, silent journey, pulling her coat aside, moving down the vee of her open shirt, wandering for a delicious moment around the soft rise of one breast and then the other. Slowly he began to work at the buttons, letting the tips of his fingers touch her tingling skin.

"Tell me when to stop," he whispered as he pulled the fabric aside.

Rella trembled and felt an engulfing rush of desire. Cort knew her better than she knew herself—to her everlasting shame. She'd never fought for long, he said, and she couldn't now. She was more than caught in his grip. She was trapped by the wonder and power of him, by the glory of his touch, by the burning love she felt for him and the need to join her body with his once again.

When he pressed her down onto the soft sand, she felt the very spinning of the earth. They seemed in some primal place, isolated, yet all the world they would ever require they held in their arms.

She would welcome him for as long as he desired her . . . *as long as he desired her.* The thought echoed in her mind. She opened her eyes to stare up at him. His gaze was on her bared breasts, his breath ragged. She knew how strong was his need. He wanted her above all else—for now. But Rella wanted so much more. A lifetime of being with him would not be enough. Maybe Cort wanted the same, but all he'd ever asked was for a time of passion. The world stopped spinning; she felt only the pounding of blood in her ears and a coldness that clutched at her heart.

Cort knew the moment she began to pull away from him . . . if not in body, then certainly in the pitch of her desire. He lifted his head and gazed down at her. Tears welled in her widened eyes and ran in a thin line to moisten her temples and the edge of her hair.

"St-stop," she managed. It came out a sob, but Cort understood.

Slowly he lifted his body from hers and fell back on the sand beside her to stare up at the stars. "You're a surprising woman," he said, his voice still husky. "I didn't think you'd say it."

Bared to the elements, she felt a chill wind pass over her. Pulling her jacket closed, she hugged her body to ward off the cold despair that held her in its grip.

"I'm surprised you stopped."

"To tell you the truth, it wasn't easy to do."

Rella's heart seemed caught in her throat. Whatever happened now, she knew she was fighting for the future of them both. Cort's lust was powerful and she satisfied him. But there were so many levels to the union of a man and a woman. Trust and respect must be mingled with that physical desire. Perhaps, somehow in her misery, she'd stumbled across the definition of love.

The thought bouyed her. She was not rejecting Cort, even though he might take it as such. But she couldn't explain what she felt in her heart. It was a discovery he would have to make for himself, and not in such a sensual setting, with ocean breezes wafting over them and the pounding of the surf giving rise to the internal rhythms of increasing need.

Slowly her breathing steadied. "It wasn't easy for me, either. But I did say it, didn't I?" she whispered, trying to concentrate on the brightest star that glimmered in the night sky. "I wasn't able to back in Illinois, and not out on the trail. And later I welcomed you into my room."

"You don't have to remind me, Rella. I remember each time."

"Then remember that I asked you to stay away from me until my problems were settled."

Abruptly Cort sat up, then drew himself to his feet. "And so I promised." He reached out a hand and pulled her upright to stand beside him. "What good is a man if he won't stick with his word?"

What good indeed, she thought as they walked

along the beach toward the horses. She half berated herself for denying what they both so sharply desired—and half rejoiced that she had done the right thing. The right thing, that is, if Cort realized the truth behind her actions; the right thing if he shared what she felt in her heart.

When Cort cupped her booted foot in his hands and helped her to mount, he knew only that Rella had pulled away from him. He wanted her now and forever. Was it fair not to tell her? Or was it better to wait until all other worries were gone from her mind?

She was a wanderer, as he had been until he held her in his arms. The real question was, had she changed in ways that mattered? He couldn't force her to love him, couldn't make her stay. He watched her ride out ahead of him, her hair streaming behind her, her slender body moving gracefully in the saddle.

Funny, but as he saw it, the main obstacle that stood in their way was that mealy-mouthed clerk Marcus Clapper. Cort's hands tightened on the reins. Clapper had talked about coming into some money and maybe leaving. Tomorrow Cort would talk to him again and find out just what money he had been talking about and exactly where he planned to head.

Alone in her upstairs room, Rella thought back over the evening. Pushing aside the interlude on the beach, she concentrated on everything else Cort had said and done. Primarily her thoughts circled around Marcus Clapper. How dare he claim to hold proof that she had killed Perry Tuttle. She'd always been able to intimidate the weak-spined man. With no more than a look from her, his attempts at flirtation had ceased. And he'd never won an argument from her, not once.

She needed to confront him herself, alone, without Cort to interfere. But if she waited until morning, she knew the chances of such a confrontation were slim. Cort had left the unsaddled mare in the Maas barn, explaining he would return her to the livery stable in the morning. It wasn't late, not nearly midnight, and she knew exactly where Marcus lived.

Greta and her father were already retired to their rooms below. Slipping into her clothes, she tiptoed down the stairs, let herself out the back door, and made a hasty line for the barn. Mindful of the way a fire could start with even a little hay scattered about, she handled the lantern with special care. In only minutes, the mare was saddled, the barn once more darkened, and she was riding toward her destination.

A low rumble sounded to her right, and she cast a glance sideways in time to see a line of lightning brighten the northern horizon. Storms came quickly to the island, and it looked as though one was on the way now.

She wasn't so brave to keep to the center of the main roads, instead taking the alleys and byways, keeping to the shadows, calling no attention to herself. Galveston was populated by visitors from all over the world, some passing through. There were bound to be those bent on mischief, or at least willing to take advantage of a female who suddenly came upon them in the dark of night.

The rumbling grew louder, but she forced herself to ignore it. Less easy was the flash of lightning that cut through the sky directly in her path. The mare spooked, and it took all of Rella's concentration to keep the horse under control.

With the storm rolling quickly in, the night shadows around her took on an ominous appearance. At least she hadn't come unarmed, she assured herself. She'd taken care to slip the knife in her boot, the knife she'd sworn never to carry again when she had finally accepted it from Sheriff Alcorn. But desperate times called for desperate means. Cort had taught her that. She certainly didn't plan to use it, but she welcomed the sense of security that came with having it within her grasp.

A loud clap of thunder sounded directly overhead, heralding her arrival on the street where Marcus lived. Forsaking caution, she quickly made her way down the center of the street for the final two blocks of her journey. His house was dark, and she found herself moving as silently as possible onto the porch. She realized how silly that was. The thunder was almost a constant rumble now, and the night turned to day by the lightning. Besides, she planned to wake him for a talk, so why be so quiet?

She pounded on the door. "Marcus!" she called out over the sounds of the approaching storm, then pounded again. She met with no response. The noises she was making echoed through the heavy night air; they seemed loud enough to wake the dead.

She tried the handle; it turned and the door creaked open. How careless of the clerk to leave it unlocked, and how typical. Marcus didn't have any more sense than a toad.

But then, neither did she, Rella decided as she groped for a lamp beside the door. She soon was blessed with a diffused gas light that illuminated the narrow entryway. "Marcus," she called up the stairs, softly, although she didn't know why. A low moan came from the room to her right. She lifted the lamp and, heart pounding so violently that it hurt, made her cautious way into the room.

She saw him lying on the floor behind a couch. Hurrying to him, she kneeled to stare into the pale face. Blood stained the front of his shirt as well as the floor beneath him, and she was swept up in a feeling of déjà vu.

"Who, Marcus? Who? she said, afraid to lift his head, afraid to leave for help.

His eyes opened, and his lips parted, but no sound emerged other than an incoherent gurgle. A trickle of blood ran from the corner of his mouth, and his head dropped back, his eyes wide and staring. Rella knew he was dead.

"Well, well, what have we here?" came a voice from behind her.

Rella twisted around with a jerk and stared, opened mouthed, at the grinning face of Deputy Ernest Bowles, who was standing in the doorway, a gun in his hand.

Chapter Twenty-two

The rain held off until Rella was once again being led down the long, dark corridor of the Galveston County Jail. On a night marked by disaster, it was the one thing she had to be grateful for.

What is Cort going to say when he finds out?

The thought came in a rush, the same as it had over and over since she first stared into Ernest Bowles' grinning face an hour before. It had pushed from her mind any thoughts of sympathy she might have felt for the slain clerk.

Behind her, the thud of the jailer Bubba's boots marked a harsh cadence to her thoughts, and she moved without protest to her fate. As far as she could tell, the back cell had not been redecorated in the five months between her visits. The same two cots, low and hard, were pushed against bare stone walls; the closest fresh air—tonight cold and damp—came from a high, barred window at the end of the corridor. Even the storm raging outside was reminiscent of the hurricane that had swept across the island just before her escape.

Worst of all, when Bubba shoved her none too gently inside, the clang of the door slamming closed behind her rang as harsh and final in the dimness as it had before.

The only things that had changed were her fellow prisoners. Instead of the dreamy Widow Welch communicating with her late husband, Rella was met with the bored stares of two undernourished whores from Postoffice and Market Streets, the ones that Deputy Bowles had mentioned yesterday as unable to pay their fines. Clad in faded dresses that rested in folds against their lank frames, they were sprawled out on the cots and looked in no hurry to make room for a fellow cell mate.

Rella brushed one hand nervously against her trousers and, clearing her mind of all else save her present predicament, nodded a greeting to the two women. Neither the thin-lipped blonde to her left nor the dark-haired woman to her right did so much as blink.

And what was she supposed to do now—lean against the bars or maybe crouch on the floor in a corner? Neither choice seemed very inviting, and it looked like a long night was ahead of her. With Cort thinking she was safely tucked away in her bed at the Maas home, he wasn't likely to come riding to her rescue anytime soon.

Not that she was in a hurry for him to appear. He had warned her to let him handle the investigation, and it wasn't likely he would take kindly to her interference—especially since it had taken such an unfortunate turn.

Unfortunate? Rather an inadequate word, she thought. As her dear mother used to say, she had come a cropper now.

What she needed was time to rest and to formulate a defense, to go over everything she knew about her situation and see if she could figure out where all the pieces fit. Ernest Bowles had generously provided her with the place and time; more than she had ever thought possible, she craved one of those cots.

The two whores continued to look up at her with glares that dared her to oust them. Rella squared her shoulders. She hadn't grown up on the stage without picking up an idea or two. She knew when a scene was needed, and she knew how to play it.

Hooking one thumb in her pants pocket, she looked from one woman to the other. "Easy to see what you're in for," she said contemptuously. "Not me. No man is gonna pay for what I've got. At least not in cash."

The blonde stirred, and the other licked her lips. It wasn't exactly a standing ovation, but it was a start.

"I make 'em pay with their lives." The two women exchanged nervous glances, and Rella realized they weren't very smart. She would have felt sorry about moving them, but she figured since they made their living lying on their backs, they could for one night fit their curiously unfeminine frames onto a single bed.

"At least," she continued, "that's what the deputy says."

"That jackass," the dark-haired one hissed.

"Now we agree there. He claims I killed two men."

The one who had spoken sat up. "You in for killing?"

"That's right. And I'm awfully tired. I aim to lie down, and if it's with one of you, that's the way of it."

The speaker moved faster than Rella expected. "Come on, Sugar, let's share. Give 'er a little room."

"Shit!" Sugar mumbled, but move she did and was joined by her fellow business woman.

Rella stretched out on the empty bed and promptly turned her back to them. She had a lot of thinking to do. Bowles hadn't let her do much of anything except what he ordered. He'd clamped handcuffs on her and led her by horseback through the dark streets to the jail. Bubba had seemed pleased to see her, but the feeling was hardly mutual.

The deputy at this moment was supposedly summoning a doctor and an undertaker to care for the late Marcus Clapper. Bowles promised to take her statement in the morning, but what could she say? The gun had been on the floor near the body. Both Marcus and the Colt were still warm.

And in a most unpleasant search of her body, he'd found Alepa's knife.

Bowles said he was just making some rounds when he heard a commotion at the Clapper home. "Had an idea with you back in town, the primary witness against you might be in danger."

"Marcus was dead when I got there," Rella had protested. "Or at least almost."

It was the sole time Bowles had seemed interested in what she had to say. "Almost, eh?"

"That's right. Unfortunately, he died before he could speak."

"Probably said your name. Same as Tuttle. You brought the knife to do him in but must have found a gun when you got there. Little lady, you should have stayed away. I can see that noose around your neck right now."

Rella had ceased to speak. And here she was back in a jail cell awaiting who knew what legal procedure that would sink her deeper in trouble. And all because she had decided to do things right. Maybe, she thought as she huddled beneath a thin blanket and tried to forget the storm, she really should quit thinking at all.

Cort didn't make it to the Maas home as early as he'd planned. He had done a lot of thinking during the long and turbulent night. Rella still wanted to leave; she had as much as told him so last night, despite her halfhearted disclaimer. But for a damned brief time she had held onto him as though he were the most important thing in her life.

Once the ridiculous murder charges against her were dropped, he had a lot of things to ask her. And to tell her. Maybe the woman didn't know her own mind. Maybe she was waiting for him to tell her how things were.

He owed her a great deal. After all his promises, in the two days since their return to Galveston he hadn't been able to turn up anything that would prove her innocence. Hints and innuendos and suspicions, that was all. And such things would hardly stand up in court.

The morning dawned clear, the only evidence of the storm the leaves that lay in sodden masses on the ground and a few fallen limbs.

He decided to call on Mollie Bigheart. She knew Perry Tuttle, maybe knew more than she had told. And she hadn't been at all glad to see him yesterday, unlike the other times he had been there. Of course then he'd been doing her a favor by settling some disturbance. Now it was time to collect on her debt.

Cort took the precaution of leaving his bay at the

livery stable. He wasn't sure why, but it made sense that if Mollie didn't want to talk to him, she also wouldn't want whoever had made her so nervous to know that he was inside.

One of the girls let him in the front door, then disappeared. The parlor was empty. Entering Mollie's office after a brief knock, he found her standing behind her desk, back to the door, her attention directed out the room's lone window. She wore the same black dress she'd had on yesterday, but instead of the curls piled high on her head, the bright red hair hung loose against her shoulders.

"Good morning," he said. "I'm glad I found you still up."

He could see her body draw tight.

"I was just getting ready to go upstairs to bed," she said, keeping her back to him. "I told you I didn't have any room here for that girl."

"That's not why I've come by this morning. We need to talk."

"Leave me alone, Marshal. I got nothing to say."

"It's not that easy. You once said that any favor I wanted, you would grant. I've got one now."

"I had something more physical in mind besides talk."

"What's wrong, Mollie? What's got you so upset?"

"Nothing."

"You want to do me a favor, you can start by turning around. It's hard talking to your back."

After a long moment of silence, Mollie slowly did as he asked. Cort gave a start. The left side of her face was red and swollen; one eye, badly bruised, was almost closed.

"Somebody wanted to play rough," she said with a shrug, then winced in pain.

"You don't go with the customers anymore."

Mollie avoided his eyes. "For a few of the old-timers, I do. They seem more comfortable with a mature woman."

"Are you saying someone you've known for a long time did this to you? That's hard to believe."

"Believe what you will. Just leave me alone."

"Unless someone's watching the front door—and I looked around before I came in—then my visit here is a secret. If that'll put your mind at rest."

"He—" Mollie caught herself. "People find out. People always find out what you don't want 'em to know. That's what got me beat up this way."

"Then you know something, Mollie. Something you're not supposed to. Did maybe one of those old-timers talk too much? Maybe brag a little and then have second thoughts about being indiscreet?"

Mollie sighed. "Damn you, Marshal. You just won't give up."

"There are lives at stake."

She laughed harshly. "You're not telling me anything I don't already know."

"I can put you under protective custody."

"Which would do about as much good as protecting a slab of meat in a roaring fire."

"Has this got anything to do with Perry Tuttle?"

"You're a persistent man," she said. "I'm going to tell you one thing, and one thing only. Then we're even. No favors owed, no favors asked. Perry Tuttle got mixed up in something he regretted. Tried to pull out when he decided to be respectable. Only someone else decided that maybe he knew a little too much to live."

"Then he wasn't killed for the money in the safe."

"Near as I can tell, that money just happened to

be extra. Made everyone think robbery was the motive."

Cort thought fast. A pattern seemed to be developing here, a web that had caught Perry and Rella and Mollie. Even insignificant Marcus Clapper was somehow involved, and beyond just having been the one to find his dying employer. Marcus had said he was coming into money. The idea of blackmail settled in Cort's mind. It was the sort of thing the clerk would try.

A wild shot had worked with Marcus. Remembering where he'd found employment, Cort tried another one now.

"So Perry was mixed up in the trouble on the dock after all," he said as if slowly figuring something out, but he kept his eyes trained on Mollie's face. "I thought he might be."

"How did you—" Again she caught herself. "Think what you will," she said. "I'm not telling you anything more." Holding herself erect, she moved slowly around the desk and past Cort. From the stiff way she carried herself, Cort knew she bore more bruises than the ones that showed.

She paused in the doorway and glanced back, giving him a last look at her injured face.

"Now I'm going upstairs and pretend that you never came by and if you did, I never said a thing that you wanted to hear. If you swear anything different, may you rot in hell."

Maybe Mollie was trying to warn him off, but Cort could look back on their conversation with nothing less than grim satisfaction—and a determination to right the injustice done her. But he'd have to move cautiously. Enough people had been hurt by whatever evil was spreading across the island. He'd always thought Galveston a beautiful place, a little unfriendly to some in this time of Reconstruction, but still, with all the immigrants pouring in from around the world, a growing, exciting city.

Evil could take the excitement out of a place fast, especially one that encouraged families to settle and businesses to start up. Rella had originally come here, like many of those people on the ship, just passing through. Circumstances had forced her to remain, in her case a fire, and she'd been trapped. Trapped by him, he thought bitterly, and his damned stubborn determination that she was guilty.

Cort had always believed in standing up to trouble; when she'd run, he had taken that as proof of her guilt. All it really showed was that she was scared, and that the opportunity for escape had presented itself.

No matter what troubles lay between the two of them, she needed to be in on the investigation. As determined as she was, she might get Marcus Clapper to break this morning. After a trip to the livery stable for the bay, he made a hasty trip to get her.

Greta, hands wringing in front of her, met him on the front porch.

"*Mein Gott,* I'm glad you've come! I was just about to hitch up the horse and try to find you."

"What's wrong?"

"She's gone. Disappeared."

An icy dread gripped Cort. "How long?"

"I don't know. Papa had already left when I got up, and I let her sleep late. Or at least, that's what I thought I was doing. But when I went upstairs to see if she was all right, her bed was empty."

"Last night I left a horse in the barn."

"It's not there now."

Cort's mind raced. It was entirely possible she knew where Marcus Clapper lived and had headed out early this morning to confront him before he left for work.

"Stay here in case she returns. I'll let you know if I find out anything."

Whatever Cort had expected to find, it wasn't a guard standing at Marcus's front door.

"Deputy Bowles asked me to keep out intruders," the man said.

"What happened here? Where's Marcus Clapper?"

The guard shrugged his shoulders. "You'll have to ask Bubba down at the jail."

"I'm asking you."

Something about Cort's manner stirred the guard. "You're the marshal, ain't you? Guess it wouldn't hurt to say. Clapper was killed sometime last night. But don't worry. Bowles already got who done it."

"A woman," said Cort flatly, knowing what the guard's response would be even before he heard it.

"That's right. Caught her in the act, or at least damned near."

A helpless rage exploded within Cort, and he bounded for his horse. He made fast time through the residential streets and then along the Strand on his way to the jail. He knew exactly where he would find Rella—in that back cell under the supervision of Bowles and his companion Bubba. What a couple of sweethearts those men were. If they'd done anything to harm her, he would see that they paid.

Damn! If they'd done anything to harm her, what difference would revenge make? It hadn't brought his father back, and it wouldn't help Rella now.

He slammed into the office and found a crowd; Bowles and Bubba as he'd expected, and they'd been joined by Alderman Hayes and a tall, thin-faced man with a sharp look in his eyes. He was in work clothes and looked as though he came from the docks.

"Thought you'd be here before now," Bowles said. "We got her for sure this time."

"Bring her here."

"She's all right where she is. We're making sure she don't have an opportunity to run again."

"You bring her out *now.*"

"Now listen here—" the thin-faced man said.

"You a lawman?" Cort asked.

"The name is Rip Griffin. I head one of the unions down on the dock. Mr. Clapper worked for me. I want to make sure his killer is punished."

Cort glanced at Alderman Hayes. "And what brings you down? Figuring with so many people here, you might hold a political rally?"

"Now, now," Hayes said placatingly, "I heard there was another murder. We public officials have to think of the town's reputation. Can't have people thinking Galveston is prone to such trouble."

"Yes," Cort said, "I can see where that would be a shame. Now Bubba," he added, without looking at the jailer, "if Miss Sandringham is not out here in three seconds, looking healthy if not exactly happy, you're going to get a taste of what Ernest here received yesterday."

Declining to argue, Bubba disappeared fast into the interior of the jail. Rella, clad in the pants and shirt he'd last seen her wearing, stood before him in not much more time than the three seconds he had allotted. Her hair fell in thick, black curls about her shoulders, and she somehow looked thinner than he remembered, as though her ordeal had robbed her already slender body of weight. He couldn't see that she had been mistreated, at least not in the way Mollie had, but there were half circles of gray beneath her eyes that told him she hadn't gotten much rest.

Rella avoided Cort's stare. This was worse than her imagining, she thought as she looked around the crowded jail office. So many witnesses to her shame. Bowles was puffed up with pride, and Bubba had the leer in his eyes that she saw every time she looked at him. And Alderman Hayes, for crying out loud! What was he doing there? She didn't know who the ferret-faced man was; she'd never seen him before.

At last she let her eyes turn to Cort. Her knees weakened. She'd expected to be overcome with fear at his rage and, worse, with embarrassment over how she had aggravated a situation that they'd both believed was as bad as it could get. Instead, with him standing so tall and strong, whatever anger he felt under control, his hat pulled low over piercing blue eyes and that wonderful black kerchief protecting the back of his neck, she had to fight the urge to throw herself in his arms.

"Good morning," he said coolly.

Rella was glad she had resisted temptation.

"Good morning," she managed in the same carefully modulated tone of voice.

"Are you all right?"

"Yes . . . under the circumstances."

"Then let's alter those circumstances." He turned to Bowles, who was standing behind the desk. "I'm taking her with me."

"Impossible!" Bowles exclaimed. "That bail doesn't extend to two murder charges. And I found her over that poor man's body. Just the way we did with Tuttle. The gun there still smoking. No one else around. We got her dead to rights."

A strange silence settled across the room as Cort fixed his gaze on the deputy. Rella recognized that silence. It was the anger she had been waiting for, the quiet kind that could strike terror in the heart of whoever was in its path.

"I wouldn't stop me if I were you," Cort said at last. "I've been doing a lot of thinking, Bowles. Everything seems to lead back to you. Somebody told me recently that being in your custody was like putting meat into a fire for safekeeping. Took me a while to figure out what that meant. You hired Bubba here from off the docks, and now this Griffin character comes from the same place to hang around the jail. And then there's the fact that Marcus Clapper found work there."

"See here—" Griffin began.

Cort kept right on. "And it's on the docks where so many rumors are swirling about kickbacks and dirty deals."

Bowles rested a hand on the gun strapped to his left thigh. "So what are you saying?"

"I'm saying you better be very careful not to make any mistakes. You started back in June when you insisted on filing charges against Rella. I might have let things go"—Rella gasped since this was the first she'd heard of any such possibility—"only you said if I didn't pursue the matter, you would. If she hadn't run away, I would not have been convinced of her guilt. Everything looked too easy. But then, as I said, she ran. And you're the one who let her get away. I don't imagine you were too happy to get the telegram that she was coming back to town."

"Ben Woods—"

"Is conveniently out in El Paso. But you're here. And you're the one I'll be stalking." Cort grabbed Rella by the wrist and headed for the door.

"I told you what you're doing is illegal," Bowles shrieked, his face red.

Cort came close to smiling. The angrier the deputy became, the calmer he felt. "I told you once to take up any complaints concerning me with Governor Davis. I don't answer to you." He threw a quick look at Alderman Hayes. "And as for you, I can't figure your part in this. If you're hooked up with the rest of them, I'll find it out. If not, then you better get out of the way to make damned sure you're not tarred by the same brush."

That was as good an exit line as Rella could imagine, and Cort took it, leading her down the long path to where his bay horse was tethered. In silence, he helped her into the saddle and mounted behind her.

Rella made one stab at conversation. "*Is* this legal?"

"Doesn't make much difference one way or the other," he said as his body pressed against hers and they began the ride. "You are not staying in there."

Rella wished she could be warmed by the protective words, but there was an edge to Cort's voice she didn't like. The anger that was boiling in him was directed at more than just Ernest Bowles.

Still, she couldn't help comparing the marshal who had practically dragged her from the jail this morning with the stern, strict lawman he had been when they first met. He was still a tough man, but now he seemed more concerned with justice than the letter of the law. Knowing she was innocent, he wanted her free and away, whether or not he had the authority to take her.

"Where do we go now?" she ventured, emboldened by the warmth of his chest against her back and by the memory of his rescue.

"Where I should have taken you in the first place," he said brusquely, his voice as darkly ominous as a roll of thunder. "So I could keep an eye on you."

Rella shut up. It didn't take a genius to realize there were black clouds on her personal horizon that portended a turbulence as violent as last night's genuine storm.

Traffic was heavy in the business district, and they didn't stop until they reached the Tremont Hotel. Rella was forced to wait at the base of the lobby stairs, under the scrutiny of a dozen well-dressed men and women, while Cort stopped by the desk. As soon as she entered the third-floor suite, she spotted a familiar valise on the floor by the wardrobe and realized she was in his room. She was surprised by the opulence of the Victorian setting, the flowered settee and Persian rug, the heavy draperies and canopied bed.

"You live well," she said, "but I guess you can afford it."

"When I'm here on business," he responded as he closed the door behind him, "I don't usually stay in such a fancy place, but I wasn't sure where you would be staying. It'll be here for now."

Not exactly a statement of romantic intent, Rella decided, but then Cort had never wooed her with sweet words.

A sudden thought struck her. "Greta! She must be terribly worried."

"I sent her a message at the desk downstairs that

you're with me."

Cort sounded calm and reasonable enough, and as much in control as ever to remember such details. He had remembered her dear friend when she had not. Even through her chagrin over such unforgiveable forgetfulness, she recognized its cause. Cort could still turn her inside out so that she forgot everything else but him. She smiled at him. Maybe the storm she had feared would not crash down on her head after all.

Watching him circle around her, she admired the graceful way he moved his lean frame; she especially liked the contrast of his rugged good looks against the background of the sumptuous room. He was angry all right—he had a right to be—but despite the firm set of his face and his brusque voice she was still ready to throw herself in his arms . . . to feel the texture of his neck with her lips . . . to let her fingers press against the muscles of his back. . . .

Cort caught the look in her eye and felt his body grow warm. Every time they got near a bed, he responded that way. Even in a worn, ill-fitted pair of trousers, with her hair a wild tangle and her face showing signs of a sleepless night, Rella was a trap—a beautiful, thrilling one, but a trap nevertheless. The coldness of reality settled around his heart. The simplest things he requested of her, she failed to do. She didn't trust him, couldn't depend upon him the way he needed his woman to.

An uneasy silence settled between them. At last Rella said, "I didn't know you weren't convinced of my guilt right away."

Her words surprised him. Of all the things they needed to discuss, his opinion of her five months ago was not at the top of his list.

"You didn't hang around long enough to find out how I felt," he said shortly. Taking off his hat, he tossed it onto the settee. "When I took you to Perry's office and asked you to reenact the day of his murder, I was looking for evidence to prove you couldn't have killed him." He rubbed at his lower lip. "What I found was that you could be a violent woman. And then I didn't see you for months."

For all his calmness, Rella knew he was angry. He had a right to be, but she couldn't let her actions go undefended. "Your kiss took me by surprise."

"You offered yourself to me."

Rella's temper flared. "I was vulnerable."

He laughed sharply. "Since when have you ever been vulnerable? At least where you would admit it. You're too damned independent for your own good. I told you to wait for me, but you thought you knew best."

Rella squeezed back the hurt. How could he talk to her this way when all she wanted was to tell him how sorry she was that she had been such a fool? But she would be damned if she let him know how she felt. He didn't see her vulnerability; in truth, after all the times they'd lain in one another's arms, he knew very little about who she really was, or how she felt.

"I had no way of knowing Marcus would be dead," she said, amazing herself at the steadiness in her voice.

"You had no way of knowing *what* you would find. The only thing you had to go on was my request that you wait for me."

"Request! Since when do you put any of your demands in such a form?"

"We're not dealing in a play here, Rella. This is real life. And real death. You want politeness, then you'll get it. Please do as I say and I'll get you out of this."

"I dislike putting you to so much trouble, since I'm obviously not worth it. I only wish I had inherited the evil eye from my grandmother. Since you seem to think Bowles is behind all of this, I could look at him and all your worries would disappear."

"You're not worth it, eh? Don't try to play on my sympathies, Rella."

"As if you had any!" Rella lashed out, wanting to hurt him as much as he was hurting her.

"Unfair as well as inaccurate."

Rella's fingers ached to slap the supercilious look on his face. During the past few months, she had developed a temper to match his; just when she wanted to rant and rave, he was keeping his under control.

She allowed herself a slight, calculated smile. "I know the problem here. I should have figured it out last night on the beach. We've been together a long time now, Cort. For most of that time, you had a willing woman—"

"You remember things different from me."

"—a willing woman," she continued, ignoring his sarcasm. "I figured that if I held myself away from you, I would learn just how you felt."

"So you've been playing a game?" he asked with soft deliberation. "Is this celibacy of yours just another role?"

Cort spoke as though he already knew the answers to his questions; his quiet conviction pierced her heart like a knife. She had wanted him to trust and respect her; instead he viewed her with scorn. Something within her died, and with great self-control she thrust herself into the most difficult part she had ever played.

"Obviously I haven't fooled you," she said with a brittle laugh. "Things went badly for me down here, and when I got in over my head, I ran. You provided a diversion." Lost in the uncaring role she was playing, she ignored the gleam in his eyes that warned she had gone too far. "Maybe I should have let you love me last night. One last time. You are good, and as you once said, I have a great capacity for lovemaking."

"A diversion, was I? Well, my hot-blooded Romany, so were you."

He stepped close and pulled her into his arms, his lips grinding against hers in a kiss that was without passion. His fingers pressed cruelly into her shoulders as he held her tight against him. Rella's heart pounded in anger and, God help her, in a quick flare of desire.

As angry as he was, Cort wanted her more than he'd ever thought possible. He wanted to hold her so tightly she became a part of him; no matter how much she tried, she would never break free. He let his kiss soften; her hands ceased to beat against his chest, and her body leaned into his.

He thrust her from him. Oh, she was a trap all right, with her lips moist and swollen, and her eyes so quickly darkened by the same need that ate at him. "You do indeed have a great capacity for making love," he said huskily.

She slapped him across the face.

"As well as for violence," he added as he stood close and yet a million miles away.

It took all her training to keep her back straight

and her head high. In that instant of time she felt a hate for him that matched the strongest desire she had ever felt, but her eyes were dry and hard. She had been fool enough to cry on that beach yesterday after asking him to leave her alone. Cinderella Sandringham who had taken care of herself all her life! Cort would never see her cry again.

"We seem to bring out the best and the worst in each other," she managed. Cort gave no notice to the tremor in her voice. "Such a scene as this must be as embarrassing to you as it is to me. I'd like to get on about our business."

Cort nodded once. "Then that's what you will get. Don't worry that I will force my attentions on you again. It will be hard enough just keeping you alive and out of jail."

With every ounce of her being in protest against this bitter time, she took refuge in the very real danger that still faced her. It was easier, she realized as she fought back those damnable, unwanted tears, to deal with charges of robbery and murder than to handle a broken heart.

"Would you like the facts about last evening?" she asked, stepping away from him. She proceeded to describe the disastrous events that had led to her incarceration.

"You didn't hear a shot?" Cort asked calmly, taking up her cue. "On a quiet street like that, I would think it would awaken half the neighborhood."

"The thunder must have covered it."

"You haven't given me much to go on, except that Bowles was in the vicinity at the time of the killing. You can testify against him as well as he can against you."

"Do you think it will come to a trial?"

He raked his fingers through his hair. "I wish I could say."

An uneasy silence descended. "I assume I'm not to be kept locked in here until such a thing happens," she said.

"Of course not," Cort answered impatiently.

"Then please take me to the Maas home, if it's not too much trouble," she asked politely. "My unexplained absence must have frightened Greta, for which I must apologize. And," she couldn't help adding, "if things are as bad as you seem to think, I need to be with someone who really cares."

Chapter Twenty-three

Whatever sympathy Rella had found missing in Cort as she related her tale of horror back in the hotel, she found in Greta.

"*Dummkopf* deputy!" her friend cried, practically flying off the settee in the parlor where the three of them had gathered. "*Dummkopf!*" And then for good measure, one last "*Dummkopf!*"

"Wily, maybe," Cort said laconically.

Greta was quick to seize on his words. "So the deputy is not stupid, you think. Could all of this have been planned?"

"No one can plan what Rella will do."

Rella's fingers started itching again. If he planned to subject her to his sarcasm over the course of their investigation, she might as well be back in jail.

"What I think," Cort continued, "is that Bowles took advantage of the situation. He found Rella hovered over another body, and he didn't bother to question her guilt."

"And the man who died?" Greta asked.

"Clapper bragged about coming into some money. Blackmail, is what I figure. Perry Tuttle must have identified someone other than Rella as his killer—Bowles, most likely, although we may never know for sure—and Clapper threatened to recant his testimony unless he was paid off."

"Why did the man ever tell such a terrible lie in the first place?" asked Greta.

"I doubt that he was thinking of blackmail at first, probably didn't even think of the consequences of such a story. As I recall, he waited awhile before saying anything about Tuttle's last words." Cort's eyes drifted to Rella for a brief, enigmatic glance. "My guess is she drove him to it. Some women can make a man do crazy things."

Rella's hands balled into fists in her lap. "So," she hissed, ignoring Greta's wide-eyed stare, "my troubles are, after all, my fault."

"That's not what I said. I'm just trying to explain how all of this mess might have come about."

Rella found she would rather face Cort's direct denunciations than this cool, matter-of-fact discussion of her shortcomings. She turned to Greta. "He also thinks this whole mess began because Perry Tuttle was involved in something down at the docks."

"Papa's trouble?" Greta asked worriedly.

"Could be," said Cort. "When do you expect him?"

Greta glanced at the clock on the mantle. "Usually he comes late. But when Rella was not here this morning and you did not return, I went down to the wharf. Perhaps, I thought, Papa had seen Rella early as he was leaving and could tell me where she was. It took some time and a great deal of talking—those men do not like women hanging around unless it is for their own purposes—but I found him. All I did," she added sheepishly, "was to upset him needlessly. He said he would be home at noon to find out if she has been found."

"I was found all right," Rella muttered. "In the

Galveston jail."

Greta shuddered. "Such an experience must have left you feeling . . . dirty."

Rella managed a grin. "It left me starving. If Gerhardt expects to find a meal waiting, some sausage perhaps and potatoes, then I would be happy to join him. As would Cort," she said with a polite nod to him. He returned the nod.

How difficult this courtesy was to maintain! Standing, she directed her steps toward the back of the house. Never, under any circumstances, would she let him see that the past few hours had left her with an emptiness that no food could ever satisfy.

By the time Gerhardt arrived, the meal was ready. He took Rella in his arms in a great bear hug.

"*Liebchen,* it does these weary eyes good to see you all right."

"She's not exactly all right, Papa," Greta said. "We will talk after you have eaten. It's good to see you with an appetite again."

Greta spoke too soon, for Gerhardt barely touched his food. In the parlor a short time later, after Rella's most recent troubles had been summarized, Cort put the matter to him directly.

"I need to know what's been troubling you. What's going on down at the dock?"

"Nothing that concerns you," Gerhardt said, his eyes averted.

"Please, Papa," Greta said, her hand on his as they sat side by side, "you don't sleep. You don't eat. It was this way before we left Germany. I hate to see it start up again, this trouble you cannot fight."

"If you don't want to tell—or you feel you cannot—" Rella said, "then forget that I'm asking. You have been too good a friend for me to ask more than ou can reveal."

Gerhardt stroked at his gray beard. "All I have are uspicions, and hints of threats. No, no," he said, his and waving away their protests, "I am not afraid or myself. But I am not alone." He glanced warmly t his daughter. "You are right, Greta. We must not e afraid here in our new country. I will tell the narshal what he needs to know."

Cort moved closer from the standing position he'd aken beside the low-burning fireplace. "I take it ou've found discrepancies in the books you keep."

"*Ja.* There is the manifest of the company, which hows what is on board each vessel. But sometimes his does not duplicate the list of what is unloaded nto the warehouses. Discrepancies must be allowed, f course, for breakage and innocent mistakes, but ot in the amount that I see and not with such egularity."

"Any particular products?"

"Whoever our thief may be, he is an eclectic one. Dry goods such as flour and sugar, furniture, fine silks and tea from the Orient. All have been missng. These and many more. As you know, Galveston s the main port through which goods travel into Texas and farther west. There is much from which to choose for a man or, what is more likely, men who have developed markets for such wares. And in a state such as this which has developed few factories of its own, there are always places for such markets."

"Such a man might be Rip Griffin," said Cort.

"He is a powerful leader among his men. When they unload the goods, I have begun to check the records most carefully. It is this that keeps me late."

"And he has found you out."

"He suspects that I suspect. And he has issued

threats. Nothing overt, it is true, but I am n
mistaken in his meaning. *Schweinehund!*"

"Any evidence that Ernest Bowles is involved?"

"For this I have been watchful, ever since I sa the deputy spending more time than seemed war ranted on the docks. After all, we have an occasiona fight among the men, some drunkenness, but noth ing that would require the frequent visits that h makes."

"And have you turned up anything?"

"*Nein.* He has a few young men, brutish sorts who stay with him. I suspect they make sure there i no trouble when the goods are being transported But again, I have no proof."

Rella broke in. "Bubba must be one of those."

Cort nodded. "And the guard I saw at Marcu Clapper's front door this morning. They look like matched pair." He remembered Mollie Bigheart face. "You are right, Herr Maas, to protect you daughter. These men don't play games."

"They have killed two men already," Rella said Two deaths for which she had stupidly let herself b blamed. She knew the thought must be burning i the minds of the others. Especially Cort.

"So what do we do now?" she continued.

"*We* do nothing," said Cort. "This is work for me now."

"If I might make a suggestion. . ." Greta spok softly into the hush of the room.

Rella could have hugged her. "I'm listening," sh said with a smile.

"Aaron can help."

Rella hid her disappointment. Thin, scholarl Aaron, with his head usually in a book, was hardl a match against the likes of Bubba and Ernes

Bowles. Not to mention that rodent Rip Griffin.

"Aaron has been doing much studying since last June," Greta continued, as though the others, even Papa, had not looked at her in polite condescension. "More than usual. He says since his father's death, his work has been in a special field called forensic medicine. Dr. Bruster and he have worked together."

Remembering the doctor as the one who had examined Tuttle's body, Cort nodded. "I've heard of such a field of study. It's using medical facts as they relate to court cases."

Gerhardt nodded. "Such work is done in Germany. Doctors are able to say what poison might have been used when a person has suffered a violent death."

"Or how long he has been dead," said Cort.

"Or," Greta ventured, "where a killer was standing when the gun was fired. And whether the . . . trajectory of a bullet might reveal whether he used a right or left hand."

"Is that what Aaron said?" asked Cort.

"He has told me only a little, of course, thinking I wouldn't understand, but yes, that is what he said."

Cort's eyes met Rella's, and for one moment they shared a common thought. "Bowles is left-handed," he said.

"And I use my right."

Cort thought back to mid June. "I don't think Perry Tuttle's body was examined closely. Dr. Bruster ruled he'd been killed by gunshot, and that was considered enough."

Greta smiled proudly. "It was Aaron who began to think that maybe all his study could be put to good use." Her smile softened to sadness. "I guess he thought to make up for his fights with his poor papa." She reached for Gerhardt's hand.

A sharp knock sounded at the door, and Greta started. From habit, Rella looked at Cort.

"Do you think it's Bowles? Come to drag me back?"

"He'll play hell doing it." He glanced at Gerhardt. "Let me see who it is." Without waiting for an answer, he disappeared into the hallway.

Cort's voice drifted into the parlor. "I'm surprised to see you here." The reply was muffled.

He returned with an embarrassed looking Alderman Hayes, who stood, hat in hand, shuffling from foot to foot.

"Didn't know I'd have an audience," Hayes said with a small laugh.

Cort introduced him, then said, "The alderman decided he'd had enough of Bowles and company."

"You put it to me bluntly enough back at the jail," the alderman said. "Bowles and Griffin had been talking to me about making political contributions for the upcoming elections, although where Bowles was going to get any money, I couldn't decide. I've known him and his family a long time. They lost everything they had in the war."

He accepted Greta's offer of a chair, settling himself down with a shake of his head. "More important, I wondered what strings might be attached. It always helps to have a politician in one's back pocket, so to speak. Issues come up in the city that affect a lot of things, such as regulations about the wharves."

Rella spoke up. "I've seen you several times since I got back, and always near Ernest Bowles. How do we know he didn't send you to find out what's going on?"

Cort nodded in agreement, and Rella felt an irritating pleasure that he thought she had said the right thing.

"She's got a lot at stake here," Cort explained to Hayes. "And reason to wonder. As a matter of fact, so do I."

"If there's bad blood in the sheriff's office," Hayes said, "then Galveston, too, has a lot at stake here. Let me help. Surely there's something a man in my position can do to uncover skullduggery."

"For all my jawing back at the jail, I don't have an ounce of proof about my speculations. Certainly about Bowles and Perry Tuttle." Cort thought with regret about Mollie Bigheart and her determination to keep secret what she had learned in bed. "But Maas here has gathered some interesting facts about irregularities on the dock involving Griffin."

"That's a start," Hayes said. "I repeat my offer of help. Can you use it?"

Cort watched him for a long moment before coming to a decision. "I might. As angry as Bowles was—and guessing, no doubt, about my lack of proof—he has probably been trying to discredit whatever good name I've got in this town. We need to go by the medical school and talk to Aaron Tuttle. And then, if we like what he says, I'll need an exhumation order for his father's body. Could be you can find a judge quicker than I can if, as I suspect, Bowles has been making the rounds at the courthouse."

He glanced at Gerhardt. "Would it be trouble for you to stay here with the women instead of going back to the dock?"

"None," Gerhardt said, the old fire back in his eyes.

"Good." He turned to Rella. "I'll let you know what's going on as soon as I can."

In dealing with her now he was all business, she thought as she watched him stride down the front walk, Hayes scurrying to keep up; but he hadn't made her swear on a Bible, and he hadn't made any sarcastic remarks about her not doing anything to foul things up.

Cort was a hard man to love, but try as she might to bring a Gypsy curse down on his head, he was an even harder man to hate.

As things worked out, it was evening by the time Aaron Tuttle was found and questioned, an exhumation order signed and delivered by a protesting judge, and Dr. Bruster summoned to aid Cort in the investigation.

"I should have done this five months ago," Bruster said by way of apology when he arrived at the Maas home, "but I didn't know all I do now. Aaron's been helping me work with this field of forensics. Did you know people leave marks behind that are like a signature? They're called fingerprints, but the country doesn't have the money to fund that kind of investigation right now."

"Whatever the cost of tonight," Cort said, "I'll cover."

Bruster shook his head. "This one's for free. Just glad I can get the chance to help. Learning doesn't mean a thing if it can't be put to use." He brushed aside Rella's thanks. "When do you think we should go to the cemetery?"

"Can you perform the examination there?" Cort asked.

"Sure can. All I need is the right surgical tools."

"And I'll help," Aaron said.

Cort glanced at the doctor. "Any objections to going right now? Just in case Bowles has heard about the exhumation and tries to get to the body first."

"None," Bruster responded with alacrity, an enthusiastic gleam in his eye.

Greta put her arms around Aaron. "Rella should have hit that deputy harder with the file."

Cort grinned, the first time Rella had seen such a pleasant look on his face since down on the beach. "See what ordinary people can do once they get mixed up in something like this?" he said.

"You're awfully understanding," Rella interjected.

"I can be."

Rella looked away. Here she was wanting to touch him again, and so soon after he'd said such terrible things to her. She decided that along with her paucity of sense, she must be totally lacking in pride.

While Dr. Bruster returned to the medical school for his bag of instruments, Greta and Rella set out a loaf of dark bread and some cheese; but they didn't get any takers on the light repast, and the food was returned to the cupboard untouched. When they were alone in the kitchen, Rella took the opportunity to make a startling request.

"Bowles took my knife. Do you have one I might borrow?"

"Your *knife,*" Greta exclaimed, wide-eyed. "Why do you need such a thing?"

"Not to help with the examination!" Rella returned, reading Greta's mind. "Please trust me. I don't like going around unarmed."

"Unarmed?" Greta's voice was a squeak. *"Gott in*

Himmel! You surely have changed."

"I sure have."

Greta's first offer was a rather frightening looking cleaver that would not have fit in Rella's boot, even if she could have managed to wield it in her or anyone else's defense. She settled on a long, narrow kitchen knife, wrapped carefully in a dozen folds of butcher paper and tucked out of sight.

They joined the others in the parlor. A short, fiery discussion ensued after the doctor returned, but no one agreed to remain behind at the Maas home. They made a curious party as they journeyed through the streets toward City Cemetery: Rella and Cort, side by side in the lead, both more courteous to each other than they'd ever been; Aaron sitting beside Greta in the old Maas carriage, Greta listening with a growing horror that she tried to hide as he described in clinical terms what must be done; and Gerhardt, Bruster, and Hayes bringing up the rear in the alderman's carriage.

Traffic was light, and the trip was made in short order. Like an inquisitive onlooker, the moon peeped out from behind a cloud occasionally to check on their progress, but by the time they arrived at their destination, the night was dark, the thick cloud cover obscuring both moon and stars.

Cort checked out the cemetery as quickly as he could, lantern held high, to make sure there was no uninvited committee waiting to greet them. He found only silence and, as seemed fitting in such a setting, a feeling of peace.

The rest of the lanterns, one for each person, were quickly unloaded, and they headed in a procession toward the vault at the back of the cemetery, the headstones of a hundred other graves acting as sentinels to guard their dead.

"Here it is," Aaron said, coming to a halt beside an arched stone structure. Carved above the keystone was a masonry angel gazing beatifically down on them.

Cort had to help Aaron open the door. The hinges cried in protest at the unwanted intrusion, and Greta gave a nervous giggle. Gerhardt moved close to her side.

Just then the moon came out once more and bathed the small party in a ghostly light. Rella started, then caught Cort looking at her.

"I'll be all right," she said.

"I never thought otherwise. Just remember to do what I say."

She let the order go by without comment.

They lit each lantern and crowded inside the vault, which was close and unpleasant, the vents built into the four walls providing an inadequate circulation of air. The lanterns cast a garish, unwelcome light onto the stones. Aaron pointed to his left, where a pair of dusty, cobwebbed caskets rested side by side. "My grandparents," he said. "My father's over here."

After a brief discussion, it was agreed that Gerhardt, Hayes, and Cort would leave their lights and remain outside on watch. Greta insisted on holding one of the lanterns for Bruster and Aaron—"to show I'll be a fine doctor's wife"—and Rella said she, too, would help.

Outside, Cort stood at attention, hand on his gun, watching the shadowy tombstones for signs of unwarranted movement. Gerhardt held a weapon of his own, an antique dueling pistol he'd brought with him from Germany. Hayes said that, unfortunately, he was a typical politician. Maybe he could talk a man to death, but he didn't know the first thing about guns.

The minutes went by slowly. Cort could hear muted talk but little else. Once Rella came out for a breath of fresh air and reported they were making progress, even though the body was badly decomposed. Cort figured he would get all the details he needed later.

A half hour went by before she came out again. "Cort," she said, "you better come here."

Gerhardt waved the pistol. "Do not worry. I can take care of anything that is alive. You see to the dead."

Cort found them gathered around the open casket ringed by the lanterns. Aaron seemed paler than he had been when they arrived; maybe, as determined as he was, he found working on his father harder than he had imagined. Cort would have rather faced a dozen gangs like Monty Slade's than do what Aaron had just done. Never in a hundred years would he understand medical men.

He glanced at Rella. Hell, he didn't understand women, either. She and Greta were standing there looking not half as queasy as he felt, and they had witnessed the whole thing. The good Lord had done right when he designed women, and not men, to bear the babies.

He forced himself to look into the casket at the remains of Perry Tuttle, then glanced at Rella and thought what a precious thing was life. He turned to Bruster. "Let's get on with it."

He got a quick course in forensic medicine from Bruster. "Not much flesh to work with," the doctor said, "but we could still tell which way the bullet came in and the exit it made from the back. In between are the broken bones."

Wiping his hands on a towel draped over the side of the coffin, he gestured at the corpse now naked from the waist up. A whisper of air passed and the lanterns flickered. "He was hit at an angle, right to left. Perry's right to left, that is. Remember, that desk of his was in the corner of the room. He was shot while he was in his chair with no room for anyone to get behind him, and the force knocked him to the floor. The bullet entered here and exited his back." He pointed to the corpse's chest and lifted it gingerly to reveal the back.

"I should have realized it at once," he continued, "but didn't until one day when I was discussing bullet wounds. Wanted to refresh my memory in case I had to testify in court."

Cort reenacted the scene in his mind. "Then the gunman must have been left-handed and shot Tuttle while he was facing him at an angle."

"Correct."

"Which means," Rella interjected, "that I didn't do it. I'm not left-handed."

Cort's gaze locked with hers. "Even I managed to figure that out already. But this is proof I can present to a judge."

By this time Gerhardt and Hayes had crowded inside to hear the last of the report.

"How many left-handed men are there in Galveston?" Rella asked.

"Too damned many," Cort said. "We may have gotten evidence to protect you, but we haven't really proved a thing against Bowles."

Rella muttered an unladylike expletive, to which Cort responded, "Let's get out of here." He took her by the arm. She didn't pull away.

The cool night air brought her little relief, and for one brief instant she allowed herself to lean against Cort. Behind him were Gerhardt and Hayes.

Reaching down, she pulled the narrow kitchen knife from her boot and unwrapped it. "This is starting to cut. Butcher paper doesn't make a good sheath."

"Why did you bring it?"

"A girl never knows when she'll need a knife. But I guess I won't be needing it now to try for another escape. Not since you proved I couldn't have killed Perry Tuttle."

"Rella—"

Here it comes, she thought, another lecture.

The moon came from behind a cloud, and a sound from somewhere in the dark stilled her protest.

"Did you hear that?" she whispered. "It sounded like shoe leather on gravel. Someone's out there."

"Get back inside," Cort ordered.

"Not without you."

Instinctively she threw herself against him just as a shot rang out. Behind her Gerhardt yelled out in pain.

Cort fell, Gerhardt on top of him, and Rella let fly with a knife in the direction of a moving shadow. She heard with satisfaction a low cry.

"Papa!" Greta cried out.

Cort knew right away from the spew of German coming from Gerhardt that the man was not seriously hurt. None too gently, Cort set Gerhardt aside and slipped silently in the direction of the thrashing sounds growing steadily fainter somewhere in the acre of tombstones. As he moved amongst the graves, trying to pick out a sign of movement, the cemetery was again thrust into darkness, and Cort muttered a none too soft curse. Just when he needed a little ghostly light, the moon decided to hide behind a cloud.

Bruster and Aaron helped the wounded Gerhardt into the protection of the vault, Greta close behind them, while Rella listened in growing apprehension for some sign that Cort was all right. It was an eternity before she heard returning footsteps along the leafy path and could make out Cort's tall silhouette.

Making little more noise than one of the dead might have done, he moved quickly beside her and said in disgust, "Whoever it was got away."

"Not exactly," Rella said. "I'm sure I hit him."

"Let's hope so. How is Gerhardt?"

"I think it's only a flesh wound. They've got him inside."

"Then as soon as the doctor gives the word, we'll move him to a bed, and I'll get you all safely tucked away."

"And then?"

"And then," Cort said in unmistakable firmness, "then I'll go see if maybe your knife throwing didn't give us just the evidence we need."

Cort found the office of the jail empty and turned his attention to the corridor leading between the cells. Silently, he crept down the dimly lighted way, drawing the curiosity of the prisoners housed on both sides. One by one they gripped the bars and watched his progress. Cort felt their sympathy with him as he placed his boots carefully in the direction of the grating sounds coming from the back cell—the one where Rella had been kept.

He didn't know how many men he would find back there—Bowles and Bubba maybe—but he didn't much care. When Rella had shoved him from harm's way outside the Tuttle vault, someone had been shooting at him, but at night under an undecided moon, the gunman could just as easily have hit her. He meant to get whoever it was, no matter the odds.

He found Bowles, alone, crouched on the ground in a back corner behind one of the cots and tugging at a section of the stone wall.

No need to hurry him, Cort decided, and waited for the deputy to get what he was after. It didn't take long. With a grunt of satisfaction, Bowles tossed a leather packet on top of the cot and pulled himself to his feet.

Cort unholstered his gun, trained it directly between Bowles' shoulders, and pulled back the hammer. The click was like a cannon shot. The deputy held still.

"Raise your hands," Cort said.

"You ain't got no right," Bowles growled over his shoulder.

"The gun says I do. And that bloodied handkerchief you've got wrapped around your left hand."

"Watch it, Marshal!" came a cry from one of the cells. Cort whirled in time to see the hulking figure of the jailer Bubba standing in the doorway at the end of the corridor.

"Take him!" Bowles yelled.

Bubba didn't stand a chance, not with the target he presented. Cort fired. The jailer jerked once, then fell to the ground and lay still.

Cort whirled in time to see Bowles grappling for his holstered gun with his right hand.

"Don't bother," Cort said, "unless you aim to get your own place out at the cemetery."

Bowles grew still, his small eyes glaring out at Cort with red hate.

"You have the keys?"

Bowles grunted, then finally nodded yes. "There on the cot."

"Pitch them here, then the packet and your gun, and step to the back of the cell."

The deputy's movements were awkward, working as he did with his right hand. When he was done, his back against the wall, Cort slammed the door to the cell closed. It made a satisfactory clang.

The same gruff voice that had warned him of danger yelled out again. "Put that bastard in here with me, Marshal! I've got a lot of tormentin' to pay him for."

"Let me at 'im," another snarled.

"You men will just have to be content talking to him for a while," Cort yelled back. "I've got someone else to go after right now. A slick thief by the name of Rip Griffin. He and Bowles will make fine companions back here in the women's cell."

Tucking the gun in his waistback, he stared through the bars at Bowles. "Tell me," he said, "why you shot at me out there at the cemetery. No use to deny it. Rella caught you in the hand with her knife."

"Why not?" The deputy's eyes were red rimmed and cold. "I heard what the bitch said. Whatever you found on that body, you decided you had me dead to rights."

"Not exactly. What we did was find evidence that

she couldn't have killed Tuttle. Nothing that said you in particular pulled the trigger. That ought to be something for you to remember a long time."

He reached for the packet and paused to look inside. "Well, well, what do we have here?" he asked. "Looks like money. Several thousand dollars, I'd say. And in the same leather container I left with Tuttle." He looked up and smiled. "Saving it for a nice trip somewhere? Or maybe just a rainy day. A bank would have been safer, although you might have had a hard time explaining how you came by so much cash."

"I should have killed you a long time ago," Bowles growled. "I would have tonight if it hadn't been for that damned woman."

Cort holstered his gun. "She does have a way of intruding herself into matters, doesn't she? When I get through convincing her of a few things for myself, I'll have to tell her what you said."

Chapter Twenty-four

At the knock on the Maas front door, Rella jumped from her parlor chair. Smoothing the skirt of her new pink dress over her hips, she checked the mass of dark curls piled precariously high on her head and licked her lips. Her breath became shallow, another sign she recognized as panic.

Rella had faced a couple of uncontrolled fires, a knife-wielding Gypsy, too many gunshots to count, and the cold stone walls of the county jail, but never has she been more on edge. Even though she had been expecting this particular caller; even though she knew exactly how she wanted the evening to end.

The knock came again, more insistent this time. Greta was keeping her father back in the kitchen, out of the way until Rella had left for the evening. There was no one to get the door but herself.

Grabbing up her woolen stole, she forced her slippered feet into the hall. "Good evening," she said, before she had the door completely open.

Her heart caught in her throat. Standing before her, hat in hand, was the handsomest man she had ever seen. Dark suited and bare headed, a string tie at the neck of a white linen shirt, one errant copper curl falling across his forehead, Cort smiled at her from out of the dark.

It seemed a lifetime since she had been alone with him, although really only two days had passed. He'd sequestered her at the Maas home while he handled the arrests of Bowles and Rip Griffin, and she had decided not to protest.

"Good evening," he answered, all politeness, but she caught the quick, thorough glance he gave to her appearance. The smile traveled to his eyes. "I have a carriage waiting outside."

"How nice," she responded, thinking it was a good thing she had rushed out to buy the gown when his message came—along with a bouquet of flowers—asking her to join him for dinner.

Knowing how her personality occasionally rubbed Cort the wrong way, tonight she needed to use all the weapons she possessed to capture his favor. The pink gown was low cut and form fitting and brought out the tawniness of her skin.

His hand rested lightly on her back as he guided her down the front walk and into the covered carriage.

"It's a beautiful night, isn't it?" he asked. "I thought, if you don't mind, we would go back to the Tremont for dinner."

"In your room?"

"I've had it catered special. But if you'd rather not. . . ."

"I wouldn't want to spoil your plans." Especially if they coincided with hers.

Rella settled back in the carriage and decided maybe she would get what she wanted after all. Not that Cort had indicated he wanted a return to their lovemaking days. All had been friendly, but no more, between them since the arrests. A dark thought passed through her mind. He could want nothing more than to discuss the coming trial. At least two more men she knew of from the docks had joined Bowles and Griffin in jail, and Cort had been tied up in court getting the charges filed.

She had about decided she preferred Cort angry than politely distant when his dinner invitation arrived. And now he offered the news that they would be dining at the Tremont. Remembering a small Missouri inn, Rella knew Cort would have a hard time remaining distant in a hotel room.

She stole a sideways glance at him, and he smiled down at her. There went her heart and breath again. Somehow she managed to remain in control.

When she strolled through the elegant hotel lobby on Cort's arm, she received a few admiring glances, far different from the unfriendly stares of her previous visit. Then she had been clad in pants and shirt and weary from a night spent with a couple of whores in jail.

The room was much as she remembered it, except that a small dining table and two chairs had been added in front of a roaring fire. Resting on the table was a wine bucket containing a cloth-wrapped bottle of champagne and two covered plates.

"I see the food and drink have arrived," he said, removing her wrap. His fingers lingered a little longer than necessary against her skin, but she didn't complain.

As she settled into a chair, he popped the cork on the champagne, filled the two glasses, and proposed a toast. "Here's to your freedom," he said.

Rella gripped the glass. Cort's words were hardly what she wanted to hear, lacking as they did the least hint of romance. When that gunshot rang out at the cemetery, all she had thought of was keeping him from injury. Pride be damned, she wanted him forever and in good health. If he gave her half a chance, she would be the most compliant woman he had ever known.

And here he was with the cursed toast.

"To my freedom," she said through gritted teeth and gave her attention to her food. She scarcely realized what she ate—some kind of oysters and shrimp, but it all seemed to catch in her throat.

Settled across the table from her, Cort ate heartily and quickly. Finally crossing his knife and fork on his plate, he poured each of them more wine. "I got a letter from the director at the state hospital in Austin," he said. "It seems the Widow Welch has practically taken over the place, claiming she is only offering advice the way her late husband directs her in their talks. He's about decided she's just fooling everybody and is the sanest person there."

Rella smiled and for a moment set her ruffled feelings aside. "He's probably right." An uneasy silence settled between them. "Did Bowles ever confess?"

"You sure you want to talk about it over dinner?"

Rella knew exactly what she wanted to talk about, and it certainly wasn't Ernest Bowles. But with Cort behaving so formally, she was struck with an unexpected shyness; she would need a little more champagne if she were ever to risk Cort's rejection by speaking what was in her heart.

"I'm sure."

"He made a statement this afternoon. He had come by the law office at noon to talk over Perry's faintheartedness about the dock thievery and found him alone with the safe open. Apparently you had just left, locking the back door after you. The safe door was open, and Bowles warned Perry he ought to be more careful."

"I told him that a few times myself."

"I'm sure you did. Anyway, Bowles said he would make sure the office was secure before leaving; what he really did was unlock the back door and go out the front. A short time later, with Bubba guarding the alley, he crept up the back stairs, shot Perry, and made a fast trip back to the jail where he hid the money."

"If I had only known. Since I was in that cell twice."

"Bowles showed a little humor there. He enjoyed putting you close to what you had supposedly killed for."

"After he left," Rella said, "Marcus must have come in, heard Perry whisper Bowles' name, and decided to blame me and blackmail Bowles."

"It cost Marcus his life."

Again the silence returned, and Rella held up her glass for more champagne. The warmth of the wine was getting to her—or maybe it was Cort sitting so near.

She looked him straight in the eye. He had often commented on her outspokenness; it was too late to change her ways now. "What's this evening about, Cort?" she asked.

His eyes widened innocently, but she caught a gleam in their depths.

"Is something wrong?" he asked.

"I just don't know why you're being so politely informative. You could have told me about Bowles anytime."

Cort waved his champagne glass. "Isn't politeness

what you want? As I recall, you said I made only demands of you, never requests."

She matched that gleam with one of her own. "And do you plan to request something?"

"I already have. Your company at dinner."

"What if I don't want dinner?"

"I thought you might be hungry."

"Oh, I am, Cort. I most certainly am."

His face softened. "If you don't see anything you like. . . ."

"I do think you're the one playing games now. You once told me you wanted a woman who would do as you said."

"It's a good thing I didn't have such a woman back at the cemetery, or I would be dead. I never did thank you for pushing me out of the way."

"No," Rella said in a whisper, "you never did. Tell me something. You haven't replaced that badge I threw away. Any particular reason?"

"I'm quitting the law. Now that Galveston has about decided to accept me, I'm ready to take on East Texas. Not that it will be easy. In fact, it will be damned hard."

"Not for you. You manage to get what you want."

"Do I? I've wanted you for a long time."

Rella caught her breath.

Cort reached out and stroked her hand. "As my wife, of course. I love you. I probably did from the moment you leaned against me for support in Tuttle's office, but I was too thickheaded and stubborn to realize it."

"I'm—" Her voice broke, and she began again. "I'm glad to hear you admit it. The thickheaded part for sure."

He moved the candle from the center of the table

and took her hand in both of his. "How about the love?"

Rella's heart raced with joy. She felt as though she could fly, but somehow she managed to keep herself in her chair. She wanted to draw this moment of sweetness out forever. "That, too, although it's easy to see why you didn't recognize how you felt at first. I probably discouraged you a little by biting your lip."

"I figure it's just your way. On the beach I said you were too damned independent. I was wrong. A mealymouthed woman would bore me in a day. I need someone to point out the error of my ways."

"Is that all I'm good for?"

"I'm not through. And to warm my bed, and bear my children, and stand with me through the good times and bad. But you have to love me as much as I love you." Cort let go of her hand and leaned back in his chair. "It seems to me I've done all the declaring. This wasn't intended to be a monologue."

"Nor should it be."

She stood, downed the rest of her champagne, and threw her glass into the fire, where it shattered in a million pieces.

"I did that in a play once, but I've always wanted to do it in real life. As for loving you, you're a part of my being. Yes, yes, yes, I will marry you. I feel as though I've been wandering around all my life just waiting to find you."

She shifted away from the table. "True," she added, her eyes twinkling, "it wasn't apparent right at first. Throwing a girl in jail tends to put a damper on her tender feelings."

Cort stood and came after her. Wrapping her in his embrace, he kissed her long and hard. "Just remember what I'm capable of," he whispered into her hair.

Rella pulled free and strolled over to the bed. "Oh, I do, my darling. I most definitely do." She began to unfasten the buttons of her dress. "You said you were wrong in wanting a subservient woman. Well, I was wrong in wanting a courteous man. At least in the bedroom, and I figure that's where we are right now. Remember that capacity of mine that you once mentioned? I figure it's time we put it to another test."

Walking toward her, Cort took off his jacket and dropped his string tie onto the floor. "I suggest we get married right away."

Rella stepped from her gown which had pooled at her feet and began to work on her chemise. "At last we're in complete agreement."

He caught her in his arms. "Let me finish that," he said huskily.

"Oh, Cort," she answered, smiling up at him. "We're not finishing anything. With all of the things that have happened between us, tonight we have just begun."